One in a Million

Sadie Gordon Richmond

Also by this author

Front Page News
Sins of Silence
Sticks and Stones
Shadow Lines
I Have Never

For Liz, who was one
in a million to me.

Wednesday 10 February

Toby Reynolds had punched in the four-digit alarm code so many times that the process had become almost automatic. This, he frequently told himself, was his principal reason for leaving it unchanged: an excuse that allowed him to dismiss the knowledge that continuing to use the date of his wedding anniversary more than two years after the divorce was weird. He also liked to think of it as a closet rebellion against all those who had passed comment on the relationship over the years. When he and Abigail had announced their engagement, there had been whisperings about Abigail's age – she had been just nineteen – nowadays it was the fact the two of them had remained in such close contact since their split. Several people had suggested, in judgement dressed up as concern, that Toby would be happier if he let go of the past. But he wasn't unhappy, and he wasn't trying to live in the past. Besides, it wasn't as if he was holding on to someone who didn't want to be held on to – more often than not, Abigail was the one who sought him out. And he cared far more about her than he did other people's perceptions. When it came down to it, she was still his best friend.

Locking the door, he retrieved his bag from the front step before heading for the car. Two paces down the drive, he realised he wasn't alone: Abigail was perching on the redundant brick gatepost, and from the look on her face he could guess what had brought her his way that evening.

'Hiya Abs,' he greeted her, setting the bag down beside the car and walking towards her. 'How'd it go?'

'You were right,' she managed, dropping her eyes to the ground. Toby sighed, moving to wrap his arms around her.

'I'm sorry,' he offered, softly, as she began to cry. He hadn't wanted to be right. All too often he found himself hoping to be proved wrong, but rarely as fervently as he had on this occasion. 'I'm so sorry.'

Abigail clung to his jumper, the wispy ends of her long French plait tickling his fingers as her body shook. As the seconds ticked by, his bad knee began to protest in response to the awkward footing the gatepost had forced him to adopt, and he tried to adjust his stance without pulling away. Across the road, one of his clients was making slow and unsteady progress along the street with a Jack Russell intent on sniffing at and peeing on everything in his path. The dog's owner raised a hand in greeting and Toby nodded in response. He frequently found himself envying dogs, with their almost boundless enthusiasm for the mundane and routine. Theirs was an existence where every meal, every walk and every squirrel seemed equally as exciting as the last. A life of simple pleasures, devoid of all responsibility.

'Have you talked to Izzy?' Toby asked, as Abigail drew her head back from his chest and raised a hand to dry her tears with her fingers.

She shook her head.

Toby didn't ask why she had sought comfort from him rather than her current partner. It wasn't the first time. He wasn't sure whom that reflected on – him, or Izzy. Izzy certainly wasn't someone whose shoulder he would have chosen to cry on, but presumably there was another side to her that he hadn't seen. Toby found her intimidating. She was searingly honest, regardless of whether or not it was appropriate, and she didn't suffer fools. On occasion, he admired her balls; at other times, he wished he could fit her with a filter. Of course it wasn't fair to raise false hopes, but there were ways and ways of framing the truth. Ways and ways of delivering bad news.

'Do you have to go?' Abigail asked, raising her wet brown eyes to meet his.

'No,' Toby replied. 'I don't have to go.'

'But – were you –' she indicated his bag with a shift of her eyes.

He shook his head. 'I was just going to drop a few things over to the folks.'

Abigail nodded slightly before returning her eyes to his. There was a moment's silence, and he wondered what she was thinking. Then she leaned to kiss him.

Thursday 1 April

Rebecca Palmer jumped awake to the sound of someone moving around her bedroom. Panicked, she flicked on her bedside light before a hazy recollection of the previous evening's events filtered into her consciousness, accompanied by the nausea of a burgeoning hangover. After the successful conclusion of a long and difficult investigation, she and her colleagues had spent half the previous afternoon and much of the evening in a pub down the road from their offices at Scotland Yard. Now, at shortly after five a.m., one of those colleagues was buttoning up the shirt he had abandoned on her bedroom floor the night before and Rebecca was peering at the scene through eyes sticky with yesterday's mascara. Her companion turned in response to the light.

'Sorry,' he whispered, as if there was someone else in the room whose sleep he might not yet have disturbed. 'Didn't mean to wake you.'

'You didn't have to creep off before I woke up,' Rebecca objected, her voice hoarse.

'No choice,' he replied, his expression apologetic, as he retrieved his trousers from the post at the foot of the bed. 'Duty calls.' As if to emphasise this, he dug his official identification from his trouser pocket and flashed it at her before stepping into the right leg of the garment.

Realising she would have to be up for work in a few hours herself, Rebecca groaned. She raised a hand to rub her eyes, hoping she didn't look too much like Alice Cooper.

'Feeling bad?'

'Mm-hmm,' Rebecca confirmed, reopening her eyes. 'You?'

'Put it this way,' he responded, as he fastened his belt. 'It's going to be a long day.'

'I have a horrible feeling it's going to get worse before it gets better.'

'Can I get you anything before I go? Water? Coffee? Drugs?' He bent to retrieve his socks and sat on the end of the bed to put them on.

'Yeah, you got any?' Rebecca joked.

'I might have some fluffy paracetamol somewhere in my jacket.'

'Wow. Move over Pablo Escobar.'

He smiled. 'You might have better luck with the drugs squad.'

'Noted. I'll be more discerning in future.'

'You do that.' He slipped his shoes on and leaned to kiss her forehead. 'I'll see you later.'

Rebecca nodded, managing a smile before he turned and disappeared out of the door. A few moments later, she heard the front door of the flat open and quietly close again. She reached for the light switch and returned the room to darkness, rolling onto her side with a moan. She had always sworn she wasn't going to fall into the trap of sleeping with a colleague, and cursed herself for allowing herself to get involved. Going forwards, she would have to negotiate not only the immediate awkwardness of working with someone she had been intimate with, but also the question of where they went from here. And, much as there was no doubt in Rebecca's mind about what she wanted, she had no idea what her colleague's thoughts might be.

An ageing Alsatian had been standing guard over the mangled body slumped on the grass of the secluded garden when Leighton Campbell first arrived at the address in Stratford, and the uniformed officer in charge of proceedings wouldn't grant him access until an RSPCA inspector had turned up and subdued the animal. Half an hour or so later, he was bagging up evidence from the scene when he heard a familiar voice berating some unfortunate soul inside the house behind him.

He turned just as Peter Rose stepped out into the garden, looking more like a Hollywood hitman than a police officer. It was the combination of black suit and skinny black tie that did it, Leighton concluded. The garment was the only skinny thing about the DCI, who was built like a rugby player gone to seed, the look completed by a crooked nose and a misshapen ear. He marched across the lawn and stood glaring at the corpse for a moment before transferring his gaze to Leighton. Not bothering with the niceties of *hello* or *good morning*, he demanded, 'This your idea of an April Fools' joke, Dr Campbell?'

'No,' Leighton replied, sitting back on his heels. Until that moment, he hadn't even registered what the date was. It was something to bear in mind if he made it into the office before noon.

'So why've I been dragged over here for something a uniform straight out of Hendon could handle?'

'I don't think it's as straightforward as it looks.'

'No?' Pete responded doubtfully, turning as his attention was diverted by loud swearing coming from the garage. Moments later, a young detective constable emerged with bloodied fingers.

'What happened?' Leighton asked, straightening up.

'Little fucker bit me!' The man responded, furiously.

Pete's frown deepened. 'Not another dog?'

The constable shook his head. 'Wild cat.'

Leighton examined the puncture marks on the detective's forefinger before rifling through his bag for antiseptic wipes and giving the wound a cursory clean.

'You'll need to get antibiotics for that, cats have a nasty bite.'

'Great,' the man sighed, dabbing gingerly at the injury with a tissue.

'You can worry about that later,' Pete cut in. 'In the meantime, get that RSPCA woman back out here.' He headed towards two scenes of crime officers on the patio, no doubt to give them a hard time about something, and Leighton moved to look into the garage.

A pile of empty cat carriers in various states of disrepair were stacked against one wall, several of them heavily soiled. The back corner of the room was occupied by a decaying pine dresser, and as Leighton's eyes adjusted to the dim light he spotted two green eyes peeping out from behind it. Snapping off his gloves, he knelt beside the dresser and slowly extended a hand, palm exposed. Although clearly frightened, the cat was tame, and it didn't take him long to get into a position where he could scruff the animal and lift it out. Grabbing an old towel from one of the cleaner carriers, he wrapped the cat in it, noticing as he stood up that the tabby's left ear was mangled and infected.

'That's your *wild* cat?' Pete remarked, derisively, to his young colleague as Leighton emerged from the garage with the animal in his arms.

'He's just scared,' Leighton put in, spotting the RSPCA inspector heading towards them with a wire carrier. Leighton had met Stephanie – an attractive woman of forty-odd – before, and guessed from the wary glance she shot Pete as she passed him that she'd come across him before, as well.

'Hello gorgeous,' she said, warmly, as she came to a halt in front of him, her eyes on the animal in his arms.

'The cat's cute too, don't you think?' Leighton joked.

Stephanie glanced up with a smile, setting the carrier down on the grass and crouching to release the top. Straightening up, she reached to take the creature from him. 'Unfortunately this is an increasing problem.'

'What, dangerous dogs?'

She shook her head. 'Dog fighting. They often throw in cats or small dogs to wind the fighters up before setting them on each other. Or to see which one gets killed first.'

Leighton stared at Stephanie, momentarily speechless. 'That's horrific,' he managed, eventually.

She nodded, lowering the tabby cat into the carrier and flipping the top shut before he could escape.

'What'll happen to him?' Leighton asked as she fastened the lid.

'Hard to say. If he's chipped, we may be able to find his owners. If not, it'll depend on several things.'

'When you've quite finished playing animal rescue, Dr Campbell?' Pete's voice snapped behind him.

Leighton exchanged a surreptitious eye roll with Stephanie before turning to face the DCI. 'I'm all yours.'

'So what's the story?' Pete asked, indicating the body further down the garden. 'Are you saying this isn't the work of a dog? Because it certainly looks that way to me.'

'I just don't think it was the dog we found with him.'

'No?' Pete made a show of looking around himself. 'So which mythical dog do you propose it was? The hound of the Baskervilles? Cerberus, perhaps?'

'I think it could be connected to the O'Leary investigation, and if –'

'Are you on drugs?'

Leighton sighed. 'All I'm saying –'

'Simple yes or no: in your opinion, was this man killed by a dog?'

'Yes, but –'

'Thank you,' Pete cut him off. 'I assume you'll be able to confirm that via the postmortem by the end of the day?'

Leighton nodded, resisting the desire to argue his point there and then. He had little enough chance of getting Pete to see things his way in private, never mind while the man had an audience.

'Right, I'll leave you to get on with it, then. Waste my time like this again and I'll file a formal complaint!'

Leighton didn't reply, watching the man stomp back towards the house and mentally giving his retreating back the finger. Why Pete thought the word *complaint* carried any real weight as a threat, Leighton wasn't sure. The detective hadn't been on good terms with Leighton's boss, Professor William Maxwell – or Max, as he was almost universally known – for months. On top of that, Max received so many petty complaints resulting from misunderstandings or unreasonable expectations that all but the most serious went unheeded. Unless Pete had grounds for something worthy of disciplinary action, Max was unlikely to do more than mutter a few platitudes and promptly forget the matter. And calling a DCI out to a suspicious death – whether or not he chose to acknowledge it as such – really wasn't going to cut it.

The BBC News Channel was running in its perpetual loop on the small television in the corner of the room when Lawrence Forrester entered the kitchen shortly after seven. He pulled a chair out from the table and sat down before making a start on loosening the laces of his running shoes. Hearing footsteps thundering down the stairs behind him, he glanced around just as his fourteen-year-old son appeared in the doorway, clad in a West Ham football strip and with his dark hair sticking out along one side of his crown as if he'd gone to bed with it wet. Lawrence opened his mouth to ask the boy where his trainers were, but Jimmy got his question in first.

'Dad, can we get a telescope?'

Lawrence blinked in surprise. 'Pardon?'

Jimmy repeated himself, his grey eyes expectant.

'What for?'

His son looked nonplussed. 'What d'you think?' He returned, insolently. 'To look at the sky.'

'I did work that much out for myself,' Lawrence replied. 'But what in particular is it you want to look for?'

He hadn't been at all sure of receiving an intelligent response, and was pleasantly surprised when Jimmy said, 'Spiral galaxies.'

'I don't know that you'd be able to see much of that nature from here, Jim.'

'Yeah, I know, Mr Cortez says you need to go out into the country to get away from all the lights. But we could do that.'

Despite the assumption inherent in this statement, Lawrence smiled. 'Yes, we could.'

'So?' Jimmy chivvied, expectantly.

'Maybe we can look at hiring one over half term.'

'That's not for ages,' the boy objected.

'A weekend, then,' Lawrence conceded, keen not to discourage his son's apparent interest in something other than football or computer games. 'I'll look into it and then we'll see what we can work out, all right?'

'Cool,' Jimmy agreed.

'Are you still coming running?'

'Uh-huh,' Jimmy confirmed, turning and bounding out of the kitchen. Lawrence moved to resume his previous activity, a familiar face on the television screen catching his attention as he looked around. He reached to increase the volume to hear what Assistant Commissioner Cora Whiting had to say.

'... to Sean Quinn was a tragedy, but in the absence of any new information we cannot justify reopening the investigation.'

Lawrence wondered what had happened to bring Quinn's now infamous case back into the spotlight. The twenty-two-year-old had been charged with his uncle's murder by one of Lawrence's contemporaries the previous spring, and had died in dubious circumstances a few months later whilst on remand. His name had been in and out of the media ever since, thanks largely to relentless campaigning by his mother, and Lawrence suspected she wouldn't stop until she either succeeded in clearing her son's name or was presented with irrefutable proof of his guilt. The assistant commissioner, meanwhile, was no doubt thoroughly fed up with repeatedly having to defend the Met for what was, at least on the face of it, a failing of the prison service, not the police.

Jimmy came scurrying back into the room and dropped his trainers to the floor in readiness to put them on, scattering slivers of dried mud across the lino.

'Oops,' the boy remarked, with an affected wince.

Lawrence sighed. 'I think it might be better if you put those on outside,' he suggested, as Jimmy thrust his right foot into the relevant shoe without bothering to untie the laces. His son rolled his eyes, but pulled the trainer off, retrieved its partner from the floor and headed for the hallway.

'Could you sweep up after yourself first, please?'

'Yeah yeah, in a minute,' Jimmy threw back over his shoulder as he left the room.

'What's your response to Aileen Quinn's claim that Sean was charged solely on the basis of unreliable witness statements?' The newscaster continued.

'I can't comment on the content or nature of individual statements,' the assistant commissioner came back. 'But the decision to bring homicide charges is not one we or the CPS ever take lightly.'

The newscaster thanked her before moving on to the next item on the program's agenda, a clean-up operation in the wake of flooding somewhere in the West Country. Lawrence's mind remained on Sean Quinn. Clearly there had been sufficient grounds to charge the man, but whether the Crown Prosecution Service would have succeeded in securing a conviction was a question that would never now be answered. The lack of any real conclusion would, Lawrence suspected, see Aileen Quinn continuing her campaign for as long as anyone in the media was prepared to listen. From experience, he knew that could be a very long time.

Only one of the bank of desks outside Lawrence's office was occupied when he arrived, considerably later than usual, at nine-fifteen. Daniel Freeman's head was leaning against the top of his chair back, his eyes were shut and a glass of something fizzy stood on the desk in front of him. In response to Lawrence's morning greeting, the Jamaican's dark eyes opened partially, the whites faintly bloodshot.

'Oh dear,' Lawrence remarked, drily. 'What time did you guys stay out until?'

'Closing,' Daniel replied, wearily. 'I think it was the Sambuca shots that proved fatal.'

Lawrence smiled and nodded. He remembered similar drinking sessions from years gone by, as well as the painful mornings after the nights before. When he had left his colleagues in the pub shortly after seven the previous evening, everyone was already more than merry, and he had guessed he was likely to be the only one with a clear head in the morning.

'And of course it would be the night Fireman Sam finally got nicked.'

'Really?' Lawrence exclaimed. The serial rapist, nicknamed for his habit of using a ladder to access first-floor windows, had been the subject of an ongoing investigation for months. His apprehension would be cause for further celebration, and no doubt there would be more sore heads in CID the following morning.

'Uniform picked him up about four a.m.,' Daniel enlarged, reaching for the glass on his desk and closing his eyes in response to the movement. 'Ugh. I didn't feel too bad earlier, I thought maybe I'd got away with it.'

'I don't suppose you're the only one,' Lawrence replied, turning as he heard footsteps approaching to see Rebecca heading towards him with a large coffee cup in one hand and a bottle of Lucozade in the other. She looked worse than Daniel, and her expression was pained.

'Morning Becky.'

Rebecca responded with something between a sigh and a groan, sinking into her chair and setting the drinks down before resting her elbows on the desktop and lowering her face into her hands. 'I'm never drinking white wine again.'

Lawrence smiled. 'Never?' He teased.

'Never,' Rebecca repeated, raising her head and reaching for the coffee. 'For at least a week, anyway.'

'And how about Sambuca?'

Rebecca's expression registered surprise. 'Sambuca?' She looked to Daniel. 'Did we do shots?'

He nodded.

She groaned again, returning her face to her hands.

Daniel's eyebrows contracted towards a frown. 'Do you not remember anything that happened after that?'

'There are fragments of recollection in the wreckage of my mind,' Rebecca replied, her voice muffled.

'That's very poetic for this hour of the morning,' Lawrence remarked.

'Not my words,' she admitted.

'Elliot's?' Lawrence guessed.

'Um-hmm.'

He nodded. Elliot was Rebecca's ex-fiancé, and the frontman of an increasingly successful hard rock band. Rebecca had broken off their engagement the previous spring, after Elliot's drinking and mental health had spiralled out of control, and by the year's end he had been in a psychiatric hospital. Since then – if what

Lawrence had gathered from the media was anything to go by – he had gone some way towards putting himself back together. And whilst the breakdown had cost him his relationship with Rebecca, it didn't seem to have done his career any harm.

'I'll leave you to re-caffeinate,' Lawrence suggested, turning for his office. 'I've booked a meeting room for debriefing at ten. Hopefully everyone will be here by then.' He paused in his office doorway. 'In body if not in spirit.'

Ingrid Watts watched her daughter talking on her mobile through the glass wall of the conservatory, guessing the caller's identity from Abigail's expression. Needlessly shaking her head in response to whatever was being said at the other end of the line, she reached up to coil the fine hair of her ponytail around her finger, just as she invariably did the cord of the landline phone in the office. As Ingrid registered the similarity between two actions with, she suspected, very different meanings, her overriding feeling was one of apprehension. She wasn't about to further complicate Abigail's relationships by sticking her oar in, but she couldn't help questioning her daughter's motives.

Turning away, Ingrid allowed her eyes to drift over the paperwork spread across the coffee table and the mess of dishes visible through the open door to the kitchen until they reached the photographic portrait of Alf that hung on the back wall of the room. As ever, feelings of affection and fond memories mingled with the anger wrought of gross injustice. Alf had been the love of her life. He had been taken violently, unlawfully and with intent – yet nobody had ever been held accountable for his suffering, or his premature death. As far as the authorities were concerned, some lives were worth more than others.

A velvety paw gatecrashed Ingrid's thoughts, delivering a sharp slap to her cheek, and she looked down to meet the malevolent stare of the scruffy blue Persian cat that had taken up residence in her lap some minutes earlier. Abigail had affectionately nicknamed the animal *Soviet death cat*, remarking, laughingly, that she could quite understand why the breed was a popular choice for the Bond villain's feline companion. The creature was nowhere near as cantankerous as her glare might suggest, but she wasn't backwards in coming forwards when she wanted something – on this occasion, Ingrid's undivided attention. Ingrid raised a hand to stroke the cat, then glanced around as she heard the glass door to her left slide open.

'So much for spring,' Abigail remarked, as she hurried inside and swiftly closed the door behind herself. 'It's flipping freezing! D'you want me to get you a blanket?'

'No, I'm going to go through to the office, I'm getting nothing done here. Can you take Hatty for me?'

Abigail obligingly scooped up the untidy grey cat, who yowled and writhed in protest, then set her rather abruptly down on the floor as she landed a powerful kick on Abigail's collarbone.

'Moody cowbag,' Abigail admonished, fondly, as the cat stalked off towards the window seat, flicking the tip of her tail in disgust.

'Was that Toby?' Ingrid asked, gathering the papers on the table together.

'Uh-huh,' Abigail confirmed, casually. 'He said he'll try to get over here later with the prescription, and he'll have a look at the dishwasher while he's here. I said he might as well stay for dinner. I thought I'd make Pad Thai.'

Pad Thai: Toby's favourite.

'Don't play with him, Abbie,' Ingrid found herself warning. So much for not sticking her oar in.

'I'm not.'

'You can't keep leaning on him. It's not fair.'

Abigail exclaimed in disbelief. 'You rely on him as much as I do!'

'In a very different way. And he's under no illusions about the nature of the situation.'

'No illusions, just obligation,' Abigail retorted.

Ingrid frowned, wondering whether there was any basis to the remark, or whether her daughter had simply thrown it at her in an attempt to end the discussion. 'Has he said something to that effect?' She asked. 'Because he shouldn't feel that way. He's under no obligation to me or the centre, and if he thinks otherwise then I will set him straight. Tonight.'

'As if he'd ever admit to it now.'

Ingrid didn't reply. Abigail probably had a point. Recent events had unavoidably altered Ingrid's relationships with those close to her, and were doubtless also behind the shift in the dynamic between Abigail and Toby. That Ingrid wasn't to blame for the circumstances in which they found themselves didn't change the fact she was the cause. And nothing could alter the fact that Abigail would bear the brunt of what lay ahead.

'Well, if you don't need anything, I've a shedload of washing up to do,' Abigail continued, briskly, turning towards the kitchen. 'Some days, I really feel as though we're making a difference. Others, it's like I'm running a giant, thankless B and B.'

Lawrence signed into the Gresham Pathology Unit shortly after four and headed for the main office. Leighton had called half an hour previously to ask if he might meet with Lawrence privately – why, and about what, he hadn't said. The pathologist was a close friend of Rebecca's, and Lawrence was intrigued by his specific request that she be excluded from the meeting. Although, given that she was clearly still feeling more than a little worse for wear, he didn't imagine she'd be sorry to miss out on the possibility of being faced with graphic autopsy and crime-scene photographs.

'Afternoon,' he greeted, as he looked into the office.

Leighton turned in his chair and smiled in response. He looked tired, but otherwise in considerably better shape than any of the other participants of the previous evening's revelry, and Lawrence wondered whether, like himself, Leighton had made off early. Then again, perhaps for Leighton the night hadn't been anything out of the ordinary. The pathologist was renowned for juggling a social life almost as busy as his job, and seemed to have the ability to sink an impressive quantity of alcohol with few apparent ill effects besides a substantial beer gut. He had clearly not long since showered, as his long dark hair was damp, so had presumably spent much of his afternoon in the mortuary. Lawrence couldn't think of many worse jobs to perform with a hangover than a postmortem.

Whatever Leighton had been doing immediately prior to Lawrence's arrival had involved an iPad and jam doughnuts, and Leighton wiped the sugar from his fingers with a paper napkin before switching the tablet to standby and setting it to one side. Noticing the iPhone also on the desktop, Lawrence said, 'Two apples and a bag of doughnuts. Is that what passes for a balanced diet in these parts?'

There was a momentary pause before Leighton got the joke and laughed. 'I like that. D'you want one?' He indicated the doughnuts.

'No thanks,' Lawrence shook his head, sitting in the unoccupied chair at the adjacent desk.

'Cheers for coming down.'

'You're welcome. Although I am curious to know what's behind the cloak-and-dagger routine.'

'That may have made it seem more intriguing than it really is,' Leighton replied, combing his hair back from his face with his fingers, gathering it together and securing it in a low pony tail. 'It's just a sensitive subject and I thought you should have a chance to work out how you want to play it before anyone else gets wind of it.'

'Now I think I'm more curious.'

'I'd best put you out of your misery, then. I had a call earlier from a pathologist in Birmingham about a case she thought might be connected to something we worked on a couple of years ago,' he leaned to reach for a cardboard folder lying atop a huge stack of paperwork that had long since outgrown its filing tray. 'She said she'd tried flagging it with the SIO, but he didn't seem very interested. She's sent me what she has so far,' he flipped the folder open and pulled out two A4 pages featuring scanned and annotated photographs, laying them in front of Lawrence without further explanation. On seeing the woman's mutilated breasts, Lawrence immediately understood his colleague's desire to speak to him alone. The case in question had involved a serial killer, and had hit much too close to home for Rebecca when the man broke into her flat in the middle of the night. Having never succeeded in apprehending him, Lawrence had been left feeling he had failed her. He had also always been acutely aware that, sooner or later, the man would kill again. Now that it had happened, he felt wholly responsible.

'Thank you for bringing this to me first,' he said, looking back to Leighton. 'I appreciate it.'

'No problem.'

'What sort of timescale are we dealing with here?'

'The body was only found this morning, but she probably died on Tuesday night.'

'Do you have much more information?'

'I've everything the pathologist could provide, but as far as the police are concerned all I can give you is the name and number of the SIO.' Leighton held out the cardboard folder. 'It's all in here. Let me know if you want to have the body moved down here.'

'I imagine I will, but I'll talk to West Mids Police first, make sure we don't trample too many toes. What time will you be here until?'

'Hopefully not much longer, but if you need anything later just give me a call.'

'Thanks,' Lawrence nodded, moving to stand and mentally planning out the remainder of his afternoon. He needed to gather and digest what information there was so far, and consult his superior about reopening the original case. The unwelcome task of breaking the news to Rebecca could wait until tomorrow, when he would be better prepared and she in better shape. He could only hope that in the interim he might find the right words with which to approach the matter. At present, he hadn't the faintest idea where to start.

Friday 2 April

The incident room felt uncomfortably warm and, with the briefing coming hot on the heels of a heavy fish and chip lunch, Daniel suspected he would soon be facing a struggle to keep his eyes open. He ought to have picked up a decent cup of coffee on his way back to the office rather than the bitter, watery substitute he'd grabbed at the last minute from the machine down the corridor. He fervently hoped his superior wouldn't deviate from his usual form of keeping meetings as brief and concise as possible.

Lawrence had affixed photographs of four women to the board and written their names underneath in capital letters. He repeated these aloud as he indicated each one in turn. Letty Winterton. Zoë Mitchell. Monica Hudson. Coralie Perrot. All but the last were familiar to Daniel, who had been a part of the original, unsuccessful effort to apprehend their killer. And all four were pretty, petite and brunette – just like Rebecca. But Rebecca was the odd one out: she was still alive.

Daniel half-listened as his superior ran through an overview of the initial investigation and the man they were looking for: an organised and sadistic serial killer called Rhys Williams. Not that he was likely to be using that name, last they'd heard of him he'd been going by Brett Lindquist, and it seemed more than likely he had since assumed another identity, quite possibly more than once. Thanks to snatches of CCTV footage and witness accounts, they had some idea of what he had looked like as Brett, but the assembled photofits would probably be of limited help – Williams had previously used both hair dye and coloured contact lenses, and had no doubt made every effort to change his appearance soon after the images were published in the national press. It wasn't even unheard of for people to go as far as cosmetic surgery in attempt to dodge the law, Lawrence pointed out. The only notable feature they were aware of, he added, was a small scar on the man's philtrum – assuming it hadn't somehow been removed.

'So we should view all moustache owners with suspicion,' Jamie remarked, stroking the mousy hair on his own upper lip.

'That's standard policy, isn't it?' Eva joked.

'Well it's not me, that's one down.'

'Thank you,' Lawrence cut in, firmly, halting the exchange. 'I'd appreciate it if we could approach this with the gravity it merits.'

'Sir.'

'Previously Williams has always gained access to properties through the front door by way of a key, obtained via a job in a locksmith's, but we can't discount the possibility he's changed that part of his MO,' Lawrence went on. 'There was no sign of forced entry at Coralie's home, so the first question we need to answer is who else had a key – family, friends, boyfriend, neighbours, cleaner, pet-sitter, et cetera. If it was a rented flat, was it managed by a landlord or an estate agent? Did she change the locks or have keys cut recently? If none of that takes us forwards, we need to check out every locksmith in Birmingham, starting with those closest to her home and workplace, and making sure we stay under the radar. If Williams clocks us, he'll disappear into the ether. West Mids have already done some door-to-door but there are bound to be plenty of people still to talk to.' Lawrence paused. 'Two years ago, we came within hours of apprehending Williams before he vanished off the radar. This time we need to do better than that.' He indicated a photograph of a woman's mutilated breasts on the wall behind him. 'We need to make sure this never happens again.'

Rebecca was bent over her desk writing when Daniel returned from the briefing, and didn't acknowledge him as he sat at the adjacent desk. He wondered whether she was actually working, or just making a concerted effort to look busy. Lawrence had spoken to her privately earlier in the day, and Daniel could only guess how she might have taken the news that the serial killer who had very nearly added her to his list of victims was active again. She was still living at the same address he had broken into some two years previously, in a week when Elliot's touring schedule had taken him hundreds of miles away, and Daniel wondered how she felt about the prospect of returning home that night.

Williams' re-emergence had no doubt also served as a reminder of the life Rebecca had shared with Elliot, just as she seemed to have succeeded in moving on from the relationship. And although she wouldn't be participating in the current investigation, Daniel didn't suppose that would do anything to take her mind off the subject. He hoped she might allow him to be there for her in the coming weeks, but he had no real idea of where he stood. He wished he could remember more of the conversation they'd had on Wednesday night.

'Hey Becks.'

She raised her powder blue eyes from the page in front of her and gave him a forced smile before returning her focus to the desk.

'Are you ok?'

'Yes thanks.'

'What you up to?'

'Paperwork,' she replied, glancing up again and reaching to tuck a chunk of her long hazelnut bob behind her ear. 'Boring but necessary. You know.'

'Do you need a hand with anything?'

'Surely you have more important things to do?'

'Yes,' he admitted. Sorry. I just –' he sighed. 'I didn't want you to think I didn't –' he hesitated. 'D'you want to go for a drink later?'

Rebecca sighed. 'Dan, do you mind if we don't do this now?'

'Of course not,' Daniel responded, with what he hoped was a sympathetic smile, wondering whether that was just her way of saying *no*.

'I'm shattered,' she excused herself. 'After the past few days I need a long bath and an early night.'

'Will your flat mate be home this evening?'

'I expect he'll make an appearance at some stage.'

'Are you going to be all right if he doesn't?'

'I think I can look after myself.'

'I know, I just meant –' he half shrugged, not wanting to articulate the question of whether logic and self-defence training would suffice to stop her mind going into overdrive in the early hours.

'I know,' she echoed. 'I appreciate it. But I don't need my hand holding. Ok?'

'Ok,' Daniel acknowledged, with a nod. He wanted to add a proviso, but hesitated, unsure how it would go down. Seemingly reading his mind, Rebecca somehow succeeded in combining a smile with a sigh, and resolved the dilemma for him.

'If I change my mind, you'll be the first to know.'

*****

The news that Coralie had rented her flat through an estate agent was a far from welcome development, as it immediately multiplied the number of people with access to her front door keys. Lawrence had handed Daniel and Eva the task of quietly investigating the agent's staff members whilst he and Jamie had set off for Coralie's one-time family home in Watford, now occupied by only her father. Father and daughter, it turned out, hadn't spoken in some four years – and he wasn't prepared to elaborate – so aside from providing a little background information, it proved a wasted journey. Jamie wondered whether any of the woman's friends would be able to fill them in on whatever it was her father was unwilling to divulge.

The first of the women they spoke to couldn't shed any light on the situation, but when Lawrence broached the subject with Kemi Okoye it was immediately clear from the change in her expression that she was a party to at least some of the story. Not surprisingly, given the circumstances, she seemed subdued, but from the photographs arranged on the sideboard Jamie gathered she had been blessed with the same stunning hundred-watt smile as Julia Roberts. Even in its absence she was a looker – approaching Jamie's six-foot height and with curves in all the right places. Drawing a host of tiny black plaits away from her face, she said, 'They fell out after her mother died.'

'Why?'

'She found out her dad had been seeing someone else.'

'Do you know whether she's had any contact with him since then?'

'None. She was devastated. She came to visit to get away from everything – and then ended up getting a job and sticking around.'

'So you knew Coralie before she moved to Birmingham,' Lawrence clarified.

'Yes. We did gymnastics classes together when we were kids.'

'Did she generally confide in you?'

Kemi nodded, her features tense. Jamie guessed she was battling to keep her emotions under control.

'Are you aware of anyone, or anything that was worrying her in recent weeks?'

Kemi shook her head, her lips pursed tightly.

'I'm sorry, I realise this must be very difficult for you.'

Kemi nodded again, swallowing hard and lowering her eyes. Several seconds passed in silence before she drew a deep breath and looked back up. 'I'm ok,' she managed, her voice wavering. 'Go on.'

Lawrence threaded his fingers together. 'Coralie didn't mention anything unusual happening, anyone hanging around or following her?'

'David, maybe,' Kemi ventured, after a moment's consideration. 'But I'm not sure he was still a problem, she hadn't mentioned him in a while.'

'Who's David?'

'An ex. Well – ex might be an overstatement. They only went on a few dates.'

'And in what way was he a problem?'

'He didn't take it very well when she didn't want to keep seeing him. He sent streams of text messages and he kept turning up outside her flat.'

'When was this?'

'Um – last autumn sometime – September, October –' she shook her head slightly. 'But she threatened to go to the police and I think he backed off after that.'

'Can you give us his full name, or a description of him?'

'No. I never met him.'

'Do you know how he and Coralie met?'

'Online, I think.'

That ought to make tracing him simple enough, Jamie thought – assuming the man had used his real name. And, if he hadn't, the process of trying to track him down might at least be worth the trouble.

'You mentioned that Coralie and David went on a few dates,' Lawrence continued. 'Do you know why she didn't want to take it further than that? Was it just a lack of chemistry, or something more?'

'She didn't trust him,' Kemi revealed. 'She said to begin with he seemed really nice, and came across as very clever and well-read – but when it came to a couple of topics she knew a lot about, she realised most of what he came out with was bull. So then she didn't know what to believe about anything he said.'

'And when he continued to pursue her, did she find his behaviour threatening? Or was it more of an irritation?'

'To start with I think it was just annoying, but it freaked her out when he turned up at her flat because she'd not given him the address.'

'Could she think of any way he might have come by it? Any nearby landmarks she might have mentioned?'

'She thought either he'd followed her home after one of their dates, or that he'd found her through her work. It's creepy however he did it.'

'Yes, it is,' Lawrence agreed. 'You said this happened about six months ago. Did Coralie mention him at all in the past month or two?'

'No.'

'Had she been dating anyone else?'

'I don't think so.'

Lawrence nodded. 'Have you any idea whether anyone – besides the lettings agency – had a key to her flat? A cleaner, or a neighbour, perhaps?'

Kemi shook her head. 'She didn't have a cleaner. And her neighbours were a bit weird.'

'Weird in what way?'

'The girl on the ground floor's nice enough, but she's a bit – I don't know – head in the clouds, I suppose. If you gave her something for safe-keeping I'm not sure you'd ever see it again. And the guy on the first floor is really awkward. I don't think they ever exchanged more than the odd hello.'

'How about people in the neighbouring buildings, did she know any of them?'

'Possibly in passing. I don't remember her ever mentioning anyone. But I don't think she ever gave anyone a key. It wasn't like she had pets or plants she needed looking after when she wasn't there. I suppose it's possible she kept a spare set at work.'

Jamie groaned inwardly: goodness knows how many more people that might mean their having to rule out. The tedious and time-consuming exercise would be made even more frustrating by the knowledge it would almost certainly be unrewarding – the chances were that Coralie's killer had been a total stranger. Even if Rhys Williams had changed his MO, it was highly unlikely they would find any obvious link between him and his victims. He was far too clever for that.

*****

A scraping sound at the door of his car interrupted Leighton's mental debate about what to do with his evening. He had been sitting outside his flat for almost a quarter of an hour, putting off going inside and dealing with his brother, who had stayed the night several months earlier and was yet to leave. Leighton had always sworn he wasn't going to return to living in the permanent state of fear that had, at age fifteen, seen him stealing his mother's tranquillizers and supplementing them with neat spirits just to find the courage to go home at night. Unfortunately he hadn't taken into account the humiliating fact that he couldn't stand up to his brother any more than he could his father.

Living with Tom was exhausting. Constantly watching what you said and did hardly made for a relaxing home life, but on its own probably would have been manageable. Tom's tendency to react to imagined slights, however, was not. There was no way to control a situation that didn't exist, although it was often impossible to know whether Tom actually believed in what he was saying or whether he was just looking for a fight. Either way, the end result was the same: home was now the last place Leighton wanted to be, and the ensuing tension was starting to seep into other areas of his life.

As he opened the door, his cat leapt up into his lap and nuzzled his chin, purring loudly. He managed a smile and reached to stroke her ears, receiving an impatient head butt in exchange: she was hungry and supper was late. It occurred to him that he hadn't given any thought to his own evening meal. Then again, he didn't feel very hungry.

Setting Pandora down on the pavement, he climbed out of the car, locked up and made for his front door. The cat trotted ahead of him and wrapped herself around his ankles as he dug into his pocket for the keys. Stepping carefully through the door to avoid tripping over her, he turned towards the kitchen, where he regarded the pile of dirty crockery and mugs in the sink with a sigh. It wasn't that difficult to stack a dishwasher, surely? As he reached for the box of Felix atop the fridge, he heard footsteps behind him.

'All right, mate?'

Leighton returned the greeting without much enthusiasm, tearing a pouch of cat food open and looking around for a clean bowl.

'D'you want a beer?' Tom asked, opening the fridge door and shunting Pandora rather roughly out of the way in the process.

'On call,' Leighton replied, shortly, locating the bowl and tipping the food into it.

'You're on call all the bloody time,' Tom grumbled, closing the fridge door and making for the magnetic bottle opener residing on the side of the boiler just as Pandora wandered in front of him.

'Stupid bloody animal!' Tom snapped, kicking her out of the way as she got under his feet. The cat yelped and shot out of the room, her paws skidding on the laminate as she rounded the corner. Leighton seized his brother's arm and slammed him against the wall.

'Touch her again and you'll wake up in intensive fucking care!'

'All right, all right!' Tom exclaimed, after a shocked pause. 'Keep your hair on!'

'Don't tell me what to do in my own house!'

'Ok! I get the message!' Tom returned, struggling to free himself.

'That'd be a first!' Leighton responded, releasing his grip. 'Now get out!'

Tom turned to face him. 'Well, there's hope for you yet,' he said, with an approving smile.

'Just get out!' Leighton replied, turning to go after Pandora.

'Lee –'

'Save it, I'm not interested!'

Leighton found the cat cowering under his bed. Although clearly spooked, she didn't seem any the worse for her run-in with Tom, and it didn't take him long to coax her out. He suspected he was more shaken than she was by the incident, not least by his own reaction. Despite repeatedly having failed to stand up for himself, it seemed he had no problem defending the animal who'd turned up uninvited at his back door two years previously and never left. His actions per se didn't unduly concern him – physical force was probably the only way to get a point through to Tom. What worried him was the fact his response had been so automatic. He hadn't even thought about what he was doing until he already had his brother flat against the wall.

The incident fed into a fear that had dogged him for the better part of two decades. Over the years he'd seen the fallout as his brother repeated their father's behaviour time and time again: his recollection of Tom's now ex-wife's swollen, battered face was still all too clear, as was his preoccupation with the possibility he might be capable of doing the same. In that eventuality, he wasn't at all sure he would be able to live with himself.

Saturday 3 April

Abigail drifted into consciousness with the uncomfortable feeling she was being watched. She sensed she had been aware of it even as she dreamed, when the eyes of countless imaginary people had stared up at her from the streets. In the dream, she had been able to fly, although she couldn't recall whether she had possessed wings. At first, swooping just out of reach of the crowds grasping at her from below, she had felt exhilarated, but as the people on the ground grew smaller and smaller, and she soared ever higher, she became consumed with the fear of falling and of the unknown alternative.

Somehow, the flight had segued into a shopping trip with an old and now largely forgotten friend; the selection of a glamorous, show-stopping dress she would never even have tried on, let alone bought; and her arrival, thus attired, at an open-air gala. The herringbone brickwork underfoot led onto a broadwalk through a grid of identikit modern apartment blocks, and one moment she was wandering, accompanied, among them; next she was alone in the dark, the voices, lights and laughter of the party far behind her, and the previously homely feel of the surrounding buildings suddenly menacing. As she began to hurry back towards the distant throng, the dream faded into a half-reality, but the accompanying sense of trepidation stayed with her. Reluctantly, she opened her eyes.

Izzy was leaning against the bedroom doorframe, her slender frame wrapped in Abigail's calf-length satin dressing gown. The deep plum colour of the fabric clashed with her curly red hair, which looked annoyingly fresh considering it had just been slept on. Abigail doubted her own had fared nearly so well: normally she awoke to find that the hair along the left side of her parting had been creased into what she could only describe as a reverse quiff overnight, and no amount of water or judicious arrangement of hair slides could undo the seemingly effortless work of a pillow. According to her high-maintenance and altogether more grown-up friend Philippa, the answer to starting the day without crumpled hair or skin lay in upgrading from cheap polycotton to silk bedclothes. But that was an expense Abigail would never be able to justify.

Seeing she was awake, Izzy approached the bed. Tucking one leg under herself as she sat down, she wedged a pillow into the small of her back and tipped her head against the padded headboard. Abigail slid a hand beneath the flimsy fabric of the dressing gown, curving her fingers around Izzy's waist, but Izzy grasped her wrist to stop her.

'Are you coming to Greece?'

Abigail sighed. 'Izzy.'

'Greece was always part of the plan. We talked about it the night we met. It was your dream as much as mine.'

'I know,' Abigail acknowledged, moving rather reluctantly to sit up. 'I know how desperate the situation is over there. If it wasn't for Mum I'd come in a heartbeat, you know that.'

'Do I?'

'That's not fair.'

'I'm the one being unfair?'

Abigail drew a deep breath. 'I'm sorry,' she offered, after a moment. 'Dreams aren't always compatible with reality.'

'Does that include me? Am I *incompatible with reality* as well?'

'Iz, you know how I feel about you. I'm choosing Mum over Greece, not over you.'

'Really? Are you sure it's your mum you're doing it for?'

Abigail frowned. 'What?'

Izzy shook her head wordlessly, her gaze fixed on a point on the opposite wall. Her pale eyes were wet with tears, and Abigail wished there was some way to make things right. Some way to rewind time, unmake promises and factor in an unpredictable future. Abigail couldn't blame Izzy for feeling let down, but she had made those promises in good faith. She hadn't known at the time that her mother was dying.

'It's not like you'd be leaving her alone,' Izzy ventured, her voice slightly unsteady. 'Charlie's here, and Meg and your Aunt Lily are in practically every day.'

'There are things they can't do.'

'It's not your job to look after her! If you weren't here the authorities would be obliged to provide care!'

'You've no more faith in the authorities than I have,' Abigail reproached. Probably even less, in fact: Izzy had precious little faith in almost anyone. Humanity, she regularly opined, represented everything that was wrong with the world. 'Besides, it's not as simple as that.'

Izzy made no reply.

'I'm sorry,' Abigail offered, again.

Izzy shook her head, her lips pursed tightly. At length, she drew breath and said, 'Well, I'm sticking to the plan.' She met Abigail's eyes. 'And if need be, I'll action it alone.' She moved to stand. 'I'll do everything I can at this end, and then I'm out of here.'

Daniel and Eva had spent the best part of everyone else's lunch hours surveilling the bizarrely named Bees' Keys shop from a parking space some fifty yards down the road. With two-thirty fast approaching, Eva had offered to fetch them a bite to eat, and, glad of an excuse to break the tedium of a day spent watching, waiting and waiting some more, had walked considerably further than necessary to find a sandwich shop. Rejoining Daniel in the car at a quarter to three, she guessed from his languid repose that he had nothing to report for the time she'd been gone.

'They were out of ham, sorry. Is chicken ok?'

'It'll do. Thanks.'

She handed him a sandwich and a can of Sprite before shedding her jacket and tossing it onto the back seat. 'Have I missed anything?'

'Other than a seagull with a sense of humour crapping on that Porsche over there, no,' Daniel replied. 'We'll give it a bit longer in case they have someone else on the afternoon shift and then we'll head on.'

'It's a good job most locksmiths don't open on Sundays or I'd have a numb bum by the end of the weekend.'

'I'm sure there'll be plenty of opportunity for that next week.'

Eva sighed, unwrapping her sandwich and thinking as the strong smell of tuna filled the car that she ought to have chosen something less pungent. 'How did Becks get out of doing the grunt work on this one, then?'

Daniel looked around in surprise. 'Did nobody fill you in?'

'Clearly not,' Eva replied, immediately feeling intrigued. 'What's the story?'

'Becky was nearly victim number three.'

Eva stopped mid-chew. 'Was she trying to arrest him?' She asked, once she'd managed to swallow what was in her mouth.

'No. He just had the opportunity to make a copy of the keys to her flat and knew from the music press when Elliot would be away.'

Eva swallowed again. 'What happened?'

'Elliot's tour got cut short, so he was home. He got up in response to a noise and disturbed the guy.'

'Wow,' Eva breathed. 'It must be horrible for her having it all dragged up again.'

Daniel nodded his agreement.

'D'you think she's ok?'

'I don't know. Probably not.'

Eva set the sandwich down in her lap and reached for her can of Pepsi Max. 'She never talks about him,' she remarked, as she snapped it open. 'Elliot, I mean, not Williams.'

'Do you talk about your exes?'

'No, but I don't keep a photo of any of them in my desk drawer, either.'

Despite the proximity of Daniel's desk to Rebecca's, it was clear from his expression that this was news to him. The fact he had a soft spot for Rebecca hadn't passed Eva by, and she felt bad for bringing it up – but not bad enough to sit on her own curiosity. 'I just can't imagine her being with someone so – I don't know – badly behaved. She seems too sensible.'

Daniel shrugged. 'He wasn't so unhinged when they got together. I think he even had a proper job.' He paused, then added, 'Besides, Becks doesn't have Forrester looking over her shoulder when she's off duty. She doesn't take life as seriously as he does.'

'*Nobody* takes life as seriously as he does.'

Daniel chuckled. 'I often wonder –' he trailed off, his attention elsewhere. Eva followed his gaze and spotted a dark-haired young man in a red polo shirt and jeans approaching the locksmith's.

'That looks like the same top the bloke I spoke to this morning was wearing,' Daniel observed, as the man opened the shop door and disappeared inside.

Eva re-wrapped the remains of her sandwich and leaned to retrieve her jacket. 'I'll go and make his acquaintance.'

The shop's name, she realised on arrival, wasn't simply a bad pun: jars of locally produced honey were prominently displayed in the window to the left of the door. It seemed an extraordinary sideline to key cutting and shoe repairs, but she supposed it would at least make for a good talking point should the conversation flounder. By the time she eased open the door, the man Daniel had pointed out just a minute earlier was behind the counter, laughing at something with an older companion, a flickering ceiling light making it difficult for her to focus on their features. The older man smiled as she approached the counter, welcoming her with a friendly, 'Afternoon.'

Eva returned the greeting and the smile before saying, 'I'd like to get copies of these made, please.' She placed a set of keys on the counter and, as he looked them over, took the opportunity to steal a glance at the other man. Frustratingly, he had turned his back, leaving her with a view of only his hair and ears.

The first man made a start on working the keys free of their ring, adding, after a moment, 'Mike, can you sort this out?' He tipped his head back momentarily to indicate the defective light above the counter.

'Yeah, will do in two ticks,' Mike replied, before disappearing through a doorway to his right, still without giving Eva a clear look at his face.

'I'll have half a cup,' the man at the counter called after him, clearly guessing where he was going, before looking back to Eva. 'I considered docking all the tea he drinks from his wages, but I was afraid it might mean him having to move back home,' he joked.

'Your son?' Eva guessed.

He nodded.

'Is it just the two of you working here?' She continued, conversationally.

Another nod. 'For the time being.'

Eva mentally crossed the shop off the list, reaching for the jar at the end of the counter. 'And who makes the honey?'

The locksmith reached for a blank key, glancing up momentarily to meet her eyes. His expression and tone such that it was impossible to tell whether he was being humorous or wholly serious, he replied, shortly, 'The bees.'

Kittle Home Security had the sort of slick high-street showroom usually reserved for outfits offering kitchens and bathrooms, and Daniel wondered how much of a premium that added to the cost of their products. It was clear from the marketing blurb on the wall to the right of the counter that the company provided much more than the average locksmith, including the installation and maintenance of a whole range of security grilles and burglar alarms, as well as CCTV. Moreover, their locks apparently took keys cut using specialist equipment, meaning replicas could only be obtained through them. Had Coralie's keys fitted that bill their provenance would presumably have been flagged by now, but as he was already there Daniel reasoned he might as well make some basic enquiries. On occasion, what seemed blindingly obvious from one vantage point turned out to have been overlooked from another.

A twenty-something man whose name tag announced him as Raj, the assistant manager, received Daniel at the front desk, and Daniel quickly fabricated a story about being in the process of purchasing a home nearby with a security-conscious girlfriend, asking what Raj would recommend. The man took one of the pamphlets from the rack on the counter and swiftly walked Daniel through everything from window locks and door reinforcements to safes and security lighting.

'That must keep you busy,' Daniel remarked, as Raj finished his spiel. 'How many people does the company employ?'

Raj paused for thought. 'You know, I'm not sure,' he admitted, before volunteering the information Daniel was really after. 'All staff members and contractors are DBS checked, though.'

'Well that should keep the lady of the house happy.'

'Sounds like a smart girl,' Raj observed.

'Smart and demanding.'

'Aren't they all?'

Daniel smiled. 'Can't argue with you there,' he agreed, reaching for the pamphlet. During Raj's run-through he had noticed that the final panel of the roll fold provided contact details for the company's head office, as well as the locations and telephone numbers of its three other branches. It wasn't information he was likely to need, and was doubtless all available online, but it couldn't hurt to have a hard copy. 'Can I hang onto this?'

'Sure. If you want more information about anything you can order a brochure or visit our website,' Raj indicated the relevant URL before reaching to take a business card from the box by the till. 'And if you've any questions, give me a call.'

Monday 5 April

Iain MacClintock glanced at his watch. It was coming up to eight, and he'd been in the lab almost an hour already. His contention that they were overstretched – as he had apologetically told his wife – wasn't untrue, but it wasn't the reason he had chosen to make such an early start. In reality, he had been desperate to avoid another breakfast with Kelly's American mother – not because she was excessively critical, or pushy, or any other mother-in-law-from-hell caricature, but because she was too *nice*. Perhaps she was sincere, he wasn't sure, but either way, after a whole weekend in her company the relentless bonhomie was setting his teeth on edge more than a bag of butter tablet.

'Clint, my man!' An enthusiastic voice interrupted his thoughts as footsteps approached from his right-hand side.

'The answer's no,' Iain pre-empted, without raising his eyes from the pipette and Eppendorf tube in his hands. 'And you need to stop letting yourself in here every five minutes, Paula'll have my balls if she finds out you've got a pass.'

'Not guilty,' came the cheerful reply over the sound of a stool being pulled out from the bench. 'Darius let us in.'

Iain lifted his gaze as Leighton sat down opposite him. 'I thought security were there to keep trouble out,' he returned, only half joking.

Leighton clasped a hand to his chest. 'Clint, I'm deeply hurt.'

'Yeah yeah.'

'I come bearing gifts,' he continued, undaunted, setting a paper bag from Pret a Manger down on the bench and digging a hand into it.

'You should've gone to Specsavers and all.'

'Eh?'

Iain nodded towards the big wall-mounted sign forbidding the consumption of food and drink in the lab.

'Have you been hanging out with Roddy behind my back?' Leighton asked, in mock consternation.

Iain flicked him a middle-finger salute, but not without a reluctant smile.

'If it'll cheer you up, I'll let you brag about yesterday's game,' Leighton continued, placing a cardboard coffee cup and a waxed paper bag containing a chocolate croissant on Iain's side of the bench. 'The Jags played a blinder.'

'Aye, well, I'll have to take your word for that.'

'Did you not see it?'

'No.'

'Now I understand the long face. You weren't working yesterday as well?'

Iain shook his head. 'The wife's folks are visiting.'

'Ah, in-law overdose,' Leighton concluded. 'You know what the best prescription is for that, don't you?'

'Yeah,' Iain came back, ruefully. 'Overtime.'

'So that's why you've been in since seven.'

Iain didn't ask how Leighton knew what time he'd arrived, saying instead, 'What's your excuse for being in so soon after daybreak? You're way too chipper to have pulled an all-nighter.'

'I'm following up on something from last year for a meeting later, and I was hoping you might be able to do me a teeny favour sometime this morning.'

Iain sighed. 'Go on, then.'

'D'you remember Quinn and O'Leary?'

Given the now infamous nature of the case, that was a bit like asking whether he remembered Litvinenko, Iain reflected, nodding his response.

'I could swear we tested the soil under O'Leary's fingernails, but there's nothing in the archive or on the system.'

Iain shook his head slightly. 'So long after the event I've no idea what was or wasn't requested, but if the results were of note they'd presumably have been submitted to the CPS?'

'Yeah, nothing doing there, either.'

'Are you sure the paperwork isn't just buried somewhere on your desk? Whole civilisations could be lost under there.'

'No. I have a system,' Leighton replied, definitively, before adding, as Iain sniggered, disbelievingly, 'Besides, it wasn't my case, I just helped out with a couple of things.'

'So what is it you want me to do?'

'Could you have a check of your lab notes? See whether you've any record of the tests being requested in the first place?'

'How's that going to help?'

'Because I'm sure they were and the fact I can't find hide nor hair of them is driving me nuts.'

Iain sighed. 'Ok, I'll see what I can do.'

'You're a star, thank you. I owe you beer.'

Iain raised his gaze from the pipette and lifted his eyebrows pointedly. This was far from the first time he had heard that.

Leighton smiled. 'Yeah, all right, a lot of beer,' he acknowledged, sliding off the stool and nodding towards the sign on the wall. 'But even I draw the line at bringing proper drinks into the lab. So if you want to claim it, one of these days you're going to have to come out to play.'

Hearing a familiar electronic chirrup, Isabel rolled over and propped herself up on one elbow to view the screen of the smartphone lying on Abigail's bedside table. In the second before it faded to black she absorbed the name and opening words of the text message, feeling something tighten inside her. She had been trying to ignore her doubts about Abigail's reasons for pulling out of the Greek arm of their venture, but instinct, as Abigail was fond of saying, never lies. Unlike Abigail herself, it seemed. After a moment's hesitation, Isabel reached for the phone and swiped it open to read the remainder of the communication, hoping she might yet be proved wrong. The message's conclusion implied otherwise.

'Your ex wants to know if tonight's good for him to come over,' Isabel informed Abigail, coolly, on her return from the bathroom. 'Or whether I'll be here.' She tossed Abigail's phone over her shoulder onto the bed before standing and reaching for her jeans. 'I wouldn't want to come between you, so I'll make myself scarce, shall I?'

'Don't be daft, he's only coming round to do me a favour. That's probably just his way of asking whether we have plans.'

'He signed off with a kiss,' Isabel snapped. 'Was that a preview of *his* plans?'

Abigail sighed. 'I doubt he meant anything by it.'

'Right.'

'Iz, this is crazy. You're making something out of nothing.' Abigail leaned to reach for the phone and, straightening up, swiped it open. Isabel watched as she read the message for herself, working up to the all-important question.

'Is he the reason you're not coming to Greece?'

'Oh for God's sake!' Abigail erupted, flinging the phone back down onto the bed. 'How many times? You know why I'm not coming, and it has nothing to do with Toby! Although I'm beginning to wish it did, given that he seems to care more about what I'm going through than you do! Mum is dying and you're behaving as if I'm being unreasonable wanting to put her first! I know you're upset about Greece, and I'm sorry, but I'm upset about my mum! And I'm sick of constantly having to justify myself and reassure you!'

'I'll go then, shall I?' Isabel threw back. 'Then you won't have to do either!'

Abigail stood staring at her in silence, her eyebrows twisted with emotion. Isabel stared back. Whether or not Abigail's reaction had been an attempt to deflect attention from Toby's message, much of what she had said was true. Isabel had been more concerned with how the change in plans would affect her than with the effect the underlying circumstances might be having on Abigail. Maybe if she'd been closer to her own mother, she would have been better equipped to handle the situation. Then again, maybe if Abigail and Toby's history had been different, she wouldn't have felt so insecure.

Eventually, with a shake of her head, Abigail replied. 'Do what you want, Izzy,' she said, turning back towards the hallway. 'You always do.'

Claire Somerset walked slowly up the road home, the handles of her shopping bags cutting into her fingers. Strands of hair stuck to her cheeks as the spring drizzle attempted an upgrade to rain, but the increase in precipitation didn't encourage her to pick up her pace. All that awaited her was awkward conversation – whether it addressed or danced around the elephant in the room – or uncomfortable silence that pervaded even the chatter of the radio. For months after her son had moved out, she had longed to have him back. Now she regularly found herself contemplating the old adage about being careful what you wished for.

She drew a deep breath, slid the key into the lock and turned. Shouldering the door open as she stepped up from the path, she was more than halfway in before she realised Evan was sitting directly in front of her. He was perching on the second step of the staircase, hunched over with his forearms resting across his knees and his thick fingers intertwined. He raised his head disinterestedly as she closed the door, his eyes barely visible through the long fringe that reached almost to the end of his nose. Despite this, Claire could see he'd been crying, and wondered what she could say that she hadn't said a hundred times already. Noticing he had his jacket on, she decided to keep things light, saying conversationally, 'You off out?'

Evan shook his head. 'I was, but –' he shrugged weakly, bowing his head. 'I can't.'

'I could come with you,' she suggested.

He shook his head again.

'I'm sure it won't be as bad as you think.'

Evan looked up, his eyes accusing. 'That's easy for you to say! You're not the one who'll get stared at and talked about!'

Claire sighed, perching on the narrow bench atop the shoe rack that stood against the wall. 'Evan, honey, I know it's hard, but it's not good for you to be cooped up indoors day in, day out.'

'I'm not going to have a choice for much longer, so I might as well get used to it.'

'It's not a foregone conclusion.'

Evan merely shook his head in response, lifting his right hand to support his forehead. 'I miss her so much,' he said, his voice wavering.

'I know,' Claire replied, reaching to take his free hand in hers. 'But you can't just give up.'

'Why not? I've lost everything. My friends all think I'm some sort of depraved rapist and – and –' he broke off, drawing an unsteady breath. 'I'm not even sure you believe me half the time.'

It was hard to know how to respond to that. Evan was as aware as she was that his version of events stretched credulity to the limit, and it was difficult to imagine any other explanation for the circumstances in which his relationship with Adriana had ended. Even Evan hadn't been able to offer a plausible alternative. And because they'd been together since the age of fifteen, his friends had also been her friends. It wasn't hard to see why few – if any – of them were on his side.

Taking Claire's failure to answer immediately as an answer in itself, Evan pulled his hand free. 'You see? What's the use?'

'Evan –'

'Don't,' he stopped her. Grasping hold of the bannister rail, he hauled himself to his feet and turned to climb the stairs. Claire watched him go, feeling helpless. She wondered how many more months of uncertainty lay ahead, and how much warning they would get of the impending court case. She didn't know where she was going to find the courage to run the gauntlet of the media, to walk into the courthouse, to face Adriana's mother. Recent events had robbed them of their friendship: an almost instant connection, and, in the end, an even more immediate disconnection. Overnight, they had become strangers again.

'You seem to be missing a corpse.'

Leighton glanced up from the laboratory bench where he was assembling a jigsaw of filthy fabric remnants on top of a schematic outline of a human. Parts of the puzzle looked to have been a pair of jeans – a detail that was apparent to Rebecca only from the style of the button on the waistband – the other some sort of sweatshirt.

'Shit, I knew there was something,' he responded, in mock seriousness, before flashing a smile. 'What can I do for you?'

'Nothing much, I was just heading out and I wondered whether you fancied going for a drink.'

'I wish I could,' he replied, turning towards the archive box standing on the bench behind him. 'But I need to get a handle on this tonight.'

Rebecca watched him rummaging around in the box. As he turned back, frowning at the piece of paper in his hand, she said, 'Are we ever going to talk about last Wednesday night? Or are you just going to keep avoiding me?'

Leighton sighed, setting the page down and clamping his gloved hands around the edge of the bench in front of him. 'I'm not avoiding you,' he replied, raising his eyes to meet hers.

'No? Because I heard more from you when you were in Hawaii than I have done in the past week.'

Leighton held her gaze for a moment before dropping his eyes to the bench. 'I've had a lot on.'

'That doesn't usually stop you finding time to play,' Rebecca returned. 'Are you honestly telling me you can't spare half an hour?'

There was another pause before he acquiesced. 'Ok,' he nodded. 'Ok. Give me five minutes.'

Lawrence pushed open the door to the Red Lion, coming face to face with a poster announcing the pub's upcoming St George's Day event: presumably a commercial ruse along the same lines as the Guinness-themed St Patrick's Day celebrations that had swept the capital a couple of weeks earlier. In other words, a night to give pubs a wide berth – not that Lawrence wouldn't happily have done as much this evening. After a frustrating few days spent chasing up dead ends in Birmingham, the last thing he had needed was to schlep back into town for a 5 p.m. meeting, but his superior, Chief Superintendent Angus MacLennan, hadn't so much asked as told him to attend. The follow-up visit to the pub was only marginally less unwelcome, and as Lawrence cast his eyes around for Max he wondered whether his friend was any more enthusiastic about it than he was.

Max glanced up from his Kindle as Lawrence joined him in an alcove at the end of the bar, and Lawrence asked what he was drinking, nodding towards the remaining inch of liquid in the pint glass on the table.

'I'll get them in,' Max replied, moving to stand. 'IPA?'

Lawrence shook his head. 'Lemonade. I'm driving.'

'Shandy?' Max suggested.

'Go on, then,' Lawrence agreed, taking a seat as Max turned for the bar. He removed his tie and began rolling it up, realising it must have been at least six months since he and Max had last been in a pub together. They had known one another more than fifteen years, and at one time rarely a week had passed when they hadn't wound up sharing a drink or four at the end of a long day. Family responsibilities had since largely put a stop to that, and, in the years since Max had taken over the running of the pathology unit, the additional demands on his time had meant Lawrence had also seen less and less of him in a professional capacity. Management and bureaucracy, as Max had more than once complained, seriously limited the opportunities for getting his hands dirty.

Quite what lay in store this evening, Lawrence wasn't sure. All MacLennan had told him before directing him to Max for the rest of the story was that he required another take on the 'shitstorm' that had blown up between DCI Peter Rose and Leighton, culminating in an official complaint. It was far from the first time Pete had clashed with one of the pathologists, and Lawrence was under no illusions about MacLennan's reasons for delegating the problem to him. Relations between Max and Pete were nearing breaking point, and MacLennan was presumably hoping to take advantage of Lawrence's long friendship with Max to smooth the waters. The man had dismissed Lawrence's protest that he already had a major investigation to oversee with a promise of more resources and the remark that the dispute between Pete and Leighton was probably nothing more than 'a storm in a teacup'. Lawrence very much doubted a *shitstorm* could ever be confined to a teacup.

Max set two pint glasses down on the table before sliding onto the bench opposite Lawrence and draining the remains of his first drink.

'What's MacLennan told you?' He asked, as he pushed the empty glass towards the far end of the table.

'Very little.'

'How circumspect,' Max remarked, sarcastically.

'So what's the story?'

'In a nutshell, Pete filed a complaint in a fit of pique and seems to expect me to give a shit that my staff don't respect someone who treats them all like dirt.'

'And how do things stand with MacLennan?'

'I told him if he wanted me to put my house in order, he'd have to do the same. Pete's default strategy for getting his own way is to bully people into submission, and as far as I can work out all Leighton's really done is stand up to him. I realise calling Pete an obnoxious myopic wanker wasn't the best way to go about it, but it's hardly a misplaced sentiment.'

'Not like him to loose his cool,' Lawrence remarked, feeling surprised. Leighton was generally very laid back – at times, frustratingly so – and Lawrence could rarely recall even hearing him raise his voice.

'I know,' Max agreed. 'I guess Pete pushed the wrong button.'

'But presumably that's not what Pete's complaining about?' Lawrence replied, guessing MacLennan would have given him short shrift if a mere insult had formed the basis of his complaint. The use of offensive language was rife in CID, and Pete was no stranger to wielding it himself: he had called people far worse than *wankers* in his time. Although Lawrence was more than a little surprised to hear Leighton had had the audacity to hurl the invective at Pete. He didn't imagine many people would dare.

'No,' Max confirmed. 'He did include disrespectful language in his rant, but his main complaints relate to insubordination – which I'm mystified by, given that my staff answer to me, not him – and poor time-keeping.'

Lawrence raised his eyebrows.

'I know,' Max pre-empted, before he could say anything. 'I'm aware he has a point where Leighton's time management is concerned. But that's not what this is really about.'

'It might not be a bad idea to address it, though,' Lawrence replied, wondering how Max would take the suggestion. They had discussed the matter more than once in the past, and to say they hadn't seen eye-to-eye was an understatement. Lawrence objected to the unspoken implication that one person's time was worth more than another's, and had argued that persistent tardiness had a knock-on effect on others. Max took the view that his staff all worked long and often anti-social hours, and a few minutes one way or another wasn't a big deal in the grand scheme of things. But if the problem had comprised only *a few minutes*, Lawrence wouldn't have raised it with him in the first place.

Max took a long drink and replaced his glass on the table. 'I'll see what I can do.'

'I'm sorry,' Leighton offered, genuinely, when he finally raised his eyes from his pint. 'For Wednesday night, I mean.'

Rebecca frowned, nonplussed. 'What is it you think you need to apologise for?'

'I shouldn't have –' he shrugged weakly. 'You were hammered, Bec.'

'And I suppose you were sober?'

'No, but –'

'Nobody spiked my drink. I'm as responsible for what happened as you are. The only regret I have about any of it is that I seem to have lost a friend as a result.'

Leighton traced and re-traced an equilateral triangle inside one of the rings left on the tabletop by his pint glass. He didn't reply.

'I miss you,' Rebecca admitted, after a long silence, hesitating before reaching to thread her fingers through his. He carefully retracted them.

'I'm sorry, I can't,' he said. 'I should never have let things go as far as they did. I'm sorry.'

'You don't have to keep apologising,' Rebecca replied, feeling irritated. 'It's not as if you made me any promises. If all it was to you was a one-night stand, I can handle that, I'm –'

'Please don't believe that's all I think you're worth,' he interrupted, his blue eyes troubled. 'I think you're amazing. Truly. But I really wouldn't be good for you.'

'Oh don't give me that. I'm not some naive teenager who's going to swallow *it's not you it's me*. At least have the guts to be honest.'

He sighed. 'Bec, you don't really know me.'

'I know I like being around you. And I got the impression the feeling was mutual.'

'It's not that simple.'

'Isn't it?'

Leighton blinked, and in the process dropped his gaze to the table. 'There's nothing I would like more than to be with you,' he said, at length. 'Really.' Here he flicked his eyes up to meet hers before returning them to the tabletop. 'It's just – I don't –' he gave up with a weak shrug.

'It's just what?' Rebecca pressed, impatiently. 'Can you stop contradicting yourself and give me a real answer? Tell me what you actually feel rather than what you think I want to hear? Because bullshit and platitudes are pretty far off the mark!'

There was another silence. 'I wouldn't be good for you,' he repeated, eventually, his voice sounding strained. 'I'm sorry.'

'So am I,' she replied. 'I'm sorry you can't be honest with me. But I get the picture.'

Leighton didn't respond.

'Ok, well I'm clearly making you uncomfortable, so I'll leave you in peace,' Rebecca continued, reaching for her handbag. 'I'll see you at work.'

Leighton put out a hand to stop her as she moved to stand. 'Bec –'

She pulled away.

'Bec, please. I don't want you to leave here thinking you don't mean a lot to me. You do. But I –'

'Yeah yeah, I know how it goes,' she interrupted. 'Let's just leave it at that, shall we?'

Rebecca made for the door to the street, trying to keep a lid on her emotions for at least as long as she was within the well-lit confines of the pub. The net result of the conversation hadn't come as much of a surprise; she had guessed from the hiatus in their usual volley of text messages that nothing further was likely to come of their night together, although a small part of her had hoped that perhaps he just wasn't sure how to proceed. What she hadn't expected was the same clichéd excuses almost every woman in Britain had probably heard at one time or another. She felt angry that he didn't value their friendship enough to approach the situation more honestly, and furious with herself for her part in putting that friendship on the line in the first place. Over the past few days, as she had repeatedly re-lived the events surrounding the original investigation of the man the media had since dubbed *the latchkey killer*, she had felt lost without it.

The break-in at her own home had been the trigger for Elliot's spiral down into drink and depression. She had never been sure how much that had resulted from the shock of having someone invade the flat while they were home, and how much it had been down to his blaming himself for leaving their door keys briefly unattended with the locksmith. Initially, his reaction had seemed self-indulgent; as Rebecca had repeatedly pointed out, no harm had come to her and he had been able to provide information taking them very much closer to the killer. Over the days that followed, his behaviour had taken her from exasperated through concerned to alarmed. From the start he had resisted seeking medical help, preferring to drown his feelings in Jack Daniels or vodka, and the worse things got the further he withdrew, leaving Rebecca feeling completely shut out. She had spent the best part of a year trying to be understanding, and encouraging him to accept treatment, before conceding defeat and bringing a definitive end to a relationship that was already well and truly over. The reopening of the investigation had brought back myriad associated emotions, which were now entangled with the feelings she had for the friend who had been there for her throughout the turmoil of the past two years. And she couldn't very well talk any of it over with him now.

Tuesday 6 April

Returning to his office at nine fifty-five, Lawrence was pleasantly surprised to find Leighton had succeeded in arriving ahead of time for their ten o'clock meeting, although he couldn't help thinking the pathologist might have spent a few minutes sprucing himself up. He rarely dressed smartly unless he was giving evidence in court, and Lawrence was accustomed to his turning up in jeans and polo shirts, but not to his looking completely unkempt. His hair clearly hadn't been brushed before being dragged into a ponytail and it didn't look as if he'd bothered shaving for the best part of a week. Lawrence could only hope it was a temporary aberration.

'Morning,' he greeted, closing the office door behind himself and heading for his chair.

'Howdy,' Leighton returned, raising his eyes from his mobile.

'I'm afraid we don't seem to have much information about Fred Ratley on file,' Lawrence began, apologetically, as he sat down. 'And I've not managed to catch up with Pete yet, so you're going to have to fill in any blanks.'

This wasn't strictly true. Lawrence had spoken to Pete first thing – or, at least, had tried to – but Pete had launched into a tirade about *your mate Max* and the way he ran his unit before storming off.

'You might find Mandy more help than Pete,' Leighton replied, pushing his phone into his pocket.

'Who?'

'DS Byrd.'

'Oh, you mean Miranda,' Lawrence realised, aloud, having never heard her referred to as *Mandy* before. In CID, the only abbreviation of her name he had come across – used behind her back – was Randy Byrd. Not being one for gossip, he had no idea whether there was anything more to the nickname than the fact she wasn't well liked. She reminded him of many a GP's receptionist: seemingly determined to make life difficult for people just because she could. Had Pete needed the human equivalent of a guard dog, she would have fulfilled the role perfectly, although Lawrence suspected she had more in common with a bad-tempered Yorkshire terrier than a Rottweiler. A lot of attitude, but not much substance to back it up.

'I'll see whether I can track her down later,' Lawrence replied, not at all sure it would be worth the effort. 'But in the meantime, according to what I have, Ratley was savaged by his dog. I'm assuming you're of a different opinion?'

Leighton nodded.

'So what do you think happened?'

'He was killed by a dog,' Leighton replied. 'Just not the one we found guarding his body.'

'How can you tell?'

Leighton opened a folder that lay on the chair beside him and drew out a set of crime-scene photographs. 'To begin with, there's no way an elderly Alsatian with dental disease and half its teeth missing could do this degree of damage,' he said, standing and placing several pictures of a badly mauled body on Lawrence's desk.

Lawrence looked the photographs over as Leighton reclaimed his seat. 'Presumably that could easily be proven one way or the other by comparing the dog's bite with some of these injuries?' He replied, indicating a clear set of teeth marks in the corpse's forearm.

'Yeah, it could, if someone hadn't mixed two dogs up and had the wrong one destroyed,' the pathologist replied. 'I'm hoping we might get something from sequencing the DNA, if we can find someone who can interpret the results, although I don't know how definitive that'll be.'

'Can we not compare it with samples from his home? There must be dog hair around the place.'

'Loads, but even without testing it it's clear it's not all from one dog, so that might not be much help.'

Lawrence nodded. 'Was there anything besides the dog that concerned you?'

'The padlock on the side gate was brand new, and we couldn't lift any prints from it. And we swabbed some fibres from Ratley's mouth. I think something was jammed in there to stop him screaming. None of the neighbours heard anything. At least, so they say.'

'Presumably the dog would have made quite a racket, though.'

'Yeah, but if you live next door to a noisy dog you're likely to be used to that. And I don't get the impression Fred Ratley was the kind of guy the average Joe was likely to challenge.'

'The kind of guy you might expect to die of unnatural causes, you mean,' Lawrence surmised. His colleague nodded, but said nothing further, and Lawrence asked, 'Was that it?' Thus far, he could quite understand why Pete hadn't had much time for the matter, and was mystified by MacLennan's apparent concern. He wondered just how acrimonious the confrontation between Pete and Max had been.

'Not necessarily,' Leighton replied. 'It's possible there's a connection to another case.'

'Which is?'

'The deceased was a man called Connall O'Leary. But the name you're more likely to be familiar with is Sean Quinn.'

The pieces of the puzzle slotted together. Given the profile Aileen Quinn had succeeded in building, there would be no burying the story should Sean turn out to have been innocent. And as the senior investigating officer on the original case, Pete would have a lot of questions to answer. No doubt MacLennan was equally concerned about the potential outcome, and this was what he had been referring to when he had used the word *shitstorm*.

'I might be remembering the details incorrectly, but I thought all that was ever found of O'Leary was part of a limb?'

'Uh-huh. His left hand and forearm. There were teeth marks on several of the bones, but those were attributed to a scavenging fox.'

'That's still perfectly possible. And, given that the arm didn't find its way around Epping Forest by itself, I'd say very likely.'

'Yeah, but there's also this,' Leighton replied, presenting a faded eight-by-ten-inch photograph of six men, flanked by two large dogs. 'It was on the wall in Ratley's living room. That's Ratley,' he indicated one of the two men crouching in front of the others, a hand resting on the dog sitting to his left. 'O'Leary had the same picture hanging in his hallway.'

'Did you work on the O'Leary investigation as well?'

'Yes. Sorry, I thought you knew.'

'No.' Lawrence paused for thought. 'Did you agree with Pete's decision to charge Quinn?'

'Not as such. Roddy did most of the work – I only got involved because he asked me to look at some botanical samples. But there wasn't a lot for us to go on, I don't think we had anything conclusive. The decision was made largely as a result of police work.'

Lawrence nodded. 'Are you sure it was the same photograph?'

'Yes.'

Lawrence looked back to the picture, understanding Pete's scepticism. The knowledge Leighton had an exceptional memory was the only reason he didn't immediately write off any potential connection.

'Presumably O'Leary isn't one of these guys?' He indicated the group of men.

'No. Maybe he was the one holding the camera?'

'Any idea who the others are?'

Leighton shook his head. 'Not at this stage.'

'Ok, well let's not worry about O'Leary for now. Our priority at this stage ought to be Ratley – we'll see where that investigation takes us and we'll bear a potential connection to O'Leary in mind. All right?'

'Uh-huh.'

'And given his involvement in both investigations, it might not be a bad idea to consider burying the hatchet with Pete.'

'You mean apologise,' Leighton interpreted, coolly. 'You know, the trouble with this place is that nobody ever deals with unreasonable individuals, everyone else just has to work around them. I'm done working around him.'

He sounded uncharacteristically angry.

'You were the one who called him an obnoxious myopic wanker,' Lawrence observed.

'He *is* obnoxious,' Leighton returned. 'And on Tuesday he was being myopic. Probably deliberately. Wanker is admittedly more subjective, but then so is fuckwit, and I very much doubt I'll get an apology for that.'

'Is that what he called you?'

'His actual words were fat, furry fuckwit, so you have to admire his use of alliteration. But I'm a lot more concerned about the fact he repeatedly ignores any evidence that doesn't suit his agenda! I do not do this job for someone to dismiss my findings out of hand!'

'Ok, ok,' Lawrence replied, holding up a hand for emphasis in response to his colleague's heated tone. 'I will deal with Pete. In the meantime, I'd appreciate it if you could look into what other means there might be of ruling Ratley's dog into or out of the equation. All right?'

'Uh-huh.'

'And on the subject of ruling things in or out, have you had the DNA results back for Coralie?'

'No, but I'm hoping to hear by the end of the day. How've you been getting on?'

'Thus far I've been coordinating an exercise in tedium,' Lawrence admitted. 'None of her friends or neighbours was much help, and we've worked our way around every locksmith in Birmingham and checked out current and former employees of the estate agent she rented her flat through, all with no joy. We're looking at her work colleagues at the moment, but I don't hold out a lot of hope we're going to unearth anything there, either.'

Leighton nodded contemplatively. 'I may have something for you,' he said, after a moment, drawing a folder out from beneath the one pertaining to Fred Ratley.

'I'm all ears.'

'I think Coralie could have been the second victim in that neck of the woods. Another woman in Birmingham was strangled in January, and that wasn't the only similarity between the two deaths.'

'Why did that not raise flags before?'

'Her breasts weren't mutilated – if it was Williams I guess he was disturbed – so it probably didn't stand out as anything out of the ordinary. The police charged the woman's boyfriend with the crime.'

'I presume they've checked his DNA against the database?'

'Yep. I'm not sure how hard they looked for DNA evidence on the body, though, there are precious few results on file.'

'They'd made their minds up before they started, then,' Lawrence concluded. 'Can I assume from the fact you thought it was worth flagging that the case against the boyfriend isn't particularly strong?'

'It's largely circumstantial, and predicated on the fact he was there the night she died. He says he came in late after a night out and didn't realise she was dead until morning. There was no sign of forced entry and the flat's on the third floor, so it's unlikely anyone accessed it any way other than the front door. Statistically, the chances he was responsible are a lot higher than those of it being a serial killer, so you can see why nobody really questioned it.'

'Were they living together?'

'No.'

'What do we have that suggests a link to Williams?'

'Nothing definitive. But aside from the geography – the flat is within a mile of Coralie's – the first thing I noticed is that there's a small tear in her upper lip,' Leighton slid a crime scene photograph onto Lawrence's desk. 'And we know Williams tends to tape his victims' mouths shut. Second, the girl fits his type – petite and brunette.' He presented another picture, this time of a pretty young woman smiling at the camera. 'The rest of what I have relates to details that don't square with the boyfriend's being involved. To begin with, he wears a signet ring, and there's nothing in the bruising on the girl's neck indicative of that. Plus there's –'

'Rings do come off,' Lawrence observed, slipping his wedding ring off as if his statement required a demonstration.

'Not necessarily,' Leighton replied, adding a photograph to the two already on the desk, this one showing a gold ring constricting the smallest finger of a pudgy left hand. 'I'm guessing you'd have a job getting that off.'

Lawrence nodded.

'And there are contusions on the victim's hands where she presumably tried to fight off her attacker, but there are no visible marks in the police photographs taken of her partner.' He delivered a final handful of pictures before leaning back in his chair. Lawrence spread them out and looked at each one in turn.

'Do we know what the story is here?' He asked, lifting an image showing several faded marks on a man's back.

'Historic abuse.'

'How historic?'

'Nothing to do with the girlfriend, if that's what you're wondering. Social services have a file from fifteen years back.'

'Father?' Lawrence guessed.

'Uh-huh.'

Lawrence returned his eyes to the photograph, feeling angry on behalf of someone he'd never even met. He could only guess at what he might do should anyone do any real harm to one of his own children; hurting them himself didn't even bear thinking about.

'Sometimes I really wish I believed in karma,' he observed.

Leighton was fiddling with his phone and didn't look up, but he nodded slightly. 'Don't we all,' he returned.

*****

The plethora of photographs captured every detail of Fred Ratley's home, garden and bloodied corpse, and went some way towards compensating for the fact Rebecca hadn't been present at the crime scene. Before departing for Birmingham, Lawrence had asked her to look into Ratley's affairs in an effort to establish whether his death had been anything more than an unfortunate consequence of keeping a dangerous dog. Ordinarily, she would have been glad of the opportunity to take charge of an investigation – as her superior had most likely assumed when assigning her the task. No doubt he had viewed it as a way to keep her occupied while the rest of the team chased after Rhys Williams. Given that Lawrence was oblivious to the events of the previous Wednesday night, he had probably supposed that working closely with Leighton would suit her, both professionally and personally. Rebecca had no intention of revealing to him why it wasn't a good time for them to be thrown together, so immediately after their meeting she had headed to the pathology unit, where she now sat flicking through the pictures on an iPad.

It wasn't the awkwardness that concerned her; working together was bound to be uncomfortable in the immediate aftermath of their night together, but that would soon pass. She wasn't at all sure her feelings would follow suit. Much as she should never have allowed herself to become so involved with a colleague, she wouldn't have taken the risk had she not thought they were headed for more than a fling or a one-night stand. And given the rather mixed messages she had picked up from Leighton so far, she wasn't even sure she *had* miscalculated his feelings for her.

'Becks?'

Rebecca raised her eyes in surprise to find Jon looking at her expectantly from his seat a few feet away.

'Sorry, what?'

'Tea?'

'Oh – no, thanks, I'm going to head off in a minute.'

Jon nodded, turning his chair through ninety degrees so that he faced Leighton. 'Dr C?'

'Ta,' Leighton accepted, handing over a mug. Jon stood and made for the door.

'Can I get a copy of these?' Rebecca asked, as the door closed behind him.

'Done,' Leighton replied, holding up a flash drive. 'I left a copy of everything else with Forrester.'

'Great,' Rebecca responded, with a perfunctory smile, leaning to take the memory stick before turning back to gather up her handbag and jacket. 'I'll give you a shout if I have any questions, ok?'

'Ok,' he echoed. Then, as she stood to go, he added, 'Bec, about last week –'

'It's fine. Let's just keep it about work.'

'It's not fine. I didn't intend to make such a mess of everything. You deserve better.'

Rebecca sighed. 'Oh please, let's not go there again.'

'But I –'

'I don't want to hear that you're thinking about what's best for me! I didn't buy that line the first time and I'm not going to buy it now!'

'I'm not trying to feed you a line. You really don't know me.' He paused. 'You're just getting over a –'

'No!' Rebecca pre-empted. 'Don't you dare imply I'm on some kind of rebound trip! That's a cop out!'

'That's not what I was going to say.'

'Oh.' Rebecca felt embarrassed. 'Sorry.'

He regarded her in silence for a moment before saying, 'You've just about recovered from one messy relationship. The last thing you need is another.'

'No, the last thing I need is more excuses!' Rebecca returned, heading for the door. 'I've had enough of those to last me a lifetime!'

'Bec, please, this really isn't about you. I just – I don't –' he trailed off.

Rebecca stopped in the doorway and looked around. 'You just *what*?'

'I don't trust myself,' he admitted, after a moment's hesitation. 'I can't.'

'What's that supposed to mean?'

He hesitated again before saying, 'I don't trust myself not to hurt you.'

Rebecca exclaimed in disbelief. 'Well here's a newsflash for you,' she shot back. 'You already have!' Flinging the door shut behind herself, she marched down the corridor, trying not to admit to herself that she wanted him to follow her. He didn't, and she made for the exit. Outside, she leaned against the wall, taking a deep breath and trying to marshal her thoughts.

In some ways, she reflected, Leighton was right: she didn't really know him. She could easily have assembled a list of personal attributes – kind, patient, witty, disorganised, impulsive – but she knew very little *about* him. Jokes and smart remarks had allowed him to maintain a largely private personal life without her ever really having noticed. The scars she had seen during their night together had told her far more about the harsh reality of his home life than he ever had. And, with that thought, she realised she ought to have given more consideration to the emotional impact that sort of abuse might have had. With a sigh, she began her trudge back to the Yard, stopping after a few paces as his final words to her suddenly took on a new meaning. Perhaps it wasn't her feelings he was so worried about hurting.

Evan Somerset looked as if he'd already given up on life. Dangerously overweight, his bulk was such that it was clear he hadn't simply piled on the pounds in the few months since his girlfriend's death. His lank mousy hair, on the other hand, probably had been presentable at the start of the year; at this stage, it badly needed cutting. He was slumped in a large armchair in front of the television, and his mother reached for the remote control as she quietly conveyed that he had a visitor, then flicked the machine to standby. Evan turned his dull blue eyes towards Lawrence, his expression disconsolate. Lawrence introduced himself and took a seat, then made a start on explaining that he was looking into a possible connection between the murder of Evan's girlfriend, Adriana, and the death of another woman. He'd barely made it through his second sentence before Evan interrupted.

'Why are you all picking on me?' He asked, plaintively. 'I've never done no one no harm!'

'I'm not saying you have,' Lawrence replied, wondering whether the words made grammatical sense in response to Evan's odd triple negative. 'And you may be able to help me help you.'

This clearly took Evan by surprise, but after brightening momentarily his hopeful expression turned to one of suspicion. He didn't challenge Lawrence, however, saying only, 'Uh-huh?'

'Do you think you might start by running through what happened the night Adriana died?'

'I've already been over it at least a dozen times.'

'I realise that, but I would like to hear it from you.'

'They tried to catch me out with that trick before.'

'That's really not what I'm trying to do.'

Evan sighed, casting his eyes down. He didn't reply.

'If you'd prefer to do this officially I can have you taken in for questioning, but I thought you might find it easier to do it informally.'

There was a long pause before Evan capitulated with a weary nod. 'Ok.'

Lawrence sat back and waited for him to go on.

'I got in late.' Evan pulled at the corner of his right eye with one finger in an apparent attempt to dislodge something. 'Getting on for two.'

'Why were you out so late on a Tuesday?' Lawrence asked, when Evan didn't immediately continue. 'Did you not have to work in the morning?'

'Yeah, we did. We didn't plan on a late one, but you know how it is,' he dropped his hand from his eye but didn't raise his gaze.

'Who were you out with?'

'Lads from the garage where I worked. Someone's birthday.'

'Given that she wasn't out with you, why did you go home to Adriana's flat rather than your own?'

'I don't know. I wish to God I hadn't.' He paused. 'I was pretty drunk, and –' he hesitated, colour rising in his cheeks, before admitting, 'Horny.'

'So what happened when you got there?'

'She was lying with her back to me when I got into bed, and I cuddled up behind her. Normally if she was sleeping and I did that she'd pull away and tell me to get off, but she didn't, and –' he swallowed. 'She was naked. So – so I started stroking her body, and – and I –' he shrugged rather than finish the sentence. 'I know I shouldn't have – without her saying ok – but if she'd said no I wouldn't have –' he closed his eyes momentarily. 'I don't remember a lot about it, I think I passed out the moment I was done. I woke up a few hours later and she was –' he shrugged again before giving up and raising a hand to shield his eyes.

Lawrence nodded to himself, guessing Evan's reluctance to repeat the sequence of events owed as much to shame over his own actions as concern about being caught out by inconsistencies between accounts. Technically, what he had just described came under the umbrella of rape, and the fact things would almost certainly have panned out differently had Adriana been alive didn't change that. But – assuming Evan was telling the truth – that wasn't relevant. The issue of consent didn't apply to corpses. The question was how Evan had come to be engaging in intercourse with a dead body.

'Could you talk me through exactly what you did between unlocking the front door and getting into bed?'

Evan took a moment to think about this before saying, 'I went to the toilet. Then I got some water from the kitchen. And then I got undressed and went to bed.'

'Do you remember hearing anything unexpected during that time?'

He shook his head slowly. 'No. I don't remember much more than what I just told you. I was pissed.'

'Can you recall whether the bedroom door was open when you got in?'

There was a pause. 'No. But it probably wasn't, the bathroom fan was really noisy and it used to take ages to turn itself off.'

'So if someone else had been in the flat when you arrived, is it possible they could have left without your hearing anything while you were using the toilet?'

'I guess,' he replied. 'D'you think that's what happened?'

'At this stage I don't know.'

Evan nodded slightly.

'Did Adriana mention any plans for that night?'

'Only catching up on some TV viewing.'

'Do you think she might have invited someone over without mentioning it to you?'

Evan shrugged. 'If she didn't mention it I wouldn't know.'

Resisting the urge to sigh, Lawrence rephrased the question. 'Had she ever done anything like that before, to your knowledge?'

'No.'

'Was she ever unfaithful?'

Evan swallowed, casting his eyes down. There was a momentary pause before he nodded. Then, after another moment, he said, flatly, 'I don't know if she ever brought anyone home, though.'

'Anyone?' Lawrence repeated. 'How many were there?'

'Only one,' Evan replied, before adding, as an afterthought, 'That I know about, at least.'

'That must have made you angry,' Lawrence remarked. 'I'd be livid if my wife did that to me.'

Evan shrugged weakly. 'Not with her, so much.'

'You mean you felt more angry with the man concerned?'

'No. Myself. If I'd been a better boyfriend she wouldn't have done it, would she?'

'Did she say that?'

'She didn't have to.'

Wondering whether the remark reflected Adriana's attitude towards Evan or simply his own lack of self-esteem, Lawrence asked what Evan could tell him about the other man. All he was able to provide was a forename and place of work – which was the same as Adriana's. With luck, the latter detail would make tracking the man down relatively straightforward. Lawrence moved on.

'Would you mind telling me where you were last Tuesday night?'

'Tuesday?' Evan echoed, hollowly. 'You said you weren't trying to pin anything more on me!'

'That's not wh–'

'Why am I such an idiot?' He berated himself, his sense of betrayal painfully apparent. 'I just walk into *everything*.'

'Mr Somerset, this really isn't a covert effort to trap you,' Lawrence returned, firmly. 'What I am looking to do is rule you *out* of my enquiry.'

Evan regarded him suspiciously for some seconds before saying, 'And how does that help me?'

'Can you please just tell me where you were on Tuesday night?'

Evan sighed, lifting a hand to rub his eye, which was apparently still bothering him. 'I was here,' he replied, flatly. 'I'm always here.'

'Was anyone here with you?'

'I dunno. Mum prob'ly was.'

'Do you not remember?'

He shrugged. 'No. She goes out sometimes, but I couldn't tell you when.' He dropped his hand a few inches and rested his chin on it before adding, disconsolately, 'Every day's the same to me.'

Claire Somerset had confirmed Evan's whereabouts on the night of Coralie's death, but hadn't been able to tell Lawrence much else he didn't already know, so he had made a start on working through the list of people who might be of more help. Having elicited no answer at any of the other flats occupying the terraced Georgian house that Adriana had called home, he moved on, guessing that if anyone had the low-down on Evan and Adriana's relationship it would be the woman's female friends.

Flora Preston answered her front door in some disarray, with a dusting of white powder – presumably flour or icing sugar – in her fringe and left eyebrow, and wet streaks down the front of her apron where she had apparently just wiped her hands. Blue catering plasters were wound around the first two fingers of her right hand, which she raised to tuck her dark bob behind her ear as she said, 'Hello?'

Lawrence introduced himself and apologised for interrupting before asking whether she would mind answering a few questions about Evan.

Flora's eyes darkened. 'Why?'

'I'm following up a few loose ends, and making sure nobody else was involved in Adriana Simonides' death.'

She frowned. 'What? Who else could have been?'

'That's a good question.'

'I don't get it,' Flora countered, her frown deepening. 'If you've nobody else in mind, how come it *is* a question?'

'Miss Preston, I can't go into all the details, but I really wouldn't be here without good reason.'

There was a brief silence before Flora nodded her apparent acceptance of this, turned from the door and headed down the corridor towards a room just visible from the doorstep. Lawrence followed, closing the door behind himself, and joined her in what turned out to be a cramped and very untidy kitchen. Workspace would have been in short supply at the best of times, as the patchwork of grey laminate distributed between the hob, the sink and the door was home to not only the ubiquitous kettle and toaster, but also a microwave oven, two wine racks and a bread bin. The remaining space had been colonised by a medley of unwashed glasses, plates and mugs, and a tower of mismatched Tupperware boxes. Two contained what looked like loaf cakes, one a tart of some description, and the final, topmost box a clutch of chocolate brownies. Meanwhile, the wreckage of the baking effort was evident in the sink: partially submerged bowls and tins listed in the murky water, while wooden spoons floated, corpse-like, at the surface.

Lawrence declined Flora's offer of a drink more on account of the kitchen's questionable hygiene than because he wasn't thirsty. She had apparently just made her own, and drew a mug of either tea or coffee out from behind the bank of Tupperwares before taking a fork from the cutlery rack that stood on the shelf above the microwave and – presumably for want of a clean teaspoon – using the handle to stir the drink.

'How well do you know Evan?' Lawrence enquired, as she shook the fork and dropped it into the sink.

'I thought I knew him pretty well,' Flora replied. ''Til January.'

'When did you meet?'

'School. We were in the same class. Although I didn't really get to know him until he and Adriana started seeing each other.'

'So about ten years ago?'

Flora nodded.

'Did you consider him a friend?'

'Yes. He was good fun.'

'And what did you think when you heard he'd been taken in for questioning?'

Flora shrugged. 'The police tend to start with the person closest to home, don't they? I didn't think much of it until they charged him.'

'So you didn't believe he was involved before that?'

'No. But I didn't have all the details either, did I?'

'Do you now?'

'No, I –' she hesitated. 'I just meant the police knew more about it than me in the first place.'

'Did Adriana ever say anything about Evan being violent, or rough with her?'

'No.'

'Was his behaviour at all controlling, or bullying?'

'No. She always seemed to be the one in charge. He was happy to go with the flow, I think.'

'And what about their sex life?'

Flora's eyebrows rose. 'What about it?'

'Was that rough? Or in any way unusual?'

'I don't think so. He wouldn't even go on top because he was worried he might hurt her. Being so big.'

'Did his size bother her?'

'Not in that sense. She always went for bigger guys.'

'You imply there was a sense in which it did bother her.'

'She was concerned about the health implications.'

'Was that something she ever discussed with him?'

'Oh yeah,' Flora confirmed. 'She was always encouraging him to eat more healthily. He just wasn't very good at sticking to it.'

'Perhaps he didn't really want to,' Lawrence remarked, thinking the comment might prompt a more honest response than a direct enquiry about how Evan had taken the suggestion.

'Perhaps,' Flora agreed, without elaborating.

'A moment ago you said Adriana *always went for bigger guys*,' Lawrence continued. 'How many others were there, given they'd been together since the age of fifteen?'

'Oh, I didn't mean like that. Just guys she'd remark on when we were out, actors she liked –' Flora shrugged rather than properly finish her sentence.

'Is there any chance she was seeing someone else?'

'No,' Flora shook her head. 'No way.'

'Relationships aren't always what they seem.'

'Nothing's perfect, I know that. They had arguments, same as anyone. But if Adriana was seeing someone else she would have told me.'

'You sound very sure about that. Had it happened before?'

After a moment's hesitation, Flora nodded.

'When?'

'The year before last. She had a fling with someone from work.'

'Does Evan know?'

She nodded.

'And how did he feel about it?'

'Pretty much as you'd expect. He was gutted.'

'How did he find out?'

'I'm not sure. He challenged her about something – I don't know what – and she admitted to it.'

'Did you know about it before he did?'

'She needed to talk it over with someone,' Flora answered, as if in mitigation. 'She was trying to decide what to do. She was really torn.'

'That must have been difficult for you, given that Evan was a friend of yours as well.'

Flora swallowed and nodded. 'I wouldn't ever have told him,' she emphasized. 'Adriana came first. But it was hard to give impartial advice when I didn't feel impartial.'

'Is it possible your disapproval – however indirect – might have encouraged her to keep something of that nature to herself if it happened again?'

'I guess,' Flora agreed, after a moment's thought. 'Do you think that's why he killed her? Because she was seeing someone else?' Then, before Lawrence could reply, her expression changed as another thought clearly struck her, and she added, in a very different tone, 'You're suggesting someone else was there before Evan that night.' Her words came across as a conclusion, not a question.

'It's possible,' Lawrence allowed.

Flora's eyebrows crinkled into a frown. 'If you don't believe he did it, why did they charge him?' She asked, at length. 'Was it a mistake?'

'I can't be sure of anything at this stage,' Lawrence replied.

'But you think he's innocent,' Flora responded, once again sounding as if she was making a statement rather than asking a question. 'You wouldn't be here otherwise.'

'The decision to charge somebody isn't necessarily the end of an investigation, and –'

'Well maybe it should be! Maybe if you did more research beforehand you wouldn't make mistakes!'

'Things aren't always cut and dried,' Lawrence replied, guessing she was as angry with herself as with the police, if not more so. It had been clear from her initial remarks that she had followed the local force in laying the blame at Evan's door, and the fact someone was now questioning that was doubtless making her do the same. 'The information we have isn't set in stone. Subsequent events, statements and forensic tests can all shed new light on a situation. Sometimes we need to reexamine what we have, and on occasion mistakes do happen. At this stage, I can't tell you whether that's the case in this instance. But I wouldn't be doing my job properly if I assumed otherwise.'

The cat in Abigail's arms jumped as a door slammed downstairs, announcing Charlie's return. She lifted the animal back into its pen and gave it a final scratch behind the ears before securing the door. By the time she reached the end of the cattery corridor, her brother was charging up the stairs towards her, and from his expression she guessed he was seeking her out in order to vent his fury about whatever it was that had pissed him off this time.

With some people, you could gauge the seriousness of the matter from their reaction, but Charlie was as likely to blow his top over a simple insult as a major betrayal. She set the bottle of tablets down on the work surface of the mezzanine kitchen-cum-storeroom-cum-dispensary, reaching for a cloth and steeling herself for the coming onslaught.

'How was the run?' She asked, lightly.

'Fine until Toby suggested we stop for a drink on the way back,' Charlie responded, pulling off his grey hoody and flinging it against the base of the washing machine. 'We might as well have gone to a bloody fighting pit! We ended up drinking with half the scum of East London, including Spencer fucking Murphy!'

'Who?'

'The scumbag who runs the book at every fight in a ten-mile radius.'

'Right,' Abigail nodded.

'The law is a fucking disgrace! Those bastards should be rotting inside, but they're so sure the cops are never gonna act they're fucking flaunting their sick idea of fun!' As he spoke, he wedged one foot against the other and kicked off his right trainer, then used his heel to help release the left one, flicking it against the washing machine with a bang.

'Chas, please, can you keep it down? I've enough of a job coaxing Noodle to eat without you scaring her half to death.'

'Sorry,' Charlie apologised, lowering his voice to near normal volume before continuing. 'I was this close to dragging Murphy out into the car park, but the gutless weasel had his dog at the ready to fight his battles for him!'

Abigail looked around to meet her brother's angry brown eyes. 'Just as well, don't you think?'

Charlie shook his head, taking hold of the worktop and balancing on one leg to peel off a sock, which he dropped onto the hoody crumpled on the floor.

'How're things here?' He asked. 'Any new ones in?'

'Three,' Abigail replied, drawing the keys from her pocket and reaching to unlock the drugs cabinet. 'A gorgeous ginger and white boy, a pregnant queen and the sweetest little old tabby girl.'

Charlie tutted, and Abigail guessed what he was thinking. Being evicted from home and thrust into a pen with no explanation was disorientating for any animal, but it seemed particularly cruel where the elderly were concerned. Their chances of ever finding another home were slim, particularly if they had health problems, and seeing them shut in the rescue equivalent of a prison cell was heartbreaking. Equally sad was the fact it represented a rare instance in which the words *you'd never see people do that to a family member* didn't hold true. Nobody gave up a child or parent because they wanted a dog instead, or because they were moving house, or because of damage done to furniture. But plenty of people seemed to have no compunction about abandoning elderly relatives, leaving them to fend for themselves or at the mercy of care homes.

'What's her story?' Charlie enquired, dropping his other sock to the floor.

'Arthritis. She can't crouch properly, so she keeps peeing over the side of her litter tray.'

'So rather than get a better tray, her owners are tossing her out like rubbish,' Charlie surmised.

Abigail nodded. In fact, the cat's owners had taken her to be put to sleep, but that information would serve only to rile Charlie further, so she kept it to herself. Replacing the tablets in the cabinet, she relocked the door.

'Here's hoping they spend their final years bedridden and alone in a dingy nursing home,' Charlie remarked, coldly, as he stripped off his wet t-shirt and added it to the growing laundry pile.

'Aunt Lil's offered to take her,' Abigail said, hoping this information might help to placate him. It had certainly come as a huge relief to her, and she was going to take the cat over first thing in the morning.

Charlie grunted in reply, abandoning his shorts and turning for the stairs clad only in his boxers. Abigail cleared her throat pointedly as he began his descent, and he looked around.

'I am not your housekeeper,' Abigail reminded him, sharply, indicating the sports kit strewn on the floor with a shift of her eyes. 'If you want that washing, put it in the machine.'

Charlie sighed heavily, but retraced his steps, scooped up the items on the floor and shoved them into the washing machine drum. 'Happy now?' He grumbled, with the air of a moody teenager. Abigail answered with a wide, sarcastic smile. Charlie pulled a face in return before turning back towards the stairs, and Abigail made a start on wiping down the counter. It seemed a long time since she could remember being *happy*.

Thursday 8 April

After two hours of scrolling wearily through computer records, Jamie had decided to take a break, and was in the process of trying to roll a cigarette. Having burned several fingers in the kitchen on Wednesday evening, the task was proving challenging, and he'd been struggling with it for a couple of minutes when Leighton strolled up to his desk.

'Forrester not about?'

'Nope,' Jamie confirmed, flinching and catapulting the cigarette filter onto the desk.

Leighton grunted his response before saying, 'Are you busy?'

'Up to my eyes, as you can see,' Jamie replied, facetiously, retrieving the filter and returning it to its rightful place.

'In that case, I have a question,' Leighton revealed, pulling the chair out from Eva's desk and sitting down.

'Shoot.'

'You worked on the O'Leary investigation, right?'

'Yeah, that was a barrel of laughs,' Jamie remarked, as he lost control of the coiled cigarette paper for the umpteenth time.

'Here, give us that,' Leighton put in, holding out a hand.

Jamie did as bid. Leighton rolled it between his fingers and thumbs, saying after a moment, 'Do you think this might be the time t–'

'Don't you fucking start. With the week I'm having I can't think of a *worse* time to quit.'

'Yeah, 'cause I'm the original health freak,' Leighton returned, amiably. 'I was only going to say you could splash out on a pack where someone's done the hard work for you.'

'Oh. Right. Sorry.'

'You ok?'

'Yeah. I'm just going stir crazy after spending all week stuck at my desk.'

Leighton licked the edge of the paper, sealed it and proffered an almost perfect cylinder.

'Nice work,' Jamie observed as he took the cigarette. 'Where'd you learn to do that?'

'Sunday school.'

Jamie smiled.

'So, anyway, I know Quinn kept changing his story, but did anyone ever manage to figure out which bits – if any – were true?'

Jamie blew out a breath, shaking his head slightly. 'I've no idea, mate, that was months ago. Why?'

'I watched some of the interview tapes, and I know a lot of what he came out with was bullshit, but –' Leighton sighed. 'When it comes to the all-important question, I believe him. And I can't get that out my head.'

Jamie gave the matter a few moments' thought before answering. 'I don't remember all the ins and outs. But I always got the sense he was more scared of someone else than of us. Although I've no idea whether that had anything to do with what happened to O'Leary – Quinn wasn't exactly a choirboy.'

'So you think he was more afraid of fessing up to where he actually was than being charged with his uncle's murder.'

'I'd say it's a strong possibility. But another is that he wasn't the only person involved in O'Leary's death.'

'Either of which could offer an explanation for why Quinn is no longer around to tell the tale.'

'Yep.'

Leighton nodded thoughtfully, then tipped his head back as one of their colleagues walked past. 'Mandy, my love, just the person.'

To Jamie's surprise, rather than objecting to this rather inappropriate address, Miranda smiled. 'What do you want?' She asked, playfully, taking hold of Leighton's ponytail and giving it a gentle tug.

'Just to wish my favourite Wolves supporter a good day,' Leighton replied, as she released his hair and turned to lean against Eva's desk. 'And maybe ask one teeny question.'

Miranda lifted her eyebrows expectantly.

'How much do you remember about Sean Quinn?'

Her eyebrows rose further. 'O'Leary's nephew?'

'Uh-huh.'

'I remember he was a lying little toe-rag,' she remarked. 'You're not still looking for a link to that bloke in Stratford, are you? DCI Rose'll have you shot.'

'Not if nobody tells him,' Leighton pointed out, mischievously.

Miranda smiled again. 'One day your luck's going to run out, you know.'

'So my mum never tires of telling me. But in the meantime, I'm trying to establish what reliable information we have on Quinn's whereabouts in the hours surrounding O'Leary's disappearance.'

'Anything we have should be on record.'

'I can't find much.'

'Then we probably didn't *get* much,' Miranda observed. 'But one way or another we must've had enough for the CPS.'

Leighton nodded.

Miranda rolled her eyes expressively. 'Do you want me to take a look at my notes for you?' She asked, with affected exasperation.

'No, no, I don't want to drag anyone else into Rose's firing line.'

'Don't worry, I can handle him,' she responded, conspiratorially, pushing off from the desk. 'Leave it with me, ok?'

'Thanks, Mandy, you're a star.'

'Yeah, you remember that,' she replied, playfully, as she turned to go.

Jamie watched her walk away before looking to Leighton. 'Have you been slipping MDMA into her coffee?'

'Eh?'

'She normally makes porcupines look soft and fluffy.'

'Really?' Leighton looked surprised. 'I've always found her all right.'

Jamie shook his head slightly in disbelief. 'You want to start a fan club, mate,' he suggested. 'You'd pull in a fortune in membership fees.'

'I dunno, that sounds like a serious admin headache,' his friend returned. 'And you know what I'm like with paperwork.' He grinned. 'A piss-up in a brewery is probably about the only thing I *could* organise.'

On meeting Barry Thorne, one of the first thoughts to go through Lawrence's mind was that Flora hadn't been wrong about her friend's penchant for *bigger guys*. The man with whom Adriana had strayed wasn't as heavy as Evan, but he was still carrying substantially more weight than could be considered healthy. That, however, was the only apparent similarity between the two men. Barry was immaculately turned out in a white shirt, navy tie and grey trousers – a work uniform that a mechanic like Evan would presumably have had little use for even before he stopped leaving the house. How real the other differences were, and how much they were simply the result of Adriana's death and the subsequent fallout, Lawrence had no way of knowing, but he suspected from what he had learned thus far that Barry's understated confidence was one thing Evan had never shared.

'I understand you knew Adriana Simonides quite well,' Lawrence began, after Barry had shown him into a small, nondescript meeting room.

'Better than I should have done,' Barry admitted.

'Would you mind telling me how long your affair lasted?'

'A few months. But I think we probably crossed the line of friendship some time before that. We both knew where it was going long before we slept together.'

'And how did you feel when it ended?'

'I was sorry, but not surprised. I always knew she wasn't really available.'

'Are you saying you never expected her to leave Evan?'

'Not really, no.'

'Could you explain what gave you that impression?'

Barry thought this over before saying, 'I suppose the fact she didn't seem unhappy with him.'

'If she wasn't unhappy, why cheat on him in the first place?'

Barry shook his head slightly. 'I don't know. Excitement, maybe?' He suggested, uncertainly. 'Or curiosity? It's not like she'd ever been with anyone else.'

'Are you saying she was bored?'

'I honestly don't know. We didn't talk a lot about her and Evan.' He paused briefly before adding, 'We didn't talk a lot full stop.'

'So it was more of a physical connection than an emotional one?' Lawrence queried, wondering what light Flora might be able to shed on how Adriana had viewed the relationship.

'Yeah, I suppose so,' Barry agreed, thoughtfully. 'As far as it went, anyway. Who knows where it might've gone given more time.'

'More time in what sense?'

'If Evan hadn't found out.'

'Was that the reason she gave you for ending things?'

He nodded.

'Did you ever meet Evan?'

'A few times.'

'Before or after your fling with Adriana?'

'Both.'

'That must have been awkward,' Lawrence remarked.

'Yeah,' Barry admitted.

'Was the affair ever mentioned?'

'No. I don't think Evan's the confrontational type. He seemed more embarrassed at running into me than anything. And he wasn't the only one.'

'Did you ever visit Adriana's flat? Either during the relationship or since?'

He shook his head. 'That was never an option. We generally went to my place.'

'But not always?'

Barry's cheeks coloured. 'There were a few occasions where things were a little more –' he hesitated before deciding on, 'Spontaneous.'

'And the venues less conventional?'

'Something like that.'

Lawrence didn't ask for further details; he had no interest in embarrassing people unnecessarily. Not if they were cooperating, at any rate. He would come back to what Barry had been doing on the night Adriana died later on; there were other questions he wanted to ask before putting the man on the defensive.

'Can you tell me what your initial reaction was to the news of Adriana's death? Or, more specifically, to how she had died?'

'Disbelief, I suppose. You expect things like accidents and illness to affect you at one time or another, but murder feels so far removed –' he held out his hands.

'And Evan's involvement?'

'That was a shock as well, but then I don't actually know the guy. Who knows what really goes on between two people.'

'Did Adriana ever have any injuries indicative of violence?'

'No, not that I noticed,' Barry admitted, looking as if this hadn't previously occurred to him. 'Is that unusual? In cases like this?'

'In domestic homicides, you mean?'

'I guess,' Barry confirmed, awkwardly.

'It's a common factor, but by no means universal,' Lawrence replied. 'Although I'm still trying to establish whether that is what we're dealing with.'

This last comment seemed to take a moment to sink in. Barry swallowed. Before he could respond, Lawrence asked what he had been doing in the hours surrounding Adriana's death.

'Not much, I don't think. I don't remember exactly. I know I was at home. I expect I was watching TV, or surfing the net.' His expression shifted from disconcerted to concerned. 'Are you saying I'm a suspect?'

Lawrence leaned back in his chair, threading the fingers of one hand loosely between those of the other. 'At this stage, as far as I'm concerned, *everyone's* a suspect.'

Leighton gathered up the selection of evidence bags scattered across the bare mattress and made for the bedroom door. Given the number of paramedics and police officers who had tramped in and out of the room before anyone had thought to preserve the scene, he didn't hold out much hope he'd collected anything of value, but at least knowing exactly what he was looking for would make the job of processing the samples straightforward. Feeling his mobile vibrate, he pulled it out and glanced at the screen, then returned the device to his pocket unanswered. Tom could talk to his voicemail.

After Friday's altercation, Leighton had hoped his brother might move on, but he hadn't, and once Leighton's initial anger had subsided the prospect of forcing the matter had been a daunting one, so he had put it off. In the meantime, he was doing his best to avoid Tom, which in the main meant finding any and every reason not to go home. He had taken his frustration over the situation – and his inability to deal with it – out on Pete, safe in the knowledge that Pete wouldn't belt him one. Not in the office, anyway. And it wasn't as if Pete didn't deserve it, the man was an arsehole. Max was of much the same mind, which was presumably why he hadn't even asked why a simple difference of opinion had escalated into a major conflict. But, even in the absence of a reprimand from his boss, recent events had left Leighton feeling on edge at work as well as home. And avoiding the workplace presented a far greater challenge than finding someone to feed the cat.

Closing the door behind himself, he looked into the adjacent living room. Evan was sitting in an armchair facing the blank television screen, his expression almost dazed, and Leighton hesitated before knocking gently on the open door to get his attention. Evan jumped.

'Sorry.'

Evan shook his head. 'It's ok. It's just – I've not been here since –' he trailed off with a weak shrug.

'Do you want to go?'

'I don't know,' he admitted, after a moment's silence.

Leighton wasn't sure whether to stay or go himself. He didn't want to intrude on Evan's grief, but the man seemed so lost he felt reluctant to leave him alone. His eyes strayed in the direction of the kitchen at the far end of the room. 'Tea?' He suggested, looking back to Evan.

Evan regarded him blankly for a moment before saying, disconsolately, 'No milk.'

'Milk I can do,' Leighton returned, opening the end pocket of his bag and rooting around for the handful of UHT sachets he'd misappropriated from the Met canteen several days earlier. Pulling one out, he held it up and regarded Evan with raised eyebrows.

The man nodded before preparing to stand.

'You're all right,' Leighton stopped him, waving him back and making for the kitchen.

From the doorway, there had been nothing to suggest it had stood idle for the better part of three months, but at closer range the spider web embroidered between the bars of the stainless steel draining rack and the layer of dust on the bread bin spoke of the reality. Leighton flipped open the lid of the kettle to find a layer of solid calcium carbonate that would take some effort to shift. He gave the vessel a quick rinse – it wasn't as if limescale had ever killed anyone – before filling it and flicking it on.

'Sugar?' He asked, glancing around.

'Two. Thanks.' Then, as an afterthought, 'She was always hassling me to cut down.'

'Been there,' Leighton remarked, ruefully, with a lift of his eyebrows.

'Not like that,' Evan countered. 'She just –' he hesitated before concluding, 'Cared.'

Leighton nodded.

'I should've tried harder. It would've made her happy.'

'She was with you for a decade, you must have been doing something right.'

Evan acknowledged the comment with a nod, but didn't say anything further, and Leighton turned his attention to a search of the kitchen cupboards.

'Does your missus give you a hard time?' Evan asked, as Leighton reached for a neatly labelled jar of sugar.

Leighton glanced around. 'Sorry?'

Evan nodded towards the jar in his hand.

'Oh,' Leighton understood, aloud. 'No. My dad.' And that certainly wasn't because *he* cared. It probably wasn't particularly personal, either – he tended to lash out at whoever was there. Leighton had long since stopped reacting to the repeated jibes and put-downs, largely looking on his visits home as offering some sort of respite to his mother. She was the only reason he ever went back.

'My dad's a bastard,' Evan replied.

Leighton nodded slightly. 'Yeah, I know.'

Evan regarded him quizzically before saying, 'Is that why you're being nice to me?'

'No. I've no reason not to be nice to you.'

Evan dropped his gaze. 'Nobody really is any more. Apart from Mum.'

It was hard to know how to respond to that. The saddest part of the situation was that even if they did succeed in connecting Adriana's death to Rhys Williams, Evan wouldn't get his life back. On top of having lost his girlfriend, his friendships had probably been damaged beyond repair.

'I'm sorry,' Leighton offered, at a loss to know what else to say.

'Not your fault, is it?'

'No, but I don't think it's yours either.'

Evan eyed him suspiciously. 'How d'you mean?'

'Well you didn't kill her, did you?'

Evan didn't reply, still looking wary.

'What did you think I meant?'

'Sometimes people blame my dad. Nobody actually believes me.'

'I guess that makes me nobody,' Leighton concluded, as the kettle boiled. He tossed a tea bag into each of two mugs and sloshed boiling water over them before realising he didn't have a teaspoon, and looking around for a cutlery rack or drawer. He struck lucky with the first drawer he tried, and was about to unscrew the lid of the sugar jar when Evan spoke.

'Why?'

Leighton turned again. 'What, why do I believe you?'

Evan shrugged. 'Nobody else does.'

Leighton leaned against the worktop, mindful of the fact he couldn't reference the investigation that had first brought Evan's case to his attention. He opted to stick to basics that were true of almost all homicides. 'There are a lot of grey areas in what we do. There are unknowns, assumptions, lies, false memories –' he paused, tapping the teaspoon against his palm. 'And then there's physical evidence. As a rule, that doesn't lie. And I can't square it with your being guilty.'

Evan's eyebrows contracted into a frown. 'But the police had the same evidence before. When they charged me.'

'There is an element of interpretation,' Leighton admitted. 'Which means preconceptions and prejudices can get in the way.'

'So how d'you know you're right?'

Leighton had been answering variations on that question for years. More often than not, they were posed by colleagues in the Met, and took the more contentious form of 'so what makes you *think* you're right?' Ordinarily, his response was a quip along the lines of *because I'm very good at my job*. On this occasion, the stakes were too high for jokes.

'I've seen a lot of homicides,' he said. 'And I've examined a lot of evidence. And if I can't join the dots, there's usually a good reason.'

The pathologists' office was deserted when Lawrence looked in shortly after four, but as Leighton's laptop was open on his desk Lawrence guessed he must be somewhere in the building. Meanwhile, the fact his mobile phone was lying beside it answered the question of why Lawrence's calls had all gone to voicemail. Lawrence quickly tracked his colleague down to the laboratory two doors along the corridor, apparently in the process of cataloguing evidence bags. Easing the door open, he said, 'Do you have a minute?'

Leighton jumped violently.

'Sorry,' Lawrence offered, pre-emptively, as his colleague spun around to face him.

'Jesus,' Leighton breathed, closing his eyes and raising a hand to his chest.

'I'm sorry, I didn't mean to startle you.'

Leighton shook his head slightly. 'You're all right,' he replied, with a weak smile. 'What can I do for you?'

'I wanted to ask about the message you left me earlier – the signal broke up at the crucial moment. I did try calling back, but I couldn't get through.'

'Oh, right,' the pathologist frowned, automatically checking his pockets.

'It's on your desk,' Lawrence offered.

'Oh, is it? Sorry about that.' Leighton reached for a nearby stool. 'I was just reporting back on the DNA results for Coralie. Or rather, the lack of them.'

'Meaning what? You don't have anything or you don't have anything that matches to the database?'

'Somewhere in between,' Leighton replied, as he sat down. 'We only managed to get a partial profile. It's sufficient to exclude ninety-nine-point-nine per cent of the population, but as you know, that's still nowhere near enough.'

'Is Williams among the nought-point-one per cent?'

'Yes. But that doesn't place him at the crime scene.'

'Taking all the evidence together, do you think there's any question over his involvement?'

'No, not really. Although it can be difficult to know whether information that ought to be restricted actually *is* these days, what with everyone having camera phones. Who knows what images might be out there on the dark web. So I suppose there is a vanishingly small chance it's a copycat.'

Lawrence nodded. 'Have you had the tox results back yet?'

'Yep. Nothing to report.'

'Not even alcohol?'

'No.'

'Was that the case for Adriana as well?'

'It was. Why?'

'Well, Williams may have changed his means of finding victims. Thanks to the press disseminating his MO the length and breadth of the country last time around, he probably knows the first place we'll look for him is locksmiths. And it's possible he could be targeting women through Internet dating sites. But – assuming both women died at the hands of the same man – that seems less likely if neither of them had been drinking. I know not everybody does, but it is the norm.'

Leighton smiled. 'You may be viewing it from a rather conventional perspective. Not everybody bothers with the trials of dating, these days. There are websites and apps out there for the express purpose of hooking up.'

'That hadn't passed me by.'

'I'm not sure I see it where Adriana's concerned, though. There's a big difference between falling for a co-worker and actively going looking to cheat.'

'There is,' Lawrence acknowledged. 'But at the very least we can try to rule it out. Assuming the guys in Birmingham ever manage to work out what they did with her mobile and get it over to us.'

Leighton nodded.

'Anything else?' Lawrence enquired.

'Not on Williams. I have been going through all the evidence we collected in relation to O'Leary, and I think it might be worth testing –'

'Your brief was to focus on Ratley,' Lawrence interrupted, with a frown. 'Does it have any bearing on that investigation?'

'Not at this stage, but –'

'But nothing. The O'Leary investigation is closed. If you want to pick it apart, you can do it in your own time and without expending Home Office resources. Otherwise, I'd appreciate it if you'd concentrate on what I've asked you to do. Are we clear?'

'Will you at least –'

'Are we clear?' Lawrence reiterated, sharply.

'Yes,' Leighton conceded, reluctantly.

'Where are you at with Ratley?'

'Waiting on the lab. And before you ask, yes, they are on it.'

Lawrence wasn't sure whether his colleague's defensive response was the result of the preceding exchange or simply his anticipating Lawrence's next question. He decided not to comment, saying only, 'Great, thank you.'

'I'll let you know when I do,' Leighton replied, sliding down off his stool and turning back towards the bench before pausing to add, 'And next time you head this way, maybe you could whistle, or something.' He flashed a smile. 'Make sure I hear you coming.'

Flora drew a deep breath before reaching to ring the doorbell. She had spent the best part of half an hour walking the surrounding streets, talking herself by turns into and out of what she was about to do. Trying to find the words she knew would never come close to being enough.

When the door opened, Claire Somerset's expression betrayed her shock at finding Flora outside, and there was a momentary pause before she spoke. When she did, her tone was cool.

'Hello Flora.'

'Hi,' Flora replied, awkwardly. 'Is Evan here?'

'Yes,' Claire confirmed, shortly. She didn't move.

'Could I talk to him?'

'I think you said more than enough at the funeral. He could do without a second trip to A and E to have his stomach pumped.'

Flora felt shaken; she hadn't heard about the first one. She couldn't recall her exact words to Evan at Adriana's funeral, they had been lost in the mists of emotion, but she did remember yelling abuse at him and challenging his right to be there. It had been one of the hardest days of her life, and that was with a host of people offering their support. Evan had been faced with open hostility. Flora wondered how he had found the courage to go at all.

'Please,' she offered, earnestly. 'I haven't come to have a go. Honestly.'

A couple of seconds passed before Claire yielded and stepped back from the door. 'He's in his room. You'll remember the way?'

Flora nodded, heading straight up the stairs before Claire could change her mind. Some seven or eight years had passed since she had last visited the house, but it still looked and felt very familiar, right down to the number-plate-style sign on Evan's bedroom door.

Flora knocked. When there was no response, she gradually eased the door open. Evan was sitting on the bed, his back against the wall, seemingly doing nothing. He glanced around disinterestedly as the door opened, then, seeing Flora, apathy turned abruptly to consternation.

'Hi,' Flora opened, awkwardly.

Evan echoed the greeting, his tone wary.

'I heard what happened – after the funeral –' Flora continued, haltingly. 'I'm sorry.'

Evan regarded her in silence for what felt like forever before saying, rather dully, 'Are you?'

'Yes.'

He nodded slightly but didn't reply, returning his head to its original position and re-fixing his eyes on the wall ahead of him.

'Can I sit down?' Flora asked, after a moment.

Evan looked back around, his eyebrows caught in a perplexed frown. 'What for? You've got what you came for.'

'Sorry?'

'Absolution,' he enlarged. 'So now you can stop feeling guilty and have a nice life. Congratulations.'

'That's not why I came.'

'No?'

'No.'

Evan made no response, reverting to staring at the wall. Flora carefully gathered up the items of clothing heaped on the chair by the wardrobe and set them on the end of the bed before moving the chair a couple of feet closer to him and sitting down.

'I'm sorry,' she offered, again. 'I know some of what I said was unforgivable, but I wasn't in a good place. I'd just lost my best friend.'

'Yeah, so had I.'

Flora nodded, more to herself than anything. 'I know,' she acknowledged, at length. 'I'm sorry.'

In the ensuing silence, Flora found herself counting the seconds as the clock on the wall ticked them away. Feeling increasingly uncomfortable, she searched for something to say. In the end, all she could come up with was, 'A detective from Scotland Yard came to see me on Tuesday.'

'Oh, right,' Evan lifted his eyebrows momentarily. 'So that's how come you're here.'

Flora wished she could say otherwise. There was another silence whilst she grappled with how to pose her next question.

'Do you know why they're involved?'

'What does it matter? It's not like it's going to make any difference.'

'You don't know that.'

Evan met her eyes. 'There's no sign anyone else was there.'

'There must be something or they'd not be looking into it.'

'Not really. The forensic scientist said he'd give evidence for me in court, but there's nothing that can't be interpreted differently.'

'That's still something, isn't it?'

Evan shrugged. 'I'm going to lose either way. Even if I don't go down people are always going to believe I did it.'

Flora bit her lip. She could hardly argue with him: events thus far had already underlined the fallacy of innocent until proven guilty.

'And I still won't have my girl,' he continued, disconsolately.

'You can't give up.'

'Nobody's interested.'

'Then we'll have to *make* them interested. Keith's brother works for the Echo, maybe we can get –'

'No, please don't,' Evan protested. 'I don't want any more publicity. Enough people hate me already.'

'This isn't just about you!' Flora exclaimed. 'This is about justice for Adriana! I'm not going to let them bury her!'

'But –'

'You should want that as much as I do,' she asserted. 'It's the least she deserves!'

Evan made no reply.

'But maybe you don't care enough to help me. In which case, I'll do it alone.' She regarded him keenly, anticipating a response. When she didn't get one, she moved to stand. 'Your choice.'

Friday 9 April

Lawrence stepped out of the lift into the foyer outside CID to find Jamie and Leighton sharing a joke that involved the pathologist gesturing wildly. Catching sight of Lawrence, Jamie raised a hand to acknowledge him before making for the toilets, and Lawrence wondered whether he had been intending to go out for a smoke – or, given his rapid departure, just returned from one. Lawrence had banned his team members from smoking during working hours unless they were on an official break, but he was well aware Jamie only observed the rule when he was in the office to enforce it.

'Afternoon,' he greeted Leighton as he drew level with his colleague.

'Howdy,' Leighton returned, cheerily, falling into step alongside him. 'I've just left a few bits and pieces on your desk, but I'm afraid there's nothing of any great note.'

'No news on our doggy DNA?'

'There's news, it's just not good news.'

Lawrence sighed. 'Well let's have it.'

'As far as the guys at the lab can ascertain, there's fur belonging to at least seventeen dogs in Ratley's house, and there are multiple samples from three animals. A couple of swabs from the body have thrown up a sequence we can't match, but there are also hits matching DNA from the house. None of it proves anything much.'

Lawrence nodded. 'Are there any other tests you think might be worth running?'

'Not for Ratley.'

Lawrence chose to ignore the unspoken reference to the O'Leary case, saying instead, 'Speaking of further tests, you were going to ask one of the SOC team to take a look at Adriana's flat. Do you know who dealt with that?'

'I did.'

Lawrence raised his eyebrows, but didn't query the fact the task clearly hadn't required a pathologist. If Max gave Leighton carte blanche to pursue whatever took his fancy, it was his problem if billable hours were wasted. 'And?'

'I've sent a bunch of samples to the lab – if we're lucky we might get something from those.'

'I hope so,' Lawrence admitted.

'You don't think Evan's guilty either, then.'

'No. I've been through every one of his accounts of that night, and there are no holes or mismatches of any note.'

Leighton nodded.

'How about you? Is your view based on anything other than what you've seen in the file?'

'Nothing material.'

'But?' Lawrence prompted.

'I don't think he'd be able to live with it if he'd had a hand in her death. I think he'd have cracked by now. He seems totally broken by it all.'

Lawrence stopped walking with a frown. 'I asked for a sweep of the flat. I don't recall authorising a meet and greet.'

Leighton looked taken aback. 'Did you expect me to guess the answers to my questions? I'm not psychic.'

The note of sarcasm in his tone grated, but Lawrence couldn't argue with his reasoning. 'Yes, all right, fair enough.'

'Chances are we're going to need to have the body exhumed. Do you want me –'

'That won't be necessary.'

'But –'

'We've more than enough evidence to nail Williams already. What we need to do is find him. A second autopsy isn't going to help with that, is it?'

'I'm not concerned with Williams, I'm thinking of Evan.'

'That's a matter for West Mids Police. I've communicated my thoughts to them.'

'They've no reason to revisit it! We have.'

'Leighton, I can't justify the cost of an exhumation unless it's likely to make a significant contribution to my investigation.'

'If we can't definitively connect Williams to Adriana, there's a good chance Evan will go down for murder. And you don't believe he's guilty any more than I do!'

Lawrence sighed. 'I understand where you're coming from, but my hands are tied.'

'Bollocks they are!'

'I beg your pardon?'

'You don't know for sure we won't learn something useful from a second PM, and given the profile of the investigation you know MacLennan will give you a lot of latitude where the budget is concerned! You just don't *want* to pursue it!'

'Evan's case is not in my remit,' Lawrence replied, shortly.

'Jesus!' Leighton exclaimed. 'What is it with everyone and their rules and remits? When did regulations and red tape become more important than justice? Are you seriously going to let a guy go down for ten to fifteen years because he's not part of our *remit*? Do you not –'

'Ok, enough!' Lawrence stopped him. 'You've made your point and you've had my decision! That is the end of it!'

For a moment Leighton looked as if he might continue to argue, but he clearly thought better of it, and turned back in the direction of the lifts without another word. Lawrence made for his office. Leighton's opinion differing from his own was nothing new – the pathologist had always had a tendency to think with his heart rather than his head where anything emotive was concerned – but usually his approach was considerably more measured, if no less persistent. It wasn't often Lawrence felt his authority was being challenged, and it was difficult to know how best to respond to that when dealing with someone who wasn't part of the same chain of command. He wondered whether Pete's complaint had arisen from a similar situation.

'What was that about?' Rebecca asked as he passed her desk.

'This week's crusade,' Lawrence replied, with a sigh. 'I'm not sure what's got into him lately, he gets wound up so easily he almost makes me feel laid back.'

This drew a laugh from Rebecca.

'Quite,' Lawrence remarked. 'Do you know what's going on?'

She shrugged. 'I suppose he's got Pete's complaint to worry about.'

'Is he worried about it, do you think?' Lawrence asked. 'He seems more pissed off than worried to me.' He didn't add that he didn't think Leighton had a lot to worry *about*. Given the circumstances, he thought it unlikely Max would do anything more than protocol demanded, and he suspected Leighton knew it too.

'Maybe.'

'Is he all right?'

'I don't know. He's not been very communicative.'

'And how about you?'

Rebecca frowned. 'What about me?' She asked, guardedly.

'Are you all right?'

'Oh. Yes.'

'I know it can't be easy for you working alongside the Williams investigation. You can take some time out if you need to.'

'Thanks, but I'm fine.'

Lawrence nodded. 'How are you getting on with Ratley? I need to report back to MacLennan on that in a couple of hours.'

'So far I've made precious little progress. His family – there's only a mother and a brother – claim not to have had a lot of contact with him, and I've had no more success tracing witnesses than uniform did. All door-to-door turned up was wise monkeys.'

Lawrence sighed again. In some neighbourhoods, you struggled to tease out relevant information from all the well-meaning but unhelpful details that poured in in response to enquiries. In others, nobody saw anything, heard anything or said anything. Fred Ratley's neighbours were apparently in the latter camp.

'His phone and Internet histories threw up nothing of note – he streamed a lot of hardcore porn, but nothing illegal – and a cursory look around his home didn't reveal much either,' Rebecca continued. 'I might extend that before I try interviewing any more of his contacts, the ones I've talked to so far were less than helpful.'

'Do you think it's worth the effort?'

Rebecca shrugged. 'Given that nobody seems to want to talk to me, I suspect I'll have more luck with possessions than people.'

'I'm not questioning your approach, Becky, I'm asking whether you think Ratley's death warrants further investigation at all.'

'Oh, right,' she nodded. 'Well there doesn't seem to be any way a dog could have got into or out of Ratley's garden, and, on top of that, none of the neighbours whose gardens abut his has a dog big enough to do more than nip your ankles. So if Leighton is correct about Ratley's dog not being a contender, it follows that someone else must have been involved. Whether or not death was the intended result.'

It was a big if. And with no way of definitively excluding Ratley's dog from the running, it was difficult to disagree with the concise summary Pete had offered up when Lawrence had finally managed to pin him down to discuss the case. 'One man killed by dog, one dog at scene, no witnesses, toss all other evidence – even if the obvious answer isn't the right one we've next to no bloody chance of proving otherwise,' he had observed. 'Why waste everyone's time?'

'And what about O'Leary?' Lawrence continued. 'Have you found anything indicative of a connection?'

'No, but there's precious little to make a connection *to*. I've yet to establish who any of the others in that photograph are, and doing so could be a bit of a mission. It's clearly at least ten years old – probably more like fifteen – and apparently it was developed from film, so I doubt there's much chance it's left a digital trail doing the rounds on social media. Ratley certainly didn't put it out there – he didn't even have a Facebook account.'

'How very sensible of him,' Lawrence remarked, cheerfully, the absence of a link between the two men coming as a relief. The last thing he wanted was any involvement in an investigation that was already a political hot potato. Pete's response to the mention of O'Leary had been predictably irate, and now Lawrence had an overview of the situation he was inclined to conclude that his own time was being wasted adjudicating a personal conflict that had been allowed to spiral completely out of hand. Pete's domineering manner and Max's relaxed approach to management had both contributed to the significance of an unexplained death being blown out of all proportion. Had a more diplomatic DCI originally been assigned the case, it could probably have been relatively quickly and painlessly shelved with an open verdict. Now, whatever decision Lawrence – and by extension his superior – came to was likely to provoke outrage from one side or the other. And he would be left with the resultant fallout.

''Ey up me duck!' A familiar voice greeted, cheerfully, as Abigail walked through the downstairs hallway of the home Izzy shared with her grandfather. She smiled, pausing in the living room doorway.

''Ey up, Hector,' she returned. 'How's tricks?'

'Magic.'

'Glad to hear it,' Abigail replied, turning for the stairs. The familiar exchange always reminded her of a recurring scene in a film she'd seen years earlier. She wondered how it played out in Hector's mind, and whether he had any awareness of the fact he lived in a real-world time loop. Perhaps it didn't seem like that to him. Perhaps there was more going on in his head than she realised.

Izzy was sitting cross-legged on the floor of the back bedroom, still in her blue nurse's uniform, bottle-feeding one of the three-week-old kittens that had been dumped outside the rescue centre early the previous morning. By the time Abigail had discovered them, the box the four siblings had been left in was soggy with the rain, the kittens cold and shivering. Fortunately, none of the little creatures seemed any the worse for their ordeal, and two of the three not in the process of eating were tottering enthusiastically around the room, all big blue eyes and oversized ears, their tiny pointed tails held aloft. Abigail crouched to pet the closest one, which promptly tried to climb her hand before losing its balance and toppling sideways onto the floor. She smiled, tickling the animal's exposed belly with her forefinger.

'Hello sausage.'

'Soldier,' Izzy corrected.

'Soldier?' Abigail echoed, looking up.

'Tinker, Tailor, Spy,' Izzy elaborated, nodding towards each of the other kittens in turn, the last of which was asleep in her lap. She almost invariably named litters along a theme of one kind or another, and her latest selection was a lot more respectable than that of the trio she'd christened Smack, Crack and Pot earlier in the year. 'Oh, like the cereal, that's nice,' Aunt Lily had remarked, innocently, causing Charlie to choke on his beer.

'Looks like they're doing well,' Abigail observed, kneeling down a couple of feet from where Izzy sat.

'No thanks to the scum who dumped them. People like that make me ashamed to be human.'

'At least they brought them to us and didn't dump them in a bin somewhere,' Abigail replied, well aware the fact would cut no ice with Izzy. They had had this conversation more times than she cared to count.

'How big of them,' Izzy returned, sarcastically. 'It's still luck they're alive. If you'd been half an hour later coming down, they'd not have stood a chance.'

'I know.'

'And some poor cat out there will still be looking and crying for her kittens.'

'I know,' Abigail repeated, wearily. 'I don't condone it any more than you do, Iz. But we can't change people. We can only do what we can do.'

'That never feels like enough. We'll be picking up the pieces forever if nobody does anything to address the root cause. People can treat animals like rubbish with little or no comeback.'

'If you want to change the law you're going to have to run for parliament.'

Izzy nodded contemplatively. 'You know, that's not such a bad idea,' she replied, at length. 'One day I might just do it.' There was a pause before she changed the subject. 'I booked my flight today.'

The news didn't come as a surprise, but Abigail felt her throat constrict all the same. Like Izzy, Abigail had seen the appalling plight of the neglected stray dogs and cats in Greece first hand, and had immediately vowed to do something to make a difference. Setting up an animal rescue centre in the country hadn't felt so much like a dream as a vocation, and until recently the biggest question had been how they would finance the project. Now, bound to her London home by a promise to her mother, Abigail would have to watch Izzy go it alone. By and large, the lot of Britain's companion animals was a happier one than that of those in Greece, but countless pets remained unwanted, neglected or abused. And somebody had to fight for them, too.

Picking out some of the higher-denomination coins from the mass of small change in his top desk drawer, Jamie debated what to request from Rebecca's afternoon coffee-shop run. The weather was unseasonably warm – one of those sunny April days that feels more like June – and he found himself tempted with a Frappuccino. But he wasn't in the mood for the piss-take the selection of a *girly milkshake* would almost inevitably attract from one quarter or another.

'What are you getting?' He asked, as if that might make a difference to his decision.

'Usual,' Rebecca replied, succinctly. A double hazelnut latte, then. Jamie himself had never been a fan of the fashion for adulterating coffee with syrups. Funny how it seemed to work when the drink was cold, though.

'I'll have an Americano,' he decided, proffering a handful of loose change. 'And can you get me a lemon muffin, as well?'

'Sure,' she nodded, taking the collection of coins and reaching for her handbag before stopping short, her eyes focused on something behind him. He was about to turn around when she answered the question of what – or who – she was looking at for him, saying, 'Coffee, Sir?'

'No thanks,' Lawrence declined, as he drew level with the end of Jamie's desk.

'Ok, won't be long,' Rebecca replied, grabbing the bag and heading for the corridor.

'How'd it go?' Jamie asked, turning his chair through forty-five degrees.

'I can't say I –' Lawrence stopped, his eyebrows drawing into a frown. 'What have you got there?' He asked, casting his eyes over the pages spread across Jamie's desk. 'Did Leighton ask you to look this out?'

'Not really,' Jamie hedged, sensing there was some backstory he'd missed. 'He asked *about* it, so I –'

Lawrence muttered something Jamie didn't catch, but his irate tone was clear enough. 'Right,' he said, decisively, after a moment. 'He's been told to leave that alone, so I'd appreciate it if you'd do the same. And if it comes up again, refer him to me.'

'Ok,' Jamie nodded, more than happy to abandon the task of reacquainting himself with the O'Leary investigation. 'Sorry, I didn't –'

Lawrence cut him off with a shake of his head. 'You weren't to know,' he replied, before immediately moving on. 'Any joy tracing Coralie's stalker, David?'

'Not really,' Jamie admitted. 'She seems to have met him through a Meetup-style app called LIFEnLOVE, but the mobile he accessed it through is no longer in use, and the address connected to the account is almost a year out of date.'

'And let me guess, it's a pay as you go phone?'

Jamie nodded. 'It has been topped up by card on a few occasions, but the card is also prepay and registered to the same out-of-date address. And there's been no credit on it for months, and so no activity.'

Lawrence sighed.

'I'm waiting on a credit check, which might answer the question of whether there's more to that than a shite credit history. But with the limited information I was able to provide they may struggle to give me much even if he *is* using his real name. Did you know there are nearly six thousand David Joneses in this country?'

'I do now,' Lawrence remarked, leaning against Eva's unoccupied desk. 'What about the address? Flat mates? Landlord? Council tax records?'

'No flat mates – it's a studio – and the landlord wasn't much help. The studio is contained within his home, and I'd be willing to bet he isn't declaring the income. Without any paper trail there's probably little way of proving he'd be over the tax threshold, especially as bills were included – or so he says, who knows whether the utility companies and council even know the building comprises more than one dwelling.'

'We could find out and apply pressure on that basis.'

'It might be worth a shot, but I didn't get the impression he was stonewalling – I think he just didn't know much about the guy because it suited him that way.'

Lawrence was silent for a moment before saying, 'I don't suppose there's any chance Jones used a photo for his profile – or whatever they call it – on the app?'

'Probably, but there's nothing showing up now. Generally when you deactivate an account on social media or networking sites it kills the photograph in historic communications. I could try contacting the company behind LIFEnLOVE, see whether they have a record of it? Although there's no guarantee it would be his picture even if they do.'

'Yes please. And I'd like to –' Lawrence's mobile began to ring and he glanced at the screen before answering it, holding up one finger to Jamie to indicate he wouldn't be long. The tone of his simple, 'Hi,' was sufficient for Jamie to identify the caller as Lawrence's wife, Katie. During the pause that followed, Lawrence's expression shifted to one of concern, and at length he said, 'Ok, I'll do that, you go –' he broke off, presumably as his wife interrupted. 'Yes … yes, I know … Kate, please don't worry about that, I've got it … yes, I will go straight there. Keep me posted. Ok.' Hanging up, he pushed off from the desk. 'I'm going to have to go and pick Elise up,' he said, heading towards his office. 'If anything urgent comes up, give me a call, otherwise I'll check back in later from home.'

'Is Elise all right?' Jamie asked, as Lawrence re-emerged from the office, slipping an arm into his jacket as he walked.

'She's fine. But Katie normally meets her from school, and her father's just been rushed to hospital, so she's heading down to Canterbury.'

Jamie nodded, trying to think of something to say that didn't sound trite. Lawrence saved him the trouble, adding, 'Can you make a start combing the system for crimes linked to dating apps – stalking, sexual assaults, et cetera? I tend to think of digital technology as leaving a trail, but as your research on Jones shows, that's not necessarily much use. And I wouldn't put it past Williams to have set up an entire identity especially for that purpose.'

Monday 12 April

'Morning!'

Toby opened his eyes in surprise; he hadn't heard Izzy come in. He echoed her greeting, his voice sounding oddly unfamiliar to his ears.

'God, are you all right?' Izzy exclaimed in concern, noticing he had a hand to his chest.

'Heartburn,' he replied, shortly, rubbing the upper part of his sternum.

'Are you sure? You look awful. Maybe I should call an ambulance –'

'No need. I didn't get much sleep, that's all.' When she still didn't look convinced, he added, 'Upset stomach.'

'So what are you doing down here?'

'It's going to be a busy morning,' he shrugged, vaguely aware of how ridiculous the idea he might be thinking of working sounded when he could barely stand up or keep water down.

'For the rest of us, maybe. You need to go back to bed.'

Toby nodded, then immediately regretted the movement. He felt as if he had the world's worst hangover. Then again, maybe that was what it *was*. His recollection of the latter part of the preceding evening was more than a little hazy. Come to think of it, he couldn't even remember getting to bed. The realisation made him feel rather ashamed. He was more than old enough to know better.

'Go on, hop it,' Izzy chivvied, kindly.

Toby forced a weak smile. 'Thanks, Iz.'

Izzy leaned to start up the main veterinary appointments system on the computer at the front desk, and Toby rose slowly to his feet. His surroundings rushed out of focus and he grabbed hold of the reception counter to keep his balance.

'Ok, sit down,' Izzy's voice instructed, firmly, as two hands pushed him back into the chair. He leaned forwards, bowing his head and waiting for the dizziness to subside. Izzy crouched in front of him and rested a hand on his arm. 'Just take it easy.'

Toby drew a careful breath, feeling nauseous again. He tried closing his eyes, but that served only to compound the vertigo.

'I really think you ought to see a doctor,' Izzy put in, after a moment. 'Your face is literally grey.'

'I'm just a bit dehydrated,' he countered. 'We've got some of those rehydration drinks somewhere, one of those should sort me out.'

'You know they're chicken-flavoured, right?' Izzy came back, lightly. 'I think it'd be a bit like drinking a bottle of gravy. You don't look like you'd be able to stomach that right now.'

That much, Toby had to admit, was true. The mere thought of it almost made him heave.

'When Phil gets here we'll get you up to bed and I'll run down to the chemist and find you something designed for humans,' Izzy offered. 'And I'll pick up some peppermint tea, as well.'

'Thanks.'

'Can I get you anything else?'

Toby didn't reply, raising a hand to his mouth.

'A bucket, I'm guessing,' Izzy concluded, reaching for the plastic bin behind the office door and placing it between his feet before straightening up. 'I must've missed out on a good night last night,' she joked, giving his shoulder a gentle squeeze.

Toby felt relieved he had an excuse to keep his gaze on the floor, because he wouldn't have been able to look Izzy in the eye. Less than twelve hours earlier, he'd been making love to her girlfriend in a room upstairs: now she was showing the same care and concern for him that she usually reserved for his animal patients. That he perhaps deserved to feel like death had already occurred to him, but he hadn't felt quite so guilty about it until now. Izzy's ordinarily hard and sarcastic demeanour made it easy to forget about the human being underneath, and the fact Abigail had been the one to come onto him had, in his mind, allowed him to push all responsibility for the affair onto her. But she wasn't the only one cheating. Toby had a relationship with Izzy, too, albeit a platonic and largely professional one, something he suspected he would no longer be able to ignore. And, much as he didn't want to press her – because he could guess what the answer was likely to be – Abigail was going to have to choose.

After a weekend spent shuttling back and forth between Birmingham, Canterbury and London, with insufficient time to devote to the investigation, his wife or his children, Monday morning couldn't have come soon enough for Lawrence. He had succeeded in offloading the Ratley investigation by the end of the previous week, but when it came to the far more pressing matter of tracing Rhys Williams, his team seemed no closer to a conclusion than they had been a week earlier. The doctors treating Katie's father didn't appear to have made much progress either, with the question of what had caused his collapse still unanswered. And, given that the man already had several serious health problems, the medics were understandably reticent when it came to offering any kind of prognosis.

Looking into the pathologists' office shortly after ten, Lawrence found Jon at his laptop and Roddy attempting to fit a warped lid onto what looked to be a very old archive box.

'Either of you know where Leighton is?' He asked, as both men glanced his way.

'He should be in later,' Jon replied, as Roddy said, 'In court.'

'Oh, he didn't mention that. Anything interesting?'

'Dangerous driving,' Roddy replied, raising his eyebrows pointedly. Jon shot him a disgusted look.

'What was he doing?'

'One eleven.'

'Miles an hour?' Lawrence exclaimed.

'Uh-huh,' Roddy nodded, as he made for the door with the archive box in his hands.

'What the hell was he thinking?'

'More like what was he on,' Roddy returned, as he shouldered the door open and disappeared out into the corridor.

'Twat,' Jon retorted, under his breath, before seeming to remember he wasn't alone and adding, 'Sorry,' as he looked to Lawrence. 'Is it anything I can help with?'

'I'm not sure. Leighton emailed me an attachment late last night and I can't seem to open it.'

'Shouldn't be a problem,' Jon responded, digging a hand into the mug full of pens on his desk and extracting a bunch of keys before relocating to the chair at Leighton's chaotic desk.

'Would it not be an idea to keep those somewhere a little more secure?' Lawrence suggested, as Jon unlocked Leighton's top desk drawer. 'What are the others for?'

'Hmmh?' Jon glanced up, eyebrows raised. 'Oh, those are his spare door keys. And they're not a lot of use to him if they're shut in my drawer, are they?'

'I'd opt for security over convenience any day.'

'Yeah, but you don't lose track of your keys every other week.'

Lawrence shook his head in disbelief. 'How is it Leighton can remember a photograph he saw at a crime scene a year ago, but not where he left his keys?'

'It's a special talent,' Jon joked, lifting Leighton's laptop from the drawer, flipping it open and switching it on.

'Do you all have access to one another's machines?'

Jon sniggered. 'Yeah, can you see Roddy agreeing to that?'

Lawrence was tempted to observe that, in this instance, Roddy had a point. On the whole, he shared Roddy's desire for everything to be done by the book, although he suspected the similarity ended there. As far as Lawrence was concerned, laws, rules and procedures existed for a reason, and it was that reason that mattered when it came to judging their importance. Roddy, on the other hand, was the quintessential jobsworth, and would probably object to Jon and Leighton sharing their access to the system because they weren't *supposed to* rather than out of any real concern about the attendant security risk.

Jon tried three different passwords before hitting on the correct one, and Leighton's desktop wallpaper – the Sheffield Wednesday owl logo – promptly filled the screen. Moments later, the dock appeared below it and Jon selected the mail icon.

'What did Roddy mean?' Lawrence asked, as the little envelope logo began jumping up and down.

'Huh?'

'When he said *what was he on*?'

'Oh, that's just Roddy stirring, as usual,' Jon replied, unconcernedly, as he tapped in another password.

Lawrence frowned. 'Tossing accusations around is more than just stirring,' he observed. Assuming they were baseless, that was. He didn't say as much, well aware of where Jon's loyalties lay, but the remark had already succeeded in raising questions in his own mind. Surely Leighton wouldn't be that stupid, though? Medics might have easy access to drugs, but abuse of that privilege carried heavy penalties. And there was a big difference between Leighton's penchant for bending the rules and breaking the law. Then again, Lawrence would never have expected him to push his luck so far on the roads, either. And he very much doubted anyone could *accidentally* exceed the national speed limit by some forty miles an hour.

*****

At some stage during every kitten season, Ingrid was reminded of lambing time on her parents' farm. Year on year, her mother had sworn she would never again allow her home to be taken over by struggling, injured and motherless lambs. Then another spring would arrive and the kitchen, warmed around the clock by the radiant heat of the AGA, once again filled up with boxes accommodating the weak, the orphaned and the victims of corvid attacks. Countless hours of Ingrid's childhood and adolescence had been spent bottle-feeding the infants, the eventual fate she knew the animals faced doing nothing to dent the joy of seeing them thrive. Her mother never had succeeded in reclaiming her kitchen.

By April, Ingrid's kitchen was generally one of the few rooms in the house *not* occupied by a queen with a litter of kittens, although only because its layout made it totally unsuitable for the purpose. She always intended to scale back the number of feline families she took into the house *next* spring, but London's population of ferals and strays only ever seemed to grow, and she could never bring herself to turn an animal away while there was still a room to spare. This year, despite her declining health, had been no different.

This was how the new downstairs shower room had come to be repurposed as a nursery for a rabble of six-week-old kittens – and why Ingrid was now watching her son carefully deconstructing the neat boxing only recently installed around the pipework. She ought to have checked more carefully for gaps in the panelling, but getting down to floor level was difficult these days, and it simply hadn't occurred to her that there might be an opening between the pipes and the unit that housed the sink above them. Neither fresh roast chicken nor tinned tuna steak had tempted the missing kitten out, and Ingrid suspected he was stuck. Either that, or he couldn't work out how to retrace his steps.

'Has Toby said anything to you about Abbie?' She asked, as Charlie sat back on his heels to delve into the toolbox.

'You mean are they shagging?'

'There's no need to be vulgar.'

He looked around from the task in hand. 'Would genteel language make the idea more palatable?'

'It's not that I find the idea unpalatable. You know how fond I am of Toby. But I don't think Abbie really knows whether she's coming or going at the moment, and I'm not sure she's being very fair.'

'Nothing new there, then,' Charlie responded, reaching for a hammer.

'Charlie,' Ingrid admonished.

'The fact you don't want to hear it doesn't stop it being true,' he returned, carefully fitting a screwdriver into the slender space between two tiles. 'She knows he'd walk over hot coals for her, and she's always taken advantage of that.'

Always was something of an exaggeration, but, on balance, Ingrid had to admit to herself, Charlie wasn't wrong. She didn't acknowledge the fact, however, and after a moment's silence he continued, 'Did she even come home last night?'

'Yes. Not long after you, actually.'

'Well, I suppose it doesn't *take* long,' he responded, tapping the end of the screwdriver before Ingrid could object to the remark, moving it along by an inch and repeating the exercise.

'Was Izzy not there last night?' Ingrid enquired, as Charlie paused at the point where the boxing met the end wall.

'No,' he returned, shortly, wiggling the panel he'd just loosened in an attempt to free it.

'Why not?'

'Oh, I dunno, maybe she didn't fancy a threesome?' Charlie came back, flippantly.

Ingrid sighed. Her son clearly wasn't in the mood to engage in a sensible conversation on the subject, and she wondered whether his peevishness was the result of Abigail's treatment of his friend, or whether it was borne of resentment over Ingrid's decision to bequeath control of the animal shelter to Abigail. She had wrestled with the matter for weeks: not because she had any doubts about her daughter's competence, but because of the difficulty of breaking the news to Charlie. The fact he was wholly unsuited to the role did nothing to change the nagging feeling she was playing favourites – or, at least, that her son might see it that way. He had said little when she had finally found the courage to broach the subject, and subsequent attempts to discuss it further had been no more illuminating. Ingrid fervently wished she had something else to offer him, but all that she owned was tied up in the charity, and she couldn't – or wouldn't – sacrifice that to spare Charlie's feelings. So perhaps, she reflected, she *was* guilty of favouritism. But it was the rescue centre, not her daughter, that had come first.

*****

The light was all but gone when Rebecca stepped out into the garden behind an unkempt but not yet rundown semidetached house in Romford, and she reached into her handbag for a torch. It was raining heavily, and a couple of scenes of crime officers were hastily erecting a tarpaulin tent in an attempt to preserve what evidence hadn't already been washed away. Leighton was standing to one side talking into his mobile, and held up a hand to acknowledge Rebecca's arrival. Rebecca flicked the torch on to try to get a better look at the dead man, who had apparently met a similar end to Fred Ratley. The pathetic glow that emanated from her torch was scarcely sufficient to illuminate the raindrops directly in front of her, and quickly faded to nothing. She gave it a sharp tap, without much hope of achieving anything, before giving up and returning it to her bag.

'I don't suppose you've a spare torch, have you?' She asked, as Leighton hung up.

'There should be a Maglite somewhere in the car,' he replied, reaching into his pocket for his key fob and handing it to her as he dialled another number.

Rebecca thanked him before backtracking, hopscotch-style, across the aluminium plates scattered between the building's front and back doors. Leighton's Aston Martin was parked several houses up the road, and Rebecca tried the boot first, then the side-door pockets, finally moving on to the glove compartment. This was jammed with a random assortment of belongings that Rebecca was forced to empty out before she could sort through them: nitrile gloves, evidence bags, a set of tiny screwdrivers, chewing gum, pens and pencils, a Ventolin inhaler, the slimline torch she was after and several packets of tablets. As she returned the bulk of the belongings to their cramped quarters, the word *Dexedrine* caught her eye. With a frown, she turned the box over, wondering how her friend had come by the drug. Then, bundling the packet back into the glove compartment with everything else, she locked the car and headed back towards the house.

On her return to the garden, Leighton was still on the phone, and from his expression it was clear he was none too pleased about whatever the person at the other end of the line was saying. As Rebecca approached, he said, irritably, 'Ok, never mind, I'll figure it out myself.' Then, after a brief pause, 'No, forget it, I'll deal with it.' Hanging up without saying goodbye, he glanced up.

'Problem?' Rebecca asked, as she returned his car keys.

'It's astounding how incompetent people can be while still remaining in employment,' he observed.

'At least by those standards we've a good chance of always being in a job,' Rebecca came back, lightly.

This drew a reluctant smile. 'I suppose that's true.'

'Is there anything I can do?'

He shook his head. 'No, you're all right, thanks.'

'What are you doing here?'

Rebecca turned in response to the sharp tone to find DS Miranda Byrd standing behind her, her pale, wispy eyebrows drawn into a scowl.

'Oh – I looked into Fred Ratley's death, so DCI Rose asked if I could come along,' she explained, choosing a rather more neutral verb than she might have done had she known Miranda better. Pete hadn't asked her to attend, he'd demanded she drop whatever personal plans she might have and get over to Stratford at light speed.

'Right,' Miranda acknowledged, with a nod. 'Well if you can tear yourself away from standing around looking pretty, perhaps you'd like to have a chat with a few of the neighbours?'

Rebecca tried not to show any reaction to her colleague's overt animosity, well aware that with Pete heading up the investigation Miranda was likely to be central to proceedings, and wondering what the other woman's problem with her was. Assuming it was with her, and not the world in general.

'Sure,' she replied, pleasantly. 'Where would you like me to start?'

Miranda gestured wordlessly to a building that shared a fence but not a wall with the property on which they stood before saying, 'Guy in there's bound to know something. He just got in with his own dog.'

The implication, Rebecca had assumed, was that the animal was a potential suspect – if you could call a dog a *suspect* – but it was immediately apparent when the neighbouring front door opened that the Jack Russell regarding her suspiciously from between his master's feet wasn't a contender.

'That brute of a dog finally get the better of him, then, did it?' The thick-set man standing over the small terrier asked, craning his neck to get a better view of the next-door front garden, where two scenes of crime officers in forensic suits were discussing something behind the uniformed police officer stationed at the perimeter to control human traffic beyond the blue and white tape.

Rebecca ignored the question, asking whether he was a resident.

'Yeah, it's my house,' he answered, rather distractedly, his eyes still on the scene playing out over Rebecca's shoulder.

'And could I take your name, please?'

'Brendan Smythe.'

'Did you know Mr Murphy well?'

'I didn't know him at all,' Brendan replied, finally giving Rebecca his undivided attention.

'You live next door to him, Mr Smythe,' Rebecca observed, coolly.

'That don't mean I *know* him.'

Rebecca sighed inwardly. 'You mentioned his dog a moment ago,' she said, the word *dog* prompting frenzied barking from the Jack Russell. 'Was he a nuisance?'

'You can say that again,' Brendan returned, over his own pet's yapping, before adding, without a hint of irony, 'Bloody animal never shut the hell up.'

'Did you ever raise that with Mr Murphy?'

'We had words a few times. Didn't do much good, though, bloke was a dickhead.' He dropped his gaze to the vociferous animal at his feet. 'Shut it!'

'And did you hear anything out of the ordinary last night, or early this morning?'

'Nah,' Brendan shook his head. 'I can sleep through anything, me, and the wife takes sleeping pills.'

Rebecca didn't believe a word: over the years she had heard both excuses an implausible number of times. 'You're telling me your dog didn't react to anything?' She responded, incredulously.

'Uh-uh,' he replied, as the animal repeated its initial response to the word *dog*. 'Shut it, Hazel!'

'Has Mr Murphy had any visitors lately?' Rebecca continued, once the dog was silent.

'Not that I saw. And with the state of that house, I'd have been ashamed to invite anyone if I was him.'

'So you've been inside, then?'

'Not really,' Brendan hedged, apparently realising he'd revealed more than he had intended. 'I mean, I've caught glimpses of the place from the doorstep on occasion, but that's all.'

'I see,' Rebecca responded, disbelievingly. 'Have you any idea whether Mr Murphy had any enemies?'

'I'd be surprised if he didn't, but I couldn't name any names.'

'Why would you be surprised?'

'Well, like I says, bloke was a dickhead.'

'Could you expand on what you mean by *dickhead*?'

'What do you think I mean?' Brendan demanded, incredulously. 'You're English, aren't you? He was a jerk. Rude. Unreasonable. Obnoxious. You follow me?'

'The kind of person you don't want living next door, then,' Rebecca surmised.

This remark apparently gave Brendan pause. 'I won't pretend I liked the bloke,' he replied, at length. 'But I had no part of whatever's gone on in there.' He thrust his hands into his pockets. 'And if you're implying otherwise, I won't be saying nothing more without consulting a lawyer.'

Tuesday 13 April

'Glad you could join us,' Pete snapped, sarcastically, as Leighton ambled into his office shortly after nine. 'Perhaps by lunch time you might even manage to switch your mobile on?'

Leighton didn't rise to the remark, setting a coffee cup down on the edge of Pete's desk and pulling up a chair without a word. He looked tired and dishevelled, and, although he appeared to be wearing clean clothes, Rebecca guessed he'd been up much of the night.

'When you're ready,' Pete chivvied, impatiently.

Leighton rubbed his eyes with the thumb and middle finger of his left hand, and made a start on describing the worst of the injuries sustained by Spencer Murphy. Pete cut him off after a matter of seconds.

'Never mind which bite killed him, was it his own dog's doing or not?'

'Not,' Leighton returned, shortly. 'Although I won't be able to definitively confirm that until Ana's compared the dental X-rays from the RSPCA vet with the bite marks on –'

'What's stopping you doing that?' Pete demanded. 'Do you have something more important to do? Muffins to eat, perhaps?'

'An argument could be made that there would be a conflict of interest.'

'Oh come off it, I'm not bloody stupid, you're hardly going to make something up that could so easily come back and bite you on the arse!'

'Ana's promised to get to it before the end of the day,' Leighton replied, without acknowledging Pete's response. 'But as the animal at the scene looks to have been drugged in the hours before our arrival, I don't think there's a lot of room for doubt.'

'Drugged?' Pete echoed. 'How?'

'Some sort of injection – there was a puncture mark on the dog's flank.'

'Was that not the RSPCA's doing?'

Leighton shook his head. 'RSPCA inspector knew nothing about it.'

Pete considered this for a moment before saying, 'That's one hell of a length to go to.'

'Uh-huh,' Leighton agreed.

'What about the victim?' Pete asked, when the pathologist didn't say anything further. 'Was he drugged as well? What stopped him making a run for it?'

Leighton lifted an eyebrow. 'You ever tried running from an angry dog? Give it a shot and see how far you get.'

'You know what I mean,' Pete snapped. 'Why didn't he fight back, yell for help, whatever?'

'I don't know,' Leighton admitted. 'I can't rule out drugs until I get the tox report, but there are no visible marks on the body I could attribute to any form of immobilization, and there are what look like defensive wounds, which suggests he wasn't incapable. There's extensive tissue damage, though, so that could be masking other injuries.'

'It's a weird way of killing people,' Rebecca ventured, when Pete didn't immediately respond. 'There are easier ways to make a homicide look like an accident.'

Leighton shrugged. 'Maybe that wasn't the intent.'

'So what do you suppose was?'

'Maybe it's some sort of message. Murphy's dog had heavy scarring on its face and front legs, which the RSPCA vet said is a classic indicator of dog fighting. The RSPCA officer who attended at Ratley's place seemed to think he had been involved in that, too. Perhaps there's some sort of turf war going on.'

'Could be,' Pete allowed, with a perfunctory nod.

'And there were two dogs in the picture O'Leary and –'

'Half the population probably owns photographs with dogs in!' Pete cut in. 'You are not dragging that investigation back into this!'

'But according to Aileen Quinn's statement –'

'Oh, I'm sorry, have I missed something? Are you a police officer?' Pete demanded, before pausing for effect. Resting one forearm on the desktop, he leaned forwards. 'If that's what you want to do, I can get you an application form! Although you'd need to do some bloody exercise! Otherwise, I suggest you put down the witness statements and get back to the mortuary where you belong!'

'I just think it might be worth –'

'No! No arguments! You are here in an advisory capacity only! You have no say in the running of this investigation or any other!

Stop trying to do my job and concentrate on your own! You might even find you get something done on time for a change!'

Leighton opened his mouth to reply, but before he could say anything Pete jumped in with, 'That is an *order*!'

Leighton regarded him in silence for a moment before reaching to reclaim his coffee and getting to his feet. 'I'll have the provisional postmortem report to you by the end of the day. Anything else comes up, I'll let you know.' He turned to go, then paused in the doorway. 'And get over yourself,' he added, coolly, as he moved to pull the door shut behind himself. 'You don't give me orders.'

Rebecca had been glad to get out of the office and put some distance between herself and Pete and Miranda; the latter's frosty demeanour didn't seem to have thawed at all, and after Leighton's parting shot that morning Pete had looked on the brink of exploding. Unfortunately, Spencer Murphy's neighbours were no more forthcoming than Fred Ratley's had been, and after several wasted hours Rebecca's limited enthusiasm for door-to-door enquiries was at an all-time low. On top of that, she was ravenous. Lunchtime had long since been and gone, and, with this in mind, she decided to redirect their focus to the local pub. At least if that exercise proved fruitless they could console themselves with a sandwich and a drink.

Turning to see the young Detective Constable who had been assigned to her that morning standing on tiptoe to peer over someone's back fence, Rebecca called him over.

'I was trying to get a look at the dog,' he explained, as he approached, clearly anticipating his actions being questioned. 'There's a beware sticker on the door.'

'Any sign of one?'

'No. Might just be for effect. Harder to call out than a fake alarm box or camera.'

'True,' Rebecca agreed. 'But we'll follow it up when someone's home. In the meantime, I think we ought to interrogate the menu at the Griffin.' She nodded towards the pub at the end of the street.

He grinned. 'Yes Ma'am.'

The menu turned out to be refreshingly down-to-earth, and Rebecca ordered a fish finger sandwich and a Diet Coke before looking around at her colleague, who was inspecting the selection of framed photographs on the wall at the end of the bar.

'Sandeep?'

'Oh – um –' he glanced back at the menu in front of him, then up at the teenage bar girl. 'Cheese and chutney, please. And an OJ.' Turning to Rebecca, he said, 'You can call me Sandy, if you like. Everyone does.' There was a momentary pause before he added, 'Everyone human, anyway.'

Rebecca smiled, guessing that was a compliment. Handing a twenty pound note to the girl the other side of the counter, she asked whether the landlord was around and, on learning that he was, voiced her desire to speak to him. The girl nodded as she gave Rebecca her change, then turned to go. Rebecca tossed her purse into her handbag and checked her mobile for messages – there were none – before perching on one of the bar stools.

'Dogs or cats?' Sandeep asked, as he sat on the adjacent stool.

'Sorry?'

'Most people prefer one or the other,' he shrugged.

'Oh, right,' Rebecca nodded. 'Dogs, I suppose,' she concluded, aloud, having never given the matter much thought. Her parents weren't really pet people, so her exposure to anything bigger than a hamster had largely been limited to visits to her paternal grandparents, who had kept border collies for the first twenty-odd years of Rebecca's life. 'Assuming they're not intent on ripping into my jugular, that is.'

Sandeep winced. 'Is that how he died?'

'I don't know the details. But it's a pretty horrific way to go however it happened.'

'Yeah, at least cats can't kill you,' he observed. 'Mind you, I had one give it a good go a couple of weeks back,' he held out a hand to display a cluster of pink marks on his forefinger.

'Ouch. What were you doing?'

'I was at a crime scene. Bloody animal made me look like a right tit – one minute it's hanging off my finger, next thing I know Dr Campbell's practically cuddling it.' He dropped his hand into his lap. 'Apparently he has the same magic touch with cats as with the ladies.'

Rebecca resisted the urge to raise her eyebrows, not entirely sure it was an innocent remark, but Sandeep didn't look as if he was expecting a reaction, so she opted to come back with a joke.

'Maybe it was a female cat.'

'Yeah, maybe,' he smiled ruefully. 'Might explain why I didn't have better luck with it and all.'

'Aye?' A shrivelled fifty-something man with salt-and-pepper stubble and something approaching a scowl interrupted from across the bar.

'Afternoon,' Rebecca greeted him. 'Are you the landlord?'

'No, I'm Santa Claus,' the man replied, sarcastically, resting his hands on the bar and leaning forwards slightly. 'You'll be Old Bill, I s'pose?'

Rebecca flashed her warrant card by way of confirmation and introduced herself and Sandeep.

'This about Murph, then, is it?'

'News travels fast,' Rebecca remarked.

'Din't it,' came the short response.

'Could I take your name?'

'Roy Aitken.'

'Did you know Mr Murphy well?'

'Depends what you mean by well,' the man returned, sounding as if he was still considering the matter himself. 'I know he liked Stella and Jameson's, he followed the horses and his dog's name was Kip. I cannae tell you what he liked for breakfast, where he grew up or 'owt he got up to when he weren't in here.'

'How often did you see him in here, would you say?'

'More often than not.'

'So he was a very regular customer.'

'Aye.'

'Do you know whether he fell out with anyone recently?'

Roy paused for thought. 'He almost came to blows with some young lad a week or so back, although I dunno why, or who the guy was.'

'In here?'

He nodded.

'Can you remember anything else about the incident or the man involved?'

Several seconds passed while Roy considered this. At length, he said, 'Not a lot. The other guy did a lot of yelling, but as I said, I dunno what about. And Kip got hi'self all worked up, which was never a good thing.'

'Kip being the dog?' Rebecca checked.

'Aye.'

'Do you have any CCTV footage that might help us identify him?'

Roy shook his head. 'Only keep it forty-eight hours.'

Rebecca doubted that very much, but there was little point in challenging the man; even if footage of the incident did exist, if Roy Aitken didn't want them to see it, it would be wiped long before they could get hold of a search warrant. She changed direction.

'You said a moment ago that Mr Murphy followed the horses. Was he a betting man?'

'Oh aye.'

'Did he run up any debts as a result?'

The landlord shrugged. 'I wouldnae know.'

'So you weren't ever aware of his being short of money?'

'No.'

'And can you think of anyone who might have wanted him out the way?'

'This ain't a church, he didnae come here to confess his sins,' Roy returned. 'We passed the time o' day, but I've no clue what he got up to the rest o' the time, or who with. I can't hang around chatting all day, this place don't run itself.'

'Well we won't hold you up any longer,' Rebecca returned, pointedly, as she put her card down on the bar. 'But if anything comes to mind that might be relevant, please do let us know.'

Roy grunted his response and slipped the card into his back pocket. Rebecca doubted there was any chance of his using it for its proper purpose, more likely than not it would wind up in the bin within the hour. Rebecca herself had no intention of being anything like as easy to get rid of.

Leaving the pub, Rebecca noticed they were being watched, and, having sent Sandeep to fetch the car, sauntered across the road in the direction of the eyes peering through an immaculately clipped hedge. They dropped to the ground the moment their owner realised he'd been spotted. By the time Rebecca reached the point at which the hedge bordered the pavement, the garden's occupant was energetically working a trowel through the soil of the narrow flowerbed just beyond it, studiously ignoring Rebecca's presence just a couple of feet away. To his right, the floral candelabra of a pink magnolia swept down over the lawn, whilst behind him a flowerbed thick with a mix of mulberry and white snapdragons ran across the front of an otherwise unremarkable house.

'Lovely garden,' Rebecca remarked to the bent head of white hair directly in front of her.

Two wary brown eyes met with hers as their sixty-something owner reluctantly raised his gaze from the ground in front of him. 'Ta,' he returned, shortly.

'It must take a lot of work.'

'Yes and no.'

'I imagine you see a lot of the comings and goings at the Griffin when you're working out here.'

'On occasion.'

'Do you drink there yourself?'

'Now and again.'

Rebecca presented him with a photograph of Spencer Murphy. 'Does this man look familiar?'

'Who's asking?'

Rebecca introduced herself and displayed her warrant card, asking the man his name.

He sat back on his heels. 'Gerald Moynihan.'

'And do you recognise this man?'

He nodded, adding a moment later, 'That's not to say I know him, mind.'

'You'd have seen him often enough though, I'd have thought. I understand he was a regular at the Griffin.'

'Was?' Gerald's brows rose marginally.

'Yes,' Rebecca confirmed. 'I'm afraid he's dead.'

The man acknowledged this news with a change in facial expression, but, to her surprise, didn't ask what had happened.

'I gather he had quite a row with another man in the pub in the past week or two. Were you privy to that?'

'I wouldn't know.'

Intrigued by the fact he hadn't said *no*, Rebecca tried a different approach. 'Have you witnessed any memorable disputes lately?'

This was initially met by silence, which Rebecca suspected marked Gerald's weighing up whether to divulge what he knew rather than any search of his memory. Apparently deciding to answer, he said, 'There is one incident comes to mind. A week or so back there was a bit of a scuffle when Roy threw a bloke out. He was yelling the odds over Roy's shoulder, then gave him an earful for his trouble.'

'Do you have any idea what it was about?'

Gerald shook his head. 'A lot of it was drowned out by some dog going berserk.'

'In the pub?' She asked, mindful of what Roy had said about Kip getting worked up.

'Yes.'

'Could you describe the man?'

'Only vaguely.'

'I'd be grateful for anything you can give me.'

Gerald thought his answer over before saying, 'Youngish, quite athletic, dark hair.' He shrugged. 'I didn't see him close to.'

'Can you remember what he was wearing?'

'Yes,' Gerald realised, aloud. 'His t-shirt was from the Paws and Whiskers animal shelter. I've seen a girl from there rounding up strays at the derelict church a few roads down.'

'Are you saying he might be a member of staff?'

Gerald shrugged again.

'Do you know any of the staff employed at the pub? You're obviously acquainted with the landlord.'

'I know his name, but nothing more,' Gerald responded, shortly. 'And I don't care for small talk. The extent of my conversation with anyone behind that bar is the matter of what I'm drinking and how much it's going to cost.' He waved an insect out of his field of view before adding, 'And that's invariably too much.'

'Hey,' Rebecca greeted, finding Leighton sitting at his desk, scrolling through what looked like chemical traces on his laptop.

'Christ, can I not have five minutes without you lot on my back?' He asked, irritably, as he looked up. 'I can't do everything at once, I'm not a magician!'

'Sorry,' Rebecca held up her hands in surrender. 'I wasn't –'

'I'll get to it after lunch, all right?'

Rebecca frowned. 'It's quarter to five.'

Leighton checked his watch. 'Bollocks,' he muttered. 'Ok, give me twenty minutes.'

'It's not like you to miss lunch.'

'Well it won't do me any harm, as my father is all too fond of telling me,' he responded, shortly, returning his eyes to his laptop screen.

Rebecca hesitated before saying, 'Are you all right?'

'I'm fine.'

Rebecca nodded to herself, and was about to say something else when he glanced up again. 'I'll get back to you as soon as, ok?'

'Ok,' Rebecca echoed.

When she didn't move, Leighton raised his eyebrows impatiently. 'What?'

After a moment's frantic internal debate, she said, 'About your car –'

'What about it?'

'You have amphetamines in your glove compartment.'

Leighton looked taken aback. 'I know what's in my glove compartment, but thanks for the inventory.'

'Dexedrine's a controlled drug.'

'Is it?' He responded, in mock surprise. 'Shit. They must've forgotten to mention that at med school.'

Rebecca felt uncomfortable. She had hoped Leighton would explain the prescription away. Clearly she wasn't going to get a straight answer without a direct question. She hesitated before saying, 'Are you using it?'

'For fuck's sake,' Leighton muttered to himself before meeting her eyes. 'Why is everyone always so quick to think the worst of me?' He demanded, angrily. 'I have never turned up to work in an unfit state to do my job and I have never taken a day off because I was out the night before, yet I repeatedly get treated like some fucking party stereotype!'

'That doesn't answer the question,' Rebecca replied, realizing as she did so that she was effectively interrogating him.

'I don't remember my giving you the Spanish inquisition over what drugs were in your flat when you lived with Elliot.'

'That's hardly the same thing.'

'No, that's true, I don't suppose he got coke on prescription!' Leighton returned, furiously. 'Now, if you don't want to rifle through my desk drawers and my pockets, perhaps I could get on with my work? I would like the chance to get some sleep tonight, it would make a nice change!'

Rebecca wondered how much of the apparent work overload was the result of his devoting time, unsanctioned, to the O'Leary investigation – and, by extension, whether he had been using amphetamines to fit more hours into the day. But she could guess what sort of reaction raising the subject of O'Leary was likely to provoke, so she simply nodded and made for the door. It seemed the more people discouraged him from picking the investigation apart, the more determined he was to prove there was good reason for doing so. Rebecca could only hope he would either succeed or accept defeat before he was facing more than disciplinary action.

Wednesday 14 April

Before eight-thirty and after five, the Gresham Building's reception was manned by the security staff employed to patrol the building out of hours, and Lawrence arrived shortly after seven to find a familiar figure lounging behind the front desk. Darius was sniggering at something on his smartphone, and hurriedly pocketed the device and snapped into the seated equivalent of standing to attention as Lawrence approached.

'Morning Sir.'

'Morning,' Lawrence returned. 'I think you ought to have something for me?'

Darius looked momentarily blank before casting his eyes across the desk. 'What was it?'

'I'm not sure,' Lawrence admitted. 'I got a message from Dr Campbell –' he reached into his pocket for his phone to remind himself exactly what his colleague had said.

'Oh, well he maybe wanted to give it you himself,' Darius replied. 'I think he's in meeting room two.'

'Meeting room two?' Lawrence echoed, surprised.

'Yep. Last I saw him, anyroad. You wanna sign in and go track him down?'

The meeting rooms were situated further down the corridor than the lab or the offices, and Lawrence glanced through the glass panels in the doors as he passed in case Leighton had relocated. Having drawn a blank, he continued on to the doorway of the small second meeting room, which was furnished with a coffee table, a couple of rather leggy plants and a handful of padded chairs. The table was swamped with paperwork, coffee cups and Chinese takeaway cartons, while the chairs had been arranged in a row down one side of the room to turn them into a makeshift bench, on which Leighton was asleep, his right arm tucked under his head.

Lawrence hesitated before tapping on the door. Leighton's eyes flickered open, then, after a momentary pause, he clearly registered where he was and pushed himself up onto his elbow, muttering, 'Morning.'

'Do you not have a home to go to?'

'It didn't really seem worth it,' his colleague replied, as he sat up. Lawrence glanced at the papers and images spread across the table, his eyes alighting on a familiar photograph. He wondered whether the text message that had brought him down here had been deliberately vague to prevent him from passing comment before now.

'What's this?' He asked, despite knowing the answer.

'The world's most frustrating jigsaw puzzle,' Leighton replied, ruefully, as he rubbed his eyes.

'I told you to leave the O'Leary investigation alone.'

'No, you told me if I wanted to pull it apart I could do it on my own time,' Leighton corrected, drawing his hair back from his face and tucking it behind his ear with his right hand while lifting his left wrist to check his watch. 'Which, as it's only ten past seven, it still is.'

'I also said you weren't to use Home Office resources,' Lawrence reminded him. 'And you know full well Jamie's time fits squarely into that category. When I tell you not to pursue something you do not go behind my back and involve members of my team!'

'I only asked if he remembered –'

'I don't care! I will not have you wasting his time as well as your own! Understood?'

'Yes, ok,' Leighton conceded. 'But I wasn't trying to slip it under your radar, I asked Jay about it because he worked on the original investigation.'

'Whatever the case, from now on you will leave my team out of it. Now what was it you wanted to show me?'

Leighton frowned. 'What?'

'You sent me a text message at –' Lawrence pulled out his mobile and checked the details, 'Three-seventeen this morning.'

Leighton held out a hand for the phone, looking perplexed. Lawrence passed it to him, and he scanned it quickly before shaking his head. 'I don't know anything about this,' he said, as he returned the device. 'I think I was comatose by then, anyway.'

'Well it came from your phone.'

Leighton reached for the mobile half buried under papers on the coffee table, and after a few moments of tapping and swiping shook his head again. 'Not according to this.'

Lawrence frowned, double-checking what was on his screen. 'It's from your number.'

'It's probably just a mobile or network glitch, resending you an old message. I wouldn't worry about it.'

'You might not, but you're not the one who came in early for nothing,' Lawrence snapped.

'Well I apologise on behalf of my service provider for the interruption to your schedule,' Leighton returned, rather curtly. 'Seeing as how you woke me up, perhaps we can call it quits?'

Lawrence regarded his colleague in silence for a moment, feeling disinclined to disregard the matter. Then, with a sigh, he shook his head. 'All right, never mind. As I'm here, perhaps I can get an update on the tests you were running on Adriana's flat. What happened to those?'

'Good question. The samples seem to have gone missing.'

'Missing?' Lawrence exclaimed. 'What do you mean, missing?'

'Missing,' Leighton repeated, before adding, with a languid wave of his hand, 'Vanished. Disappeared. Vamoosed.'

'You mean you've lost them,' Lawrence surmised.

'I mean they've disappeared. I sorted out a bunch of samples and sent them to the lab, but they have no record of them.'

'How is that possible?' Lawrence demanded.

'I don't know. Maybe they got put somewhere daft while in transit. Or maybe someone's trying to sabotage everything I touch.'

'Oh, so now it's somebody else's fault you can't keep track of what you're doing?'

'I have flagged it with everyone in the pathology unit and the lab. Short of getting you lot in to search the place I'm not sure what more I can do.'

'I want to know the moment they turn up.'

'Yeah, all right,' Leighton responded, wearily, rubbing his eyes.

'And if they don't, is there anything else we can do?'

Leighton appeared to consider his answer for a moment before saying, 'What, aside from exhuming the body, you mean?'

'Yes, aside from that,' Lawrence confirmed, wondering whether the samples really had gone missing or whether Leighton was simply trying to force his hand. 'Because that is not happening under any circumstances.'

Leighton nodded contemplatively. 'Then I think we'd be all out of options.'

*****

Having established that the Paws and Whiskers animal shelter didn't sell t-shirts, Rebecca had looked into the charity's affairs and quickly discovered that it had just three members of staff, all of whom lived on site. A DVLA search furnished her with a photograph of the only man among them, whom Gerald Moynihan tentatively identified as the individual ejected from the Griffin the week before. On arrival, Rebecca was surprised to find the rescue centre located in a residential street, a black and white sign in the front courtyard the only clue that the large detached house was anything more than a normal suburban home.

As Rebecca neared the front gate, she spotted a petite woman in blue jeans and a baggy grey jumper approaching from the opposite direction, lugging a long, low metal cage containing a large black cat. She glanced up in response to Rebecca's opening greeting, then set the cage down on the pavement.

'Can I help?'

Rebecca introduced herself and afforded the woman a glimpse of her warrant card before asking for her name.

'Abbie Watts,' she replied, raising a hand to draw the multitude of mousy hairs that had strayed from her wonky French plait out of her eyes. The wind immediately whipped them back again.

'Do you work here?'

Abbie's reply to the affirmative was almost drowned out by a howl of protest from the cat at her feet, and as a black paw shot out between the metal bars Rebecca instinctively took a step back.

'Someone's not too happy,' she remarked, lightly.

'He'll calm down when I get him out the trap.'

'Where did he come from?'

'An industrial estate over Upminster way. We run a TNR program covering several local sites.'

'TNR?'

'Trap, neuter, return,' Abbie replied. 'To control the feral population. A lot of businesses are happy to provide shelter and basic care for feral cats in exchange for pest control, but if you don't stop them breeding you end up overrun with cats instead of rats.'

'That sounds like a Herculean task.'

'Yeah, you could say that.'

'So he'll be going back to Upminster when he's been done?'

'Yes.'

'And where do the dogs come into the equation?' Rebecca asked, nodding towards the picture on the sign.

'We take in unwanted pets – cats more than dogs – and where possible we re-home them.'

'Do you see much in the way of dangerous dogs?'

'Quite a bit. Unfortunately certain breeds are often viewed more as weapons than as companions, and people who keep dogs as status animals tend not to care that much for them. All too often they view animals as disposable. Plus if a dog is mistreated or improperly trained, its behaviour can get out of control, which only increases its chances of being dumped.'

'Can you do much to rehabilitate dogs like that?'

'It really depends. We do have to euthanise some because we can't safely re-home them.' Abbie shifted her weight from one leg to the other, prompting the tomcat on the ground to hiss loudly, which, in turn, made Rebecca jump. It also brought to mind another question.

'Obviously you use traps, do you have access to any other means of catching or disabling animals?'

A puzzled frown tugged at Abbie's fine, mousy eyebrows. 'Like what?'

'Drugs, maybe? Sedatives, tranquillizers, that kind of thing?'

'Oh, I see. No. I think you'd need a vet on hand for that.'

'So you don't stock anything of that nature?'

'I don't think so. I can check, if you want?'

'Do you not know what drugs you have on site?'

'I don't, but Mum will. Do you want to come through?' She indicated the house behind her with a flick of her wrist.

'I'm actually looking for Charlie.'

'Oh,' Abbie blinked. 'How come?'

'I'd just like to ask him a few questions.'

'I don't know that he's about, but I'll check with Mum. Come in.' She bent to retrieve the trap. Its irate occupant yowled, then spat, and Rebecca kept her distance as she followed Abbie towards the building.

As outside, there was initially little about the building's interior to indicate Rebecca was in anything other than a normal family home. The entrance hall was scarcely more than a cloakroom, featuring a row of overburdened coat hooks, a narrow wooden bench that doubled as a shoe rack, and a waste-paper bin serving as an umbrella stand. The long galley kitchen leading off it was cluttered with an unremarkable selection of small appliances, storage jars and foodstuffs, a stack of stainless steel bowls on the tiled windowsill the only thing that stood out. Beyond it, a handful of wicker chairs lounged around a glass-topped coffee table in a conservatory, the room's perimeter dotted by large terracotta pots. Several of these were overflowing with the long, tapered leaves of Miltoniopsis orchids, while a plant with more compact foliage was sharing its vessel with a fluffy grey cat.

The homely feel extended only as far as the back door. All that was visible beyond the conservatory were rows of wooden huts and chicken-wire enclosures, and, in the immediate foreground, a hutch containing an apricot-coloured rabbit that stared out impassively as it chewed a mouthful of hay. Rebecca had little opportunity to absorb the scene before Abbie planted the trap and its sooty prisoner on the floor by the door and continued on her way into a large room that ran almost the full width of the building. Rebecca surmised from its two desks and multiple shelving units that the room's intended function was as an office, although it clearly doubled as a storage area, with much of the floor space taken up by pallet upon pallet of cat-food boxes. Meanwhile, a large cage in one corner was serving as a feline nursery, with a cat that looked little bigger than a kitten herself nestling in a blanket with three tiny fluffy bundles.

Only one of the desks appeared to be in use – unless you considered a ginger cat asleep in a filing tray a *user* – and a plump woman whom Rebecca put at fifty-something raised her eyes from a desktop computer as Rebecca followed Abbie into the room. From the likeness, Rebecca had already guessed who she was before Abbie said, 'Mum, this is –' she hesitated, looking to Rebecca for assistance. Rebecca introduced herself, and Abbie continued, 'She wants to talk to Chas, but she also has a question about the dispensary.'

The woman's eyebrows rose. She pushed herself back from the desk, at which point Rebecca realised she was in a wheelchair. 'Ingrid Watts,' she offered, by way of introduction, as she manoeuvred herself out into the room. 'What is it you want to know?'

'Primarily what you keep on site in the way of tranquillizers or sedatives.'

'Not a lot. Certainly not enough to have ever been of interest to the police. What's this about?'

'I can't go into detail, but it would help if you could answer my questions. I'm not looking to make trouble for you.'

Ingrid looked unconvinced, but nevertheless obliged, saying, 'We do use drugs like Xanax when we're taking nervous or traumatised animals for veterinary treatment, but it's not something we'd ever have a big stock of. Vets hand out those kinds of drugs quite sparingly, for obvious reasons.'

'So you don't use tranquillizer darts, or anything like that?'

'Goodness, no,' Ingrid shook her head for emphasis. 'That's beyond our capability. I'm not sure it would even be legal.'

'That being the case, how do you handle dangerous dogs?'

'That's hardly a day-to-day occurrence for us. Out in the community, incidents involving dangerous dogs are the preserve of police dog handlers and RSPCA officers, and those dogs don't wind up in rescue. Where dogs we take in do turn out to be dangerous, they generally aren't with us very long.'

'You mean you have them destroyed?' Rebecca asked, noticing the cat on the desk pushing itself up into a sitting position and registering as it did so that it had only one front leg.

'Sadly, yes.'

'That must be difficult,' Rebecca remarked.

'Rescue work often is.'

'But it hasn't stopped your son and daughter following in your footsteps.'

Ingrid half smiled. 'It's not all doom and gloom.'

Rebecca nodded. 'Is Charlie here at the moment?'

'Why?'

'Is he here?'

'He's out in the cattery,' Ingrid conceded. 'I can't get down there in the chair, I'm afraid. But if you wait two minutes, Abbie can show you through.'

'Are you responsible for this?' Lawrence demanded, throwing a copy of the Birmingham Echo down on the laboratory bench beside the rack of test tubes Leighton was ministering to. The front-page headline read *Wrong man charged, says forensic expert.*

Looking nonplussed, Leighton reached for the paper and briefly gave the article his attention.

'It depends what you're referring to,' he replied, levelly, as he raised his eyes from the page.

'Don't play games with me! Yes or no?'

'I had nothing to do with the inception of the article,' Leighton responded, setting the paper back down. 'But I did say I didn't think Evan was guilty.'

'You did what? What the hell were you thinking? You know full well not to talk to the press!'

'Yes, I know, and I –'

'This is *not* the way to get Evan's case heard!' Lawrence exclaimed, snatching the paper up again and holding it aloft.

Leighton stepped backwards, raising his hands defensively. 'Ok, calm down, I only –'

'Don't you dare tell me to calm down!' Lawrence cut him off, furiously. His colleague flinched and took another step back. 'You've potentially compromised two investigations! And don't pretend you weren't well aware of the fact!'

'I didn't expect it to end up in the paper,' Leighton defended himself, meekly. 'I was talking to Evan and I said I could –'

'What reason did you have to talk to Evan?'

'I was concerned about him.'

'Heavens alive, Leighton! You cannot get involved with witnesses, suspects or anyone else connected to an investigation! Quite aside from –'

'Ok, cut,' a decisive voice interrupted from behind him. Lawrence turned to see Max standing in the doorway. 'What's the problem?' He asked, advancing into the lab and releasing the door.

Lawrence handed him the newspaper without a word. Several seconds passed while Max scanned the limited text on the front page. Looking up, he glanced in Leighton's direction.

'Can you give us a minute, please?'

Leighton didn't argue, heading for the door. Max waited until it had closed behind him before saying anything further.

'I understand why you're angry, but I'd appreciate it if you didn't shout at my staff.'

'And I'd appreciate it if your staff didn't speak to the press!' Lawrence fired back.

'I realise that, and I will have a word with him, but that's my job, not yours.'

Lawrence only just managed to hold back from observing that if Max had done his job properly in the first place, the problem might never have arisen. Tempting as it was to deliver a few home truths about his friend's relaxed style of management, falling out with Max wasn't going to help.

'While you're at it, perhaps you might also remind him he needs to maintain a degree of professional bloody detachment!' He returned, instead. 'He's a scientist, not an agony aunt!'

'First and foremost, he's actually a doctor,' Max pointed out. 'And you're never going to get him to stop caring about people.'

'Ignoring the offensive implication that I don't, whether or not he cares is irrelevant! His loyalty is to the Home Office, *not* to Evan!'

'I'm not saying you don't care,' Max countered, reasonably. 'And I'm not disagreeing with you. I'm just asking you to leave it with me. Ok?'

Lawrence sighed heavily, not at all convinced Max would take anywhere near as firm a line as he should. Not, he conceded, that there was much more he himself could do about the problem. 'Ok,' he agreed, at length. 'But you need to do more than slap him on the wrist.' He made for the door, planting a finger on the paper in Max's hands as he passed. 'This *cannot* happen again.'

Whilst Rebecca wasn't a fan of the fashion for close-cropped beards, she had to admit the look suited Charlie Watts. His dark hair was nowhere near as neat, although it was impossible to know whether its ruffled appearance was intentional or simply the result of his having spent most of the afternoon outdoors. He was apparently in the process of constructing a new cat enclosure a few feet from the rear fence of what had presumably once been an extensive garden. The walk down from the house had afforded Rebecca a closer look at some of the existing pens, all of which appeared to have an indoor and an outdoor component. Most were occupied by one or more cats, a few contained dogs – and one, much to Rebecca's surprise, was busy with a family of hedgehogs.

On arrival at the partially constructed wooden hut, Abbie made basic introductions and handed her brother a mug of tea before muttering something about a visiting vet and hurrying back towards the house. Charlie bent to set his screwdriver down on the ground before raising his wary brown eyes to meet Rebecca's.

'I'm sorry to disturb you,' she opened. 'This shouldn't take long.'

'Ok,' Charlie responded, uneasily.

'I'd like to talk to you about a man called Spencer Murphy. I believe you're acquainted?'

'I wouldn't go as far as *acquainted*.'

'But you do recognise the name?'

'Yes.'

'I understand from a couple of the customers at the Griffin that you threatened Mr Murphy in the bar last Tuesday.'

'Nothing he didn't deserve.'

'And what did you think he deserved?'

'A slow and painful death.'

'Did you see to it that he got that, as well?'

Charlie frowned. 'What?'

'Mr Murphy was found dead two days ago.'

There was a brief silence. Charlie swallowed. 'I didn't know that.'

'Really?'

He shook his head slightly. 'I didn't – I never –' he gave up with a shrug.

'Could you tell me why you think he deserved a slow and painful death?'

'Because he was scum,' Charlie returned, shortly, almost spitting the words out.

'How so?'

'He was a big name in dog fighting. He liked watching animals tear one another apart. That's some people's idea of entertainment round here. The law's done next to nothing about all the blood on their hands. Funny how you care about what happens to them, though.'

'I think you'll find dog fighting is very much on the Met's radar.'

'Then why does nothing ever change? Why do we still see maimed and dead animals every week?'

Rebecca wondered whether *every week* was an exaggeration. Not that she understood the mindset of those who viewed such wanton cruelty as sport; she didn't imagine it was something she could even bear to watch. But that wasn't why she was there.

'When did you last see Mr Murphy?'

'In the pub that night.'

'The sixth?'

'If that's when they say it was. I don't remember the date, but I've only been there the once.'

'And what took you there on that occasion?'

'I'd been for a run with a mate and he suggested stopping for a pint on the way back.'

'So the Griffin was his choice?'

'I s'pose. But I'm not sure it was a choice, as such. We just passed it on the way.'

'What's your mate's name?'

'Toby Reynolds.'

Rebecca made a note of this before asking what Charlie had been doing on Sunday evening.

'Uh –' he paused for a moment's thought. 'I was round at Toby's place. My sister was there too.'

'Until what time?'

Another pause. 'I'm not sure – I didn't check. Nine, maybe? We had a barbecue earlier in the afternoon, and a few beers. Then I walked back.'

'Alone?'

'Yeah. Abbie fell asleep on the sofa, so I left her there.'

'Can anyone confirm where you were after that?'

'Mum was home.'

'How late was she up?'

'I don't know, later than me. I checked she was ok before I went up.'

Rebecca nodded. 'I'd also like to know where you were on the thirty-first of March, although I realise that's going back a bit, and that you may need to check your diary.'

'I don't have a diary. What happened in March?'

'Perhaps you could take a look at your mobile communications for that week, see whether that helps you narrow it down?' Rebecca suggested, ignoring his question.

'I'll give it a go, but I don't use my phone that much,' Charlie replied, sounding slightly apologetic.

'I'm sure you'll be able to piece things together,' Rebecca returned, assuredly, perching on a nearby crate to indicate she wasn't going anywhere in a hurry. 'It wasn't *that* long ago, was it?'

'I'm out of action for a couple of days and everything goes to pot,' Toby grumbled, glancing up from rooting through a box containing an assortment of needles, syringes and blood-collection tubes as Abigail joined him in the rescue centre's makeshift consulting room. His evident irritation washed over Abigail, her overriding emotion one of relief that he was back on his feet. When she'd last seen him, on Monday afternoon, he had looked ghastly, and she had shared Izzy's fear that he might wind up in hospital.

'Feeling better?' She asked, unnecessarily, as she set Willow, a fluffy calico cat, down on the table between them.

'Much, thanks,' Toby nodded, reaching to stroke the animal. 'Hello trouble,' he greeted her, lightly, before adding, to Abigail, 'I have no idea how I managed to get so drunk, though. I've never felt so ill in my life.'

'Maybe the wine was off,' she suggested, plugging in the electric razor and handing it to him.

'I don't know. Half the night is a complete blank. I remember us –' he lifted his eyebrows rather than articulate what he was referring to. 'And after that, the next thing I remember is you kissing me goodbye when you left.'

'That was at six,' Abigail informed him, wrapping one hand around Willow's sternum and taking hold of her head with the other.

'I know, the hours that followed are all *too* memorable,' he replied, ruefully, leaning to shave the fur over the cat's jugular vein before Abigail could respond. Willow held still for a couple of seconds before trying to wriggle free of Abigail's grasp, and Toby caught a flailing black and ginger paw before the claws could make contact with his hand. 'Easy, missy!'

'Sorry,' Abigail offered, gripping the cat more firmly. Toby examined Willow's neck and reached for a syringe, and Abigail gently pulled the animal's chin up to grant him access to the vein. As he slid the needle in, the cat jerked away, and he sighed.

'You torties are all the same, nothing but trouble,' he remarked, tossing the bent needle into the sharps bin and reaching for another. Abigail smiled. Tortoiseshell cats were known for their attitude, and Toby had once offered a scientific explanation for this anecdotal connection between temperament and coat colour. As a rule, he had pointed out, female cats were decidedly feistier than males – and, thanks to a genetic quirk, torties were almost invariably female. Izzy's objection to what she saw as sexual stereotyping had seen him extend the theory:

in his experience, he had said, female cats were also the brighter of the two sexes. Izzy hadn't been impressed.

'Can we wrap her, please?' Toby asked, looking to Abigail.

She nodded, releasing the cat and turning towards the cupboard beneath the sink for a towel. A split second later, Willow launched herself upwards, landed on the topmost of the three shelves above the table and disappeared behind a plastic crate.

'I think that's what you call a catapult,' Toby joked.

'You div,' Abigail sniggered, reaching for a chair and positioning it next to the table before grasping hold of the backrest and stepping up onto the seat. The chair wobbled, and Toby grabbed her arm to steady her. As Abigail climbed gingerly up onto the table, Willow panicked and shot along the shelf towards the cupboard in the corner, knocking into boxes as she went. Bubble packs of worming tablets rained down, and Abigail dissolved into giggles, lowering herself into a crouching position before she could lose her balance. Toby reached to help her off the table, and as she landed on the ground in front of him Charlie came striding through the door, stopping short when he saw Abigail's hands on Toby's shoulders and his at her waist.

'I thought as much,' he remarked, sardonically. 'Anyone told your girlfriend you've switched teams again?'

Toby muttered something unintelligible, releasing Abigail and turning to move the chair towards the cupboard.

'What did the policewoman want?' Abigail asked, deciding the best way to deal with the situation was to ignore it and change the subject.

'Spencer Murphy's dead.'

'Who?' Toby asked, without looking around.

'Fight organiser, bookmaker, arsehole. You remember, from the Griffin.'

Toby grunted in response, climbing onto the chair.

'Mauled to death by a dog, apparently,' Charlie enlarged, sounding almost triumphant. 'That's poetic justice for you.'

Abigail frowned. 'Why did the police want to talk to you?'

Charlie shrugged. 'Seems they think there was something suss about it.'

'But what's it got to do with you?' She persisted.

Toby turned. 'Someone got a little hot under the collar with Murphy when we were at the Griffin,' he revealed. ''Fact, we were asked to leave. Several times. 'Fore being *forced* to.'

Abigail shook her head, raising her eyes heavenwards. She wished she could say the news came as a surprise, but Toby's account sounded perfectly plausible.

'You didn't do anything else stupid, did you?' Toby asked, beating Abigail to the punch.

'No I bloody didn't!' Charlie returned, indignantly.

'All right, I'm only asking.'

'Oh, and they want to speak to you as well.'

'What?' Toby exclaimed, consternation sweeping across his face. 'Why? What for?'

Charlie shrugged. 'I s'pose 'cos you were there too.'

'Great,' Toby returned, sarcastically. 'Thanks a bunch.'

'Sorry,' Charlie replied, contritely. 'I didn't mean to involve you – I didn't think –'

'No,' Toby responded, irritably, as he looked back to the cat. 'That's your problem. You never bloody do.'

On entering the laboratory, Rebecca was met with an unfamiliar sound: Miranda was giggling. The normally sour-faced sergeant was smiling as she watched Leighton lower a coverslip onto a microscope slide from her vantage point on the laboratory bench. Leighton said something about a box of cornflakes and she laughed again. Rebecca immediately felt irked, and wondered whether she would have felt as resentful had she not so disliked Miranda.

'Sorry to interrupt,' she opened, trying – and, she suspected, failing – to keep her tone light.

Leighton glanced around. 'Hiya Becks,' he greeted her, with an easy smile, the previous day's exchange apparently forgotten. 'How you doing?'

'Good, thanks. I just came to see whether the DNA results were back yet.'

'Ah, Mandy beat you to it,' Leighton replied, tipping his head in Miranda's direction.

Mandy? Rebecca's eyebrows rose.

'I told you I'd look after it,' Miranda put in, innocently. She had done no such thing, but Rebecca wasn't going to give her the satisfaction of arguing about it, and instead asked what the result had been.

'Positive,' Leighton answered. 'Canine DNA match.'

'With Ratley?'

'Not literally,' he joked, moving the slide towards the rear of the bench. 'But yes, the same dog was at both scenes. I've sent the sequence to a veterinary geneticist to see whether he can give us some idea of what breed or mix of breeds it is.'

'Do you have any idea of the ETA for that?' Rebecca asked, knowing it would be Pete's first question.

'Hopefully within twenty-four hours. But if I have time later I might do a bit of research and see whether I can make sense of it myself. There are a couple of other sequences I'd like the low-down on.'

Rebecca frowned. 'Why not just send those to the vet as well?'

'No authority,' Leighton returned, with a lift of his eyes ceilingwards and a quirky smile.

'O'Leary,' Rebecca concluded, with a sigh.

'You're incorrigible,' Miranda added, lightly, giving his shoulder a playful dig with her right forefinger. 'How much time did you spend sitting outside the headmaster's office when you were at school?'

Leighton grinned. 'A lot less than I might've done if I'd actually turned up every day.'

'Oh, out collecting ASBOs in the community, were you?'

'What a suggestion!' Leighton returned, in mock indignation. He tutted and shook his head before adding, 'What sort of amateur do you take me for? As if I ever got caught.'

This drew a laugh from Miranda, and Rebecca wondered whether she had any idea how much truth there was to the remark. Despite the recent realization that her own perspective on Leighton's personal life was little more than a series of snapshots, she suspected she knew more than most at Scotland Yard.

'How's your O'Leary investigation going?' Miranda enquired, bringing Rebecca back to the present.

'Nowhere fast,' Leighton admitted. 'There are a whole bunch of tests I'd like to order, but in the absence of anyone to sign them off I'm having to do what I can myself.'

Miranda nodded. 'There's not much I can do on that score, but if there's anything I can help with, let me know.'

Rebecca swallowed a sharp response, feeling angry with Miranda for encouraging him – and, she reluctantly admitted to herself, for flirting with him. She also felt angry with him for reciprocating, which she knew was irrational. He had always flirted with just about everyone, so it was unlikely he was doing it to provoke her. On top of that, she felt angry with herself for letting it get to her. Guessing that if she stayed she would probably wind up saying something out of line, she was mentally composing an excuse to leave when her mobile did the job for her. She could only hope the investigation didn't drag on. The sooner it was in the bag, the sooner she would be shot of Miranda.

Unusually – and much to Lawrence's relief – there was a parking space almost directly outside his front door. Swinging into it in one swift movement, he made a mental note to straighten the car later before climbing out and heading for the house, glancing needlessly at his watch as he hurried up the steps.

Given the reason for his wife's absence, it wasn't the time to discuss whether their eleven-year-old daughter really still needed someone to collect her from school, and as Lawrence couldn't duck out of work every afternoon he had reluctantly decided to try giving his son the responsibility of meeting Elise on his way home. The previous year the idea would have been unthinkable – Jimmy had succeeded in getting himself arrested not once but twice, on the second occasion having been caught travelling in a stolen car. But given that the boy's behaviour seemed to have improved in recent months, Lawrence had hoped putting him in a position of trust would do him good, and, by way of motivation, had made reference to adding a bonus to the boy's allowance.

Initially, the strategy had been a success, and on Monday and Tuesday Jimmy had dutifully seen his sister home. Earlier this afternoon, however, Lawrence had had a call from Elise to inform him that not only had Jimmy not turned up at her school, he wasn't at home either, and she was without a door key. Some forty miles away and with no way of contacting any of the other parents without involving Katie, Lawrence had called on Rebecca for help before heading home. He had spent much of the drive mentally concocting scenarios to explain Jimmy's absence, and desperately hoping the task had simply slipped his mind.

The mortice wasn't locked, and Lawrence called his son's name as he opened the front door. Jimmy came wandering out of the kitchen, a sandwich that looked to be heavily laden with Nutella in his hand.

'Uh-huh?' He responded, rather incoherently, his mouth full.

'What happened to you? You were supposed to meet your sister at four!'

Jimmy looked taken aback. 'It's Wednesday,' he replied, on swallowing, as if this offered a full explanation.

'So?'

'I had athletics training.'

'And it didn't occur to you to mention that?'

The boy shrugged. 'Thought you knew.'

Lawrence sighed. He probably *ought* to have known. He certainly ought to have thought to ask whether there were any days Jimmy might not be able to meet Elise. And he could hardly blame a teenage boy for not thinking of something that hadn't occurred to him either. 'Well, I do now,' he conceded. 'Do you have anything on after school tomorrow?'

Jimmy shook his head, taking another bite of his sandwich.

'So can I rely on you to meet your sister?'

'If you want,' came the careless response as Jimmy turned for the stairs.

'Is that a yes?'

'Yeah, all right,' the boy answered, unenthusiastically, without looking around. Lawrence nodded to himself, taking his mobile from his jacket pocket before slipping the garment off and folding it carefully over the bannister rail. He was still working his way through his recent messages when a knock at the door announced the arrival of Rebecca and Elise.

Elise scarcely glanced his way as she made for the stairs, with a distracted, 'Hi Dad,' as she passed. He followed her with his eyes for a moment before looking to Rebecca with a rueful smile.

'I hope she was more personable for you. Come in.' He stood back from the door. 'Can I get you a drink? Coffee? Juice? Wine?'

'Coffee, thanks, you made it back before she succeeded in driving me to drink,' Rebecca joked as she stepped inside.

'Small mercies,' Lawrence remarked, closing the door. 'But I am sorry for putting you in this position. And thank you for your help, I really do appreciate it.'

'It was no trouble.'

'All the same, I'm aware I shouldn't even have asked.'

'Don't worry, I'll store it up for the next time I need a favour.'

'Fair play,' Lawrence smiled, turning towards the kitchen. 'How much do I owe you for cab fare?'

'You don't. Leighton gave me a lift.'

'Does he still have his licence?' Lawrence exclaimed.

'Apparently so.'

'How on earth did he manage that? Usually if you're doing over one hundred a ban is more or less automatic.'

'I don't know. Maybe he charmed the magistrate.'

Lawrence shook his head slightly. 'I know we joke about people getting away with murder, but I sometimes think he really could.'

'Probably, given his knowledge of forensic science.'

'That wasn't quite what I meant,' Lawrence replied, reaching to fill the kettle and reflecting that speeding wasn't the only thing the pathologist seemed likely to get away with that week. Max had called a few hours earlier to inform Lawrence that Leighton hadn't actually spoken to the journalist responsible for the article in the Echo, but had kept in contact with Evan and offered to give evidence in his defence as and when the case came to court. That Leighton should never have been communicating with Evan ended up taking second place to Max's rejoinder that Lawrence ought to have established the facts before launching an all-out verbal assault. Whilst Lawrence had to admit that much was true, the fact remained that Leighton knew better than to get involved in the first place, and the likelihood Max would now do nothing to address his actions was infuriating.

Lawrence had made several attempts that afternoon to get hold of the paper's editor with the intent of quashing any further reporting or comment on the case. In all likelihood, Rhys Williams would be following the media attention closely – during the original investigation it had seemed he was actively seeking press coverage – and the last thing Lawrence wanted was for the man to get a sense of the scrutiny the Birmingham homicides were under. His team might have made little obvious progress in the past fortnight, but they had covered a huge amount of ground; work that stood to be wasted should Williams move on to look for victims elsewhere. If, indeed, he hadn't done as much already.

Thursday 15 April

'What the hell are you playing at?' Claire demanded, the moment Flora opened her front door. 'Do you not think Evan's going through enough without you making things worse?'

Flora frowned. 'What?'

'His solicitor just read him the riot act for talking to the papers!' Claire returned. 'Except it wasn't Evan that talked to them, was it? It was you!'

'Well someone had to do something.'

'To what end? It's done nothing to help Evan! The paper should apparently never have printed it, so you've probably lost someone their job! And goodness knows whether the pathologist will still be allowed – or even prepared – to speak up for Evan now! One of the few people who's treated Evan with any humanity and that's the thanks he gets for it!'

Flora swallowed.

'All to make yourself feel better about the fact you weren't there when it really mattered!'

'That's not true,' Flora countered. 'I didn't do it for me.'

'I doubt you believe that any more than I do.'

'People deserve to know what's going on!' She protested. 'Despite the fact there are clearly unanswered questions, Evan still has to go on trial and some psycho out there is walking around scot-free! And nobody is *doing* anything!'

'You don't know *what* the police are or aren't doing!' Claire exclaimed. 'None of us do! And making them look bad isn't going to endear Evan to them, is it?'

'Evan isn't the one who's dead!' Flora flared. 'It's Adriana the police should be worried about! She's the real victim here!'

Claire stared at her in disbelief, seemingly speechless. 'So you just used Evan to further your own agenda!' She concluded, at length. 'Never mind whether it tips him over the edge! Have you no conscience?'

'The police are the ones at fault here, not me! *They're* the ones who charged him!'

'And you think that absolves you of any responsibility? The police didn't *know* Evan! You did! Yet you and his other so-called *friends* were quick enough to find him guilty by kangaroo court!'

'Like you really believed him either,' Flora threw back cynically, immediately regretting the remark. She opened her mouth to offer some form of apology, but before she could get a word out Claire had seized hold of her shoulders and slammed her against the wall inside the door.

'You spiteful little bitch!' She spat, delivering a powerful slap to Flora's face. 'You really are a piece of work! Evan's better off without friends like you!'

For a moment, Flora was too stunned to respond. Myriad entangled thoughts raced through her mind, among them the immediate panic of what to do. Then, as Claire moved to strike her again, fear finally filtered through the shock and she screamed.

On learning that Charlie Watts' friend Toby was a vet, Rebecca had promptly tapped his name into Google, and by the time they met had already established that he was thirty-nine, had studied veterinary medicine at Bristol University and had additional qualifications in veterinary acupuncture and animal behaviour. She arrived at his East End practice to find that, far from ministering to the furry patients she'd expected, he was up a ladder to the rear of the building attending to a broken gutter. Clambering down in response to Rebecca's introduction of herself, he said, 'This'll be about last Tuesday, I suppose?'

'What makes you suppose that?'

'Chas said you wanted to talk to me,' he replied, reaching ground level and brushing nothing in particular from his Paris Marathon t-shirt. It was dated two years previously, and from his athletic physique she guessed he had earned rather than bought it. 'Well – not necessarily *you*, but the police.'

Rebecca nodded. 'Perhaps you could start by running me through what happened that evening.'

'There's not a lot to say. We went for a beer after a run, then had to abandon the better part of a pint after Chas kicked off and the landlord asked us to leave.'

'Can you explain what you mean by kicked off?'

'He had a go at someone.'

'The landlord asked him to leave simply for having a go at someone?'

'It got a bit heated,' Toby admitted.

'More than a bit, from what I've gathered.'

Toby shifted his stance, but didn't speak to confirm or deny the suggestion.

'Did you know Mr Murphy?'

'No.'

'But Charlie did.'

'He knew who he was, I don't know that that's quite the same thing.'

'And how did he know that much?'

'I didn't ask,' Toby replied. 'We've both seen more than our fair share of the fallout from dog fighting, and it's heartbreaking. Charlie knows more about the perpetrators than I do, because he's tried to sabotage fights a couple of times. I have warned him to stay out of it, because it's a dangerous business, but –' he held his hands out helplessly. There were a number of scratches down his left arm, and Rebecca supposed it was an occupational hazard.

'Has he ever said anything to make you think he might try to do more than sabotage a fight?'

'No.'

'You didn't have to give that much thought,' Rebecca observed.

'It's hardly the kind of thing you'd forget.'

'I shouldn't think it is, but it seems you've already forgotten that Charlie threatened Mr Murphy last week.'

Toby wasn't easily rattled, and shrugged this off with, 'That was just the heat of the moment. Chas mouths off a lot. But – if you'll excuse the pun – his bark's worse than his bite.'

'And how about you?' Rebecca asked. 'I understand you do a lot of work for the rescue centre. I can't imagine what it must be like seeing the aftermath of dog fights on a regular basis. Have you ever felt tempted to take the law into your own hands?'

'I'm sure you see all manner of horrors in the course of your work, too,' Toby returned. 'Do you respond by going around killing people? Or do you redouble your efforts to make a difference?'

'You're a vet, not a police officer. What difference *can* you make to the rise of dog-fighting, exactly?' Rebecca baited. 'Is it not more a case of endless mopping up?'

'I didn't say I was doing it in a professional capacity, and I don't need validation from you,' he returned, bluntly. 'If you're hoping to provoke me, you're wasting your time. You can't work on the frontline of animal rescue if you're a hothead.'

'No? I'd say Charlie's a classic example of a hothead.'

'Charlie doesn't deal with the public.'

'So you agree that he's a hothead.'

'I don't think anyone would dispute that. But it doesn't make him a killer.'

'Not necessarily, no,' Rebecca agreed. 'Come to think of it, premeditated murder probably requires a considerably cooler head. Where were you on Sunday night and in the early hours of Monday morning?'

'Sunday night?' Toby echoed, his dark eyebrows pulling towards a frown.

'Where were you?' Rebecca repeated.

'Here,' he replied, simply. 'Well, not right here, I was inside.'

'Were you working?'

'No – I live upstairs. Above the practice.'

'Was anyone with you?'

'No. Not after about ten, anyway. Chas and Abbie were here before that. First barbecue of the year.'

'And how about the thirty-first of March?'

'Hornchurch,' Toby replied, without a moment's hesitation.

'You didn't have to think too hard about that,' Rebecca observed. 'One might almost think you were prepared for the question.'

'One might,' Toby agreed. 'Although if one was less suspicious, one might simply assume it was a memorable date.'

'And was it?'

'Yes. March the thirty-first is my dad's birthday.'

Lawrence and Jamie were met at Flora's front door by the next-door neighbour who had telephoned Lawrence a short while earlier, a heavy-set woman of sixty-something called Jacinta. She welcomed them in, offering teas and coffees as she ushered them through to the living room, where Flora was sitting in a scruffy yellow armchair, her hands twisted together in her lap. She raised her bloodshot eyes as Jacinta showed Lawrence and Jamie into the room, then cast them back down. The skin over her left cheekbone was a vivid pink that would no doubt darken as it turned into a bruise, and a long scratch ran down her cheek.

Lawrence sat in the armchair's mismatched blue companion, and Jamie perched on the windowsill, flipping his notebook open and beginning a search of his pockets for a pen.

'I understand from your neighbour that someone attacked you,' Lawrence began, holding a biro out in Jamie's direction without shifting his focus from Flora. 'Can you tell me what happened?'

Flora swallowed. 'She really scared me,' she managed, her voice wavering.

'Who?'

'Claire.'

'Claire Somerset?'

Flora nodded.

'Is she the person who attacked you?'

She nodded again.

'And why did she do that, do you think?'

'We were arguing,' Flora admitted. 'And – I know I said some things I shouldn't have – but – I never expected –' she gulped. 'She just lost it.' There was a pause before the girl looked up and added, 'What if she lost it with Adriana?'

Jamie had already asked himself the same thing. Hopefully one of the pathologists would be able to answer the question of whether a female assailant was a likely possibility.

'What was the argument about?'

'My friend's brother wrote an article for the local paper. Claire and I were disagreeing over the rights and wrongs of it – and –' Flora hesitated. 'She had a go at me for not giving Evan the benefit of the doubt in the first place. Then –' the girl's cheeks coloured, and she lowered her eyes before finishing, 'I questioned whether she'd really believed him herself.'

Jamie's eyebrows rose. He could certainly understand why Claire had reacted to that, and it seemed he wasn't alone, because Flora added, 'I know it was terrible thing to say, and I would have apologised, but –' she shrugged. 'I didn't get the chance.'

'Could you describe what happened?'

Flora nodded. There was a moment's silence before she said, 'She shoved me up against the wall and started hitting me – calling me names –' she paused. 'I was so shocked – I never thought she'd –' she stopped again. 'I didn't know what to do – I just started screaming – and some guy who was walking past outside came running in. I don't know what would've happened if he hadn't.' She swallowed before adding, haltingly, 'What if – if she and Adriana –'

Jacinta appeared with three mugs gathered in her hands, and placed two on the small side table that stood between the armchairs before handing the third to Jamie. He nodded his thanks and turned to set it on the windowsill, guessing from its anaemic appearance that it contained either too little tea or too much milk.

'What was Adriana's relationship with Claire like?' Lawrence asked, once Jacinta had withdrawn from the room.

'Ok, I guess,' Flora shrugged. 'I know she found Evan's reliance on Claire frustrating – and I think she felt Claire should have pushed him to be more independent – but they got on ok. Most of the time, anyway.'

'In what way did she think Evan was too reliant on Claire?'

'Emotionally. He seemed to want her approval for everything. And he almost always followed her advice, even if he'd not asked for it.'

'You said they got along *most of the time,*' Lawrence continued. 'Can you give me any examples of when they didn't?'

Flora didn't need to give this any thought, saying, immediately, 'After the affair.'

'Well that's hardly surprising.'

'No, I know,' Flora conceded. 'But –' she hesitated. 'Afterwards, when Evan agreed to give Adriana another chance, Claire told her that if she ever hurt Evan like that again, she wouldn't know what had hit her.'

'And why did you not mention that to us before?'

'I never thought about it,' Flora admitted, her tone apologetic. 'It was ages ago – and –' she swallowed. 'I never thought she meant it *physically.*'

Having failed to raise any response at Claire Somerset's front door and had no more success making contact by phone, Lawrence had reluctantly decided to head back to London and return to Birmingham the following morning. Claire's mobile wasn't the only one going straight to voicemail, and, rather than wait for another message to go unanswered, Lawrence had paid an impromptu visit to the pathology unit. It proved a wasted trip, and, on his way towards the exit, he stopped off at Max's office.

'Unless you're here to invite me out for a beer, can it wait?' Max asked, wearily, as Lawrence put his head around the door.

'Not really, no.'

Max sat back in his chair with a sigh, gesturing wordlessly towards the other seats in the room. Lawrence sat down.

'So. What's up?'

'First of all, I want an explanation for this,' Lawrence passed him the photocopy of two mobile-phone screenshots that had been waiting in his *in* tray when he arrived back from Birmingham. 'You told me Leighton said he hadn't put anything in writing to Evan.'

Max took the page and, from the length of the ensuing pause, Lawrence guessed he was reading the exchange in full. His expression when he looked up was perplexed.

'Is this *real*?'

'According to the paper's editor. I demanded to know where the journalist got his quotes from, and this is what she provided.'

'I will look into it,' Max responded. 'But Leighton's English is above the level of *would of* and *different than*.'

'He also knows that's exactly the sort of thinking we employ.'

'Oh come on, that's hardly his style. I know he has a tendency to jump in without thinking things through, but he's not devious.'

Lawrence didn't reply, and Max reached for the phone on his desktop. 'I'll see whether I can track him down.'

'Good luck with that. I haven't been able to get hold of him all day. He's not answering his phone or his email, and when I was in the office just now Roddy said he hadn't been in today.'

This was clearly news to Max, who referred to his laptop before saying, 'He should be around. Unless I've missed a message somewhere along the line.'

'This is getting beyond a joke,' Lawrence objected. 'He's not here when he's supposed to be, when he *is* around more often than not he isn't doing what he *should* be doing, he's argumentative, he's talking to people he shouldn't be, he's lost track of a raft of evidence – at this rate Pete isn't going to be the only one complaining!'

Max sighed. 'I'm aware he's not been himself lately,' he acknowledged. 'But I couldn't pull him up over Pete's complaint for obvious reason, so in the absence of any others there's not been a lot I could do. Any expression of concern is generally deflected with jokes.'

'Was a charge for dangerous driving not sufficient cause?'

Max frowned. 'Who told you about that? Roddy?'

'Yes.'

'He doesn't know all the details and he shouldn't be disseminating an abridged version of events.'

'Well it seems quite simple to me, either Leighton was driving at an incredibly irresponsible speed or he wasn't.'

'Life is rarely black and white,' Max responded. 'And frankly, what goes on in his personal life is neither your nor Roddy's concern. Suffice to say I have spoken to Leighton about it and I am not worried about that particular incident. What I am concerned about is whatever it is that is affecting his performance at work, and I will have a word with him.'

'I can answer that one for you! The problem is his fixation on O'Leary, to the detriment of everything else! And you need to do more than have a word!'

'Yes, all right, you've made your point,' Max returned, curtly. 'Was there anything else?'

Lawrence's mobile interrupted before he had a chance to reply, and, seeing the name on the display, he took the call. 'Jamie, hi.'

'Are you still in the building?' His colleague asked, breathlessly.

'No, but I can be in five minutes. Why?' Lawrence stood and signalled his intention to depart with his free hand. Max nodded, looking relieved to see the back of him.

'I've got an address for David Jones.'

When there was no response to the very audible doorbell of David Jones's Maidstone flat, Lawrence tried its companion, and moments later the front door to the building was thrown open by a scruffy but attractive young woman. Her wavy blonde hair was crowned by inch-long roots, and she was clad in faded combat trousers and a baggy grey t-shirt, which, Jamie guessed from the little he could make out, hid a pretty decent figure.

'Uh-huh?' She greeted them, eyebrows raised expectantly.

Lawrence introduced himself and Jamie before asking for her name – Xanthe – and whether she had any idea of the whereabouts of her upstairs neighbour. When she replied that she had seen him come in not ten minutes earlier, they tried his first-floor front door and, getting no response, forced it open. The flat was empty, the open window in the rear bedroom and the garage roof below it answering the question of how the occupant had departed, unseen, after their arrival. In the interest of saving potentially vital seconds, Jamie had been straight out of the window and on down into the passageway that ran behind the row of postage-stamp gardens, only to find it deserted. By the time he had searched the length of the alleyway and completed a circuit of the terrace, Lawrence was on the phone, by the sound of things issuing a description to the local police force. The resident of the ground-floor flat, meanwhile, was leaning against her doorframe, one ankle tucked behind the other, and gave Jamie a smile as he re-entered the building.

'What'd he do, then?' She asked, curiously, indicating the upstairs flat with a slight jerk of her head.

'That's a good question,' Jamie returned, amicably. 'Do you know him well?'

'I don't really know him at all. He's just the guy who lives upstairs.'

'How long has he lived there?'

Xanthe's dark eyebrows crinkled in thought. 'A few months, I guess?'

'Do you know who owns the flat?'

She shook her head.

'And does he have many visitors?'

'No,' she answered, sounding faintly surprised by this realisation. 'Actually I don't know if he's ever had any visitors.'

Jamie nodded. 'I realise this is a long shot, but you don't happen to remember whether he was here on the night of March the twenty-ninth, do you?'

Xanthe's expression said *fat chance*, but she appeared to give the question some thought before shaking her head. 'Sorry, no. To be honest, I don't even remember what *I* was doing that night.'

'Would you mind having a check of your diary?'

'Seeing as you asked so nicely,' Xanthe replied, coyly, turning back into her flat and returning, moments later, with her mobile. 'The twenty-ninth?' She checked, lifting her gaze briefly from the screen.

'Yes. It was a Tuesday, if that helps.'

'Oh, then I was probably playing squash. Unless I got caught up with work.'

'What do you do?' Jamie enquired, conversationally.

'I'm a plumber.'

Jamie laughed.

'Guys always laugh when I tell them that,' Xanthe remarked, with a wry smile.

'Are you serious?' He asked, after a moment, still not certain she wasn't joking.

'Yep.'

He raised his eyebrows in response. 'Neat.'

When he said nothing further, she glanced up from the mobile. 'Ten points for not making lewd jokes about hoses and ballcocks,' she said, playfully, with another smile.

'Never crossed my mind.'

She held his gaze for a moment, then her eyes flickered leftwards and she returned them to her phone. 'So, the twenty-ninth,' she said, her tone more business-like, as Lawrence joined Jamie in the corridor. 'Yeah, I was at the squash club, which doesn't really help me narrow it down,' she dropped the hand holding the phone to her side as she looked back up. 'Sorry,' she shrugged.

'Don't worry, it was a big ask.'

'Thank you for your help,' Lawrence put in, when Jamie didn't continue. 'The local police force is sending someone around shortly to keep an eye on things upstairs, and then we'll get out of your hair.' He turned to Jamie. 'I'm just going to pop up for a couple of things.'

Jamie nodded, and Lawrence made for the stairs. Xanthe leaned out through her flat's doorway and watched him go, waiting until he disappeared from view before shifting her gaze to Jamie. 'So I'm guessing you're not allowed to ask for my number,' she ventured, with a coy smile. 'But is there any rule that says I can't ask for yours?'

Jamie returned her smile. 'Well, we will need to leave you a contact number, in case you think of anything that might be relevant to our enquiry,' he drew a copy of his card from his inside jacket pocket and held it out for her to take. 'And I can't stop you from calling me, now, can I?'

Friday 16 April

The news that David Jones's fingerprints didn't match those of Rhys Williams came as a huge relief. Considering how completely Williams had succeeded in disappearing two years earlier, Lawrence wouldn't have staked much on their chances of pinning him down after the event had it been his flat they had stormed the previous evening. In the hours since the event, Lawrence had repeatedly berated himself for his poor planning of the venture and his failure to take the precaution of surrounding the property prior to entry. And, much as he was still responsible for Jones's escape, he was less pessimistic about the odds of their having another chance to apprehend him.

In addition to confirming that Jones and Williams weren't one and the same, the fingerprint hit explained why Jones had made off so rapidly; he was wanted for questioning in relation to an aggravated burglary. More interestingly, he had previously been questioned over a serious sexual assault. Given the lack of any hard evidence connecting Williams to either Coralie or Adriana – or, indeed, anything to definitively link the two deaths – the possibility remained that someone other than Williams might have been responsible. In that eventuality, Jones would seem to be the prime suspect for at least one of the crimes. With that thought, Lawrence reached for a Post-it note. There might be a way to establish what the likelihood of Jones's involvement was.

He stepped out of his office to find the open-plan area beyond it deserted but for Rebecca and Jamie, whose conversation came to an abrupt halt as he appeared.

'What was that?' He asked, having caught the tail end of what Rebecca was saying.

'Oh – nothing,' she responded, with a dismissive a shake of her head.

Lawrence raised his eyebrows. 'If it's nothing then you won't mind filling me in on who it is that has amphetamines in their car, will you?'

There was a tense silence.

'I'm waiting.'

'I found a packet of Dexedrine in Leighton's glove compartment,' Rebecca admitted, at length.

Lawrence looked to Jamie. 'Did you know anything about this?'

Jamie hesitated. 'I was just trying to get hold of him –' he began, haltingly. 'Ana said Max sent him home – I asked Becks whether –'

'*Did you know*?' Lawrence pressed.

'Not until just now,' Rebecca answered on Jamie's behalf.

Lawrence returned his attention to her. 'And how long have you known?'

She swallowed. 'A few days.'

'A few days?' He exclaimed. 'If you suspect someone is abusing controlled drugs do you not think perhaps it's in your job description to report it?'

'I –'

'If you want to turn a blind eye to what people are doing in your personal life, that's your choice, but you do *not* do it here!'

'What?'

'You know very well what! Elliot uses cocaine, doesn't he? And you lived with him for – what? Eighteen months?'

'He didn't use it when I was there!'

'I should bloody well hope not! But that doesn't make it ok! And it certainly doesn't excuse your choosing to ignore the fact that one of your colleagues is using class B drugs!'

'That isn't a fact, though, is it? The only fact is that they were in his car! Having prescription medication in your vehicle isn't a crime!'

'Well I think we can trust Max to get to the bottom of that one, don't you?' Lawrence responded, as he turned back towards his office. 'Not least the question of who wrote out the prescription!'

Claire's first words to Lawrence and Jamie as she led them through to the living room were an apology for the fact nobody had received them the previous afternoon. 'Evan won't answer the door when he's here alone,' she explained, as she paused in the doorway. 'Take a seat and I'll go and call him for you.'

'It was you we wanted to speak to, actually,' Lawrence replied. 'Do you have five minutes?'

'Oh – yes – yes, of course,' the woman nodded, apprehension creeping into her tone. 'Would you like a drink? I can –'

'No, thank you,' Lawrence cut her off, as he sat down. He waited for her to do the same before saying, 'I gather you had cause to visit Flora Preston yesterday morning.'

Claire nodded.

'She alleges that you attacked her.'

Claire closed her eyes briefly before nodding again and admitting, 'I'm so ashamed I did that.'

'Could you explain your actions?'

'We had a row. I brought up the fact she'd turned on Evan the moment he was charged, and –' Claire hesitated. 'She said something like *as if you really believed him yourself*.'

Jamie wondered what the real answer to that might be. Or, rather, what it might have been before Leighton queried the case against Evan. Assuming Claire didn't already *know* what had happened to Adriana.

'Is that why you hit her?' Lawrence asked.

Claire nodded. 'I just saw red. She's already caused so much hurt, and I know that's no excuse, but –' she trailed off with a weak shrug.

'Have you ever seen red like that before?'

'No. I think I just reached the end of my tether. The past few months have been incredibly hard – I've been so worried about Evan – and we've had so little support from anyone – although I realise that's no excuse, either.'

'So you never lost your temper like that with Adriana?'

Claire looked shocked by the question. 'No,' she answered, rather hollowly. 'What are you suggesting?'

'I think what I'm suggesting is probably quite clear.'

'I never hurt that girl,' Claire asserted. 'She was like a daughter to me.'

Lawrence raised his eyebrows disbelievingly. 'Even when she was unfaithful to your son?'

'That was hard,' Claire admitted, at length. 'And we did have words, but nothing more.'

'From what I gather, you told her that if she did it again she wouldn't know *what had hit her*. What exactly did you mean by that?'

'I didn't really mean anything in particular. It was an expression of how angry I felt, not a threat. In retrospect, I can see how it might have come across as one, but that wasn't how it was intended.' She paused, and her anxious frown shifted to one of perplexity. 'How is this relevant? It *didn't* happen again.' She sounded less than certain, and after another momentary pause asked, 'Did it?'

Lawrence ignored the question, saying, 'How did you feel about Evan taking her back?'

'I was concerned she would hurt him again. As any parent would be, I think. But it was what he wanted, so I did my best to put it behind us.'

'And can you tell me where you were the night she died?'

Claire swallowed. 'I was here.'

'Can anybody confirm that?'

'No,' she admitted. 'No – but – surely you don't believe I could have watched Evan go through all this if I'd –' she shook her head. 'This has ruined his *life*! How could you even *think* that?'

'I've seen people do a lot worse,' Lawrence replied, levelly. 'But I think we've covered enough ground for today. I'd like a quick word with Evan before we go, though, if you wouldn't mind fetching him?'

Evan appeared as dejected as ever, and didn't even look up as he sank down into the armchair his mother had recently vacated. Much as it didn't excuse Leighton's actions, Lawrence could understand why his colleague had expressed concern for the man.

'You'll have seen this by now, I presume?' Lawrence began, presenting the front page of the local paper.

Evan lifted his gaze for long enough to take it in before closing his eyes despairingly. 'I had nothing to do with that,' he defended himself, weakly. 'But I don't s'pose that'll stop you joining everyone else in having a go.'

'If you had nothing to do with it, how is it that the journalist who wrote it had access to quotes from a conversation you had, via text message, with one of my colleagues?'

'Flora,' Evan replied, shortly.

'And what part did Flora play? Did she simply provide the screenshots of the conversation, or did she instigate it?'

'Both.'

'So you gave her access to your phone.'

'I didn't really *give* her access. She just took it.' He met Lawrence's eyes briefly. 'I did try to stop her,' he added. 'But Flora doesn't take *no* for an answer. And I didn't have the energy for a fight.'

*****

Adriana's mother had left Lawrence two voicemail messages over the course of the morning, and, guessing what they were likely to be about, he decided to respond in person. They had met, briefly, when he had first taken an interest in Adriana's death, and he had hoped that by their next meeting he would have more to offer her than an apology for the front-page article in the Echo. He made a start on explaining that he was looking into how the story had come to be in the public domain, but Katerina Simonides interrupted before he had even finished his second sentence.

'I don't care *how* it got into the paper! I want to know if it's *true*!'

'I'm still trying to establish the answer to that, which is precisely why the story shouldn't have been published.'

It was clear from her expression that this wasn't what Katerina had wanted to hear, and Lawrence wondered which way she had been hoping the investigation would go.

'I realise the uncertainty must be very difficult for you, and I will let you know as soon as I have any news,' he added.

Katerina nodded in response.

'When we last met, we talked quite a bit about Adriana's relationship with Evan,' Lawrence continued. 'Can you tell us much about how she got on with Claire?'

'Claire?' Katerina echoed, in surprise. 'What does that matter? You can't possibly be suggesting she's a suspect? My daughter was raped!'

Lawrence didn't want to have to spell out the fact Evan didn't deny having sex with Adriana, nor that there was no evidence to indicate intercourse had been forced upon her, and prepared to say something about trying to build up a complete picture of the girl's life. But Katerina wasn't finished.

'If you'd asked about Brian I might understand, but *Claire* –' she shook her head in disbelief.

'Evan's father?'

She nodded.

'My understanding from Claire was that he hadn't been around for some time. Is that not the case?'

'No, it isn't,' Katerina answered, with an expressive lift of her eyebrows, before adding, hastily, 'I'm not saying she was lying. She may not have known.'

'So it was Evan that Brian was in touch with?'

'Well – trying to be. His desire for contact wasn't reciprocated. Hardly surprisingly.'

'How persistent was he?'

'Very. Some of it sounded like it bordered on harassment.'

'For example?'

'When his initial attempts at reconciliation weren't successful, he started using more underhand ways of getting a window on Evan's life. Online, largely. At one point he created a fake Facebook page purporting to be an old friend of Adriana's, and once he had access to what she was posting he could track a lot of what Evan was up to, as well. And access all Adriana's photographs.'

'Did Evan report that?'

'I don't know. I only ever heard about it second-hand.'

'And despite being a close friend of Claire's, you didn't mention it to her?'

'I didn't think that was for me to do. Evan wasn't a kid. If he didn't want her to know, that was up to him, wasn't it? I expect he wanted to avoid upsetting her. Brian put them both through a lot.'

'Did Adriana ever feel threatened by Brian?'

'I don't know. She didn't say as much, but obviously she was aware of his record. Primarily I think she was concerned about the effect it had on Evan.'

'And how did it affect him?'

'She said he was having nightmares.'

'Was that in the weeks before she died?'

'Brian was bothering them for a lot longer than that.'

'How much longer?'

Katerina considered her answer before concluding, 'I couldn't say exactly. At least eighteen months. Probably more.'

'Do you know whether Evan ever acted out any of his dreams?'

'No. And I hardly think he could have killed her in his sleep.'

Lawrence didn't contradict her, but, far-fetched as it might sound, it wasn't impossible. History was scattered with killings alleged to have occurred in the throes of parasomnias such as sleepwalking and night terrors, and there appeared to be reasonable evidence to support some of those claims. The fact that the odds were vanishingly small wasn't a reason to summarily dismiss the idea. However, the chances of Brian – or Claire – being responsible were much greater, and Lawrence steered the conversation back to the subject of Adriana's relationship with Claire. To complete the picture, it seemed they would need to pay Evan another visit.

Evan was still sitting in the chair in which Lawrence and Jamie had left him an hour or so earlier. He didn't appear to have been doing anything ahead of their return – the television was off, and there were no books, magazines or tablets in the immediate vicinity of the chair – leading Jamie to wonder whether he'd moved since their previous visit. Jamie himself would have gone stir-crazy sitting around for hours at a time with nothing but his own thoughts for company. But, he reflected, perhaps in some circumstances there was no activity that *could* distract from the tumult in a person's mind. And no way to focus on anything beyond that.

On this occasion, Lawrence took up Claire's offer of a drink, no doubt to give them a few minutes alone with Evan. Sitting down, he got straight to the point.

'When did you last have contact with your father?'

The question clearly took Evan by surprise, and there was a shocked silence before he said, 'I dunno. A while back.'

'What's a while? Weeks? Months? Years?'

'Not this year,' Evan replied, apparently reluctant to commit himself.

'Last year?'

He shrugged weakly.

'When last year?'

'Christmas,' he admitted, after a long pause. 'Christmas Eve.'

'Was that in person?'

'Sort of. He turned up in person. I didn't actually speak to him.'

'So you didn't answer the door,' Lawrence concluded.

'He gave up quicker if I ignored him.'

'Did Adriana take the same approach when she was there with you?'

'No. She generally threatened to call the police.'

'Did she ever follow through with that?'

'A couple of times.'

'And what happened?'

'Not much. They said they'd speak to him, but it didn't stop him coming back.'

'Was his behaviour ever threatening?'

Evan shrugged.

Lawrence frowned. 'What does that mean?'

There was a long silence. Eventually, eyes on the floor, Evan admitted, 'It was to me.'

Jamie wondered whether Evan had said as much to the police at the time. He would have hoped that information might have prompted them to take the situation more seriously. At times like this, he felt less regret at having grown up in a family that comprised only himself, his mother and his elder sister.

'How did your father react when Adriana threatened to call the police?' Lawrence continued.

'*Brian*?' Claire's voice exclaimed, from the doorway, prompting all three of them to look her way. 'You're in touch with *Brian*?'

Evan returned his eyes to the carpet, making no reply.

'From what I gather, the contact wasn't welcome,' Lawrence offered, after an uncomfortable silence.

This information did nothing to assuage Claire's evident dismay. 'Why in God's name didn't you say?' She demanded.

'What good would it have done?' Evan asked, finally finding the courage to meet her eyes. 'You'd only've got upset. You couldn't have *done* anything!'

'To the *police*!' Claire shrilled. 'You *know* what he's capable of!'

'He didn't hurt Adriana,' Evan responded, with a shake of his head.

'You can't know that!'

'I can.'

'How?'

'He wasn't around,' Evan revealed. 'When – she –' he faltered, before abandoning the sentence and closing his eyes. At length, he reopened them, adding, 'He sent me a postcard. He was in Florida the night she died.'

Rebecca hesitated as she reached to ring Leighton's doorbell, unsure how he might react to her showing up uninvited, then jumped as something brushed past her leg. She looked down to find her friend's petite black and white cat staring back at her, her markings such that it looked as if she was wearing black eyeliner.

'Hello,' Rebecca greeted, with a smile, crouching to stroke the creature. Pandora rubbed her cheek against Rebecca's wrist before turning towards the door and daintily batting the cat flap open with a pristine white paw. It swung in by about forty-five degrees, back through ninety-odd degrees, then returned to its starting position and shut with a clunk. The cat immediately repeated the action, but made no effort to use the flap for its proper purpose, simply watching it swing one way, then the other. When she hit the tiny door for a third time, Rebecca stopped stroking her, thinking perhaps she was confusing the animal, but it made no difference. Pandora gave the plastic flap another smack, and as it thwack-thwack-clunked for a fourth time Rebecca shook her head slightly.

'You daft critter.'

Pandora lifted her paw to try again, but before she could make contact the door housing the flap opened.

'Sometimes I think I –' Leighton stopped short, regarding Rebecca in surprise as the cat skipped past him into the flat. He looked sleepy, and Rebecca felt glad she hadn't been the one to disturb him. 'If you want to use that door you're going to have to start by finding the little bottle labelled *drink me*,' he remarked, drily, raising a hand to rub his eyes.

Rebecca smiled, straightening up. 'Does she not know how to use it?'

'She knows,' he replied, wearily. 'She just likes to use me more.'

Rebecca nodded. There was an uncomfortable silence before she said, 'I just – I was worried – you've not been at work, and you weren't answering your phone –'

'So you thought you'd better check I'd not been sacked?'

Rebecca shrugged. 'I guess,' she admitted, awkwardly.

Leighton looked taken aback. 'That was a joke.'

Rebecca felt herself blush. 'Sorry,' she offered, after a moment. 'It's just – I know Max sent you home – but that's all anyone seems to know, and –' she trailed off. 'Are you ok?'

'I'm ok,' he returned, with a smile that didn't look real.

'Are you sure?' She asked. 'You seem a bit –' she hesitated.

'I've had better weeks,' he admitted. There was another pause before he said, 'Do you want to come in?'

Rebecca suspected the invite had more to do with his need to fill the silence than any real desire to entertain her, but took him up on the offer regardless.

She had visited his flat several times before, and the living room had generally been what she described as 'untidy around the edges', with clutter on the coffee table, an overflow pile of books stacked on the floor beside the haphazardly packed shelves, and the odd magazine and a handful of cat toys knocking around the floor. It was now chaotic. One of the etched glass panels was missing from the door, and the furniture had been shunted to the far side of the room and pictures taken down to free up a wall, which was plastered with photographs, maps, computer printouts and Post-it notes. The coffee table was buried beneath more of the same. It didn't take Rebecca more than a few seconds to identify the purpose of the project: the O'Leary investigation.

'Does Max know about this?' She asked, indicating the wall.

'Not yet.'

Rebecca sighed. 'Do you not think perhaps this obsession is getting a bit out of hand?'

'It's not an obsession.'

'You shouldn't have all this stuff here.'

'What, now you're going to police the contents of my house as well as my car?'

Rebecca bit her lip. 'I'm sorry,' she offered, after a moment. 'I just don't want to see you getting into trouble.'

'I think you missed the word *more*,' he replied, in a lighter tone.

Rebecca managed a smile.

'Coffee?'

'Yes please.'

'Grab a seat,' he suggested, turning towards the door. Pandora tore across the floor in front of him, slid to a stop on the laminate in the hallway and galloped back across the living room. Rebecca slipped off her jacket and perched on the sofa, sitting between a pile of unfolded laundry and a cat bed. Spotting a ball bedecked with bright red and yellow feathers under the coffee table, she bent to reach for it and tossed it in the cat's direction, then retrieved the papers it had been lying atop. One featured a photocopy of the photograph from Fred Ratley's living room – an image that had, a week earlier, lain on her desk in the office. But the copy she now held wasn't identical. It had been annotated with names.

A postcard scarcely constituted hard evidence of a person's whereabouts, and Lawrence and Jamie had spent much of the afternoon trying to locate Brian Somerset, without success. The return to London had been frustrated by rush-hour traffic, and after a brief pause to put in a request to Border Force for information on Brian's movements, Jamie had headed straight out to meet up with friends. Lawrence, meanwhile, had sat down to wade through the latest tranche of reports on the hunt for Rhys Williams. He was nearing the end of the task when a movement in his office doorway caught his eye.

'Evening,' Max greeted him, as soon as he saw he had Lawrence's attention. 'Leighton asked me to deliver these.' He held up a folder, which Lawrence guessed contained lab results.

'I gather you sent him home,' Lawrence replied, sitting back in his chair.

Max nodded.

'What did he have to say for himself?'

'Not much, other than that he wasn't feeling at all well. I couldn't take him to task, he was quite clearly in no state to be at work.' Max sat in one of the chairs scattered in front of Lawrence's desk.

'If he felt that bad, why did he come in?'

'I asked the same question. He pointed out that I'd left a message telling him to be in my office at nine a.m. sharp and that I didn't want to hear any excuses,' Max sighed. 'I felt like some kind of dictator – all I meant was that I didn't want him waltzing in late like he usually does. I didn't mean he should drag himself in if he didn't feel up to it.' Max paused. 'He did apologise for yesterday's mix-up. I suspect he wasn't thinking very clearly.'

'If it was just yesterday I could write it off as a bad day. But he's been out of sorts for weeks.'

'I know, and I will have a chat with him when I see him next. He's clearly been under a lot of stress and I think –'

'Stress?' Lawrence exclaimed. 'Is that the line he's taking? I don't think I've met anyone less susceptible to stress in my entire life!'

'That's not his line, it's my interpretation.'

'Well you might want to factor amphetamines into your interpretation. According to a member of my team, he keeps Dexedrine in his car.'

This information didn't generate the shocked reaction Lawrence had expected. Max's expression barely changed. 'The fact certain drugs are widely abused doesn't stop them having legitimate uses,' he replied.

'You can't turn a blind eye just because you like the guy!'

'That's not what I'm doing, and I don't need you telling me how to run my department,' Max returned, coolly.

'I'm not sure the chairman would see it that way!'

Max sighed heavily. Standing, he leaned to close the door before reclaiming his seat. 'I'm aware he takes Dexedrine,' he admitted. 'He has it on prescription. All right?'

'What on earth for?'

'ADHD. Without it I doubt he'd ever get anything finished. As it is getting him to apply himself to anything that doesn't hold his interest is nigh on impossible.'

Lawrence regarded his friend in silence for a moment before responding. 'Do you not think it might have been an idea to mention that before?'

'I shouldn't be telling you now! It's confidential information and the only reason I'm sharing it at all is to avoid unnecessary embarrassment!'

Lawrence didn't immediately reply, trying to think of a way to convey his scepticism of Max's explanation without potentially digging himself into a hole. Eventually he said, 'The past few weeks aside, I'm a little confused as to how someone routinely taking speed can be so chilled out.'

'I know it seems counterintuitive. It's a function of brain chemistry. Although I suspect to some extent his laissez-faire attitude is a cover for the fact he *can't* actually keep on top of everything.'

'Well perhaps you ought to be keeping on top of it for him.'

'That's easier said than done. Besides, a lot of the things he gets sidetracked by produce results. Roddy's the epitome of organisation and efficiency, but that doesn't make him better at the job.'

That much, Lawrence had to agree, was true. There was - at least in the normal run of things - a reason why he grudgingly tolerated Leighton's chaotic working practices.

'I don't deny he's very good at his job,' Lawrence countered. 'That's not at issue here. And frustrating as it is chasing around after him, I can live with a degree of disorganization. What is unacceptable is his inclination to go way beyond his official remit, and your reluctance to stop him! You *need* to keep him in line! He knows full well he can't go talking to witnesses and suspects without authorisation, and there is no excuse for his doing so!'

'Yes, I know,' Max conceded. 'I will reiterate that very strongly.'

'And as for putting privileged information in text messages –'

'I am doing my best to get to the bottom of that, but I'm yet to hear back from the journalist.'

'Have you asked Leighton?'

'Briefly. The only explanation he could offer was that there are apps out there that allow you to falsify numbers.'

'What, so he's suggesting Evan contrived the whole thing? I really can't see it.'

'No, I don't think that's what he meant. But I can't imagine why he would lie about it. Even leaving aside the fact it seems totally out of character, he knows that if it comes down to it we can trace exactly where a message came from.'

It was a valid point, although Lawrence remained unconvinced. Clearly sensing this, Max added, 'I'm not discounting the seriousness of the matter, and I will push harder for answers if necessary, but it really wouldn't have been fair to do that this morning.'

Lawrence hoped Max would be as good as his word. The last thing he wanted was to have to force the issue.

'And I will talk to him about the limits of his remit when he comes back in,' Max promised. 'In the meantime, let me know if you need me to pick up anything on his behalf.' He moved to stand. 'I wasn't planning on working this weekend, but I won't be far away. So if anything comes up, you can consider me to be on call.'

Saturday 17 April

Rebecca had been awoken long before her alarm by a phone call delivering the news that what looked to be another dog-attack victim had been found in East London. By the time she, Pete and a couple of others met with Jon late in the morning for a preliminary report on the body, she felt ready to go back to bed, and was attempting to reinvigorate herself with a large cappuccino. Jon had also resorted to caffeine, and carried a mug of tea with him into the meeting room. The beverage was as dark as his skin, and Rebecca wondered, not for the first time, how anyone could stomach tea without milk; it was barely palatable sweet and white.

'Right, what've you got so far?' Pete asked, without waiting for everyone to sit down. 'Aside from the obvious.'

Jon swiped open his iPad and presented a photograph showing the top of a man's back. 'First, what look like stun gun injuries,' he said, indicating two small welts at the base of the man's neck. 'It's hard to say when these were received, further than that the marks look relatively recent, but a dog would struggle to overpower a healthy adult without some form of assistance, so logic would suggest it played a part in proceedings.'

The description left Rebecca with a mental image of a dog wielding a stun gun, and she bit her tongue to keep her face straight as Pete observed, 'So that could be how the killer incapacitated our other victims, as well.'

'It's a strong possibility,' Jon agreed. 'They both had extensive injuries, which could easily have masked the damage.'

'Assuming it wasn't just missed.'

'I very much doubt Leighton would miss something like that once, never mind twice,' Jon responded, coolly. 'And there's nothing visible in any of the autopsy or crime-scene pictures to indicate otherwise.'

'Oh, so it's ok for you to double-check, but if I query it you get shirty.'

'It's standard procedure.'

'If you say so,' Pete retorted. 'Anything else to report at this stage?'

'Yeah, I found a small red feather in his mouth.'

'The assumption being that it came off whatever was shoved in there to keep him quiet.'

Jon nodded.

'Can we find out what sort of feather?'

'I think it's undercoat, or whatever they call the fluffy downy feathers birds have beneath their –'

'No, what kind of bird it came from.'

'Oh, right, sorry,' Jon smiled, rolling his eyes comically. 'We can try asking an expert, and if that doesn't get us anywhere we might be able to find out from sequencing the DNA – although I'm not sure whether there are many reference sequences available for birds.'

Pete looked to Rebecca. 'You said the rescue centre had animals besides cats and dogs.'

She nodded, feeling surprised he had remembered that; she hadn't thought he was paying much attention when she reported back on her visit to Paws and Whiskers. 'Rabbits and hedgehogs.'

'So it's not beyond the realms of possibility they've also had birds in there. And if the feather's from something exotic, we might be able to trace it.'

'It's more likely to be a dyed feather from a cat toy,' Rebecca ventured, thinking of the one Pandora had been playing with the previous evening.

'I still want it followed up.' Pete looked to Jon. 'If we find any feathers on site – be it from live birds or toys – we can work out whether they match, right?'

'Probably. For the live ones, at least. It could require more in-depth sequencing than human DNA fingerprinting, though.'

'Well that's for the lab to worry about.'

'I meant it could be expensive.'

'So be it,' Pete replied, unconcernedly. 'I want this wrapped up immediately, if not sooner. Before the papers have any chance to bitch about us not knowing our arses from our elbows.'

Charlie Watts was on his knees in one of the rescue centre's many cat runs making a fuss of a waif-like tabby when Abigail showed Rebecca through. In response to Abigail's one-fingered tap on the wooden frame of the wire-mesh door, he glanced around and, on catching sight of Rebecca, sighed and pushed himself up onto his feet. Rather than leave the enclosure, however, he scooped the cat up into his arms, opened the door and leaned against it, bidding Rebecca a rather grudging hello.

'Good morning. I've a few more questions, if you don't mind?'

Charlie shrugged his consent, tipping the cat onto her back and cradling her in the crook of his left arm. To Rebecca's surprise, the animal didn't struggle or protest, and, as Charlie began rubbing her belly with the fingers of his right hand, started to purr.

'First of all, could you tell me where you were last night, between ten p.m. and two a.m.?'

'The A12.'

'You were on the A12 all that time?'

'Unfortunately. The van broke down about a mile south of Marks Tey, and by the time I'd hung around for the RAC, the guy had established he couldn't fix the problem there and then, and I'd waited for someone to come and pick me up, it was gone three by the time I got in.'

'What time did you break down?' Rebecca asked, noticing that the cat had started paddling her front paws in the air, her eyes shut and face a picture of bliss.

'Um – about half ten.'

'And how long did you have to wait for the RAC?'

'Just over an hour.'

'Did it take the mechanic long to establish that the problem wasn't fixable?'

'Long enough for me to miss the last train back to London.'

'Who did you call to pick you up?'

'Toby.'

'And what time did he show up?'

'I don't remember exactly – a bit after two, I think.'

'Presumably your mobile phone log will allow you to tell me exactly what time you called him, though?'

Charlie sighed, giving the cat in his arms a quick tickle under the chin before bending to deposit her on the floor. He drew his mobile phone from his back pocket and, after consulting it, said, 'Twelve-thirteen.'

'I wouldn't have thought it would take more than about an hour to get from Stratford to Marks Tey,' Rebecca observed. 'So why did it take him double that time, give or take? I can't imagine the traffic would have been heavy at that hour.'

'I dunno,' Charlie shrugged, unconvincingly.

Rebecca raised her eyebrows. 'You mean to tell me you were waiting around in the middle of the night for all that time and you didn't think to ask what kept him?'

There was a brief silence before Charlie replied. 'When I called, he said he couldn't come straight away because he was in the middle of something.'

'In the middle of *what*?'

'Some kind of emergency. He said he'd come when he could.'

Rebecca guessed from Charlie's reluctance to share this information that he either knew it to be untrue or didn't believe the excuse any more than she did.

'That being the case, did you not consider calling someone else? Your sister, for instance?'

He shook his head. 'Abbie was the one supposed to be going to Colchester in the first place, but Mum wasn't well, so she asked if I could go instead.'

'And what were you doing in Colchester?'

'Collecting a load of stuff from one of our supporters. Cat food, beds, towels, that kind of thing.'

'I presume you'd be able to give me the supporter's name and contact details?'

'If you want.'

Rebecca nodded. 'Speaking of names, do you know a Caleb Frey?'

'Frey?' Charlie repeated, appearing to consider the question, before shaking his head. 'No. Sorry.'

'Does he look familiar?' She asked, presenting Charlie with a photograph. Charlie took it and gave it his attention for a couple of seconds.

'I don't think so, but I'm not great with faces. Who is he, anyway? Or is he dead and all?'

'Why do you ask? Do you know something about it?'

Charlie swallowed. 'I wasn't –' he faltered. 'I didn't mean –' he trailed off.

'Can you answer the question, please?' Rebecca pressed, more for the record than anything. It had been clear from Charlie's expression in the wake of her response to his flippant remark that he hadn't been aware of Frey's death, much less been responsible for it.

'No,' he answered. 'I mean, I don't. Know anything. And I don't know why I make stupid comments that get me into trouble.' He sighed. 'One of these days maybe I'll learn to keep my mouth shut.'

Leighton had spent two days avoiding answering the front door or the phone, and when the bell rang shortly after midday he briefly considered putting off the inevitable for a little while longer. Reluctantly deciding against it, he pushed himself up off the sofa and made for the front door. The uniformed police officer outside greeted him with a familiar nod.

'Mr Campbell.'

'Hi.'

'Do you mind if I come in for a minute?'

Leighton stepped back to allow the man to pass before closing the door and turning to face him.

'How are you doing?' The uniform asked.

'Fine.'

'I think you know why I'm here. I need you to take me through what happened on Wednesday night. Shall we sit down?'

Leighton didn't move. He had spent the past forty-eight hours trying *not* to think about the evening that had culminated in his neighbour, Margaret, calling the police after Tom lost his temper in spectacular style. His greatest concern in the aftermath of the police dragging his brother away – perhaps because it offered a distraction from the bigger picture – had been the risk the shattered glass of the living room door posed to Pandora's paws. He had been physically unable to bend over to attend to it himself, and someone had obligingly cleared it up on condition he agreed to go to A and E. The news that he had two fractured ribs hadn't come as much of a surprise, and by the time, shortly after three, that the police had tried to take a statement, a combination of exhaustion and opioid medication had rendered him barely coherent. They had suggested leaving it until the following day, and Leighton had been too tired to argue that the exercise would be a waste of time. That conversation was now unavoidable.

'An argument got a little out of hand,' he said. 'I'm sorry you had to get involved.'

'A little out of hand is putting it mildly.'

Leighton didn't reply.

'Mr Campbell, I'm go–'

'Dr Campbell,' Leighton corrected, feeling irritated with himself even as he said it. He normally only set someone straight if they were being an arsehole and he wanted to make a point.

'Right,' the man nodded. 'Sorry. As I was saying, I need a detailed account from you of what happened.'

'There's no point. I don't want to press charges,' Leighton replied, wearily, knowing how frustrating it was for the police when people were unwilling to take action in cases involving domestic violence. He was well versed in all the arguments in favour of doing so, but giving evidence against his brother went against the ethos of the culture he'd grown up with, and, despite the circumstances, he knew it was something his father would never forgive. Although why he even cared when the man had rarely had a good word to say to him in thirty-five years, he had no idea. As far as his mother was concerned, it would be best all round if she never found out about Tom's latest arrest, and there would be no chance of keeping her in the dark if he was handed a custodial sentence.

'Dr Campbell, we will be pursuing a charge against your brother whether or not you make a statement. I realise it's difficult to file a report against a family member, but I would urge you to give the matter serious thought. This is far from your brother's first offence, and there's a real risk of something like this happening again, either to you or to someone else.'

Leighton was all too well aware of that, but the knowledge served only to heighten the contempt he felt for himself, it didn't change the fact he wasn't brave enough to deal with the fallout such action would inevitably beget.

'I can't.'

'Next time, someone could get killed.'

'I *can't*.'

The man sighed. 'All right, I'll leave you in peace,' he conceded, taking a step towards the door. 'But please do give your decision some more thought. And think about how you'll feel if Tom does serious harm to someone else.'

Leighton wanted to object to this blatant manipulation, but it wasn't as if the remark had really made much of an impact. The thought – and the accompanying sense of guilt – had already been foremost in his mind. He opted to say nothing, and after a moment the officer turned to go.

'If you change your mind, you know where we are.'

*****

Rebecca had a long wait to speak to Toby, who was apparently in the middle of a complex operation when she arrived at the practice, but dismissed the receptionist's suggestion that she return later. Considering the explanation given for the wait, she had been expecting the vet to emerge in surgical scrubs, and was surprised when he finally joined her in the waiting room clad in jeans and a grey polo shirt embroidered with the practice name and logo.

'Afternoon,' he greeted her, cordially, as she peeled herself off the chair she'd been sitting in for the best part of an hour. 'Sorry you've had to wait around.'

He didn't sound sorry at all. Rebecca asked whether there was somewhere they could speak privately and, with a rather pointed sigh, he showed her through to one of the consulting rooms, checking his watch as he closed the door.

'Could you run me through where you were and what you were doing last night and in the early hours of this morning, please?'

'I was here until about one a.m., and then I had to hightail it out to Essex to collect Charlie after he got stranded by a breakdown.'

'And what were you doing here?'

Toby appeared perplexed by the question. 'I live here.'

'I realise that,' Rebecca returned, shortly, wondering whether his misunderstanding of the question was genuine. Charlie had been easy enough to read, but Toby was inscrutable. 'What I'm asking is what you were doing with your time.'

'Oh, I see,' he nodded. 'Nothing very interesting, I'm afraid. I spent way longer than I intended on a tonne of paperwork – not my favourite part of the job – and after that I grabbed something to eat and watched a bit of TV.'

'Really?' Rebecca queried. 'So did Charlie get the wrong end of the stick? Because he told me you couldn't go straight to collect him when he called because you were dealing with an emergency.'

Toby affected a grimace. 'That might have been an exaggeration on my part,' he admitted. 'But I was about to get into the shower when he called, my dinner was in the oven and I'd not eaten since lunch time.'

'You call that an exaggeration, do you?' Rebecca mused, aloud. 'To me it sounds like a straight-up lie.'

'It's not as if he was standing in the dark in the middle of nowhere,' Toby defended himself, sidestepping Rebecca's real point. 'He was in Burger King.'

This was news to Rebecca. 'Whereabouts?'

'Feering. The guy who towed the van dropped him off at motorway services.' He stole a glance at his watch.

'I'm sorry, am I keeping you from something?' Rebecca snapped.

'I was supposed to make a house call twenty minutes ago, so since you ask, yes.'

'Well I'm afraid that'll have to wait a few more minutes,' she informed him, tartly. 'In the meantime, does the name Caleb Frey mean anything to you?'

There was a moment's silence before Toby shook his head. 'No.'

Rebecca drew Frey's photograph from her bag and handed it to Toby. 'Do you recognise him?'

'No.'

'Are you sure?'

He met her eyes as he returned the photograph. 'Yes.'

'That's strange, because when I spoke to your receptionist, she confirmed he – or at least his dog – is registered here.'

'A lot of people have pets registered here,' Toby replied, unconcernedly. 'That doesn't mean I know all of them. I'm not the only vet working here.'

'Perhaps not, but I'd have expected him to be on your radar. The RSPCA vet noted a number of injuries on Frey's dog consistent with its having been used in fighting. That seems like something you'd be all over.'

'As I said, I'm not the only vet working here. But if I do see something that causes me concern, I flag it with the RSPCA, and I would hope my colleagues do the same. I've no authority to do anything more.'

'You're happy to go on taking their money, though.'

'Are you seriously advocating leaving an animal to suffer for the sins of its owner?' Toby demanded, incredulously. 'Or do you live in the same never-never land as the people who think that because animal welfare is our first priority we should be working for free? Never mind the cost of things like drugs, equipment and utilities, or the fact we can't live on fresh air!'

‘Not so cool and collected in the face of provocation, after all,’ Rebecca remarked, with a lift of her eyebrows.

‘Well I’m glad you enjoyed having a chance to prove your point,’ he retorted. ‘Now if you’ll excuse me, I have more important things to do with my time.’ He turned and yanked the consulting room door open before stopping in his tracks and looking back around. ‘Frankly, I’d have thought the same would apply to you.’

Sunday 18 April

'DCI-and-mighty let you out for good behaviour?'

Rebecca turned from her perusal of the coffee shop's cake selection to find Jon grinning at her.

'Something like that,' she responded, rather flatly.

'Things not going well?'

'I've spent the past five hours going through boxes of our victim's paperwork with Cruella de Vil.'

Jon used his right hand to mime the action of shooting himself in the head before saying, 'If you're stuck with Miranda I think it's only fair I buy you some cake.'

'So it's not just me she has it in for,' Rebecca surmised from the fact reference to the literary villain was sufficient for Jon to guess who she meant.

'Nah, I think it's just about everyone. It's probably one of her appraisal objectives.'

Rebecca smiled.

'What about the paperchase? How's that going?'

'On forever,' she replied, ruefully. 'Frey had two rooms piled high with boxes and stacks of documents, magazines, photographs, junk mail, you name it – and none of it seemed to be in any kind of order. Sorting through it all and working out what was what took hours.'

'A bit like trying to find something on Leighton's desk, then,' Jon joked.

'Yeah, imagine his desk after twenty years.'

Jon laughed. 'We'll all have been buried by then.'

Rebecca sighed. 'I used to think the shift towards paperless billing and online banking would cut down the amount of junk people hang onto, but from our perspective I suspect it's going to make things worse. You don't have to find space to file stuff electronically, so there's no incentive to manage what you do or don't keep. The majority of us are going to end up digital hoarders by default.' She paused. 'Although, on the bright side, at least you can't get spiders and dead rodents buried in amongst emails.'

'Rodents?'

'A desiccated mouse.'

'Nice.'

'And for some reason he had five bank accounts. Who needs *five* bank accounts?'

'He probably just couldn't be bothered closing old ones,' Jon suggested.

'Probably,' Rebecca agreed. 'A couple of them have seen next to no activity for years.'

'And the others?'

'One of them has a series of big payments from the same source as a bunch of entries on Murphy's statements.'

'What is the source?'

'I don't know, yet, the reference doesn't mean anything to me. I'll find out when the banks open tomorrow. But Frey had several notebooks full of what look like lists of odds, and we've been told Murphy was a bookmaker at dog fights, so it could well relate to that.'

'I don't get it,' Jon responded, with a shake of his head. 'What do people get out of blood sports that they can't get from something humane?'

'I know,' Rebecca concurred. 'If a person kills an animal in cold blood it's a red flag they might go on to be a serial killer, but call it a sport and politicians will come out in favour.'

'I'm not sure politicians are the best comparator where psychopaths are concerned,' Jon returned.

'Yeah, maybe not,' she conceded. There was a pause before she went on, 'I know there's a financial incentive for the fight organisers, and clearly there's a lot of money to be made for those in a position to run a book, but I'm not sure what motivates the uninitiated punter to go to a fight in the first place, let alone pay for the privilege.'

'Status?' Jon ventured, after a moment's thought. 'If they or their mates have vicious dogs, I mean. If you run with that kind of crowd, you probably don't want to look like you can't hack it.'

Rebecca nodded contemplatively. 'I wonder whether the odds are better?' She mused, at length. 'It's not as if backstreet bookies will be paying tax.'

'I guess not.'

'And they might also offer credit.'

'No doubt with very unfriendly collection protocols for those who don't pay up when a bet doesn't go their way.'

'I don't imagine that's much of a deterrent for a gambling addict.'

Jon grunted and nodded in agreement before saying, 'If it's anything like horse racing, presumably there's also money to be made from breeding successful fighters. If you've a male, anyway.'

Rebecca frowned. 'Why only for males? Do the females not fight?'

'I don't know, but if you've a bitch I should think it'd be an expensive and involved process. For one thing, there's the risk of complications during pregnancy and labour, and then there's the cost of additional food during lactation, and when it comes to weaning the pups. Meanwhile, until they're old enough to go to their new homes, the little critters will be making endless mess and destroying everything around them.'

'True.'

'Whereas if you've got a male, all you have to do is turn up with your randy dog, let nature take its course and collect your stud fee. Job done. Money can't get much easier than that.'

Monday 19 April

The prevailing gloom made it feel more like seven p.m. than eight a.m. when Lawrence reached Birmingham, and a couple of scenes of crime officers were rigging up floodlights beyond the vehicles deliberately parked to obstruct the entrance to what had rather optimistically been labelled a mews. In reality, it was little more than an untarmacked alley running behind a parade of shops, a considerable proportion of its area occupied by lurid commercial rubbish bins. Lawrence presented his warrant card to the uniformed officer guarding the blue-and-white plastic cordon strung between a drainpipe and the wing mirror of a police car, and was halfway through asking who was managing the scene when he spotted a familiar figure a few yards beyond the tape.

Leighton turned in response to his name, then zigzagged towards the cordon across aluminium floor plates.

'All right?' He greeted, brightly, as he arrived on the other side of the tape.

'Wishing I was elsewhere,' Lawrence admitted.

'Aren't we all?'

Lawrence raised his eyebrows. 'I'm not sure how to take that.'

Leighton smiled mischievously. 'Wishing we were elsewhere, obviously.'

'Well let's see if we can make that happen. Where are you at?'

'Trying to preserve a swamp. We'll be lucky to get much at all from this scene.'

'Do you think it's Williams' doing?'

'Hard to say. If I had to put money on it, I'd say no, but the girl's his type and there are a number of basic hallmarks in common with his MO, so I can't discount it just yet.'

'So what makes you think no?'

'Too messy. There is evidence of strangulation, but there's also a wound to the back of her head, and at this stage I can't tell you which killed her. Her thorax has been slashed, but the cuts don't appear to follow any real pattern. It looks like a more frenzied attack than any of the others, but as we have no information on Williams' mental state I can't exclude the possibility he's taken things up a notch. Plus we have to factor in the location – outdoors he'd have less control over his environment, and I imagine a corresponding sense of urgency. And on the basis of past form, presumably if he did come to be grabbing a victim off the street, it was because his original plans fell through, which would also raise the pressure.'

'Most likely.'

'Hopefully I'll be able to give you more of an idea later on, when I've done the PM, but I suspect we'll have to wait for DNA results to rule Williams in or out. Assuming we get any at all. Everything's soaked.'

This was the last thing Lawrence wanted to hear. Until – or unless – they could dismiss the possibility, he would have to throw time and resources at a crime that probably had no relevance to his investigation. As if they didn't have enough to do already.

'Any idea who she is?' He asked, turning his thoughts to how they might narrow down the details of her last hours.

'Nope. No sign of any ID.'

'How about time of death?'

'Probably not before Saturday night is about as specific as I can be at this stage. She's dressed for a night out, so late Saturday or early Sunday seems likely. But that's obviously just conjecture.'

'Understood,' Lawrence nodded. 'If that is the case, we should be –'

'Have we considered the possibility Williams is working as a cab driver?' Leighton interjected. 'A lot of people chat to cabbies with little or no thought for the fact they don't know them from Adam. And if you're taking a cab home, you direct them straight to your front door. It would be easy enough to go back a day or two later on the pretext of something having been left in the car.'

'We've considered it,' Lawrence replied. 'But for us to establish that someone has used a given cab company – or even Uber – depends on factors such as their being the one who booked the car, or having paid by card. And although cabs are licensed within a specific area, they also travel between areas. We've taken it as far as we can, but it's impossible to conduct a truly exhaustive search.'

'Sorry,' the pathologist offered, ruefully. 'You don't need me teaching you how to suck eggs.'

Lawrence dismissed the apology with a shake of his head. 'Any ideas are more than welcome,' he responded. 'We've drawn blanks at every turn, and I've little doubt we're still missing something.' He sighed. 'And, as and when we work out what, I have a feeling it's going to seem so obvious we're going to be kicking ourselves that we didn't think of it before.'

'This is a fucking farce!' Roy Aitken objected, as Rebecca started the audio recorder and detailed the time and the names of those present in the interview room. 'I don't have time for this crap! My business don't run itself!'

Pete's eyebrows rose. 'Your launderette not self-service, then?'

'It's a pub, you twat!'

'Sorry, my bad,' Pete replied, with heavy sarcasm. 'I mistook these for laundry receipts,' he slapped a handful of pages down on the table and spread them out with a sweep of his hand. Green highlighter pen picked out entries on photocopied bank statements, sizeable payments made into the accounts of Spencer Murphy and Caleb Frey from the Griffin's business account.

'What the fuck you on about?'

'What are these payments for?'

'My business ain't none o' your business!'

'Wrong,' Pete informed him, shortly. 'And unless you want us to shut the place down until we've been through every receipt and accounted for every single fucking thing, right down to the last square of bog roll, you'll tell me what these transactions are!'

Several seconds passed in silence before Roy yielded. 'Just payment for some work about the place,' he answered, grudgingly.

'What kind of work?'

Roy shrugged. 'Decorating. DIY.'

'What you decorating with, gold leaf?' Pete exclaimed. 'These sums aren't exactly in keeping with a spot of Polyfilla and a lick of paint!'

Roy made no reply.

'I'll answer the question for you, shall I? You've been laundering the proceeds of illegal gambling, and no doubt taking a hefty cut for yourself!'

Roy shook his head.

'No? You got invoices for all these improvement works?' Pete gestured towards the pages on the table.

'Somewhere.'

'Somewhere *where*?'

'I dunno. I ain't the one does the accounts.'

'So who does?'

'The accountant,' Roy returned, derisively.

'If you want to make this difficult, I'm more than happy to go that route,' Pete retorted. 'But I'm not going to waste my time on your paperwork, that's a job for the boys in financial crime. What really interests me is how both bookmakers came to wind up dead in the space of a week. Care to shed any light on that?'

'I've no fucking clue about any of it.'

'Where were you on Friday night and early Saturday morning?'

'I was working 'til gone midnight. Then I went to bed.'

'Can anybody verify that?'

'Not after we closed up the bar.'

'Which was when?'

'Midnightish.'

'How about Sunday night a week ago?'

Roy appeared to think about this for a moment before saying, 'Same, give or take an hour or so.'

'And were you alone again after you closed up?'

'Aye. Naebody told me I was gonna need an alibi! An' if I were making as much profit as you seem to think, why would I even want them dead?'

'Anybody else on your DIY payroll?' Pete returned, shortly, without bothering to acknowledge Roy's question. 'Or any other payroll besides your bar and cleaning staff?'

'No.'

'Sure? We've applied to the courts for access to your bank statements, so it won't take us five minutes to check.'

'Perfectly fucking sure.'

'You didn't have any arrangements with a man called Fred Ratley?'

'Never even heard of him.'

'He didn't drink in your pub?'

'How the fuck should I know? I don't run passport checks!'

'Do you have a dog?'

'What?' Roy exclaimed, the change in direction apparently taking him by surprise. 'No. Bloody animals stink.'

'That doesn't stop you letting them into your pub.'

'Aye, well, I let people I wouldn't have in my home into the pub an' all.'

'Have you ever been to a fight?'

'I've watched a lot on Sky Sports.'

'Don't take the piss. You know full well that's not the kind of fight I'm talking about.'

'Do I?' Roy came back. 'You a mind-reader, then?'

'Have you ever been to a dog fight?' Pete enunciated, furiously.

'I wouldnae know where to start wi' finding one.'

'You're wasting my time, and if you carry on down that road I've no compunction about doing the same in return!' Pete spat. 'So if I were you, I'd stop pissing me about! Otherwise, I'll book you into one of our zero-star en suites for the night, with a view of the gutter and an aroma of stale sweat and piss! Comprendé?'

Rebecca had returned to her desk to find a note asking her to contact an RSPCA vet. Several phone calls later, she had managed to get hold of the woman in question, who revealed that the bruising to Frey's dog's flank indicated the animal had been darted. Moreover, the fact the location of the injection site was within centimetres of that documented for Murphy's dog suggested that the person responsible not only had a gun, but knew how to handle it. On top of that, dart guns were prohibited weapons that could be held only with an appropriate exemption of the Firearms Act. Rebecca's excitement at finding a familiar name in the records was dampened by Pete's demanding to know why she'd not looked into the matter before. This was swiftly followed by an order to bring the gun's owner in for questioning and organise a search warrant. Ninety minutes and one arrest later, they were back in the interview room.

'According to our records, you have a firearms licence and own a dart gun,' Pete began.

'Yes,' Toby confirmed.

'Given the stringent restrictions on ownership, you're presumably aware that there aren't many dart gun holders in London?'

'Presumably,' Toby retorted.

'Yes or no?' Pete demanded.

'Yes,' Toby replied, with affected weariness.

'When did you last use yours?'

'Without checking *my* records, I couldn't tell you. It's not a regular occurrence.'

'Are you not required to undertake regular practice?'

'I hardly think you brought me in here to discuss target practice.'

'You'd do well to cut the smart remarks and stick to answering my questions,' Pete warned him.

'Yeah?' Toby leaned back in his chair. 'What you going to do, charge me with impertinence?'

'If I could, it would be the least of your concerns! We've at least two homicides involving a dart gun, you've not been able to give us an alibi for either of the crimes, and we can connect you to both the victims! Do you know how many years you could be looking at for that?'

There was a pause as Toby apparently processed this information. 'None of that's really evidence, though, is it?' He concluded, eventually.

'We're working on that,' Pete replied, taking a handful of photographs from the file that lay in front of him. 'Starting with the contents of your gun cabinet.' He placed three pictures on the tabletop. 'And whether you can explain the discrepancy between the number of darts in your possession and the number detailed in your log book?'

For the first time since his arrest, Rebecca detected a flicker of concern in Toby's expression. 'I'm not aware of a discrepancy, but I suppose it's possible I miscounted something somewhere along the line.'

'You might get away with that defence for one dart,' Pete conceded. 'But four is quite a stretch.'

Toby swallowed. He didn't comment.

'Unless you suffer from some kind of numerical dyslexia?' Pete suggested, regarding him expectantly for a moment before concluding, facetiously, 'No, that wouldn't make for a very convincing defence either, would it? I can't see the Royal Vet College letting someone loose to prescribe drugs if they couldn't manage basic arithmetic.'

Toby cast his eyes down, looking as if he was trying to maintain an air of calm.

'Does anybody else have access to the gun?'

'No.'

'Right. I'll ask you again, then. When did you last use it?'

Toby lifted his gaze. 'I couldn't tell you,' he responded, impatience creeping into his tone.

'Interesting choice of words,' Pete observed. 'Not an unequivocal *I don't know*. I suppose you couldn't tell me where the missing darts are, either?'

'No, I couldn't.'

'Ok, this time I want a simple yes or no. Were you at the scene when Fred Ratley, Spencer Murphy or Caleb Frey were killed?'

Toby appeared to consider his answer, then said, 'I think I'd like to speak to a solicitor now.'

'Were you at the scene, yes or no?' Pete demanded.

'I said I'd like to speak to a solicitor,' Toby reiterated, coolly. 'And I believe you have to wait until I've done that before you can ask me anything further.' He tipped his head to one side before raising his eyebrows and adding, pointedly, 'Yes or no?'

Rebecca rang the doorbell of the small modern terraced house and stepped back. After the interview with Toby, Miranda had informed her that, in her absence, *some crazy bint* by the name of Isabel Harris had turned up demanding to speak to her. The name meant nothing to Rebecca, but a quick Google search identified Isabel as a senior veterinary nurse at Toby's practice, and less than an hour later Rebecca was standing on the woman's doorstep.

The flurry of barks that preceded the opening of the door was sufficient to tell Rebecca that the house had at least two canine inhabitants: one turned out to be a red setter, the other a stockier fawn-coloured dog Rebecca couldn't identify. The willowy twenty-something gripping their collars to keep them on her side of the threshold regarded Rebecca with a suspicious frown, tipping her head to one side as her thick, wavy red hair slid forwards, obscuring her vision. 'Yes?'

'Detective Sergeant Palmer,' Rebecca introduced herself over assorted barks and yelps, displaying her warrant card. 'I understand you wanted to speak to me. May I come in?'

Isabel looked less than thrilled by the request, but she pulled the dogs back to grant Rebecca entry, then turned to shepherd the animals into a room across the hallway. The volume dropped as she closed the door, carefully avoiding trapping a wagging tail, but the dogs' excitement over the arrival of an unfamiliar visitor didn't sound in any way diminished.

'You arrested Toby,' Isabel said, accusingly, as she turned back around, as if in so doing Rebecca had acted alone. 'You have to let him go. There is no way he was involved in killing anybody!'

'Do you know that for a fact?'

'I know *him*!'

'So that's a no,' Rebecca concluded, aloud. 'Tell me, if he wasn't responsible, why do you suppose he doesn't deny it?'

Isabel managed the first syllable of a response before apparently absorbing what Rebecca had said and stopping short. 'He what?' She exclaimed, after a moment's silence. There was a pause while she apparently considered this before she shook her head. 'You're lying,' she said, definitively.

'Why would I do that?'

Isabel threw her hands up in an exasperated *I don't know* gesture, raising her eyebrows for good measure.

'Do you think he might be trying to protect someone?'

'Like who?'

'I was hoping you might be able to tell me, you're the one who knows him.'

Isabel didn't seem to have an answer.

'Are you and he involved?'

'No!' Isabel returned, vehemently. 'For God's sake! He's my friend and I care about him! That doesn't mean we're screwing!' Then, apparently feeling the need to add something approaching evidence to her case, she added, angrily, 'I'm gay, ok? Does that clear that one up for you?'

'All right, there's no need to get so worked up,' Rebecca responded, guessing Isabel had probably been *worked up* ever since hearing the news. 'How about you take me through what you remember of the events surrounding the deaths and see whether you know anything that might help us get to the bottom of where Toby was or wasn't?'

Judging by her expression, this suggestion didn't do much to placate the other woman, but she grudgingly agreed and Rebecca asked what she could tell her about the preceding Friday night.

'I was here.'

'Alone?'

'No, my granddad was here, too.'

'Any idea what Toby was doing?'

Isabel shook her head.

'And how about Sunday the eleventh?'

'The eleventh?' Isabel echoed. 'I was at a Ruby wedding do, otherwise I would have been round at the –' she broke off abruptly. 'There is no way Toby was out doing anything that night! When I saw him next morning he could barely stand up!'

'Why not?'

'Food poisoning, I think. He said he'd been throwing up half the night.'

'You don't think it's possible that was his attempt to create an alibi?'

'He wasn't faking, if that's what you mean. He was in a really bad way. I would've called an ambulance if he'd've let me.'

'Was anyone else who'd been at the barbecue ill?'

Isabel considered this for a moment before saying, 'No. At least, Abbie wasn't. But she's vegan. Anyway, if he'd been making it up, why didn't he tell you?'

That was a good question. Rebecca was on the verge of asking another of her own when a crash came from the room containing the dogs. Isabel muttered something under her breath, then a grudging apology, before easing the door open and lunging to grab the two animals' collars as they came charging out. She half-walked, half-dragged them into the kitchen – presumably with the intention of taking them outside – and disappeared from view. Wondering what the source of the commotion had been, Rebecca stepped forwards and looked into what turned out to be a rather untidy sitting room. The cause of the crash was immediately clear: one, or both, of the dogs had knocked a side table over, and some now-unidentifiable items of crockery lay in smithereens on the floor. Feeling relieved she wouldn't be the one clearing that up, Rebecca turned back towards the hallway, stopping short in surprise as a cheery northern voice behind her greeted, ''Ey up me duck!'

Spinning around to find nobody there, it took her a moment to identify the speaker. Then she spotted a keen pair of eyes looking straight at her from across the room. Their owner was an African grey parrot.

Lawrence had returned from Birmingham for six to meet with Leighton for a preliminary report on the postmortem, but, as ever, the pathologist was running late, and it was getting on for seven by the time he emerged from the mortuary.

'Sorry, sorry,' he pre-empted, on catching sight of Lawrence. 'I'm not sure where today went. Can we do this in the kitchen? I'm in dire need of tea and biscuits.'

Lawrence nodded, and followed as his colleague headed down the corridor. 'Did the PM throw up any surprises?'

'Well, she was six weeks pregnant, but I don't imagine that's the sort of surprise you had in mind.'

'No,' Lawrence confirmed.

'Do we have any idea who she is yet?'

'Name's Donna Redmond. Her husband reported her missing yesterday morning – apparently she went out with friends on Saturday night and didn't come home.'

'Have you spoken to her friends?' Leighton asked, pushing open the door to the kitchen.

'They say she got a taxi shortly after midnight. We're still trying to track down the driver.'

Leighton nodded.

'Any advance on the odds of Williams being involved?'

'I'd stake a macchiato and a jam doughnut on not,' the pathologist responded, checking the water level in the kettle before turning towards the sink.

'Well that's confidence for you,' Lawrence joked.

'Doughnuts are not a laughing matter,' Leighton replied, in mock seriousness. He filled the kettle, then added, as he switched it on, 'But she didn't die in the alley where her body was found. Someone just made a good job of making it look that way.' He reached for a packet of chocolate Hobnobs, turning around and leaning against the worktop. 'And I think Williams is much too careful to put himself in a position where he'd have to dispose of a body.'

Lawrence nodded in agreement. 'Any idea how long she'd been dead before she was dumped there?'

Leighton began uncoiling the twisted cellophane at the open end of the biscuit packet, saying, 'It's hard to be precise, but not long. An hour or two, maybe.'

'Had she been raped?'

'She'd had intercourse in the hours before she died, but I can't say whether it was against her will. The defensive injuries could all be attributed to the struggle when she was strangled.'

'Is that what killed her?'

'Yep.' He offered Lawrence the biscuits.

Lawrence declined with a shake of his head, asking, 'Anything else?'

'I think it's very unlikely she died in a car.'

'Meaning the cab driver probably isn't our perpetrator,' Lawrence concluded.

'No. But he may be an important witness. We need to know where she went after she left her friends,' Leighton fished three biscuits from the packet. 'If it was home, I'd guess you need to look at the husband.'

'The oldest story in the book.'

'Uh-huh.'

Lawrence considered what his colleague had shared so far before saying, 'So if she didn't die in the alley or the car, is there anything that might give us a clue to where she did die?'

'Very little. And what I can give you is really only supposition. But I don't think the head wound was inflicted intentionally – it made quite a mess, but it's a relatively minor injury. I would guess she was slammed against a wall and strangled, and that there was something like a hook or a bent nail protruding from the wall.'

'The sort of scenario that smacks of a domestic dispute.'

The pathologist nodded.

'Right. I need to get a warrant to search the Redmonds' home for fixtures and fittings that might fit the bill, then,' Lawrence concluded. 'Which should at least be a fairly straightforward job.' He glanced at his watch. 'And if I can get hold of a magistrate and a SOC team, we might even get it done tonight.'

Charlie Watts had clearly played no part in Caleb Frey's death, and from his reaction to the news Rebecca very much doubted he had been a party to a conspiracy to kill any of the three dog-attack victims. What Toby's involvement might or might not be remained an open question; meanwhile Rebecca's visit to Isabel's home had brought to mind another possibility. The talkative parrot's red tail was a plausible source of the feather found in Frey's mouth, and where animal cruelty was concerned Rebecca could easily imagine Isabel taking the law into her own hands. If she had done as much, she couldn't have acted alone: her alibi for the time of Spencer Murphy's death was solid. And Toby wasn't the only individual who might have served as an accomplice. So Rebecca found herself revisiting the animal shelter, and waiting in a living room that contained more cats than chairs. Loath to get myriad shades of fur on her clothes, she chose to remain standing, and spent the time it took for Abigail to join her studying the plethora of framed photographs placed cheek by jowl on the walls.

'Hiya,' Abigail greeted, amicably, as she slipped in the door and scooped up a cat trying to sneak out the other way. 'Minnie said you wanted to ask me something?'

'Yes,' Rebecca confirmed. 'First of all, I'd like you tell me where you were on the night of the thirty-first of March.'

'Where *I* was?' Abigail exclaimed, seemingly surprised by the question. 'Here, I expect. I usually am. Mum often needs my help in the night, so I can't go far.'

'Could you give me something more definitive?'

A couple of seconds passed while Abigail apparently thought this over. 'What day of the week was it?' She asked, planting the cat on the sofa.

'Wednesday. If it helps, Toby told me it was his father's birthday.'

'Oh – yes – I think Izzy was here that night.'

'Overnight?'

'Yes.'

'Would your mother and Charlie be able to confirm that?'

'I should think so. Our relationship isn't a secret.'

'And how about Sunday the eleventh? Where were you that night?'

Abigail hesitated before admitting, 'I was with Toby.'

'All night?'

She nodded.

'In his bed?'

Her cheeks colouring, Abigail nodded again.

'He told us nobody could vouch for his whereabouts that night.'

'Yeah, well, he's hardly going to advertise it, I'm in a relationship with one of his colleagues!'

'Are you saying he'd rather risk prison than admit to an affair? That seems unlikely in the extreme.'

'No, I didn't mean –' she stopped. 'I guess he's hoping it won't come to that.'

Rebecca nodded thoughtfully. 'It's not the first time you and he have been involved, is it?'

Abigail frowned. 'Sorry?'

'You were married,' Rebecca indicated the wedding photograph among the many on display, wondering why it had been left out.

'Oh,' Abigail realised, aloud. 'Yes.'

'Who ended it?'

Rebecca had expected Abigail to object to the question, but to her surprise, the woman replied, unconcernedly, 'I did. I was too young. I didn't know what I wanted.'

'It doesn't seem as if anything's changed there,' Rebecca remarked, bluntly.

'I'm watching my mother die, and he's been there for me,' Abigail snapped, in return. 'It wasn't my intention for things to go the way they have.'

'Perhaps you could give me your account of that night?' Rebecca suggested, returning to her original line of questioning. 'The eleventh?'

Abigail nodded. 'We had a barbecue,' she began. 'Me, Toby and Charlie. On Sunday afternoon. I pretended to fall asleep so Charlie would go home without me. He left about half nine.' She paused. 'We made love on the sofa, and then had a couple of drinks before bed. We were in bed by twelve, and I had to be off at six to get home for Mum.'

'You said before that she often needs your help during the night. Did you conveniently forget that?'

Abigail sighed. 'I know,' she admitted. 'I shouldn't have stayed out. But Chas was here, it wasn't as if she was alone.'

'Was Toby awake when you left?'

She nodded. 'I woke him up, actually. I thought we could –' she averted her eyes, looking mildly abashed. 'Before I left.' She paused. 'But he was feeling a bit rough.'

'More than a bit, according to Isabel,' Rebecca observed. 'She told me that when she arrived for work that morning he was so poorly she wanted to call an ambulance. Did she mention that to you?'

Abigail nodded.

'But clearly you weren't particularly concerned, because you left him and went home.'

'He said he was ok,' Abigail defended herself. 'Just a bit of a dodgy stomach.' She shrugged. 'Maybe he played it down because he didn't want me to be there when Izzy arrived.'

'And where were you last Friday night?'

'I was here, with Mum. I told you that before. When you were here on Saturday.'

'How about Isabel? Do you know where she was?'

'At home.'

'Are you sure about that?'

'I'm sure that's what she told me,' Abigail returned, bending to stroke a lithe white cat that had wrapped itself around her ankles. 'But I can't be absolutely sure about where she was, I wasn't tracking her movements.' She straightened up. 'And I'm hardly the only person in the world with secrets.'

Tuesday 20 April

'I just tried to call you.'

Leighton turned from the doorway of Lawrence's empty office looking tired and harassed. Folding his forearms on the filing cabinet overlooking Rebecca's desk, he lifted his eyebrows expectantly. 'Uh-huh?'

'If you used sleeping pills – or sedatives – or something along those lines to knock someone out, could that make them sick?'

'Of course it could,' Leighton returned, sounding surprised she needed to ask. 'Most drugs have the potential to make you sick if they're not used responsibly, or if you're sensitive to one of the ingredients.'

'Sorry, I get that,' Rebecca replied, with a brief shake of her head. 'I meant literally. Could they make you throw up?'

'It's not a common side effect, but they can. Particularly if you're mixing something like benzos with booze. A drug like lorazepam can fast-track a handful of drinks to alcohol poisoning. It's a very dangerous combination and it kills a lot of people.'

'How easy would it be to get hold of those kinds of drugs?'

'Too easy. If you said the right things you could probably get a short course from your GP. Or you could help yourself to a relative's. Failing that, you can buy all sorts online.'

'Would a vet have access to those kinds of drugs?'

'Some. Offhand I couldn't tell you which ones. Do you want me to find out?'

'No, don't worry, I think you've covered enough ground for me. Thanks.'

'No problem,' he responded with a rather half-hearted smile. Rebecca was about to ask if he was all right when her superior strode into view.

'Dr Campbell,' he greeted, coolly. 'Something wrong with your watch?'

'No, I jus–'

'And was there anything unclear about the words *I want everyone in the incident room at eight-thirty*?'

'No, I'm sorry, I –'

'I don't want to hear it! It's high time you learned to behave like a responsible adult! You're not a student and this morning's meeting wasn't an early morning lecture you could get away with cutting!'

'I didn't –'

'I've said I don't want to hear it! What I *do* want to know is whether you've got any of the test results back yet!'

Leighton shook his head. 'No. But I wasn't taking the piss, I did have every intention of getting here for half eight.'

'So what happened?'

'I couldn't find my car keys.'

'You couldn't find your car keys?' Lawrence echoed, incredulously. 'And you expect me to believe it took you –' he consulted his watch. '*Forty-five minutes* to find them?'

'No, that's just where the domino effect of cock-ups began,' Leighton replied, his voice sounding strained. 'I am genuinely sorry, I have had a really bad morning. Ok?'

'No, Leighton, it's not ok! At the very least you could have let me know! You've got a phone, haven't you?'

'I couldn't find that either, I think I left it in the office last night.'

'So you don't actually *know* whether or not the lab has come back to you!' Lawrence surmised. 'Well you might have had the guts to say as much!'

'That wasn't what I –'

'I have had it with chasing around after you! It was bad enough when you were doing a bloody good job, but these days you barely seem to be managing an adequate one!'

'Yes, all right, I'm sorry –'

'Enough with the bloody apologies!' Lawrence exploded. 'I don't want you to be sorry, I want you to show some respect and consideration for the rest of us, and register that our time is just as valuable as yours! Now get out of here and come back when you've something useful to contribute!'

Leighton didn't argue, he simply turned and headed for the corridor. Feeling acutely uncomfortable, Rebecca kept her eyes fixed on her computer screen. She wondered how many of her colleagues were doing the same.

'Why the hell does he do that?' Lawrence demanded, looking around at Rebecca as the pathologist disappeared from view.

She raised her eyes from her laptop. 'I don't think he means you any disrespect,' she ventured, cautiously. 'I think time just gets away from him.'

Lawrence shook his head dismissively. 'That's not what I meant,' he replied. 'Although I'm not sure I agree with you. But he pushes his luck time and again, and then when I lose my temper he jumps half out of his skin and looks at me like I'm some sort of monster who's about to batter him with the nearest blunt instrument!'

Rebecca hesitated before saying, 'I don't think it's any reflection on you.'

Lawrence regarded her closely. 'You say that as if it is a reflection on someone.'

Clearly reluctant to give a definitive answer, Rebecca half-shrugged – a response Lawrence knew her well enough to interpret. Indicating with a small hand gesture his desire for her to follow him, he stepped into his office, and, as she joined him, closed the door.

'Do you think you might fill me in?' He asked, taking a tone that he hoped conveyed it wasn't really a request.

Rebecca swallowed. 'I'm not sure it's my place,' she responded, at length.

'Not your place,' Lawrence summarised, leaning against his desk. 'In the same way it wasn't your place to report his being in possession of a controlled drug?'

'No. I just –'

'Does it have anything to do with Pete?'

Rebecca looked surprised by the question. 'No, I don't think so.'

'Are you sure? It wouldn't be the first time he'd used physical intimidation.'

'I don't think it has anything to do with anyone here.'

'Ok,' Lawrence conceded. 'What has he got himself into, then?'

'I didn't mean –' she stopped. 'I don't think it's anything in particular, I think it's –' she hesitated, seemingly searching for the word she wanted, before finishing, 'I think it's a learned response.'

'Learned?' Lawrence echoed, a moment passing before he guessed what she meant. 'What, at home?'

She nodded.

Lawrence absorbed this information. He wasn't sure what to say. The revelation certainly explained a few things – Leighton's preoccupation with Evan among them – but, at the same time, it raised several other questions. Thinking aloud, he said, 'Presumably that's not all there is to it, though?'

'All?' Rebecca echoed, in disbelief. 'Do you –'

'I'm sorry, that was a poor choice of words,' Lawrence stopped her. 'I'm not trivialising the situation. But he doesn't live at home, and he hasn't always been so jumpy. So it stands to reason there must be something else going on.'

Rebecca didn't reply.

'And it's hardly as if he's been going out of his way to avoid conflict lately, is it? Hurling insults at Pete was asking for trouble. Why push his luck so far if he can't handle the reaction?'

'What, so it's his fault?'

'No –' Lawrence sighed. 'No, of course not. I'm just trying to make sense of all this. Do you have any idea why he's so on edge?'

'No.'

'None at all?'

She shook her head.

'Ok,' Lawrence concluded, moving to sit down. 'I'll let you get on.'

Rebecca turned to go, then paused, her hand on the door handle. Looking back around, she said, haltingly, 'You won't – I mean – could you not –'

'I won't mention this conversation to Leighton,' Lawrence put in, guessing what she was trying to say.

'Thanks,' she nodded.

'And I will try to bear it in mind going forwards. I don't want him to feel intimidated, whatever that stems from.' Lawrence reached for a pen. 'But he could make life a lot easier for himself, too.'

Shortly before midday, Rebecca sat down to re-interview Toby, who treated proceedings with the same affected weariness as on the previous afternoon. Rebecca repeated the basic questions regarding his whereabouts late on Friday night, and the Sunday night before that. When Toby reiterated his claim that he had been home alone, Rebecca lifted her eyebrows.

'Really?' She queried. 'Abigail Watts told me she was with you on Sunday night. Is she mistaken?'

Toby hesitated. 'No,' he admitted, after a moment.

'And why did you keep that to yourself?'

'Why do you think?' Toby retorted.

'Given that I don't believe you'd risk going to prison simply to spare Isabel's feelings, I did think you and Abigail might have acted together to kill Spencer Murphy,' Rebecca replied. 'That is, until I had a chat with a few of your colleagues earlier today.'

Toby's eyebrows contracted slightly, but otherwise he didn't respond.

'When Isabel told me yesterday why she didn't believe you could have been responsible for Mr Murphy's death, I thought it was a misguided attempt to provide you with something approaching an alibi. But now I'm not so sure it was, because everyone who saw you last Monday morning says the same thing. It's clear you were very unwell, which doesn't really square with your running around overseeing homicide by dog a few hours earlier, does it?'

Toby regarded her impassively from across the table, saying nothing.

'Why did you not mention that?' Rebecca asked. 'Why allow us to believe you were responsible for a crime you didn't commit?'

There was a long pause before he said, 'It is my responsibility. The gun. There shouldn't be any circumstances where someone else would be able to get hold of it.'

'No, there shouldn't, but I very much doubt you kept quiet solely because you believed your gun had played a part in proceedings. So how about you tell me who else might have had access to it?'

'I couldn't say.'

'Now that's just not true, is it?' Rebecca countered. 'You know who has access to your office – presumably all the practice staff, for starters – and to your home, and you know where you keep the key to the gun cabinet. Where is that, by the way?'

'In the safe.'

'And who else knows the code?'

'Nobody.'

'Who might have guessed it?'

'How am I supposed to know?' Toby exclaimed.

'In most cases people use a memorable number, so I imagine anyone who knows you well would stand a reasonable chance of working it out.'

Toby reverted to silence.

'Not that I need you to tell me,' Rebecca continued, after a few seconds. 'I hope she appreciates it. It must take a special kind of devotion to put yourself on the line for someone who inadvertently almost added you to the body count.'

'You've lost me.'

'I very much doubt that. I'm sure you'd already added two and two by the time your gun came into the equation.' Rebecca paused. 'Abigail's account not only serves to give you an alibi, it provides one for her, as well. Or it would do, if you'd not been unconscious. Does she realise her little drug cocktail nearly killed you?'

'It's not Abbie's fault I had a few too many.'

'A few too many,' Rebecca echoed. 'Well it must have been quite a few, because from what your colleagues have said it sounded more like alcohol poisoning than a hangover. In fact, one of them even said if she didn't know you better, that's what she would have put it down to. And I can't see a moderate social drinker losing track quite that spectacularly on a quiet Sunday evening.'

'We all make mistakes.'

'That's true. Yours was getting back into bed with Abigail, so to speak. She's quite the master of manipulation, isn't she? She exploited the feelings she knew you still had for her to get into your gun cabinet and your pharmacy.'

'You know nothing about Abbie.'

'I know she was prepared to drug you. And that she didn't say a word when we pulled you in. Isabel was the one who came running to your aid, which is rather ironic, isn't it? Abigail only spoke up when she herself needed an alibi.'

Toby didn't reply, and Rebecca gave him some time to think about what she'd just said before adding, 'I'm guessing you've served your purpose.'

Toby regarded her in silence for a time before saying, 'Well, like I said, you don't know Abbie. And you don't know me.' He folded his arms emphatically. 'The day we first got *back into bed*, as you put it, she found out her mother has motor neuron disease. She came to me for support, and I ended up taking her to bed.' He paused. 'So if anyone was in the wrong, I'd say it was me.'

'Watch it, you might actually be getting some work done there.'

Leighton glanced up from his laptop. He had the kind of hangover that comes of attempting to compensate for insufficient sleep with an excess of caffeine and sugar, and had been rubbing his forehead as he tried to make sense of the information on the screen. He had slept badly, having inadvertently run out of painkillers, and had either forgotten to set his alarm or slept through it. He had stumbled out of the bedroom with scarcely ten minutes to spare before he needed to leave the house to find he wasn't alone: Tom had let himself in and was sitting on the sofa. When his brother hadn't turned up after first being released on bail, Leighton had wrongly assumed he wouldn't have to face Tom any time soon. He doubted he would have been in the mood to hear a jumble of apologies and excuses at the best of times; in the circumstances he had resorted to threatening to report his brother for breaching his bail conditions if Tom was still there by the time he was done in the shower before slamming the bathroom door shut behind himself.

Emerging a few minutes later, he had been more than a little relieved to find Tom had disappeared. The icing on the cake of a hellish start to the day had been stepping in a pool of cold cat sick while hunting for his car keys. Things hadn't improved much since, and the last thing he needed on top of it all was snide comments from Roddy. He opened his mouth to reply, but Roddy beat him to it, saying, in a different tone, 'Are you all right?'

'Fine, ta.'

'You don't look it.'

'I'm tired, ok?' He returned, rather more sharply than was justified.

'Sorry I asked,' his colleague snapped, pulling the chair out from his desk and sitting down.

Leighton sighed. 'No, I'm sorry,' he relented, resting an elbow on the arm of his chair and propping his head up with his hand. 'I've barely slept in about three days and I'm having a really shitty day.'

'If you're feeling bad, then go home. I can pick something up if it would help. What is it you're doing?'

Leighton managed a smile, thinking it was a shame his colleague didn't drop the sarcasm more often. But then maybe Roddy felt the same way about Leighton's jokes. Either way, there was no way he would be willing to take over the current focus of Leighton's attention once he knew what it was.

'I'm trying to work out whether someone's fucking with an investigation, or just with me.'

Roddy's eyebrows rose. 'What's the investigation?'

'O'Leary.'

'Oh for crying out loud, are you *trying* to get sacked?'

'I swear it's stalking me. Every time I try to put it out of my mind, something new crops up to bug me.'

Roddy sighed pointedly. 'So what's bugging you now?'

'You know those soil tests I couldn't find? When I asked Clint to double-check his records a couple of weeks back he turned up nothing either, but he's just come across a misfiled lab book with a bunch of notes relating to the tests. So we did run them.'

'And what did they show?'

'I don't know, what he's got predates the results. But what most concerns me is the fact the whole trail has disappeared almost without trace.'

'Paranoid much?' Roddy responded, sceptically. 'It's more likely to be human error than a conspiracy.'

'Yeah, but it's not the first thing that's gone AWOL lately. What I don't know is whether someone's expressly interfering with evidence, or just trying to make me look like an idiot.'

'Well what else are you missing?'

'I think one of the samples might have been switched, and a bunch of stuff from another investigation has vanished into thin air.'

'Not the Stratford one?'

'No. I think that link was a red herring, anyway. Those killings converge on the law of retaliation. O'Leary may well have known Ratley – at least in passing – but the MO was completely different.'

'I don't recall us ever reaching a conclusion on O'Leary's cause of death.'

'We didn't,' Leighton returned, with a brief lift of his eyebrows.

Roddy raised his in turn. 'Interesting. So how did he die?'

'Ah, that would be telling.'

'Can you prove it?'

'I think so. Assuming the evidence doesn't follow the trend and go walkabout before I get my ducks in a row.'

'Have you got new evidence?' Roddy exclaimed.

'Of sorts,' Leighton confirmed, rubbing his eyes.

'All the same, maybe you should call it a day for now?'

'I'm all right. I just need to take a break,' he lifted his wallet from the desk. 'Do you want anything from outside?'

'Where are you going? If it's for coffee I'll join you.'

'French coffee, maybe,' Leighton returned, with a half-hearted smile.

There was a brief pause before Roddy shook his head slightly and reached for his jacket. 'The Ship it is, then.'

This was far from the reaction Leighton had expected: he could count the number of times Roddy had joined in a lunchtime pub trip on one hand. Given that he didn't drink and wasn't the most sociable of people, it probably didn't hold much appeal. His motivation became clear moments later when he added, 'You can fill me in on what it was we missed last year.'

'Just give me one minute,' Leighton replied, calling a number up on his desktop phone. 'If someone can make a set of tests disappear, they can presumably mess with the back-up samples, as well.'

'Sounds a safe bet,' Roddy agreed, leaning to look at the phone's display. 'Although I'm not sure what Clint can do about it.'

'He can check out the additional samples I lined up before the whole thing got shut down,' Leighton answered, raising the handset to his ear. 'I still have them in the storeroom. Maybe they can tell us why someone's so keen for evidence to disappear.'

Having released Toby from custody, Rebecca had driven over to the rescue centre, intending to take Abigail in for questioning. On arrival, however, she was received by a volunteer, who went to look for Abigail only to return alone, bearing the news that Ingrid Watts was keen to have a word. Curious, Rebecca consented to the request, and the volunteer led her through the kitchen and conservatory to the office.

Ingrid looked up as Rebecca entered, greeting her with a surprisingly relaxed smile. 'Good afternoon. Would you like a drink?'

Rebecca demurred, taking the same seat she had occupied on her first visit, and shrugging off her jacket. Setting her handbag down on the floor, she regarded Ingrid expectantly. 'You wanted to speak to me?'

Ingrid nodded, sliding open one of the desk drawers and pulling out a handful of thick brown envelopes before leaning across the desk to pass one of them to Rebecca. Rebecca guessed its likely contents from the feel of the package, and looked inside to find she was right: the envelope held about a dozen photographs. She drew them out to find what she could only assume was a snapshot of a dog fight, the two animals at its centre a blur of movement. The second image was a grainy close-up of one of the spectators gathered around the low wooden walls of the makeshift arena, and, despite its low resolution, Rebecca immediately identified the man as Spencer Murphy. The series of graphic pictures that followed documented the battle between the dogs, their injuries after the bout and, finally, Murphy dragging one of the creatures away. The sight of the animal with half a leg torn off left Rebecca struggling with how to respond. She drew a deep breath before raising her eyes to meet Ingrid's, hoping the other woman would say something to break the silence.

She didn't. After holding Rebecca's gaze for a second, she simply proffered another envelope. The contents came as no surprise: the crowd, the dogs and the series' main subject – Caleb Frey – were different, but the theme remained the same. As Ingrid handed over the third envelope, Rebecca's mind turned to the fact that the number of envelopes outweighed the number of homicides under investigation, and the possibility Connall O'Leary might be among the individuals pictured. Identifying the subject of the latest selection within a couple of images as Fred Ratley, Rebecca quickly flicked through the remaining pictures, her mind already focused on what the next batch might contain.

Resisting the urge to sigh in response to Ingrid's drip-feed approach, she tipped out the contents of the fourth envelope. Having expected more of the same, the scene in the first photograph took her by surprise – in terms of not only its content, but also its familiarity. A similar shot lay on her desk in the office, among the plethora of pictures gathered at a crime scene.

'Are those going to be along the same lines as these?' Rebecca asked, nodding towards the remaining envelopes in Ingrid's hand and holding up a picture of Ratley's lifeless body.

'Essentially.'

'Perhaps we could cut to the matter of who took them?'

'The fight pictures are a friend's work. They're stills of covert film footage I asked him to gather.' Ingrid leaned to set the final two envelopes on Rebecca's side of the desk. 'I took the rest.'

'Right,' Rebecca responded, sceptically. 'And are you going to tell me you were responsible for this man's death, as well?'

'In a manner of speaking. Although the teeth marks aren't mine.'

Rebecca lifted her eyebrows and shook her head in an expression of disbelief. 'Unless you want to be charged with wasting police time, I'd advise you to stick to the facts.'

'Those are the facts.'

Rebecca didn't immediately reply, trying to decide how to approach the situation. Eventually, she opted for, 'Who helped you?'

'Hercules,' Ingrid replied, presenting Rebecca with a photograph of a surprisingly demure-looking brown and white dog that Rebecca tentatively identified as some sort of bull terrier.

'Hercules and who else? Your daughter?'

'Nobody.'

'Do you think you might explain how you managed to access and navigate three secure and fairly inaccessible back gardens in a wheelchair?'

'I didn't,' Ingrid responded, rather confusingly. There was a pause before she added, with a wry half smile, 'Do it in the chair, that is.'

'No comment.'

Jamie resisted the desire to roll his eyes in exasperation. They'd been in an interview room with David Jones for almost a quarter of an hour, and so far he'd given the same answer to every question. The practice was frustrating enough when you suspected someone *had* committed the offence under investigation, but even more so when you simply wanted to rule them *out* of the running. And, as dislikeable as the man was, Jamie didn't believe he'd been responsible for Coralie Perrot's demise, and he doubted his superior really thought so, either.

'All right, we'll leave it there,' Lawrence concluded, wearily. 'I was under the impression you cared about Coralie, but clearly we were misinformed. And if you're not interested in helping us to catch her killer, then I've no reason to –'

'*Killer*?' David exclaimed. 'You never said –' he stopped abruptly.

'Well we're hardly in the business of investigating deaths by natural causes, Mr Jones.'

'No, but –' he swallowed. 'What happened?'

'Perhaps if you try answering a few of our questions, I might fill you in.' Lawrence returned. 'Starting with when you last saw Coralie.'

The man thought this over before saying, 'It was in March. I don't remember when, exactly.'

'Try.'

'Before Easter,' he offered, after a long pause.

'What does that mean?' Lawrence pressed. 'In the days leading up to Easter, or at some stage between the beginning of March and the Easter weekend?'

'A few days before.'

'Right. Where was that?'

'In the street.'

'Are you purposefully wasting my time, or just trying to skirt around the fact you were loitering near Coralie's flat in the hope of seeing her?' Lawrence asked, bluntly. 'Because if so, you're wasting your own time. She's dead. She can't make a complaint against you now.'

David sighed.

'So. Which street did you see her in?'

'Fernley Close,' he admitted, confirming Lawrence's hunch.

'Did you speak to her?'

'No.'

'Did she see you?'

'No,' David repeated, his voice barely audible.

'And how long were you there?'

'I don't know. A while.'

Jamie half expected Lawrence to push for a more specific timeline, but he didn't, instead asking when David had last been in Fernley Close.

David's eyebrows crinkled in suspicion. 'You already asked me that.'

'No, I asked when you last saw Coralie,' Lawrence replied. 'That wasn't necessarily the last time you were there.'

'Oh. It was.'

'Are you sure about that?'

'Yes.'

'But it wasn't a one-off, was it?'

The man shrugged.

'I'll take that to be a no,' Lawrence went on. 'So, on your visits to watch Coralie and her home, did you notice anybody else hanging around the area?'

'Depends what you mean by hanging around.'

'Any form of hanging around,' Lawrence returned, shortly, his tone betraying the fact he was struggling to keep a lid on his temper.

'There were a couple of guys doing some work on the road,' David revealed. 'Or at least, that's what it looked like they were supposed to be doing. But they weren't really doing much on either of the days I saw them there.'

'What made you think that's what they were supposed to be doing, then?'

'There were cones out, and those red and white plastic barriers. And they had on reflective vests and hard hats.'

'Was there anything printed on the vests?'

David thought this over for a moment before shaking his head. 'I don't remember.'

'And could you describe the men?'

'Not really. They were white. Twenties or thirties, I guess.' He shrugged.

'Anything else?'

'No. Sorry.'

Jamie drew an exasperated emoji in his notebook, despite the fact the paucity of information was unlikely to pose any real problem. It shouldn't be difficult to track the men down through the local council. If he could get hold of the right person by the end of the day, they might even be able to identify and interview the two men before returning to London. Assuming the individuals in question were genuine maintenance workers. In the unlikely event that they weren't, Jamie doubted their presence in Fernley Close would have been in any way connected to Coralie's death – sadistic sexual crimes were almost exclusively the preserve of lone psychopaths. There was certainly less chance of two perpetrators being involved than of Williams having found employment in road maintenance, although even the latter possibility struck Jamie as highly unlikely. Individuals working on the roads and pavements were, by the very nature of the job, conspicuous, and a serial killer needed to blend in, not stand out. The best they could hope for, Jamie suspected, was that one of the men might prove to be a valuable witness.

*****

'I hope you've more for me than overtime forms,' Pete remarked, as Rebecca stepped into his office, clutching a handful of papers.

She nodded. 'A confession. Well, of sorts.'

'Of sorts?' Pete echoed, directing her to sit with a singular hand gesture.

'The woman making the confession has motor neuron disease,' Rebecca began, perching on the nearest chair. 'She uses a wheelchair, but says she's not yet unable to walk, it's just that it can be difficult. Thus, she claims, she was perfectly capable of darting resident dogs, getting herself into our victims' gardens, temporarily incapacitating them with a stun gun, shoving a cloth into their mouths to shut them up and setting a very aggressive pit bull on them. All without any assistance.'

Pete considered this for a moment before saying, 'I presume you've checked what the medical perspective is on the likelihood of that?'

'Unlikely, but not impossible. Apparently the effects of motor neuron disease vary hugely from person to person, as does the rate of progression, so there's little chance of anyone being able to definitively disprove what she's saying. Particularly after the event.'

'Including operating a dart gun? Does she even have the relevant training?'

'She says she learned to shoot as a child, growing up on a farm. And that she'd be happy to demonstrate her gunmanship if we have any doubts.'

'Unless we've a queue of suspects who are adept at handling a gun, I'm inclined to believe she *was* involved,' Pete remarked, bluntly.

'It's not that I don't think she was involved,' Rebecca replied. 'She was clearly complicit in the killings – she may even have been the driving force – I just don't believe she acted alone.'

'Who's your money on for her accomplice?'

'Her daughter, Abigail. But we've no actual evidence, and technically she has alibis for at least two of the crimes.'

'Technically? What does that mean?'

'Well, both crimes occurred in the small hours, and on each occasion she was sharing a bed with someone who swears she was with them. I suspect she drugged her respective bedfellows to give her the opportunity to come and go unnoticed – but again, I've no evidence.'

'Then what's your theory based on?'

'She spent one of the nights with Toby Reynolds – who turns out to be her ex-husband – and, according to his colleagues, he was violently ill the following morning. Leighton said something like lorazepam could have that kind of effect. I'm guessing Toby came to the same conclusion, and that's why he didn't deny responsibility for the crimes.'

'It doesn't sound as if there's much ex about their relationship,' Pete observed.

'No,' Rebecca agreed. 'Although who knows whether –'

Pete's desktop phone interrupted, and he answered with an impatient, 'Yes?' After a few seconds, he frowned and said, 'What?' During the pause that followed, his expression grew darker. 'No. No, it isn't ... well, you can tell her I'm sorry about that, but it's not happening. And if you see Dr Campbell, you can tell him he's a dead man when I catch up with him!' He returned the handset to its cradle without bidding the caller goodbye, then looked back to Rebecca. 'Who was she with on the other occasion?'

The abrupt return to their conversation took Rebecca by surprise, and a couple of seconds passed before she managed to focus and answer the question. 'Her girlfriend. Name of Isabel Harris.'

'Girlfriend? You mean she's a dyke?'

'They're in a relationship.'

'Presumably the girlfriend doesn't know her other half is banging her ex?'

'No.'

'I wonder whether she'd still vouch for her if she did?'

'I suspect her devotion to the cause would outweigh any desire for revenge. The venom she has for the dog fighters is palpable.'

'And, given the mother's involvement, a defence barrister would almost certainly make short work of any DNA evidence on the grounds it could be circumstantial,' Pete concluded. 'What about the stun gun? Do we have that?'

'Yes, she surrendered it willingly. But the only prints are her own.'

'So she wiped it first,' Pete concluded.

'Presumably. And there are no prints at all on the dart gun. As things stand, we've nowhere near enough for the CPS to do more than charge the mother.'

Pete nodded thoughtfully. There was a long pause before he said, 'The question is how much we care about nailing the daughter.'

Rebecca didn't reply. The response hadn't come as a much of a surprise. Ingrid's confession offered a means of tying the case up, and Pete was rarely inclined to pursue a line of enquiry if an argument could be made that the outlay wasn't in the public interest. To Rebecca, it often seemed to be little more than lazy policing dressed up as pragmatism, but in this instance, she conceded, Pete might have a point. She didn't condone vigilantism, but the scenes in some of Ingrid's photographs made it hard to feel any sympathy for the murdered men, and there was no reason to believe either Ingrid or Abigail posed any real risk to the rest of society.

'Ok,' Pete concluded, at length. 'Let's look at charging the mother – although if her diagnosis checks out I doubt the CPS will have any interest in prosecuting – and in the morning you can pull the daughter in and go over everything umpteen times, see where that gets you. And then have a word with the girlfriend. She might not be so keen to stick up for someone who's been screwing around behind her back.' He stood and reached for his jacket. 'I'm out tomorrow, so we'll revisit the matter first thing on Thursday. And unless you've found a very good reason not to, I want to wrap the whole thing up.'

Rebecca reached for her phone as an electronic chirp announced the arrival of a text message. She had scarcely had a chance to read the brief communication – *Can you call Forrester?* – before another arrived. *If he's going to listen to anyone, it'll be you.*

Rebecca hesitated. She desperately wanted to make the call, but she could imagine only too well what her superior's reaction would be. And that was before she even factored in the hour: it was almost midnight and Lawrence was probably asleep. Ordinarily, Rebecca would have been getting ready for bed herself, but the quiet evening in she had originally planned had been anything but.

Shortly before nine, the doorbell had interrupted the BBC drama she was already three episodes behind on, and she had been more than a little surprised to find Elliot outside. It had been over six months since she had last seen him in person, standing in exactly the same spot. Then, he had looked gaunt, dishevelled and ill after months of relentless drinking. During his subsequent stay in hospital, he had penned several rambling, rather incoherent letters, whether as part of his therapy or of his own volition she didn't know. Now, he was looking better than he had done in a long time, and she had found herself feeling pleased to see him.

Ostensibly, the purpose of his visit had been to organise collection of the large number of his belongings still at the flat, but that could easily have been arranged with a brief telephone call, and Rebecca guessed his real reason for doing the job in person had been to give him the opportunity to apologise for his behaviour during the final months of their relationship. It had been well over a year since she had seen him both sober and on good form, and she had enjoyed the conversation that followed from their initial, rather awkward exchange. They had still been chatting when her mobile rang at five past eleven.

Her first thought on seeing Jon's name on the screen had been that perhaps Ingrid's confession hadn't marked the end of the killing spree, but, in the event, her colleague hadn't been calling about work. And when he had revealed his reason for contacting her, she hadn't thought much of it. Forty-five minutes later, it was a different story.

Coming to a decision, she placed the call to Lawrence, and held her breath as she waited for a response.

'Becky,' he answered, hoarsely, after seven rings. 'What's up?'

'Hi – I'm sorry to bother you – it's just –' she faltered. 'I think Leighton might be in trouble.'

'If Pete's to be believed I don't think there's much doubt about that,' Lawrence returned, shortly. 'Are you aware of the time?'

'Not like that,' Rebecca countered. 'He borrowed Jon's car earlier to follow something up and he was supposed to be back two hours ago. We can't get hold of him, and I'm worried he might have put himself in danger.'

'No offence, Becky, but Leighton going AWOL and not having the courtesy to keep in touch isn't something that causes me grave concern.'

'I know, but –'

'I expect he's just lost track of time. That's if he's even still awake.'

'But –'

'I'm sure he'll turn up in the morning.'

Rebecca swallowed.

'Becky, it's late. Get some sleep. I'll see you tomorrow.'

'Ok,' Rebecca agreed. 'Sorry for waking you.'

'Goodnight.'

Rebecca sat and stared at her mobile screen for several seconds before selecting Jon's number. He answered almost before it had a chance to ring, and Rebecca quickly updated him on her conversation with her superior. He didn't immediately reply, and she wondered what was going through his mind.

'I know he's scatty,' Jon acknowledged, after a moment. 'But there's no way he'd take off in my car without a word. And I'm not just going to sit tight and wait and see what happens.' Then, when Rebecca didn't respond, he added, 'Can you have someone trace his phone?'

It wasn't a request Rebecca could action alone, and she hesitated.

'Please, Becks.'

'I'll see what I can do,' she conceded. 'But I'm going to have to go into the office, so it'll be a while before I can get onto it.'

'Ok, I copy,' Jon returned. 'I'll let you go. And I'll see you there.'

'Did you help her?'

Abigail turned her eyes from Alf's portrait. She had once overheard Ingrid tell a friend that Alf's loss had been harder to bear than the death of her husband. More often, her mother described the chunky black-and-white cat as her *soul kitty* or *one in a million*. Abigail wasn't sure she believed in soul mates, but she did understand that, as much as you loved every pet that shared your life, some animals touched you particularly deeply.

Alf had been orphaned at three days old, and for several weeks Ingrid had cared for him and his sister around the clock. He had grown into a gentle giant of a cat, one who had loved but never monopolised human company, apparently content to be a quiet presence on life's periphery. Sadly, his life had been all too short. That he had been fitted with a microchip had proved to be both a blessing and a curse. It had brought an end to the uncertainty that had followed his disappearance, but with it the heartbreaking news he had died at the hands of dog baiters.

Ingrid had channelled her grief into fighting for something approaching justice, appealing to the police and, later, politicians for more resources to tackle the crime, and badgering local and national newspapers, pushing to raise awareness of the perpetrators' opportunistic habit of snatching pet cats and dogs from the streets, and even private gardens. She had never let up on the campaign, despite the absence of any observable effect. On more than one occasion, she had remarked that were she ever to find herself on borrowed time, she wouldn't hesitate to take more extreme action. For years, Abigail had wondered whether she really meant it.

'Did you?' Charlie repeated, from the doorway. 'Because someone must've.'

There was a long pause before Abigail nodded.

'Is that why you've been screwing Toby?'

'No.'

'Right,' Charlie retorted, disbelievingly, as he dropped into a nearby chair. 'You just happened to take up with him again at the same time you wanted at his gun, and now, what, you're suddenly in love? Don't make me laugh.'

'He's always been special to me,' Abigail protested. 'You know that.'

'He's always been there for you, you mean,' Charlie retorted. 'It's always about *you*. Would you have been there if it was his mother who was sick?'

Abigail didn't reply. She wasn't even sure she had the answer.

'Did he know?' Charlie asked, after a moment. 'Before the police came looking for his gun, I mean.'

Abigail shook her head.

'And Izzy?'

'No.'

'Well I suppose there's some consolation in knowing I'm not the only one who was left in the dark.'

'What, would you rather have been an accessory?'

'Oh, so you did it for me?' Charlie snapped, disbelievingly.

'Chas, it wasn't my fight. Mum would have done it alone if she could have done. She wanted to protect you.'

'She didn't trust me, you mean.'

'You know that's not true.'

'You're the one she's leaving this place to. Assuming you don't get locked up. I can't believe you took that risk!'

'What should I have done?' Abigail demanded. 'Told her no?'

'Yeah, you should.'

'Would you have? Really?'

'Yes!' Charlie exclaimed. 'There's a massive difference between wishing those bastards dead and actually *killing* them!'

'Says the one who described it as *poetic justice*.'

'That was when I thought it was his dog's doing!'

'Right,' Abigail responded, sarcastically. 'Like Scotland Yard's CID have nothing better to do than investigate a single dangerous dog. Thanks for leading them straight to our front door, by the way.'

She had expected an angry retort, but none came, and there was a long pause before Charlie replied. 'How many were you planning, then? Before they started sniffing around.'

'I don't know,' Abigail admitted, honestly. 'That was Mum's department. I just borrowed the gun for her, and did a few physical things she couldn't manage.'

'Actually killed people, you mean?'

'Neither of us killed anybody.'

'Yeah, keep telling yourself that,' Charlie returned. 'You might not have inflicted the injuries, but you're the reason they're dead. The dog couldn't have done it alone.'

Wednesday 21 April

The clock at Lawrence's bedside read 2.37 when he finally abandoned the attempt to sleep and reached for his phone. Thanks to the activity updates provided by a messaging app he'd consulted shortly before one, and on two occasions since, he knew Rebecca was still awake, and he dialled her number. He had tried, repeatedly, to dismiss her concerns as an overreaction, but there was no getting away from the fact it wasn't hard to imagine Leighton rushing headlong into a situation with little regard for the risks. And, whatever the reality, allowing his mind to continue running in metaphorical circles wasn't going to resolve anything.

Predictably, it didn't take Rebecca long to answer.

'Has Leighton turned up yet?' Lawrence asked, unnecessarily. Had she succeeded in tracking her friend down, she wouldn't still be up.

'No.'

'Is his mobile on?'

'Yes, but he's not picking up.'

'I assume by now you've traced it?'

'Yes, it's out near Knebworth.'

'Knebworth?' Lawrence exclaimed. 'What's he doing all the way out there?'

'I don't know – all Jon seemed to know was that it had something to do with a farm.'

'I've no idea what that's about,' Lawrence admitted. 'Have you tried contacting the relevant SIO? Assuming there is one?'

'Jon did,' Rebecca admitted. 'But he thinks it's something to do with O'Leary.'

Lawrence sighed. He should have known. 'Right.' He paused for thought. 'Presumably the farm is somewhere around Knebworth, then.'

'There are loads of farms out that way.'

'Of course there are,' Lawrence remarked, wearily. 'Have you checked Leighton's desk?'

'Yes.'

'And his laptop? I know Jon has access to that.'

'There's nothing obvious there, either.'

'Ok,' Lawrence paused for thought. 'Check what the PNC, Companies House and Google can tell you about the farms closest to the mobile signal and we'll go from there. Are you in the office?'

'Uh-huh.'

'Katie's down in Kent, so I can't join you, but I'll log in and run some searches. Is Jon with you?'

'No.' Rebecca hesitated. 'He's somewhere between here and there.'

'Between London and Knebworth, you mean?'

'Yes.'

'Oh for heaven's sake,' Lawrence muttered.

'I did try to stop him.'

'The last thing we need is to be looking for the both of them!'

'I know.'

'I'll give him a call. And I'll be online shortly.'

Lawrence's calls to Jon had gone unanswered. He had left more than one voicemail, but when he did finally get a response, it was via Rebecca.

'Leighton isn't in Knebworth,' she imparted, the moment he took her call. 'He must have left his phone in his car.'

Lawrence frowned. 'I thought you said he had Jon's car?'

'And now I know why. His is upside down on the hard shoulder of the A1.'

'What? When did he do that?'

'He didn't. That was Tom.'

'Who's Tom?'

'His brother.'

'Oh,' Lawrence nodded to himself, another thought occurring to him. 'Do you suppose he was responsible for the speeding charge, as well?'

'I don't know. But I've run an ANPR check on Jon's car, and that's somewhere over near Cheshunt.'

'Well that makes more sense, given that O'Leary's remains were found in Epping Forest. What time is the last record of it?'

'Eight twenty-three.'

Lawrence glanced at his watch: it was coming up to four. He was still debating what the best course of action might be when Rebecca said, 'If you need someone to stay with Jimmy and Elise, I can come over.'

It took Lawrence only a moment to agree. He didn't enjoy directing operations at a distance, especially not when he had no idea what he was dealing with. And if something had happened to Leighton, Rebecca was the last person Lawrence wanted to be faced with that on the ground.

Had Jamie known he would be up at five to embark on a tour of farms scattered between Hertfordshire and Essex, he wouldn't have sat up playing computer games until after one. He was still eating a hastily assembled peanut butter sandwich as he climbed into Lawrence's car, lamenting the fact he didn't own a travel mug. As he fastened his seatbelt, his superior handed him a list of addresses and an AA road map, reiterating his oft-cited complaint about the shortcomings of Sat Nav. Where country lanes and private farm tracks were concerned, Jamie conceded, he probably had a point.

The first property on the list appeared to be deserted, although in good repair, and a circuit of its buildings and outhouses revealed signs they had been in relatively recent use. The second farmstead felt immediately more lived-in, thanks to the distant chatter of a radio, but wasn't, it turned out, being used for its original purpose. Beyond what looked to be the original farmhouse stood an expansive and very modern indoor parking lot, accommodating some fifty luxury cars. These, the man waxing the bonnet of a royal blue Lotus hastened to tell them, all belonged to clients of his vehicle-storage business. For reasons of security, he added, without prompting, the site's address wasn't available online, and the company was headquartered elsewhere, which explained why Rebecca had been unable to turn up any current data for the property. The high-tech alarm system and abundance of security cameras lent credence to the explanation, and after taking down the man's details and checking his driving licence, Lawrence and Jamie returned to the road.

A car was one of the first things to catch Jamie's eye on their approach to the rather quaintly named Holly Brook Farm, on this occasion because it looked familiar. At closer range, the licence plate confirmed that the navy Golf belonged to Jon, and it took scarcely a moment for Jamie to establish that the car was both empty and undamaged. The only other vehicle in the vicinity of the red-brick farmhouse was a battered, rusty tractor. The building behind it was a jumble of extensions, two of them single-storey, the walls scarred by the tracks of long-dead climbing plants. And although the window frames were in good condition, the glass clearly hadn't been cleaned in years. The front door, meanwhile, looked almost new. Presumably it had been replaced in the interests of security, because when, after knocking yielded no response, they attempted to force it, the task proved impossible. Jamie stood back to survey the building's facade for an alternative means of entry as Lawrence made his way around the side.

In the end, they gained access through a small rear window, aided by a heavy-duty spanner and the fact the latch had been shut but not locked. Climbing into a filthy bathroom, Jamie stepped down over a toilet that he wouldn't have been surprised to learn hadn't been cleaned in at least as long as the windows. Keen to escape the dank air, he immediately opened the bathroom door, whereupon the temperature and humidity surged. Ahead of him, an expansive kitchen with a black-and-white checkerboard floor appeared to have been repurposed as an indoor greenhouse, with pots of various sizes scattered across the floor, and heat lamps hanging from a makeshift scaffold above them. Jamie's immediate assumption – that the room had been set up to grow cannabis – was swiftly followed by realisation that the plants looked neither particularly familiar nor alike. A selection of palms and ferns mingled with other plants he couldn't identify, while orchids clustered on a stretch of worktop between two sizeable humidifiers.

'It feels like a hothouse in here,' Lawrence remarked, as he emerged from the bathroom.

'I think that's the idea,' Jamie responded, stepping through the kitchen doorway and picking his way between the pots. 'Although God knows why, I can't see anything illegal.' He ducked under one of the lamps and reached to open a cupboard. It was empty, as was the next, while others contained the usual miscellany of dishes and utensils one would expect to find in a kitchen.

Skirting around a giant pineapple of a plant almost as tall as he was, he reached a low, windowless extension. Given that the kitchen was devoid of white goods, Jamie guessed the annex might once have served as a utility room, but whatever furnishings it possessed had been obscured by stacks of identikit boxes. These were all printed with the same logo and, beneath it, the words *Premium Russian Vodka.* Hearing footsteps behind him, he glanced around.

'Ten to one this is no more Russian than I am.'

There was a momentary pause before Lawrence replied. 'Chances are it's not vodka, either.'

The barn was dark, and, with the light behind him, the first thing to hit Lawrence was the metallic smell of blood, mingled with other foetid odours, including sweat and excrement. A quick sweep of his torch beam around the building's interior revealed no obvious signs of activity: the space appeared to be empty, and the dirt floor and wooden walls looked incongruously normal. He walked slowly towards the wall to his right, wondering when the farm had last been used for its original purpose, and whether it had ever housed livestock. If what they had seen so far that morning was anything to go by, the area's farms were exclusively arable. In another decade or two, half of them would probably have been built on.

'Sir?'

He turned. Jamie was standing near the centre of the barn, scraping the dirt on the floor to one side with his shoe to expose the rough concrete underneath. As Lawrence neared, he could make out dark stains that were almost certainly blood, and by the time he reached his colleague, the young man was crouching over them.

'Smells like disinfectant,' he remarked, after a moment, straightening up.

Given where they were, it was impossible to know whether either the stains or the faint chemical smell was relevant. Bleach's ability to obliterate forensic evidence had been overstated on popular TV programs, and it wouldn't have been the first time Lawrence had come across attempts to use it as such at a crime scene, but it was much more likely to have been used for its intended purpose as a cleaning product. He nodded in response before returning to his circuit of the perimeter.

He hadn't yet reached the far end of the barn when the sound of a car engine took him outside, and he stepped out into the yard just in time to see a familiar red hatchback turn in beside his Honda. Jon didn't bother straightening his girlfriend's car, nor locking it after climbing out, and was halfway across the courtyard by the time Lawrence caught up with him.

'Is it too much to ask that *one* of you might behave like a responsible adult?' He demanded, furiously. '*What* did I say when we last spoke?'

Jon ignored the question in favour of one of his own. 'Have you found him?'

'I told you I would let you know, and I will! In the meantime, you will sit in that car until I say otherwise!'

'I thought –'

'No! It's not negotiable! And the longer you stand here arguing, the more time we're wasting!'

'But what if you need a medic?'

'Then I will know where to find you! Now get back in that car or I swear to God I will charge the both of you with wasting my bloody time!'

This time Jon didn't argue, turning back in the direction of the vehicle. Lawrence retraced his steps, and Jamie met him at the barn door.

'The place is definitely empty.'

'Ok, let's move on.'

Beyond the barn stood what Lawrence took to be a hay-storage building – a naked frame topped by a pitched roof. Three metal storage containers were lined up within its confines, and the hum of a generator was audible. The first container was secured with a heavy padlock, and Lawrence handed Jamie his car keys with instructions to fetch the bolt cutters from the boot before walking on to the next container. This had been bolted shut, but didn't appear to be locked, and it took Lawrence only seconds to release the doors. They were heavier than he had expected, and the blast of cold air that hit him as he pulled them apart filled him in on the container's purpose. Shining his torch into the walk-in freezer, it took a moment to grasp the reality of the scene that met him.

The space ahead was half filled with rows of plastic vats stacked three or four high. Against the back wall, a body, white with ice crystals, was frozen in position in a manner that called to mind the plaster-cast bodies of ancient Pompeii. In front of it was a pile of what appeared to be rubbish – a stack of flattened cardboard boxes with a bundle of thick polythene gathered on top of it. Then, through the plastic, he spotted the bottom of a shoe. Shouting to his colleague as he hurried into the container, he drew a portion of the plastic aside to find Leighton curled up, unmoving in a foetal position on the cardboard mat, more plastic wrapped around his torso.

'Oh Jesus –' Jamie breathed, from behind him.

'Let's get him outside,' Lawrence suggested, moving around the body huddled on the floor. Jamie nodded, crouching to grasp the sheaf of cardboard. Lawrence did likewise, and they used it as a makeshift stretcher, shifting it the few feet to the doorway and setting it down a short distance outside. By the time Lawrence straightened up, Jon was sprinting down the track towards them. He dropped to his knees immediately upon reaching them, directing Lawrence to call for an ambulance as he reached to check for a pulse. Lawrence did as bid, feeling increasingly concerned when Jon didn't look up or move his fingers away from Leighton's neck. Foremost in his mind was the question of whether the situation might have been different had he acted earlier.

Jon had turned anxiously towards Lawrence as the paramedics began their return trip to the ambulance and, casting an uneasy glance in the direction of the freezer container, had stammered something about prioritising the living. Lawrence had cut him off with, 'Jon, he's your friend. Go.' Jon had nodded his thanks before hurrying after the paramedics, and Lawrence had taken a deep breath before placing a call to Max. A little over an hour later, the cherry red Audi Max had been driving for at least a decade came into view on the farm's access road. Lawrence hadn't expected Max to attend the site himself. Then again, with both Leighton and Jon unexpectedly out of action, he supposed the pathology unit would be seriously short-staffed.

They had walked the short distance to the freezer container in silence, and it was only when Lawrence opened the heavy doors, revealing the white, rigid corpse inside, that Max showed any real emotion.

'Fucking hell,' he breathed, training the beam of his torch slowly around the rectangular tomb. 'What must go through your mind –' he shook his head slightly.

Lawrence had been more preoccupied with the mind of the person who had closed the door, seemingly on more than one occasion. A psychopath devoid of empathy, or a coward who couldn't kill with his own hands?

'I don't suppose at this stage there's any way of knowing how long he's been in here?' Lawrence asked, as Max pulled on plastic shoe covers and stepped into the container.

'None at all,' Max confirmed. 'I know the frost makes it look like it's been a while, but if you had the door open long enough to bring that lot in –' he indicated the barrels, 'Or take others out, that could form quite quickly.'

'It was a long shot,' Lawrence conceded.

'I'm not sure I'll be able to make any sort of estimate even after a PM,' Max admitted, illuminating the corpse at closer range.

'Let's hope we can identify him and work back from there, then,' Lawrence replied, as his mobile began to ring. Seeing Jon's name on the screen, he hesitated before stepping away from the container and answering the call.

'Hi. Any news?'

'Not yet. I'm calling because there was something written on his arm, it looks like a brief description and a vehicle registration number, and I thought we ought to follow it up.'

'I can have someone do that. I don't have a pen to hand, would you mind texting it to me?'

'Will do.'

'And if you can, get some photos.'

'Already done. I'll send them through.'

'Great, thanks.'

Hanging up, Lawrence headed back towards the farmhouse. Two crime scene officers were working their way across the courtyard, and he could see another through the building's open front door. He didn't suppose there was much more he could do on site – his time would probably be better spent elsewhere. Noticing as he approached that somebody had blocked in his car, he sighed. He cast his eyes around in the hope someone nearby might be able to tell him who, and spotted Jamie perching on an old tractor tyre, a cigarette between his fingers. He didn't notice Lawrence approaching and looked up sharply in response to his name before hurriedly getting to his feet and stamping out the cigarette while muttering an apology.

'I don't suppose –' Lawrence stopped, realising with one look at Jamie's colourless face that Jon wasn't the only person he should have excused from the site that morning. 'Are you all right?'

'Yes,' Jamie nodded, almost automatically.

'Would you like to go home?'

'No. I'm ok. Thanks.'

'You don't have to work on this if you'd rather not.'

'I'll be fine.'

'Ok. Well I don't think there's a lot more we can do here, so we'll leave the scientists to it. I'm going to let Max know we're heading off – can you find out who that black Lexus belongs to and get them to shift it?'

'No problem.'

'I want to be on the road in ten minutes.'

On his return to the office, Lawrence was surprised to find Rebecca at her desk, having suggested during an earlier phone conversation that she take the afternoon off. She was poring over a makeshift map assembled from photocopied sheets of A3, and, as he neared, his eyes were drawn to the single splash of colour – heavy yellow highlighter picking out the words *Holly Brook Farm*. The only other noteworthy feature of the piecemeal document was stretches of cross-hatching along the sides of some of the roads. From the uneven nature of their rendering, he guessed they had been hand-drawn on the original map.

'Becky.'

She raised her eyes and forced a smile. 'Hi.'

'Have you heard any more from Jon?'

'No. He said it could be a while.'

'I thought you might have gone to the hospital.'

'I'd go mad sitting in a corridor all day. It's not like I can do anything to help.'

Lawrence nodded. He could certainly identify with that sentiment.

'I checked out that registration number,' Rebecca continued, reaching into a filing tray for a computer printout. 'The vehicle belongs to a Norman Healy.' She indicated a passport-sized photograph with her index finger. 'I've put a call out for him and the van.'

'Thank you,' Lawrence replied, taking in the man's picture before looking to the patchwork of paper on the desk. 'What's the map for?'

'I'm not sure,' Rebecca admitted. 'I went round to Leighton's flat this morning – he had some bits and pieces there relating to O'Leary – and this was among them.'

'Any idea what this relates to?' Lawrence asked, gesturing towards a section of cross-hatching that ran along a road at the farm's periphery.

She shook her head. 'But this isn't his writing,' she observed, indicating the notation *ECS Map #37* and a date in the top right-hand corner. 'So presumably he didn't annotate the original.'

Lawrence nodded.

'And this was stuck to it,' she added, presenting an evidence bag containing a Post-it note bearing the chemical formula $CaMgAc_4$ and, below it, the letters NCBA. 'I've tried looking this up,' she indicated the formula. 'And I can find all the individual elements, but the combination doesn't seem to exist.'

'Calcium, magnesium and –' Lawrence paused for thought.

'Actinium,' Rebecca finished for him.

Lawrence was none the wiser.

'Google also pulls up a lot of different things with the acronym NCBA, but nothing that jumps out at me.'

'I'll see whether Max can answer that one,' Lawrence suggested, his eyes alighting on a familiar image that had been obscured by the bag containing the Post-it. 'Was this in his flat as well?' He asked, reaching for it.

'Yes.'

Lawrence took in the names superimposed on the picture. One immediately stood out. 'Patrick Quinn?' He exclaimed. 'What the hell was he sitting on this for?'

He hadn't expected Rebecca to have an answer, and was surprised when she said, 'I don't think he was. He did flag it with DCI Rose.'

'How do you know that?'

'He told me. I saw this a few days ago, and I asked the same thing.'

'What, and when Pete didn't act on it Leighton just let it go? That doesn't sound like him.'

'He said he didn't think it was relevant.'

'Did you not think it was worth a mention?' Lawrence asked, wondering whether his impatience with the pathologist had made her reluctant to speak up.

'If he'd been concerned about it I might have, but he thought it was a red herring,' Rebecca shrugged. 'And he knew a lot more about it than I did.'

'I'll have a word with Pete.'

'I think he's off today.'

'I'm sure I can track him down. Was there anything else relevant in the flat?'

'I'm still trying to figure that out,' Rebecca admitted, sounding apologetic. 'Do you want to have a look?'

'When you're done. In the meantime, I'm going to see what I can find out about the farm. Could you let me have what information you managed to gather this morning?'

'There's next to nothing. All I've been able to establish is that it's owned by what appears to be a shell company registered in Nevis.'

Lawrence sighed. 'I won't waste my time on that, then. I'll check the farm isn't on the radar of the organised crime unit before we start trying to work back from what there is on site. Or in the archives,' he turned towards his office. 'Leighton managed to find it that way, so one way or another, we must be able to do the same.'

Catching herself in the eye with her mascara wand, Rebecca flinched and inadvertently daubed a black crescent just beneath her right eyebrow. Tears came to her eyes again, and she reached for a tissue. She'd been coping perfectly well until she arrived at a point where there was nothing left to do besides wait on other people. Realistically, she was unlikely to hear from many of them before the next day, but she couldn't face going home to sit staring at her mobile, or to the hospital to stare instead at unfamiliar walls. In any case, the latter option seemed inappropriate; she wasn't Leighton's girlfriend and she wasn't a part of his family. And the medical staff probably had more than enough people getting under their feet already.

Hearing the door to the room open, she resisted the natural urge to look around and hurriedly wiped the smudge of make-up from the rim of her eye socket. There was a brief silence before the newcomer spoke.

'Are you ok?'

Rebecca nodded. 'Just poked myself in the eye,' she responded, ruefully, holding up the mascara and flicking her eyes heavenwards in emphasis.

'I'm always doing that,' Eva replied, turning her back to the mirror and leaning against the counter. After a moment, she went on, 'Were you up all night?'

'Uh-huh,' Rebecca confirmed, wondering whether the question was a subtle comment on how tired she looked. 'Jon called before I'd made it to bed. Leighton was supposed to drop his car back by ten.'

'Good job he didn't have his own car, or no one would've missed him 'til this morning,' Eva observed, echoing a thought that had already gone through Rebecca's mind countless times. 'If I had a car like that, I'd not be lending it to anyone.'

Rebecca didn't say that there was no way Leighton would have *lent* the car to his brother. It was quite possible he hadn't even known it was missing; he'd mislaid the keys plenty of times in the past without any help from Tom.

'Is his brother all right?'

Rebecca glanced around with a frown. 'What?'

'He crashed the car, didn't he? Last night.'

'Oh,' she realised, aloud. 'Yes. No lasting damage.'

'He's going to have some explaining to do,' Eva replied, with a lift of her eyebrows.

'Well let's hope he gets the chance.'

'I'm sure he will.'

'Are you?' Rebecca exclaimed. 'Because Jon isn't! And if he's worried, the rest of us should be too!' She returned her focus to the mirror, trying to blink back another rush of tears.

'Sorry,' Eva offered, awkwardly. 'I didn't mean to sound glib – I just –' she trailed off, then repeated, 'Sorry.'

Rebecca swallowed and used her right forefinger to quickly dry her eyes.

'Do you want a hug?'

Rebecca shook her head. She set her mascara down on the counter and dug into her handbag for her compact.

'Have you been friends a long time?' Eva asked, at length.

'About two and a half years,' Rebecca replied, after a moment's thought. 'Which doesn't sound very long. It feels like longer.' She paused. 'But then a lot has happened in the past couple of years.'

There was another pause before Eva ventured, 'Do you love him?'

Rebecca's first instinct was to object to the personal nature of the question; the second to shut the conversation down with a definitive *no*. In the end, she opted to do neither, instead admitting, 'I don't know.' She needlessly tucked a lock of hair behind her ear. 'But he's been a very good friend to me, and I can't imagine –' she shrugged in lieu of finishing the sentence.

Eva nodded.

Not wanting to go into any detail about her feelings, Rebecca sighed and changed the subject with, 'I'm not sure mascara's going to cut it as a rescue remedy this evening.'

'Sleep might be more effective.'

'I don't think I'd be able to.'

'You mean you don't want to,' Eva surmised, bluntly. 'Because the idea you might be able to switch off feels disloyal.'

Her colleague probably had a point, Rebecca conceded, although she didn't say as much.

'So what are you going to do if there's still no news in six hours?' Eva went on. 'Or twelve?' She regarded Rebecca in silence for a moment. 'Last night, staying awake made a critical difference, but it's not going to achieve much tonight, is it? All it's going to do is make you next to no use tomorrow.'

Thursday 22 April

Lawrence arrived at Scotland Yard shortly after eight to find Max waiting in his office. He didn't look as if he'd had much sleep, and Lawrence wondered for how long he had been sitting there.

'Morning.'

'Hi,' Max returned, shortly, in a tone that betrayed nothing of the answer to the question Lawrence didn't quite dare to ask. Max waited until he had sat down before continuing, 'I gather from Jon that I have you to thank for the fact all my team members are still alive.'

Feeling hugely relieved, Lawrence shook his head. 'Not at all. He was the one who was jumping up and down insisting something was wrong.'

'Yes, but you could easily have dismissed that. Especially in light of recent events.'

Lawrence frowned. 'Leighton and I may have exchanged some cross words, but that doesn't mean I don't care what happens to him.'

'Of course not, that's not what I meant. It's just –' Max hesitated. 'I could understand why you might not have taken Jon's concerns seriously.'

'Well hopefully Leighton will think twice about running around playing detective in future,' he replied. 'Do you know whether he's said anything about what happened yet?'

'It's going to be a while before he's capable of saying anything at all. Right now he's on a ventilator in intensive care.'

'Intensive care?' Lawrence echoed, hollowly. He had assumed – perhaps naively – that, providing it hadn't gone past the point of no return, reversing hypothermia would be a relatively simple rewarming process. 'Is that normal?'

Max nodded. 'If your temperature drops below a certain point it has all sorts of knock-on effects. And that's even before you take into account the danger of rising carbon dioxide levels when you're breathing in an enclosed space. He's still seriously ill, and it's likely to be at least a few days before they have any real idea how much damage has been done or what the prognosis might be.'

'I didn't realise.'

'But he's lucky he's here at all. He came this close.' Max held up a finger and thumb.

Lawrence wasn't sure what to say, and, in the end, opted for, 'Do you have any idea what he was actually looking for? Or how he came to be there?'

'No. I've found nothing on his desk or laptop that obviously relates to the farm.'

'How about in Jon's car?'

Max shook his head. 'I've left a message for IT asking if they can get the contents of his email account to me – including deleted messages – hopefully I'll find something in there. I'll let you know what turns up.'

'And is there any news on the body from the freezer?'

'Not yet. We've no clues to his ID, and we couldn't very well cut him up while he was frozen solid. I'm hoping to make a start on the PM later this morning, so I'll try to have something for you by close of play.'

'Thanks. While you're here, there's something else I'd like your thoughts on,' Lawrence drew a folder from his bag and flicked through it until he found a photocopy of the Post-it note Rebecca had retrieved from Leighton's flat. 'Do either of these mean anything to you?' He asked, holding it out. 'Google wasn't much help. We think they relate to the O'Leary investigation.'

Max took the page and regarded it for a moment. 'I'm not a chemist, so I couldn't tell you what this is offhand,' he admitted, indicating the formula as he looked back up. 'But I'll check it out for you.'

'I wondered whether it might be used for refrigeration purposes.'

'It's not a coolant, if that's what you mean. For that you'd most likely be looking at HFCs or CFCs, depending on the age of the system. But I suppose it's possible it's something like a de-icing product.'

'Was there any evidence to indicate O'Leary might have died in a freezer?'

'Nothing that raised flags. The original investigation established that the body – or at least, the arm – had been frozen at some stage, but O'Leary was last seen immediately before a severe cold snap, so that on its own wasn't particularly noteworthy. Even when you've got a whole body, establishing cause of death as hypothermia is often a diagnosis of exclusion.'

'So there's no way of working out whether the freezing occurred before or after death?'

'Not from what's left of him,' Max replied. 'But I'm not sure that really matters. What we need is evidence connecting him to the container on Holly Brook Farm. And if he was shut in there long enough for it to kill him, chances are there'll be something for us to find.'

Pete appeared in Lawrence's office doorway within moments of Max's departure, and, with a nod towards his retreating back, asked, 'Any news on our little pathologist friend?'

'I think it's still touch and go.'

'Christ,' Pete responded, with a lift of his thick eyebrows. 'Have you got the little shit who was responsible?'

'Not yet, although we've a relatively firm ID. Leighton took down a vehicle reg and a brief description that matches the photo held by the DVLA. We'll find him sooner or later.'

Pete nodded. 'You left a couple of messages yesterday. I was up in the Peaks, so they didn't come through 'til late. Did you manage to answer whatever it was in the meantime?'

'Not fully. I've a few questions about the O'Leary investigation, given that that seems to have been what took Leighton out to Cheshunt.'

Pete sighed heavily, bending to rest his forearms on the back of a chair. 'I warned him a hundred times to leave that alone.'

'I know. You weren't the only one. What I'm trying to establish is what made him so determined to pursue it. For starters, I'm not clear why he was so convinced Quinn wasn't involved in O'Leary's death.'

'There's not really any question over whether or not he was *involved*, we know they were together the night O'Leary disappeared. Leighton just didn't think he was responsible.'

'Why not?'

Pete shook his head slightly. 'Your guess is as good as mine. Last time he brought it up it he was on about that bloody Quinn woman's statement. As if that was ever going to be worth the paper it was written on.'

'But he must have had more to go on than that,' Lawrence persisted. 'I can't imagine he would have gone through the statements simply on account of a tenuous link to an old photograph.'

'Nothing that made much sense to me. But then following his notes is like trying to navigate a maze blindfold and with your hands tied behind your back.'

Given that the pathologist's notes tended to jump from one thought to another without any real explanation of how he'd got there – calling to mind the perennial complaint of maths teachers about pupils not showing their working – it was difficult to dispute this contention. But Lawrence suspected the real reason for Pete's limited grasp of Leighton's theory was that he hadn't given it a fair hearing in the first place.

'Do you have any of those notes?'

'I think I've one or two electronic communications,' Pete admitted, after a pause. 'I'll have a look back and see whether I can find them.'

It wouldn't have taken a minute to search the inbox on his mobile, but Lawrence suspected *I'll have a look back* probably translated to *I'll have IT retrieve my deleted emails*. Or, possibly, *I'll get back to you when I've fudged the evidence*. A comparison with the contents of Leighton's sent mailbox might prove illuminating.

'If you were able to do that today I'd be very grateful.'

Pete nodded. 'I'll take a look this morning.'

'And how about the list of men in the photo?'

'What photo?'

Lawrence presented the image, complete with Leighton's annotations. 'Patrick Quinn,' he said, indicating the man in the picture before adding, for emphasis, 'Sean's father. O'Leary's half-brother.'

'Oh, that,' Pete realised aloud, rather unconvincingly. 'Someone did look into it. I'll dig out what came back.'

'Great, thanks,' Lawrence nodded, wondering whether the task really had been assigned.

'Ok,' Pete responded, turning to go. 'Tell Becky I'll tie up the loose ends on the dog deaths. And if there's anything else I can do to help, let me know.'

'Thank you,' Lawrence replied, feeling surprised by the offer.

Pete paused briefly in the doorway. 'He might be a pain in the arse, but he's still one of us.'

'They found Healy's van,' Rebecca announced to Jamie, as she replaced her phone handset in its cradle. Her colleague didn't respond, eyes fixed on his computer screen, and after a couple of seconds Rebecca tried again. 'Jay?'

Jamie started. 'Sorry, what?'

'Are you all right?'

He nodded.

Had it been later in the day, Rebecca would have suggested going for a drink, but it wasn't even lunchtime. Instead, she settled for, 'Do you want to talk about it? Yesterday, I mean.'

'No. Thanks.' Jamie forced a smile. 'What was it you were after?'

'I was just saying they found Healy's van.'

'Oh, right. Whereabouts?'

'Wasteland on the outskirts of Walsall. I don't know how much it's going to help us, though, it'd been torched.'

Jamie gave a rather indifferent grunt. There was a pause before he said, seemingly irrelevantly, 'You know what they say about university lectures and information transferring from the notes of the lecturer to the notes of the student without passing through the brains of either?'

'Yes.'

'Sometimes I see parallels with this job. I read through part of an interview transcript and it sounds vaguely familiar, so I think maybe I overheard someone talking about it, and then I realise I was actually there. That's not good, is it?'

Rebecca smiled. 'In your defence, a lot of interviews really aren't very interesting, contrary to what popular culture would have people believe.'

Jamie nodded slightly.

'What's the interview?'

'Sean Quinn.'

'Did you think he was guilty?'

'I don't know,' Jamie admitted. 'I don't doubt he and O'Leary had a fight – it wouldn't have been the first time, and there's no evidence or witnesses to support his claim that the blood on his clothes got there after O'Leary had a fight with someone else – but that doesn't mean it was fatal.'

'Who reported him missing?'

'Nobody. First we knew about it was when the DNA results on the remains came through.'

'Was that another factor in the case against Quinn?'

'Yeah. They were thick as thieves – right up until the night O'Leary dropped off the face of the earth. After that, Quinn never tried to call or text him again.'

'What was his explanation for that?'

'He blamed his mum,' Jamie replied, with a derisive roll of his eyes. 'As if the fact she couldn't stand the sight of O'Leary had made any difference up until that point. She backed him up, but until we presented her with evidence to the contrary, she claimed he was home the night O'Leary disappeared, as well.'

Rebecca nodded. 'If it wasn't because he already knew O'Leary was dead, maybe he cut contact over whatever the fight was about.'

'Probably,' Jamie responded. 'Anyhow, I figured it was worth checking whether there was anything in the transcripts that might allude to the farm. It's only three miles from the forest boundary.'

'Do you think the rest of the body might be somewhere on the farm?'

'I suppose it's not inconceivable, but I'm not sure how his arm would have made it all the way to the forest from there. I can't see something like a fox being able to carry it that far. They're not that big, foxes, are they?'

'No, I guess not.'

'I reckon there's a good chance he died there, though,' Jamie observed, returning his eyes to his screen. A brief silence followed before he sighed. 'None of this is going in,' he admitted, leaning to peer past the filing cabinet beside his desk and through the glass wall of Lawrence's office.

'Just go,' Rebecca suggested, guessing what he was thinking. 'Nobody's going to begrudge you a break today.'

Jamie hesitated, and she added, 'If it makes you feel better, I'll come with you.'

'Yeah?' He responded, looking surprised.

'Sure,' she smiled, reaching for the Snickers bar that lay on the desktop and holding it up. 'Providing you don't mind if I eat while you smoke?'

Lawrence returned to his office late in the afternoon to find Max slumped in a chair with his eyes shut, his head supported by his left hand and his elbow on the armrest. Wondering whether his friend was asleep, he hesitated, and before he had a chance to decide on a course of action, Max's eyes opened and he straightened up. 'Hi.'

'You look done in,' Lawrence observed, moving to sit down.

'I'm out of practice with this working around the clock lark,' Max responded, ruefully.

'Getting old, you mean.'

'Well I suppose you would know.'

Lawrence smiled. 'Only on account of my extensive investigative experience.'

'Perhaps you'd like to extend that experience to the contents of the barrels from the freezer,' Max suggested. 'Because they certainly aren't what I was expecting.'

'So not simply an earlier incarnation of whatever was bottled and boxed in the house,' Lawrence guessed, feeling intrigued.

'No. That was your bog-standard, potentially lethal fake vodka. Something we see the end result of all too often. But the freezer was full of what looks to be nothing more than unusually strong beer.'

'How strong?'

'Some vats were stronger than others, but between about fifteen and twenty per cent.'

'Presumably it would have been even stronger had the liquid component been drawn off straight from the freezer?'

Max nodded. 'I should think that would have nudged it up by a couple of percentage points.'

'Curious. I wonder what the market for that kind of thing is?'

'That's the sort of random trivia I'd normally look to Leighton for an answer to. I did try an online search for super-strength beer, but all I got was special offers on extra-strong lager, and if your search terms –' Max trailed off and looked around as Lawrence's attention was diverted by Jamie's appearance in the office doorway.

'Brewing-related question for you,' Lawrence put in, remembering that Jamie had an interest in the subject. 'Any idea why someone would put beer in a freezer? Other than simply to chill it.'

Jamie blinked and there was a momentary pause before he said, 'To make something like Eisbock?'

'Which is what?'

'A German beer. You take a particular type of strong lager and freeze off some of the water to make it even more alcoholic.'

'What sort of price would it fetch?'

'I don't know, but it's expensive to make. None of the big breweries do it. Not in bulk, at least.'

'So there could be profit to be made in counterfeiting the stuff,' Lawrence concluded. 'But why try to mass-produce the real thing?'

Jamie shrugged. 'Maybe someone *thought* there was money in it. I'm not sure how you'd calculate the potential yield – or costs – for something like that, but there's probably plenty of room for error.'

'Good point,' Lawrence conceded. 'Most criminals are not masterminds.' Then, guessing Jamie hadn't intruded on his conversation with Max without good reason, he asked, 'Any updates?'

Jamie nodded. 'Loads and loads of fingerprints,' he revealed. 'The place is awash with prints from seven individuals, and we've four of them on file. Guess who's among them?'

'O'Leary?'

'And Sean Quinn.'

'Well that's a result,' Lawrence remarked, feeling heartened by the news.

'I can see why Quinn kept his trap shut now. Prison's got to be a picnic compared with death by freezer.'

'Assuming anyone actually died in there,' Max observed. 'The man whose corpse we retrieved yesterday didn't.'

'Are you sure?' Lawrence asked, surprised.

'Yes. His neck was broken and he had other injuries consistent with a fall. I couldn't tell you whether or not that was accidental, but I can say it didn't happen in the freezer.'

'So shutting people in there alive may not have been a repeat MO,' Lawrence mused. 'Did Leighton have any injuries that could have been associated with loss of consciousness?'

'Not to my knowledge, but I'll check.'

'What else do we know about the ice man?'

'Precious little. We've no clue to his ID – hopefully fingerprints or dental records might help us there – so I can only provide the limited information I gleaned from the body. Caucasian, probably somewhere in his thirties, five eleven, athletic. And if I were you, I'd start the search for missing persons with those last seen in December.'

'December? Why?'

'He'd been eating mince pies.'

*****

Abigail unlocked the door to Toby's flat and eased it open. Toby was slumped on the sofa, a cold compress held to the left side of his face, and raised his right eye as she looked in.

'What happened?' Abigail asked, closing the door behind herself. 'Kylie said something about an accident?'

'If Izzy punching my lights out is what you call an accident,' Toby responded, ruefully. 'You might've given me a heads up you were going to tell her about us.'

'I didn't. I think that was the police.'

'Oh. Right.'

'Can I see?' Abigail asked, perching beside him.

Toby drew the compress back by a few inches. His eye was swollen shut.

Abigail winced. 'Sorry.'

'It's not your fault,' he replied, replacing the compress. 'I knew what I was getting into. As far as Izzy goes, at least.'

'Sorry,' she repeated. 'I didn't mean for you to get dragged into Mum's crusade.'

He looked incredulous. 'What, did you not think using my gun would be a bit of a giveaway?'

'I wasn't expecting Chas to attract the cops' attention,' Abigail countered. 'And I didn't expect you to put yourself on the line for me, either. I know I owe you big time.'

'What else could I do? Ingrid needs you.'

Abigail didn't believe he had stood by her on her mother's account, but saying as much would have sounded presumptuous, so she held her tongue.

'Chas said they're not going to take any action against her,' Toby went on.

'No. I guess it's not worth their while.'

He nodded. A couple of seconds passed in silence before he said, 'And what about you?'

'I don't think they have enough evidence. They spent most of the day trying to trip me up, and I guess they tried to turn Izzy by telling her about you and me, but without something concrete there's probably not a lot they can do.'

'Until this afternoon I assumed Izzy was in on it,' Toby admitted. 'Although I didn't imagine she'd have sanctioned your use of sex to access my gun.'

'I didn't sleep with you to get my hands on your gun.'

Toby's only response was a disbelieving lift of his one visible eyebrow.

'I didn't,' Abigail insisted. 'You and I had already slept together before Mum said a word about what she had in mind.'

Toby still didn't reply.

'And it's not as if I didn't already have a key to the place,' she pointed out. 'I didn't need to make love to you to get into the office.'

'So why did you?'

'Because I wanted to,' Abigail responded, simply. 'I love you. I realised I didn't choose the wrong person to marry, I just chose the wrong point in my life to get married.'

Toby shook his head slightly. 'If that was true you'd have finished with Izzy before now.'

'It's not that simple.'

'It is, Abs. Or it was.'

Abigail didn't answer immediately. 'I didn't want to upset her,' she offered, at length, aware, even as she spoke, of how inadequate the words sounded.

'Do you have any idea how often I hear that sort of excuse from pet owners who really mean *I didn't want to pay for an appointment*?' Toby asked. 'What you're actually saying is that you didn't want to deal with the fallout.'

'Maybe,' Abigail acknowledged. 'But I do love her. And I wish there was a way we could have remained friends.'

'If you'd been honest with her in the first place maybe you could have been.'

'I doubt it.'

Toby didn't respond.

'Can I stay here tonight?'

'Aren't you forgetting something?'

There was a moment's silence as Abigail tried to guess which of several possible *somethings* he was referring to.

'Your mum,' Toby clarified.

'Aunt Lily's there.'

He didn't reply, and she reached to take his free hand. He moved his away before her fingers could make contact.

'The fact I didn't drop you in it doesn't mean I'm not mightily pissed off about being put in that position,' he observed. 'And it doesn't stop me feeling used and manipulated.'

'I'm sorry. That was never my intention.'

'I can believe you never meant for me to *feel* that way,' he returned. 'But only because you never intended me to realise the lengths you'd go to for an alibi.'

'I had no idea that would turn out like it did.'

'That's not really the point, is it?'

Abigail thought her response over for some time. Eventually, she said, 'So is that it?' Then, realising the ambiguity inherent in the question, she added, 'For us, I mean.'

'I don't know, Abs,' he responded, resignedly. 'I love you, and I've always loved you, but after the past week I'm not sure I can trust you.' He paused. 'Right now, I really don't know what I want.' He turned his head to meet her eyes. 'And, to be honest, I'm not sure you do, either.'

Friday 23 April

'Knock knock.'

Lawrence raised his eyes from a search of the Police National Computer to see Max standing in his office doorway. He wondered whether his friend was privy to any of the information currently on his computer screen. With a number of questions about the past few days still unanswered, he was attempting to track down Leighton's mobile phone, starting with locating his car. But an initial search for Tom Campbell in an effort to identify the arresting officer from Tuesday evening's RTC had turned up far more than Lawrence had bargained for. Leighton's elder brother had a criminal record that went back some two decades, covering myriad driving and public-order offences, as well as convictions for several violent crimes. And, only days earlier, he had been charged with GBH after an assault that had left Leighton with two broken ribs. On that occasion, Tom had given Leighton's address as his own, and Lawrence guessed he had found the answer to the question of why his colleague had been so on edge of late.

'How's it going?' Max asked, moving to sit down.

'Slowly,' Lawrence admitted. 'Working out how Leighton got to where he did is proving something of a challenge.'

'Well I don't know whether it's of any help, but I do have an ID on that compound you asked about yesterday.'

'What is it?'

'Calcium magnesium acetate. And it is a de-icing product, but not one destined for freezers.'

'So what is it used for?'

'Roads.'

'When did they stop using rock salt?'

'I don't think they did, but salt's quite harsh on the environment. It's possible they use CMA in and around Epping Forest on account of it being a site of special scientific interest.'

Lawrence nodded. 'Do you know why Leighton came to be looking at it?'

'I do,' Max replied, presenting a graph featuring elongated troughs and sharp peaks that Lawrence immediately recognised as a read-out from a mass spectrometer. 'This is from a swab taken from O'Leary's hand, and –'

Lawrence frowned. 'What, last year?'

'Yes.'

'Why did nobody look into it at the time?'

'People come into contact with all sorts of chemicals every day. We don't have the resources to investigate every one, so unless we have reason to we just keep things on file. In this particular instance, I expect that by the time the results came through Quinn had already been charged.'

'So what do you suppose made Leighton think it was meaningful?'

'I suspect he's been through everything relating to the case with a fine-toothed comb and this forms part of a bigger picture. No doubt that map fits into the equation somewhere, as well, but without knowing what it represents it's hard to add up.'

'Becky got to the bottom of that. It came from a local conservation group and apparently represents the known locations of a rare type of clover,' Lawrence sifted through several of the pages on his desk in search of the relevant document. 'Sulphur clover,' he remembered, aloud, as it came to light. 'Found mostly on road verges and railway banks.' He glanced back to Max. 'Any idea what that might relate to?'

'There were a couple of botanical samples retrieved from O'Leary's remains – a seed under a fingernail and a plant fragment caught in his watch strap,' Max replied. 'Have you got the map to hand?'

Lawrence passed Max his copy and watched as he cast his eyes over it. At length, Max looked back up, saying, 'NCBA – that acronym you asked about – is a thiazole that was among the other compounds that showed up on O'Leary's skin. It commonly arises in particulate matter from tyre wear. I'm wondering whether Leighton's thinking was along the lines of O'Leary having been hit by a vehicle. It's quite possible his hand could have come into contact with both the road surface and the verge in that eventuality, and the clover might have helped to narrow down where that happened. There's a stretch along one of the farm's boundaries,' he tapped a finger on the map before handing it back.

'I can see that's possible,' Lawrence agreed, taking the document. 'Were there any injuries consistent with an RTC?'

'It's hard to say when we only got one limb, and there was significant post-mortem damage.'

Lawrence nodded. 'Did anything stand out in whatever paperwork Leighton had on the case?'

'To be honest, there's little more than what was in the original file,' Max admitted. 'He doesn't tend to write much down unless he's required to do so. I'm hoping Jon might have more idea of what his thoughts were.' As he spoke, his mobile buzzed, and he drew it from his pocket and glanced at the screen. 'Speak of the devil,' he remarked, swiping the message open. There was a momentary pause before he said, 'Although we may not need his help after all.' He raised his eyes from the phone. 'Apparently Leighton's awake.'

'Police?'

Rebecca wondered how the mumsy senior nurse whose name badge identified her as Connie had reached that conclusion just from looking Lawrence up and down. In response to his answer to the affirmative, she informed him, rather curtly, that Leighton wasn't up to 'being quizzed' and recommended he call ahead in future. The revelation that they were, in fact, colleagues didn't change her stance, and Connie only reluctantly relented when Rebecca protested that she was a friend, agreeing to grant them access - briefly - if Leighton recognised her first name. Apparently he was cognisant enough to do so, and a couple of minutes later they were shown into an uncomfortably warm, rather colourless ward whose soundtrack largely comprised lowered voices, footsteps, and the regular beeps and hisses of hospital equipment.

Rebecca had been expecting her friend to look pale, but in fact his face was flushed, his hair damp. He was propped up in bed with a breathing tube affixed to his nostrils and a series of leads connecting him to an ECG recorder, his hands bound by lengths of spotless gauze and surgical tape. He raised one slightly in greeting and managed a small smile as Rebecca neared. She leaned to give him a gentle hug.

'Thank God you're ok.'

'I prefer to thank the Metropolitan Police,' Leighton croaked in response as she released him.

'Hello,' Lawrence said, joining Rebecca at the bedside. 'How are you doing?'

'Oh, I'm high on diamorphine, so I'm having a lovely time.'

Lawrence smiled. 'It's good to have you back with us.'

'I bet you never expected to say that,' Leighton joked, before starting to cough.

'We won't disturb you for long,' Lawrence continued, when Leighton managed to catch his breath. 'But before we go, do you think you might be able to answer a few questions?'

'I'll do my best.'

'Can you remember much about your trip to Holly Brook Farm?'

Leighton's eyes rolled sideways, and he blinked and corrected them before saying, 'Some.'

'Is there any chance you might recognise the person – or people – responsible for what happened out there?'

'Um – yeah – maybe.'

Lawrence pulled the table up from across the end of the bed and laid out five photographs in turn. 'Any of these look familiar?'

There was a long pause as Leighton visibly struggled to focus on the images. 'Number two,' he concluded, at length, raising his gaze. 'How'd you find him?'

'You wrote his vehicle registration number on your arm.'

'Oh, right.' He half smiled, his eyes closing briefly. 'Forgot about that.'

'Did he say much?'

'No. Just pointed a gun at me.'

'And was there anybody else there?'

'Not that I saw.'

Lawrence nodded. 'How did you come by the site's location?'

Leighton coughed. Several seconds passed before he said, 'Sorry, what?'

'What was it that took you to the farm?'

'Message. From the lab.'

'Saying what?'

He had to think about this. Eventually, he said, 'Something about chemicals – historical contamination – in some soil samples.'

'Do you remember who the message came from?'

'Clint.'

Lawrence frowned. 'Who?'

'Iain MacClintock. Central Lab tech.'

'What format did it take?'

Leighton blinked. 'Sorry?'

'What sort of message was it? Printout, voicemail, email?'

'Oh – um – Lync, I think,' Leighton replied, weakly.

'Ok,' Lawrence nodded. 'Just one more thing and we'll leave you in peace. Max seemed to think from your notes that O'Leary might have been involved in an RTC. Is that what you were thinking?'

There was a long pause. At length, Leighton said, 'Sorry, what was the question?'

'Did you think O'Leary might have been hit by a vehicle?'

'Maybe,' Leighton responded, uninformatively, his eyes looking out of focus.

'We'll let you get some rest,' Lawrence suggested. 'If anything comes to mind, have someone call us for you.'

Leighton nodded slightly, his eyes closing again. Lawrence turned back in the direction they had come and, reluctantly, Rebecca followed. She suspected the chances her friend would think of much at all without prompting were remote.

Iain MacClintock had looked blank when Lawrence first enquired about the message relating to Holly Brook Farm, and further questions had proved no more fruitful. Guessing that in his current pharmaceutical haze Leighton might be confusing dates, times and people, Lawrence contacted the building's IT department to ask whether they could retrieve Lync correspondence. Apparently they could, and the discovery that the pathologist's recall of the message hadn't been incorrect sent Lawrence back to the Central Lab, still to no avail. Iain's response when presented with a printout of the brief communication was a shrug and a shake of the head, whilst the revelation that the message had almost led to Leighton losing his life was met with seemingly genuine shock. An investigation of the security system's log in an effort to establish who else might have had access to Iain's laptop on the evening in question threw up a thoroughly unexpected result that took Lawrence back to the technician for a third time.

'Apparently you were in two places at once,' Lawrence observed, presenting Iain with a highlighted copy of the access-card log. 'Would you like to explain how?'

Iain muttered something under his breath, closing his eyes.

'Sooner rather than later,' Lawrence chivvied, sharply.

There was a pause before Iain revealed, 'I have two cards. Sort of.'

'Sort of?'

'I don't actually *have* both of them,' he admitted. 'But there are two.'

'We'll come back to how there came to be two in a minute,' Lawrence replied. 'Right now I think the more pressing question is who has the one not in your possession.'

'I'm not sure that's relevant.'

'I'd say it's pretty damn relevant, given that whoever has it may well have sent that message!'

Iain shook his head. 'That wouldn't make sense.'

Lawrence was about to ask why not when he guessed the likely answer. 'Because Leighton wouldn't have sent a message to himself,' he concluded, aloud.

Iain nodded.

Lawrence sighed. 'Who else knew he had an access pass?'

'I don't know. He wasn't supposed to use it on a regular basis, it was –'

'He wasn't *supposed* to have it at all!' Lawrence exclaimed. 'What were you thinking giving it to him in the first place?'

'I didn't, really,' Iain protested, weakly. 'I lent him mine one evening so he could run some tests before the next day, and he cloned it. I did ask him not to keep using it.'

'Oh, well, that's all right then!' Lawrence returned, sarcastically. 'You didn't think perhaps you ought to report it to someone?'

Iain shrugged weakly. 'He wasn't doing any harm. Besides, the security office must've been aware he had it, it's not like they don't do the rounds out of hours.'

'That doesn't mean they knew he *shouldn't* have it! Their job isn't to police where staff members are once they're in the building!'

Iain didn't respond.

'Do you know how he cloned it?'

'I didn't ask.'

Lawrence suspected Iain hadn't *wanted* to know, and returned to the matter of the messages sent from Iain's computer on Tuesday evening.

'From the brief exchange on Lync I presume he was expecting test results of some sort back from you?'

Iain nodded. 'Yeah, he left a couple of soil samples with me earlier in the afternoon.'

'Where from?'

'The fingernails of a man called O'Leary.'

'Do you have any idea what he was looking for?'

'I think he was hoping to find a clue to why the original results had disappeared from our records.'

Lawrence's eyebrows rose. 'Disappeared?'

'Well, there's no official record of the tests being requested and no sign of the results, but we definitely ran them.'

'Is that your contention, or Leighton's?'

'Both.'

'And what were the results of the re-run?'

'Unremarkable. If we had a site we were trying to connect the body to they might be useful, but there's nothing unusual about them that might give us anything more.'

'So what motive would anyone have to make the first set disappear?'

'I wish I knew.'

'Who else might have known Leighton was expecting to hear from you? Was there anyone around when he brought you the samples?'

'He was barely here a minute,' Iain replied, sounding mildly apologetic. 'We'd already spoken on the phone. I was out at lunch when he called and he said he wanted to hand the samples over in person. I told him to run them up when he got back.'

'Back from where?'

Iain looked momentarily puzzled before apparently realising he had omitted that piece of information. 'He was heading out for lunch himself.'

'Did he say where to, or whether he was going with anyone?'

'The pub, I think. With Roddy.'

'Roddy?' Lawrence echoed. 'I didn't think he and Leighton got on.'

Iain shrugged. 'I think they just like winding each other up. I was more surprised he'd got Roddy into a pub. That doesn't happen often.'

'And did you have any further communication with Leighton after he left the samples with you?'

Iain shook his head. 'I did send an email to let him know when the results came through,' he offered. 'But that wasn't until Wednesday morning. And they weren't much use to him by then.'

*****

'Becks?'

Rebecca glanced up to see Miranda standing a couple of feet away, her expression anxious. Rebecca wondered what had happened to *bitch-face Byrd*, as she had mentally taken to calling the woman. Miranda had never called her *Becks* before.

'Hi.'

'Were you at the hospital earlier?'

Rebecca nodded.

Miranda hesitated. 'How was he?'

'Reasonably with it, considering. He seemed quite cheerful.'

'Did he say much about what happened?'

'No, not really.'

'Do they think he's going to make it?'

'I don't know,' Rebecca admitted, mindful of a warning Jon had given her about the likelihood of complications. 'But he's awake, so that must be a good sign.'

Miranda nodded slightly, pursing her lips. Despite her previous animosity, Rebecca felt for her. 'He's made it this far,' she offered.

Miranda nodded again and Rebecca guessed she didn't trust her voice. After a moment's indecision, she suggested, 'Coffee?'

The other woman nodded for a third time, forcing a smile. 'Thanks.'

Max glanced up from his laptop as Lawrence put his head around the office door.

'This isn't a great time, mate, can it wait?'

'No, not really.'

Max sighed, sitting back in his chair and saying, as Lawrence took a seat, 'Did you manage to get any sense out of Leighton?'

'We did. And he succeeded in ID'ing the man responsible for events at Holly Brook Farm.'

Max nodded.

'I understand he sometimes uses the facilities in the labs upstairs.'

'On occasion, if it means getting a result faster than sending it through official channels.'

'I'm trying to track down the access pass he has for that.'

'We don't have passes for the fourth floor. It's a separate department.'

'So you weren't aware Leighton was using a copy of one of the technicians' passes to come and go as he pleased.'

'No, I wasn't,' Max replied, sounding nettled. 'And I'm struggling to see how that could possibly be urgent, given that he's unlikely to be going anywhere near the labs in the foreseeable future. I certainly don't need you to point out that had I been firmer with him he might not be where he is now.'

Lawrence shook his head. 'You're not responsible for Leighton's cavalier attitude to his own safety. And I'm not here to score points. My main concern isn't the fact he had a pass, what I want to know is who knew about it and where that pass is now.'

'Does it matter? Surely security can just cancel it?'

'It matters because it looks as though someone may have used the card to access one of the technicians' computers and write the message that sent Leighton out to Cheshunt.'

There was a brief silence as Max absorbed what Lawrence was saying and grasped the implications. 'Someone *planned* that?' He exclaimed. '*Here*?'

'Here, the Met, the lab –' Lawrence held his hands out to emphasise the uncertainty.

'*Why*?'

'Good question. Clearly it has something to do with the O'Leary investigation, but what that might be I don't yet know.'

Max didn't reply. He looked stunned.

'Is there anything you're aware of that might serve as a motive? Any individuals he's raised concerns about?'

Max considered his answer before shaking his head. 'Not that I can recall.'

'We may be able to identify the person or people responsible from the signing-in book and CCTV footage, but as there's a good chance Leighton used the security office to clone the access card I can't discount the possibility a member of the security staff might be involved. I was hoping you might be able to contrive some reason for checking the tapes, because at this stage I'd like to keep the fact we may be looking at conspiracy to murder off the record.'

Max nodded. 'I'm sure I can come up with something.'

'And I realise it's a long shot, given his chaotic record-keeping, but could you have a sort through everything he's been working on and see whether you come across anything that might be relevant? Particularly anything on O'Leary.'

'Of course.'

'On that subject, it seems Leighton and one of the technicians were both convinced some test results relating to the original investigation had disappeared from the system. In light of what's happened since, they may well be right, but the rerun threw up nothing of note and apparently neither of them recalls the original findings being anything out of the ordinary. You said this morning that a lot of results tend to be kept on file – why would someone interfere with one ostensibly unremarkable piece of evidence and not another?'

Max thought this over before saying, 'The clue may lie in the word *ostensibly*. Just because the results seem unremarkable doesn't mean they would be irrelevant if we had the whole picture.'

Lawrence nodded. On reflection, it seemed a glaringly obvious point. As, it turned out, was Max's second suggestion.

'Or perhaps they just didn't know much about what they were looking at.'

'Sorry, I didn't expect to be gone long,' Rebecca apologised, as she hurried into Lawrence's office. 'I popped out for coffee, but I was with Miranda and she was upset, so –' she broke off as Lawrence signalled for her to close the door. 'What's happened?' She asked, panic rising in her chest. 'Is Leighton –'

'I've not heard any more since we were there this morning.'

Relaxing in relief, Rebecca pushed the door shut and turned to sit down.

'Is that what Miranda was upset about?'

'Yes. She didn't do much to discourage his fascination with O'Leary. She said she feels responsible.'

'She's not the only one. Max has been beating himself up over it, as well.'

'I don't think there would have been any stopping him.'

'No,' Lawrence concurred. 'And someone was so determined *to* stop him I think he would have come to grief even if he'd not made the trip to the farm.'

Rebecca frowned. 'How would they have known, if he'd not pitched up there?'

'The test results that prompted his trip over there weren't genuine. Someone engineered that.'

For a moment Rebecca couldn't breathe. She stared at her superior in horror. '*Seriously*?' She managed, at length.

'So it would seem.'

Rebecca didn't respond, feeling dazed.

'Do you have any idea who might have had reason to do that, or who might have known what he was working on?'

'Just about everyone,' Rebecca replied, before adding, hurriedly, 'In terms of what he was working on, I mean. He's pretty sociable – I don't think there are many people in this building or his own who don't know him – and between his obsession with O'Leary and calling DCI Rose an obnoxious wanker he's hardly been keeping a low profile lately.'

Lawrence sighed. 'I suspect you're right,' he agreed. 'How about anyone with reason to want him out of the equation?'

Rebecca hesitated, and, apparently guessing the thought she was reluctant to voice, Lawrence said, 'Besides Pete.'

'Not that I can think of. He's pissed a few people off recently, but nothing that would merit more than a complaint to Max.'

'He hasn't raised concerns about anyone?'

Rebecca thought this over before responding. 'Not to me. There've been *things* that have concerned him, but I don't think he'd ever name names without facts. He's not one for snide insinuations or bitching about people behind their backs.'

'What things? Aside from the obvious.'

'I don't really know,' Rebecca admitted. 'He thought someone was trying to undermine him, but I didn't have much time for what seemed like conspiracy theories. Jon's probably the best person to ask, I should think he's had his ear bent a few times. Or maybe Miranda. She had a lot more time for his fascination with O'Leary than I did.'

'Why did she even entertain it when Pete had made his feelings about the matter so clear?'

'I think she's quite fond of Leighton,' Rebecca revealed, awkwardly, heat rising in her cheeks.

'What do you mean by that? She fancies him? Or is there something more between them?'

'I don't think so. But he doesn't give a lot away where his personal life's concerned.'

'True enough,' Lawrence agreed. There was a brief silence before he said, 'I think we can safely conclude his concerns someone was interfering with his work weren't unfounded. And the likelihood is O'Leary is at the root of that. What we don't know is whether someone was trying to frustrate the investigation itself, or simply looking to conceal mistakes or misconduct.' He paused. 'I will try to get a clearer picture of which pieces of evidence are missing or in contention, and of who might have had the opportunity to direct him to the farm. I'd like you to scour everything you can find on O'Leary and see whether you can find any holes, inconsistencies or errors. I'd also like a list of everyone who had any involvement with the original investigation – officers, scientists, SOCOs, et cetera.'

Rebecca nodded.

'And please keep the purpose of the task to yourself. Only a handful of people have any idea that Leighton didn't find his way to the farm by way of genuine evidence, and for the time being I'd like to keep it that way.'

Lawrence returned to the pathology unit shortly before seven to find Max sitting a few feet from Leighton's desk with a stack of paperwork in his lap and a collection of partially filled archive boxes arranged in a horseshoe on the floor around him. Relegating the bundle of pages in his right hand to the box at ten o'clock, he glanced around in response to the sound of the door, and, on seeing Lawrence, abandoned what he was doing and leaned back in the chair.

'I'd ask if you want the good news or the bad, but I've yet to come across any of the former,' he opened.

'So what's the bad news?' Lawrence asked, reaching for the chair at Jon's desk.

'We have zero CCTV footage for Tuesday evening.'

'What? Why?'

'Some sort of system outage.'

'Now there's a coincidence,' Lawrence remarked, sceptically.

'I thought the same, but it turns out it happened four times in twenty-four hours, so it may be a genuine technical glitch. Not that that helps us any.'

Lawrence sighed, mentally trying to picture the building and its surrounds in an attempt to recall whether there might be external cameras covering the main entrance and side exits.

'I do, however, have copies of the relevant pages in reception's logbook for you, as well as a list of resident staff the security records place in the building,' Max continued, when Lawrence didn't respond. 'There's a folder on my desk if you want to pick it up on your way out.'

'Thanks,' Lawrence nodded. 'Have you found anything of interest in here yet?'

'No. Unless you count this,' Max reached behind himself and presented Lawrence with a triangular yellow sign bearing a large black exclamation mark and the words RISQUE D'AVALANCHE.

Lawrence smiled. 'Very apt.'

'A gift from Jon, I imagine,' Max replied, returning it to Leighton's desk.

'How's he doing after Wednesday?'

'I don't really know, to be honest. I've not seen him. I told him to take yesterday off, and he wasn't rostered to work today.'

Lawrence nodded, glancing at his watch. 'Is Roddy still around?'

'No, it's just me this evening.'

'Will he be working over the weekend?'

'He should be in tomorrow, but if you tell me what it is you're after I can look into it for you now.'

'I need to speak to him.'

Max's eyebrows rose. 'About what?'

'Tuesday evening.'

'Is that really necessary?'

'He worked on the O'Leary investigation and he was in the building on Tuesday, so yes.'

'I really can't see his being involved. Besides, if he'd known Leighton had a pirated security pass I'd have known as well, believe you me. Much as he wastes an awful lot of energy on petty nonsense, from time to time he does bring more important matters to my attention. And I know you think I let the lunatics run the asylum, but if I'd been aware Leighton had a clone of someone else's pass I would have contacted the lab. Not least because we could probably have come to some sort of arrangement on granting him official access.'

'It is possible Roddy learned about it after he had reason to keep it from you.'

Max sighed. 'I'm really not comfortable treating my staff like suspects.'

'None of us is comfortable with it!' Lawrence exclaimed. 'But the most uncomfortable part of this whole damned mess is the fact a member of staff from either your building or mine willfully directed a colleague into harm's way!'

'I know, I know,' Max conceded. There was a brief silence before he admitted, 'I just can't get my head around it. Generally I can either understand – on some level – what made someone act as they did, or that a person's thinking was as incomprehensible as their actions. But on the basis of what we have so far, it seems likely someone's opted for an incomprehensible solution to a comprehensible problem.' He shook his head slightly. 'And making sense of that is like nailing jelly to a wall.'

Saturday 24 April

Roddy was always in early, and had already started work in the lab when Lawrence arrived at the pathology unit shortly after eight. He glanced up from the microscope as the lab door opened, and from his look of surprise it was clear he had been expecting someone else.

'I don't think Max is in yet,' he offered, helpfully.

'It's you I was looking for, actually.'

'Me?' Roddy's grey eyebrows drew together in consternation, and Lawrence wondered whether he was anticipating being asked to take on extra work.

'I was hoping you might have time for a quick chat.'

'What about?'

'I'm just looking to fill in some blanks about Tuesday evening.'

Roddy grunted in response, whether by way of agreement or simply acknowledgement, Lawrence wasn't sure. He decided to take it as the former, and reached for a nearby stool.

'Did Leighton say anything to you about some soil samples?' He asked, as he sat down.

'Yeah,' Roddy confirmed, turning a few degrees towards Lawrence. 'He was convinced somebody was interfering with his work. I thought he was being paranoid.'

'Do you still think that?'

Roddy appeared to consider this before answering. 'The fact he ran off half-cocked and almost got himself killed doesn't give me any more information either way, does it? But sometimes stuff does get misfiled or lost, and it's a lot more likely than the alternative.'

'Is that a yes?'

'On balance.'

Lawrence nodded. 'Have you any idea what took him out to the farm?'

'Reckless abandon?'

Lawrence didn't acknowledge the remark, regarding Roddy in silence and waiting for him to give a proper answer.

'No,' Roddy capitulated, at length. 'But I know earlier in the day he was chasing Clint to re-run some tests, so he might be able to tell you.'

'I spoke to Clint yesterday. He mentioned that you'd been for a drink with Leighton on Tuesday lunch time.'

'A soft drink.'

'Even so, it's not something you normally do, is it? What made Tuesday different?'

Roddy shrugged. 'He said he was having a crap day. I felt bad for the guy.'

'And what did you talk about?'

'How does that concern you?'

Lawrence reworded his question. 'Did you discuss the O'Leary investigation?'

'A little.'

'Presumably, then, he updated you on where he'd got to?'

'Hardly. I think his exact words were *if nobody else knows the details, the only person who can fuck it up is me.*'

'You didn't press him?'

'No. He wasn't obliged to fill me in. I just told him not to do anything too stupid. For all the good it did.'

'So do you think he deserved what happened?'

'Nobody *deserves* that!' Roddy exclaimed. 'Don't twist what I'm saying! You're normally the first to object when people conflate risk and blame!'

He wasn't wrong. Few things riled Lawrence more than kneejerk cries of 'victim blaming' in response to sensible suggestions on crime prevention. The implication that people had no power to maximise their personal safety struck him as irresponsible, while the idea of refusing to take steps to protect oneself because one *shouldn't have to* seemed alarmingly naive. Why people couldn't see the absurdity of neglecting to mitigate real-world risks on the grounds that in an ideal world the dangers wouldn't exist was a mystery to him. None of them was living in an ideal world.

'But clearly it didn't come as a surprise to you.'

Roddy's eyebrows contracted into an expression of incredulity. 'Are you *serious*? I meant something that might get him sacked, not killed!'

'Like accessing the labs upstairs without permission, you mean?'

'Yes, exactly like that.'

'So you were aware he had a copy of someone else's access pass.'

'I wasn't, but it doesn't surprise me. He's always been under the misapprehension he's above the rules.'

'That's always bothered you, hasn't it?'

'Like I'm the only one,' Roddy returned, pointedly.

Lawrence chose to ignore the comment, saying instead, 'Can you think of anyone who might have had reason to want him out the way?'

'I'd say the guy who locked him in the freezer would be a safe bet,' Roddy responded, rather flippantly.

'Anyone here.'

'Here?' Roddy echoed, looking perplexed. 'What do you mean, here? Nobody here told him to go haring off to investigate a potential crime scene without back up, did they? Most of us have had to tell him *not* to do that at one time or another.'

'Maybe, but someone gave him the coordinates.'

'Well, yes, but they weren't to know what he was going to do with them.'

'Why not? As you've just said, he's done it before.'

'That's hardly a reason to withhold test results, much as it might seem like it with the benefit of hindsight.'

'No, you're right, but the ones that sent Leighton over to the farm were fabricated. So I suspect whoever provided them did so in the hope he *would* follow them up.'

This revelation was met with silence, and after a moment Lawrence added, 'Which, of course, indicates that the person responsible knows him well enough to guess he might well do as much.'

There was another silence before Roddy spoke. 'Is that a roundabout way of asking whether I was involved?'

'That is a question I have to ask, and I am going to need to know where you were between five-thirty and six on Tuesday evening, but as you, Jon and Ana share an office with Leighton you're also likely to have more idea of what he's been working on than the rest of us.'

'What, and of who might want him dead?' Roddy asked, doubtfully. 'I know he's not exactly made himself popular recently, and I can see someone like Pete losing it with him in the heat of the moment, but premeditated murder –' he raised his eyebrows and shook his head slightly in lieu of completing the sentence.

'How about work? Was there anything – besides O'Leary and the soil samples – that he was concerned about?'

'He mentioned some other stuff going missing, but I expect it'll turn up sooner or later. Organisation isn't exactly his forte.'

'No, but he's not in the habit of losing track of evidence.'

Roddy conceded this point with a change of expression and a small nod.

'Did he say which investigation the missing samples related to?'

'I know it wasn't O'Leary or the dog deaths in Stratford, but that's all he told me.'

'And how about Tuesday evening? What were you –'

'Actually, there was one other thing,' Roddy interrupted.

'What was that?'

'It's probably nothing. There was a sample in a batch from the O'Leary PM that was labelled in different handwriting from the rest. That's not necessarily meaningful – between us and the technicians there's often more than one person involved in bagging stuff up. But Leighton was determined to read something more into it.'

'Do you know what the sample was?'

'A hair belonging to Sean Quinn.'

Lawrence frowned. 'But that would prove nothing. We know O'Leary was with him in the hours before his death. The CPS would dismiss that as circumstantial.'

'That wasn't what bothered him,' Roddy replied. 'His concern wasn't that someone was trying to incriminate Quinn. His thinking was that the sample was replaced because the original might incriminate someone *else*.'

'Morning,' Lawrence greeted Rebecca, finding her in his office on his arrival at the Yard, an A4 pad balanced on her knee. 'Any news?'

'Healy's been picked up in Manchester,' she replied. 'He should be here by midday. And Max called two minutes ago.'

Lawrence sighed. 'I must have just missed him.'

Rebecca shook her head. 'He wasn't in the office, said he'd be in after lunch. He was calling to let you know he'd found no sign of the pass, if that means anything to you?'

'Right,' Lawrence nodded, slipping off his jacket and hanging it over the back of his chair before sitting down. 'Do you know a lab technician called Iain MacClintock? Goes by the name Clint.'

'I've met him in passing a few times.'

'Were you aware that Leighton had a copy of his access pass to the Central Lab?'

'I knew he had a pass,' Rebecca admitted, her evident discomfiture betraying the fact she had also known he shouldn't have done. 'But I didn't know whose it was.'

'Have you any idea how many other people knew?'

'No. But he didn't make a secret of it. Why?'

'The bogus test results that directed Leighton to the farm were sent at five thirty-seven on Tuesday evening from Clint's computer, and someone used the pass at about the same time. It could be that Leighton was up on the fourth floor himself, but it's also possible someone else used the pass to access Clint's laptop. The card wasn't among the belongings Leighton had on him when we found him, and apparently Max hasn't turned up anything on or in his desk.'

'Does Clint have an alibi?'

'Not a water-tight one. But I think it's very unlikely he was responsible. His reaction to the news seemed genuine, and if he'd wanted to direct Leighton to the farm he could have done the job in person. Lync might not leave an obvious trail, but it's still risky.'

Rebecca nodded.

'The message related to something Leighton asked Clint to do at lunchtime on Tuesday, so assuming Clint wasn't involved, whoever was must have heard about it during the course of Tuesday afternoon. Clint couldn't think of anyone at his end who knew the details, so presumably the information came from Leighton.'

Rebecca nodded.

'Do you know how he's getting on?'

'Not great. He's got pneumonia.'

'Asking him isn't an option, then.'

'He was pretty out of it when I was there last night,' Rebecca admitted. 'I could try calling his mum, though, see whether he has any idea which way is up?'

Lawrence shook his head. 'I don't want to put too much pressure on him. Besides, if he's not thinking clearly, his version of events may be more hinderance than help. But if he's compos mentis next time you visit, see whether he can give you any names.'

'I'm going to head over there later, so I'll see what I can do.'

'Thank you. In the meantime, the signing-in and access-card logs for the Gresham Building might give us some ideas. Have you had a chance to go through those yet?'

'Uh-huh,' she confirmed, a note of apprehension in her tone. 'I've made a list of all those who were in the building on Tuesday afternoon, and highlighted those who also worked on the original O'Leary investigation.' She proffered an A4 page. Lawrence scanned it quickly. In addition to Iain and Roddy's names, several others had been tagged fluorescent yellow, and Lawrence immediately realised why Rebecca appeared on edge. One of the people on the list was a member of their team – and, in her case, a friend.

'And did you come across anything of concern in the records for the original investigation?'

'Not really, no,' Rebecca admitted. 'I'm not sure whether the CPS would have secured a conviction, because the physical evidence could all be considered circumstantial, but Quinn didn't do himself any favours changing his story every five minutes.'

Lawrence nodded.

'Would you like me to follow up on the witness statements? See whether what we've got on file tallies with people's recall of events?'

'Not at this stage. Let's see what we can get out of Healy.' Lawrence suggested. 'Although even if we can get him to talk, I very much doubt he'll have all the answers. From his record, I suspect he's nothing more than one of the organ grinder's monkeys.'

'I have three pieces of bad news for you, Mr Healy,' Lawrence began, setting a cardboard folder down on the interview room table and taking a seat beside Rebecca. 'Number one – and this is pure bad luck – the man you locked in the freezer at Holly Brook Farm has a photographic memory. And before hypothermia got the better of him, he made a note of your vehicle registration number.' Lawrence flipped the file open. 'Number two, he's still alive. So we have a witness who can identify you, as well as your van.' He rested his forearms on the table and threaded his fingers together. 'Number three, he also happens to be a colleague of ours. In other words, you are in deep, deep shit, and I would urge you not to make things any worse for yourself by messing us around.'

Norman Healy didn't move, his eyes fixed on the table. Rebecca, in turn, kept her focus on him. The sallow, pitted appearance of his skin made it hard to put an age on him – not that she had ever been a particularly good judge where age was concerned – but from the volume and colour of his hair she guessed he wasn't older than thirty-something. He wore his mousy fringe relatively long, presumably in an effort to hide the ugly scar that cut his forehead and left eyebrow in two, and she wondered whether he had considered growing a beard to disguise his pock-marked skin and prominent underbite. Even if he hadn't been in dire need of a wash and a shave, he wouldn't have been an attractive man.

'I have to say, I'm mystified as to why you took the risk of shutting someone in the freezer alive,' Lawrence continued. 'Especially considering you had a gun on you. Why not take him out on the spot?' He paused, eyebrows raised. When Norman didn't answer, he went on, 'Did you have a reason for not dispatching him immediately? Or do you get off on torturing people?'

'I didn't shut anyone in a freezer.'

'Don't waste my time.'

Norman finally raised his gaze. 'I don't know what you're on about!' He protested, rather desperately.

'You know *exactly* what I'm on about!'

Norman shook his head.

'Ok,' Lawrence replied, after several seconds had passed in silence. 'Let's talk about Connall O'Leary.'

Norman frowned. 'Who?'

Lawrence repeated the name, slowly and deliberately, presenting Norman with a photograph.

'Dunno him.'

'Don't know much, do you?'

No answer.

'Perhaps if we start with the basics we can jog your memory,' Lawrence suggested. 'You are familiar with Holly Brook Farm, at least?'

Norman gave a half-hearted shrug. 'I might've been there once or twice.'

'Well you must have been exceedingly busy on those one or two occasions, because your fingerprints are all over the buildings and half their contents,' Lawrence revealed. 'You clearly played a part in the preparation of a potentially lethal concoction masquerading as vodka – we will be charging you in relation to that, by the way – and your prints are on the freezer door. That being the case, can we take it you were aware of the container's existence?'

Norman shrugged again.

'Yes or no?'

'Yes,' the man admitted, sullenly.

'We also found prints on site belonging to several others, including Mr O'Leary. Did you shut him in the freezer, as well?'

'No! I didn't kill anyone!'

'So you don't know him, but you do know he's dead,' Lawrence concluded, with a lift of his eyebrows. 'That's interesting.'

'That's not what I meant!'

'No? Who were you referring to, then?'

'Nobody!'

'You didn't kill nobody,' Lawrence summarised, aloud. 'I have to admit, I'm a little confused.' He paused. 'I think we might have to start again.' He began leafing through the contents of the file in front of him. 'My colleague – the one who remembered your number plate – once told me visual memory is far superior to other kinds.' Coming to a photograph of Leighton, Lawrence turned it around and pushed it in Norman's direction. 'So perhaps this will aid your recall of events at Holly Brook Farm last Tuesday evening.'

'I wasn't *there*!'

'Does anybody else use your van?'

'No! I don't know how your colleague got my registration number, but it wasn't at the farm! I wasn't nowhere *near* there!'

'Our traffic cameras indicate otherwise.'

'They don't prove nothing, though, do they?'

'I think they'll prove to be a nail in your coffin when all this comes to court,' Lawrence returned. 'Speaking of which, I've been looking over your record,' he drew the relevant page from the file and ran his finger down it as he read, aloud, 'Theft, forgery, theft, obtaining money by deception, taking and driving away, theft again –' he raised his gaze. 'Attempted murder seems quite a leap. Particularly given that allowing someone to freeze slowly to death is hardly a spur-of-the-moment act. It makes me wonder whether that was what you had in mind.' He paused. 'Perhaps the freezer was only intended to be a temporary arrangement. Maybe it wasn't even your idea, and you were just acting on someone else's instructions.' He paused again, then leaned forwards, resting his forearms on the table. 'What I do know is that you were there. I know you closed the freezer door. And I will personally make damn sure you go down for it. So if you want to do yourself any favours, you'd better hurry up and start filling me in on what I *don't* know.' He sat back in his chair, crossing his arms and regarding the man expectantly. 'Your move.'

Returning to his office to find Jamie waiting for him, Lawrence immediately referred to his watch. 'Sorry, have you been here long?'

'Nah,' Jamie replied, switching his mobile to standby. 'Just long enough to waste a few minutes on social media.'

Lawrence nodded, saying as he closed the office door and moved to sit down, 'It's a good job you can't play sport online, or Jim would never have reason to leave the house.'

Jamie smiled. 'You might wish he didn't when he discovers girls.'

'Too true,' Lawrence agreed.

'Did you get much out of Healy?'

'No. He's denying everything.'

'D'you think someone has him by the balls?'

'It wouldn't surprise me.'

'I thought the same with Quinn.'

'Did you believe he was guilty?'

Jamie wrinkled his nose. 'I think he was guilty of something. I don't know that it was murder.'

'Leighton seems to have been certain it wasn't.'

'I know. He was trying to nail down Quinn's movements the night O'Leary disappeared.'

'Is that what he wanted your help with?'

'Yeah, but my memory of the details was fairly sketchy. I was going to check back to see what I could find, but –' he hesitated. 'Then you told me not to.'

'So you didn't give it any more attention after that.'

'No.'

'Did he say anything about it more recently? Or mention some soil samples?'

'Nah, I told him to leave me out of it because I could do without –' Jamie broke off, then re-phrased, 'Because you said no.'

'Because you could do without what?'

'Getting my arse kicked,' he admitted, his cheeks colouring.

Lawrence allowed himself to smile. 'Very wise,' he remarked. 'And did he respect that?'

Jamie nodded.

'Were you aware he had an access pass to the Central Lab?'

Jamie's brow furrowed and he sounded perplexed as he said, 'Obviously. He works there.'

'No, he works in the pathology unit.'

'Isn't that the same thing?'

'No.'

'Oh,' Jamie lifted his eyebrows. 'I thought it was.' And then, as an afterthought, 'Wasn't he supposed to have access, then?'

'Not unfettered access, no.'

'Oh,' Jamie repeated. 'You wouldn't have known. Nobody up there ever seemed worried. And it always looked like he knew what he was doing.'

'So you've been in the labs with him.'

'A few times.'

'Do you know your way around up there?'

'I wouldn't say that. The lab names are largely jargon to me.'

'How about the members of staff? Do you know many of them?'

'Not particularly.'

'Have you come across Iain MacClintock?'

'Iain?' Jamie echoed, with a frown. 'No, I don't think so.'

'You might know him as Clint.'

'Oh, right. Yeah. Scottish bloke.'

'I understand he's friendly with Leighton.'

'Isn't everyone?'

Lawrence smiled. 'True enough,' he agreed. 'I gather you were in the Gresham Building on Tuesday evening.'

Jamie thought for a moment before nodding.

'For what?'

'I was going for a beer with Jon,' Jamie replied, before adding quickly, 'After we were done for the day, I mean.'

'And you went to the trouble of signing in?'

'Yes.'

'Would you mind telling me why?'

'I wasn't pretending to be working, if that's what you're getting at.'

'It's not. I'd just like to know why you didn't wait for Jon in reception.'

'Because you never know if you're going to be there five minutes or fifty,' Jamie replied. 'And it's bloody boring in reception. In the office there's usually either someone to talk to or something to read.'

'And was there?'

'There was a copy of the Evening Standard knocking around.'

'Was anybody in the office?'

'Leighton was, and Jon was in and out.'

'Did Leighton have much to say?'

Jamie shook his head. 'He was up to his eyes in something. Even the offer of a pint didn't shift him.'

'Did you see anyone else, or go anywhere other than the pathologists' office?'

Jamie frowned. 'No. And with respect, I don't get why you care what I was doing after I was done working. I had a couple of beers with a mate when I was off duty and I was sober when you picked me up at stupid o'clock the next morning.'

'I'm just trying to build up a picture of events in the Gresham Building early on Tuesday evening, because during that time somebody used a computer on site to send Leighton bogus lab results directing him to Holly Brook Farm.'

There was a pause while Jamie presumably processed this information. He swallowed. 'So what you're actually asking is whether I'm guilty of conspiracy to murder.'

'No, I'm asking where you were and who you saw.'

'That's exactly what you're asking!' Jamie exclaimed, angrily. 'You can dress it up however you like, but that's the bottom line!'

'Jamie –'

'I know any of us can screw up and wind up on the wrong side of the law, but what sort of sick fuck leaves someone to die in a freezer container? That's not just premeditated, it's sadistic!'

'I'm not suggesting you –'

'Like hell you're not!' Jamie retorted, standing abruptly and shunting his chair backwards in the process. 'You didn't ask why I signed in out of idle curiosity, did you?'

'Sit down!' Lawrence ordered. 'All I am doing is gathering information! The fact I am asking what you remember of your time in the Gresham Building doesn't mean I am accusing you of anything!'

'It might not be an explicit accusation, but that doesn't change the implication!'

'I don't want to have to do this any more than you do! Throwing an adolescent tantrum will only prolong the process, and it certainly won't do you any favours! Now *sit down*!'

Jamie shook his head, turning for the door.

'Get back here! We're not finished!'

'I am!'

'Jamie, I'm warning you –'

'You know what?' Jamie returned, wrenching the office door open. 'Right now, I really couldn't give a shit!'

The door slammed shut behind him.

Lawrence had arranged to meet Max in his office, but arrived to find a note on the door directing him to the mortuary. Down in the basement, Lawrence eased open the door, then immediately recoiled in response to the sickening smell of the partially decomposed corpse Max and Ana were working on. From experience, he could imagine what the body would look like closer to – swollen, putrefied flesh alive with maggots – and he had no desire to see the reality. He couldn't begin to fathom what drew anyone to a job that necessitated the handling of such nauseating material, and he remarked on the fact a couple of minutes later as Max joined him in the corridor with a folder in his hand.

'Well, be thankful someone's willing to do the dirty work for you,' his friend remarked, amicably, as he removed his face mask.

'Would you rather I came back later?'

'No, no, Ana doesn't need me to hold her hand. And I've several things for you today. Starting with the work-up on the freezer.'

'And there's no sign O'Leary ever went near it,' Lawrence responded.

Max smiled. 'How did you know?'

'We tracked the freezer container, and until about six months ago it was in Suffolk.'

Max's eyebrows rose in surprise. 'That's got to be quite an outlay. Was it stolen?'

'Yes.'

'Far from the only thing, I suspect,' Max replied, opening the envelope wallet he held and presenting Lawrence with a photograph showing the charred interior of what was presumably Healy's van. Knowing there was no question over the vehicle's ownership, Lawrence examined the picture closely before looking back to his friend.

'What am I not seeing?'

Max handed him a close-up view from the same image, showing what looked like a grubby heavy-duty plastic bag. 'It seems Healy took the precaution of keeping his spare tyre in a fire-retardant bag,' he revealed, before providing another picture in which the bag had been slashed from one side to the other to reveal the tyre inside. 'And then shoved a few extra things in there for good measure.' He presented a photograph of several scorched pieces of fabric laid out side-by-side in evidence bags. Despite the fire damage, they were clearly identifiable as polo shirts – one grey and two in different shades of green – and all had letters or logos embroidered in place of a breast pocket, although from the way the garments had been folded into the bags the details weren't clear.

'You're looking at uniform t-shirts for three prestigious botanical gardens,' Max revealed. 'The SOC team are still going over them, but I think there's a good chance they're going to find traces of rare plants that are listed among those stolen from collections at places like Kew.'

'So the plants in the farmhouse were probably stolen,' Lawrence concluded.

'More than likely,' Max agreed. 'We're trying to get hold of an expert who can identify them, but I suspect that's not going to happen before Monday.'

'Normally that sort of thing is stolen to order,' Lawrence remarked. 'I wonder why they were keeping so many of them at the farm?'

'Who knows. But if they do turn out to be valuable, someone involved must have a good knowledge of plants. To the uninitiated – yours truly for one – a lot of cycads and ferns look much the same. And if you're not passing them straight on, they'll need specialised care, particularly if they've just been uprooted.'

Lawrence nodded.

'And one other rather interesting result,' Max went on. 'Regarding the message sent to Leighton from Clint's machine.'

'Oh?'

'It turns out the information wasn't actually made up.'

During Friday evening's visit to the hospital, Rebecca had met Leighton's mother, and, although she had been determined not to impose, almost two hours had passed before she departed. In the circumstances, it wasn't surprising that Lorna Campbell should be anxious and restless, but from the unconscious way she worried her bracelet around and around her wrist, one link at a time, Rebecca guessed she was highly strung by nature. She had talked and asked questions almost incessantly, and despite having stayed far longer than intended, Rebecca had felt guilty when she finally took her leave.

Lorna wasn't at her son's bedside when Rebecca arrived late on Saturday afternoon, and he wasn't awake. Rebecca perched on the empty chair by the bed, her eyes wandering over the cards scattered on the bedside unit, a hand-drawn one of a racing car catching her attention. Peering in to see whom it was from, she frowned, thinking she must have misread the contents. She reached for the card, opened it and read it several times, struggling to absorb the implications of the words inside, which began, 'To Dad'. The card was signed off 'Dylan'.

Rebecca couldn't recall ever even hearing the name. Leighton hadn't been kidding when he'd said she didn't really know him. She felt hurt that he'd shared so little with her.

As she replaced the card, she saw a petite woman clad entirely in black, complete with a thick, choppy black bob and black eyeliner, heading towards her. The newcomer looked quizzically at Rebecca as she approached and Rebecca gave her a small smile. 'Hello.'

'Hi. Are you from the police?'

'Yes. We work together,' she explained, indicating Leighton and moving to stand. 'I'm Rebecca.'

'Millie,' the woman replied, before nodding towards the card and adding, 'Dylan's mum.'

Rebecca had no idea how to respond: she'd no more heard of Millie than Dylan, and without knowing the status of Leighton and Millie's relationship it was impossible to gauge what information the other woman might expect her to know already. At the same time, there were countless questions Rebecca desperately wanted to ask. In the end, she opted to focus on the here and now.

'How's he doing?'

Millie shook her head slightly. 'I don't really know,' she admitted, her eyes flickering towards the bed. She took a couple of steps back before adding, in a muted tone, 'I mean, I know it's serious, but nobody seems prepared to commit to how bad, or what might happen next – and when he's been awake he's not made a lot of sense.' She paused. 'I know he'd probably just give me the answers I want to hear, but somehow I think that would still help.'

Rebecca understood what she meant: Leighton was good at finding words of reassurance. In fact, when it came to anything but his own feelings, he was good at finding the right words full stop.

'I guess it's better for him this way, though,' Millie continued, pensively. 'Hopefully by the time he's with it enough to worry about the damage to his hands they'll have more idea how bad it is.'

'What damage?'

'From the frostbite,' Millie replied. 'They said he might end up losing some of his fingers. And he's almost certainly going to lose a degree of movement.'

Rebecca swallowed. Jon had said something about frostbite injuries, but he hadn't given her any idea of the seriousness of the situation. Perhaps he hadn't had the full picture himself.

'I didn't realise,' she responded, weakly.

'Have you got the guy who did this to him yet?'

Rebecca nodded. 'We picked him up earlier today.'

'I'd like to say that's a relief, but I don't have much faith in the system,' Millie admitted, rather bitterly. 'No doubt attempted murder will get watered down to ABH and instead of going down for life he'll get six months.'

It was an exaggeration, but Rebecca could identify with the woman's frustration. Attempted murder was notoriously difficult to prove, and the Crown Prosecution Service was often unwilling to pursue anything more than GBH.

'We will do everything we can to see that that doesn't happen,' Rebecca replied, wondering whether Millie's perspective was borne of personal experience or what she had seen of Leighton's work.

'I know,' Millie acknowledged. 'I'm sorry, I'm not knocking the police, I know the lengths you guys go to. But the courts' decisions don't always reflect that. And for some unfathomable reason, human rights legislation seems to be used primarily to protect those who've willfully violated the rights of others. What sort of justice is that?'

Monday 26 April

Hearing Rebecca grunt in surprise, Lawrence glanced up from the highlighted statement in his hands. 'What is it?'

'Paperwork mix-up. There's a bunch of pages here from a historic investigation neither of us worked on.'

'Turn to page three.'

Rebecca did as bid, and there was a moment's silence whilst she presumably read the two sentences Max had underlined.

'It's the same as the Lync message,' she said, as she raised her eyes from the document.

'Word for word,' Lawrence replied. 'Just for a different location.'

'So whoever sent the message probably worked on this, too.'

'Most likely,' Lawrence agreed. 'Although as Pete was SIO on both cases there are quite a few personnel in common.'

'And it's probably not someone from the lab. They'd be able to come up with something off the cuff.'

'They would. Although we can't rule out the possibility someone wants us to draw that conclusion.'

Rebecca nodded, returning her eyes to the file. When she didn't say anything further, Lawrence went back to what he had been doing, and was almost immediately interrupted by a knock at the door. He looked up to see Jamie hovering in the doorway.

'Morning,' Lawrence greeted him, sitting back in his chair. He hadn't been at all sure Jamie would turn up for work that day, and hoped the fact he had was a good sign. That the young man's first action was to hand over a folded piece of paper made him suspect it might not be. He moved to unfold it.

'I wrote down everything I can remember about Tuesday evening,' Jamie offered, as Lawrence flattened the page on his desk. A list of biro bullet points detailed the half-hour period he had spent in the pathology unit. There was a pause before he added, awkwardly, 'Sorry for losing it before.'

Lawrence raised his gaze from the document. 'It was a tough week for all of us,' he acknowledged. 'Thank you for putting this together.'

Jamie shrugged. 'Leighton has a lot more than hurt feelings to worry about. I'm sure I'll get over it.' He turned to go, and Lawrence returned his attention to the account that lay on his desk. As he scanned the page, one detail immediately stood out.

'Jamie?'

He looked around. 'Uh-huh?'

Lawrence beckoned him back into the office, and, as Jamie retraced his steps, gestured for him to close the door.

'You've said here you saw DS Byrd in the corridor on your way to the office.'

Jamie nodded.

'Are you sure that was on Tuesday?'

'Yes.'

Lawrence frowned, wondering whether Rebecca had missed Miranda's name during her examination of reception's logbook. 'I wasn't aware she was in the building.'

'Well she was, because she'd been in the office and when I got there I made a joke about it.'

'To who?'

'Leighton.'

'Did he say why she was there?'

'No. It wasn't a conversation, just a few daft remarks. After a moment he went back to whatever he was doing.'

Lawrence turned his eyes on Rebecca. She was already flicking purposefully through a stack of papers, presumably in search of the answer he was after. Apparently sensing his gaze, she glanced up. 'I'm pretty sure she wasn't on the list,' she said. 'But I'll double check.'

'Writing in a book is hardly a fail-safe system,' Jamie remarked. 'Anyone with a key card could probably slip through the net if the person on the front desk was distracted.'

'I know,' Lawrence replied. 'And Leighton may not have been alone in having a cloned card. But I'm not sure where we would even start with identifying duplicates. They show up as one and the same on the log.'

Jamie nodded thoughtfully. 'There's got to be a pattern to people's card use,' he remarked, at length. 'Or the occasional mismatch where people are using duplicate cards.' He drew his mobile from his pocket. 'And we might not be able to spot it, but I bet there's a computer program out there that could do the job for us.'

*****

Rebecca had been relieved to find she hadn't omitted any names from the list lifted from the Gresham Building's signing-in book, and had spent much of the morning trying to track down CCTV footage from the surrounding buildings in an effort to confirm Jamie's recollection of events. By the time she and Miranda joined Lawrence in his office, it was lunch time.

'I'd like you to run me through what you did last Tuesday afternoon and evening, please,' Lawrence began, as soon as everyone was seated.

'Tuesday?' Miranda echoed, with a frown. 'Why?'

'Tuesday,' Lawrence repeated, ignoring her question.

'Um –' she paused for thought. 'I was doing house-to-house for a stranger rape over in Brentford, and then I was here doing paperwork 'til about nine.'

'You didn't have cause to visit the Gresham Building?'

'Oh – maybe,' she allowed, sounding flustered. There was a momentary pause before she went on, 'Yes, I did, sorry. I popped in for a quick word with Leighton on my way back from Brentford.'

'About what?'

'He'd been in touch with Aileen Quinn, and DCI Rose was on the warpath.'

'Not surprisingly,' Lawrence remarked.

Miranda hesitated. 'He said Leighton would be a dead man when he caught up with him.'

'Were those his exact words?'

'More or less.'

'What do you think he meant by that?'

'I don't know.'

'And how did Leighton take it?'

'He didn't seem bothered.'

Lawrence nodded. 'Did he mention some soil samples?'

'He might have done, but I wasn't interested in encouraging him, he was in enough trouble as it was.'

'You'd given him plenty of encouragement up until that point, though, hadn't you?'

Miranda sighed. 'I know, and I shouldn't have done. I never expected him to go so far. I didn't think he'd risk his job, let alone his life.'

'How long were you there, would you say?'

'I don't know – a few minutes, I suppose. Not long.'

'Were you in the pathologists' office?'

'Yes.'

'So then why did you not sign in at reception?'

Miranda blinked. 'Did I not?'

'If you had, I wouldn't be asking.'

'Sorry, I didn't mean –' she faltered. 'I just didn't realise I hadn't. Darius and I were chatting – I guess I forgot.'

'You and him both, it would seem,' Lawrence returned, sceptically. 'And did you go anywhere besides the pathologists' office?'

'No.'

'That being the case, perhaps you could explain what kept you in the building nearly forty minutes?'

Miranda's eyebrows rose. 'Was it that long?'

'Yes.'

'I must have been messing about with Darius for longer than I thought.'

Lawrence nodded thoughtfully. 'So how is it that someone who was in the pathologists' office after you, but who left the building before you, doesn't recall seeing you in reception?'

Miranda's cheeks coloured. 'I might not have been visible from the front of the reception desk,' she admitted, coyly.

'And why might that have been?'

She swallowed. 'Do you really need me to spell it out?'

'Yes.'

She lowered her eyes before admitting, 'I was performing a sex act.'

'While Darius was manning the front desk?'

She nodded.

'And there was me imagining it was a tedious job,' Lawrence remarked, drily, leaving Rebecca struggling to keep a straight face.

Miranda didn't reply.

'Did you go anywhere besides reception and the pathology unit? The fourth floor, perhaps?'

'No.'

'Are you sure? A few minutes ago you didn't remember visiting the building at all.'

Miranda didn't rise to the bait, saying only, 'I didn't leave the ground floor.'

'You didn't send Leighton any messages?'

She frowned. 'Why would I when I'd just seen him?'

'I'm not clear why you felt it necessary to see him at all when you could have conveyed Pete's wrath by phone,' Lawrence returned. 'Or were you just playing hard to get with Darius?'

Miranda's only response was a weak shrug.

Lawrence regarded her in silence for a couple of seconds before saying, 'I think that's all, for now. In future, please make sure you sign in *every* time you visit the Gresham Building.' He paused before adding, pointedly, 'Even if you are there only to pleasure the security staff.'

'Well that answers the question of how she got her nickname,' Lawrence observed, once he and Rebecca were alone.

Rebecca's eyebrows contracted into a puzzled frown. 'Sorry?'

'Randy Byrd.'

The frown didn't lift.

'Have you not heard that one?' Lawrence asked, trying to remember where and when he had.

She shook her head.

'Are you aware of her having a reputation?'

'Not in that way. I know a lot of people think she's a bitch.'

'*People*?'

Rebecca smiled. 'It's not just the women, if that's what you mean. Jamie calls her the Wicked Witch of the West.'

'A view apparently not shared by Darius,' Lawrence remarked. 'Or Leighton, if the impression I got from you was correct.'

'No.'

'Do you think she really made a trip to the pathology unit just to warn him about Pete?'

Rebecca shrugged. 'DCI Rose did say he was a dead man. I was in his office at the time.'

'I hardly think Pete meant to shut him in a freezer over a conversation with Aileen Quinn.'

'Of course not, I'm just saying it would have been a genuine excuse to visit Leighton if Miranda was looking for one.'

'Yes, I suppose so.'

'Or Darius, come to that.'

Lawrence nodded. 'Can you find out whether he's working this evening?'

'Sure.'

'Thank you. If he is, I'll –' Lawrence stopped. 'Actually, before I speak to him, could you go through the CCTV again and cross-reference it with the names in the signing-in book? I'd like to know whether Miranda was an exception, or whether he *forgot* to register anyone else.'

Rebecca nodded, getting to her feet. Lawrence's mobile buzzed to announce the arrival of a text message and he glanced at the screen to assess the communication's importance, then did a double-take: it contained what appeared to be nothing more than a string of random words. Before he had a chance to do anything more than register this, another message arrived. 'Sorry,' his sister had written. 'Client's kid got hold of my phone.'

Lawrence nodded to himself, deleting the messages and thinking back to the time when he had had to keep his phone out of reach of Jimmy and Elise. These days he was far more concerned with what might be on their mobiles than about either of them having access to his. He flicked the device to standby and set it aside, then stopped short, picked it up again and selected a number.

'Hi,' Max answered, several rings later, 'Can you give me five seconds?'

He didn't wait for an answer before putting Lawrence on hold, and considerably more than five seconds passed before a click announced his return. 'Sorry, mate, trying to do three things at once here,' he apologised. 'What can I do for you?'

'I'm after some more security footage.'

'Right,' Max acknowledged, sounding distracted. There was a brief pause before he continued, 'D'you want to tell me what you're looking for and I'll see what I can get my hands on?'

'I'd like everything for the pathology unit on the afternoon of the ninth of April.'

Max repeated the date in a manner that indicated he was noting it down as he spoke before continuing, 'Anything else?'

'The early hours of the fourteenth.'

'The fourteenth. That it?'

'Yes. Thanks.'

'I'll see what I can do,' Max promised. 'And there's something else that might be of interest to you. Are you on Instagram?'

'What do you think?'

'Yeah, me either,' Max admitted. 'But see if you can find someone who is. And when you do, check out Burke and Hare.'

Lawrence frowned. 'As in the Edinburgh body snatchers?'

'The very same.'

Tuesday 27 April

Rebecca had scarcely shed her jacket before Lawrence called her and Miranda into his office. He had positioned his laptop so that it faced the near side of the desk, and the screen bore a fuzzy monochrome image with few recognisable features. At closer range, Rebecca realised from the row of icons across the bottom that it belonged to a video, which was set on pause. She sat down, and, as Miranda did likewise, Lawrence closed the office door and returned to his seat.

'Right,' he opened, looking to Miranda as he rested his forearms on the desktop and linked his fingers loosely together. 'I'd like you to start by telling me why you initiated a text-message dialogue using Leighton's mobile phone on Friday the ninth of April.'

'What?' She exclaimed. 'I did no such thing!'

'No?' Lawrence queried. 'That's odd, because CCTV puts you in the pathologists' office at the time a call came through from a young lady named Flora. She tells me she spoke to a woman who said Leighton was a bit tied up and suggested Flora – or the friend she was calling on behalf of – send him a text message. And if you compare the times logged by the phone company against the CCTV footage, you'll find that a series of messages were sent to and from Leighton's mobile while he was away from the office.'

'You're assuming his phone was in the office,' Miranda pointed out. 'It's called a mobile for a reason.'

'That hadn't escaped me,' Lawrence returned, coolly. 'But his phone certainly wasn't in the lab – which is where he was at the time – because there was nobody else in there who could have answered it.'

'That doesn't mean it was in the office.'

'No, that's true,' Lawrence agreed. 'But it wasn't the only time someone used his phone to send messages purporting to be from him. On another occasion, a message was sent to me. And when I confronted Darius with the CCTV, he told me you put him up to it, claiming it was payback for some prank or another. Why would he would point the finger at you if you weren't involved?'

Miranda shrugged.

'Presumably the idea was to distract from the O'Leary investigation and at the same time make life more difficult for Leighton,' Lawrence continued. 'Which you largely succeeded in doing.'

Miranda shook her head.

'Unfortunately you didn't manage to quash his interest in the case, which is why you had to go to more extreme lengths last Tuesday evening.'

'How many times?' Miranda demanded in exasperation. 'I didn't have anything to do with that!'

'So you keep saying,' Lawrence returned. 'That being the case, perhaps you could explain this,' he reached to select *play* on his laptop.

It took Rebecca a couple of seconds to work out what she was watching: two rats, one white and one grey, scrambling over obstacles. She looked back to her superior in bewilderment, wondering whether he had picked the correct video clip and, at the same time, why he would have footage of two domestic rats on his computer at all.

'Meet Burke and Hare,' Lawrence went on. 'I gather they're big stars on Instagram.' He paused. 'They belong to one of the managers at the Central Lab. That's her office,' he indicated the backdrop of the rats' enclosure before pausing the clip. 'The door opens onto the corridor just beyond the lifts. And if you didn't visit the fourth floor on Tuesday evening, I'd love to know how you came to feature on camera passing that office at five thirty-two.' He presented Miranda with a printout showing a close-up of the narrow fire-door window. She paled.

'Or perhaps you'd prefer to talk about the end result of that little foray?' Lawrence went on, when Miranda remained silent. He placed a row of photographs on the desk in front of her, one at a time, as if he was dealing cards. They included a picture of the freezer container, one of the frozen body inside it, and one of Leighton in intensive care on Wednesday afternoon. Despite having seen them before, Rebecca felt her throat constrict.

'That's got to be a hell of a way to die,' Lawrence observed. 'I cannot even begin to comprehend how anyone could abandon another human being to freeze slowly to death. That, as one of my officers said, is truly sadistic.'

'I didn't do that,' Miranda protested, her voice choked.

'You may not have closed the freezer door, but you made sure he ended up there!'

'I didn't know.'

'What didn't you know?' Lawrence demanded. 'Because you must have known he wouldn't be coming back!'

She shook her head, tears in her eyes. 'I *didn't*.'

'No? What did you think was going to happen? A nice little chat and a request to please, pretty please, leave the investigation alone?'

'I didn't expect anything like *that* to happen!' Miranda defended herself, weakly. 'Honestly. I didn't even know about most of it. I just –' she broke off. After drawing a deep, unsteady breath, she concluded, 'I was just following orders. I had no idea it would end like that.'

'And whose orders would those be?'

Miranda closed her eyes, pursing her lips. She didn't respond, and after several seconds Lawrence repeated his question. The silence that followed was broken only by Miranda's heavy, uneven respirations, and the ticking of the clock on the wall. At length, she answered, her voice little more than a whisper.

'DCI Rose.'

Pete's reaction to Miranda's allegation was considerably more controlled than Lawrence had expected. After a moment of seemingly stunned silence, he responded, incredulously, 'One of my colleagues said *what*?'

'And, as unbelievable as it sounds, we are obviously obliged to look into it,' Chief Superintendent MacLennan added.

There was a pause before Pete replied. 'What exactly is it I'm being accused of? Perverting the course of justice, or conspiracy to murder?'

'At this stage that's not entirely clear.'

'And what reason did I have for doing this?'

'That's also something of an open question, but it obviously relates to the O'Leary investigation.'

'Why the hell would I kill someone over that when I could just pretend to look into the matter and then make something up to get him off my back?'

'I realise it all sounds very unlikely.'

'Besides, that would have been the least of his concerns if I'd reported him for talking to Aileen Quinn without authorization!'

MacLennan frowned. 'You should have done that regardless. Why didn't you?'

'Because I only found out late on Tuesday, when I had a hundred and one other things to deal with, and after that –' he raised his eyebrows in lieu of completing the sentence.

'Was his contact with Aileen your reason for telling a colleague he was *a dead man* that Tuesday afternoon?' Lawrence queried.

Pete sighed. 'Yes. In retrospect, a regrettable choice of words. But it's far from the first time I've used the expression, and nobody else has come to any harm.'

'Can you think of any reason why one of your colleagues might have made the allegation?'

Pete considered this for a few moments before shaking his head. 'I'm at a loss to explain any of it,' he admitted. 'I'm still struggling to comprehend the fact what happened was premeditated. Leighton getting himself into hot water seemed perfectly plausible. It never occurred to me to question it.'

'Until I followed up something he told me, it didn't occur to me either,' Lawrence replied. 'Presumably that was the idea.'

'What's he had to say about it?' Pete asked, before adding, 'The allegation obviously didn't come from him.'

'What makes you so sure of that?'

'Because it's not true and he's not vindictive.'

'He's not been up to saying much,' Lawrence responded. 'All we've really managed to get from him so far is that someone sent him a message purporting to connect results of a test he'd requested with Holly Brook Farm. And we're confident the person whose machine that message was sent from wasn't involved.'

'Putting a message through the system wasn't very bright, was it?' Pete remarked.

'No,' MacLennan agreed. 'But all the same, we're going to have to check your communications, mobile and otherwise.'

For a moment, Pete looked as if he was going to respond with something along the lines of *you can't be serious?*, but then he shook his head slightly, drew his phone from his pocket and tossed it onto the table. Lawrence put the device to one side. He thought it highly unlikely they would learn anything from it, and not only because Pete knew better than to make such an obvious mistake. Had the man been behind Leighton's visit to the farm, Lawrence very much doubted he would have dismissed Jon's concerns later that night; taking control of the rescue mission and steering it in another direction would have made much more sense. But he couldn't rule out the possibility Pete might have assumed nobody else senior enough to mount a meaningful operation would have been persuaded to do so. It wouldn't have been an unreasonable assumption – Lawrence wasn't sure he would have been unduly worried had Rebecca not been so concerned. Her anxiety had been contagious.

Pete's point about Leighton's contact with Aileen Quinn was less convincing. That he would have been in a position to report the pathologist for misconduct wouldn't have made any new evidence Leighton might have come by – or any counterclaims he might have made about wrongdoing in the O'Leary investigation – any less valid. And given how protective Max was of his staff, not to mention the animosity between him and Pete, Leighton wouldn't have been fighting that battle alone.

A knock came at MacClennan's office door, and his PA appeared. 'Sorry to interrupt,' she said, directing the apology to her boss, before shifting her attention to Lawrence. 'DCI Forrester, there's someone outside needs to speak with you urgently.'

Lawrence looked to his superior, who dismissed him wordlessly with a small nod, then stood to leave the room. Jamie was hovering in the corridor beyond the PA's desk, and his expression was sufficient to convey that he came bearing bad news. As Lawrence neared, he answered the necessary question.

'It looks like Williams has killed again.'

'Are you and his mum doing shifts?' Rebecca asked, arriving at the hospital early in the evening to find Millie at Leighton's bedside.

'Kind of, I suppose,' Millie replied. 'Insofar as I don't have much to say to her.'

Her tone took Rebecca by surprise, and, apparently feeling the need to offer some sort of explanation, Millie added, 'We have very different ideas about parental responsibility.'

'You mean his dad?' Rebecca guessed, tipping her head in Leighton's direction.

Millie looked thrown; clearly she hadn't expected Rebecca to have much idea of what she was referring to. Recovering herself she nodded. 'Nobody should have to go through that. And she let it happen.'

Rebecca didn't reply. For years she had had precious little sympathy for people who stayed in abusive relationships, but that had changed over the course of the year she had lived through Elliot's descent into depression and alcoholism. Although drinking hadn't made him abusive, it had made him incredibly difficult to live with – yet it had taken countless attempts for Rebecca to bring an end to the relationship. And that had been without the added concern of what it might mean for her personal safety. Admittedly she had often feared Elliot might harm himself in the aftermath of a breakup, and the biggest barrier to walking away had been the feelings she still had for him. Seeing him distraught at the prospect of life without her had been heart-wrenching, and, when he begged for another chance and promised to seek help, made it easier to override common sense and the weight of experience to convince herself *this time* might be different. It never was.

'And he *still* runs round after her,' Millie continued, sounding exasperated. 'When we met I loved how much he cares about people. Now it just winds me up watching everyone take advantage of it.'

'How did you meet?' Rebecca asked, out of a mixture of curiosity and a desire to change the subject.

'Dylan had a febrile convulsion in a supermarket and I screamed for someone to help. He did.' She shrugged. 'He drove us to the hospital and stayed to make sure we were both ok.'

'So he isn't –' Rebecca hesitated.

'No. Not biologically. But he has been in every other sense. Even after we split and he moved down here.'

The remark answered a question Rebecca had been dying to ask ever since learning of Millie's existence. She felt relieved in more ways than one. She had hated the idea of having, however inadvertently, gatecrashed another woman's relationship, and the possibility that her friend might have cheated on his partner had shaken her faith in him. Her work offered regular reminders that you can never really know anyone, but that didn't stop it coming as a shock when those close to her behaved in a manner that seemed completely out of character. Meanwhile, the fact Dylan wasn't Leighton's flesh and blood was also reassuring – not sharing the fact you had a relationship with your ex-girlfriend's child was very different from saying nothing about your own son.

‘I should get going, I have a train to catch,’ Millie went on, gathering up her jacket and bag, and getting to her feet. ‘I’ll be back on Saturday, so I guess I might see you then.’

Rebecca nodded. Millie turned back towards Leighton, kissed the first two fingers of her right hand and touched them to his cheek. Then, after a moment’s hesitation, she made for the corridor without another word.

Sitting in the chair Millie had just vacated, Rebecca spotted an iPad in the half-open drawer of the bedside unit and, wondering whether it might give her some insight into the life she knew so little about, reached to pick it up. Once switched on, it issued a demand for the PIN, and she tried the number Leighton used for the tablet in the office. She hadn’t really expected it to work, but the home screen promptly appeared, and she tapped the colourful photo icon.

It took only a couple of pictures for her to realise what she was viewing wasn’t personal: the iPad contained crime-scene photographs, and the folder that was currently open related to the Williams investigation. Presumably Jon had inadvertently left the tablet behind, or perhaps Leighton had uploaded the images to a personal one. Either way, the device shouldn’t have been lying around in a public place, and when Lorna returned Rebecca would try to establish where it had come from. In the meantime, she couldn’t resist the temptation to flick through the photographs. Williams’ resurgence had provoked a mix of emotions, chief among them frustration at being forced to watch the ensuing investigation from a distance. Being an effective outsider among the people she worked with every day had left her feeling strangely lonely, and had done nothing to keep her mind off Rhys Williams. And with few details of his recent crimes available to her, her imagination had been filling in the blanks.

Wednesday 28 April

Lawrence hadn't needed a pathologist to deliver the sombre news that Laura Ancona had died at the hands of Rhys Williams: the girl's mutilated body was almost a carbon copy of one he had seen in London some two years earlier. The better news, which Roddy had imparted within minutes of his arrival, was that they had a considerably better start than in Coralie's case. But, despite the fact Laura had been dead less than twelve hours, immediate enquiries turned up no valuable witness reports, and by the time Lawrence left Birmingham shortly before midnight, the only major change since his arrival was the gathering of journalists and TV crews beyond the police cordon.

He had returned home long after everyone else in the house had gone to bed, and departed again before anyone was up. Popping into the office en route back to Birmingham, he was more than a little surprised to find Rebecca already at her desk, apparently in the process of drawing a schematic outline of a house. She didn't respond to his arrival, and he felt intrigued.

'You're in early.'

Rebecca started and looked up, her tired eyes telling another story: clearly she hadn't slept. But there was an intensity to her expression that immediately conveyed she had something important to impart.

'I need to talk to you about Williams,' she said, urgently, gathering some papers together.

Lawrence frowned. 'Becky, you're not –'

'I think he's working for an estate agent,' she cut in. 'This was taken outside Coralie's flat,' she set a photograph down on the desk and pointed to a board advertising a property through Oakworth Estates a few houses down the street. 'And this outside Laura's.' She repeated the process, indicating a board for the same estate agent before adding an advertisement for a flat in the same road, apparently printed from the agent's website. 'Both properties are in Georgian terraces, and many of those still have interconnecting loft spaces – so if you can access the top floor of one dwelling it's possible to get into others,' she presented her line drawing of a Georgian terrace and drew repeating semicircles in the roof space from one house to the next to illustrate how someone might move from one to another. 'Burglars sometimes take advantage of that to do over more than one place at once.'

Lawrence nodded. Rebecca's final point wasn't news to him, and he silently berated himself for not considering the possibility before.

'Thank you,' he said, indicating the pages on her desk. 'May I take these?'

'Sure,' she gathered them up and held them out.

'How did you come to be looking at this?'

'I was at the hospital. Some of the crime scene pictures were on Leighton's iPad – and then I saw the same estate agent's board in the news footage on the TV.'

'Have you been in here ever since?' Lawrence exclaimed, wondering why she hadn't called to share her thoughts the night before.

'That was only a couple of hours ago. I dozed off – the news was on when I woke up.'

'Were you at the hospital all night?'

'Uh-huh. His mum went to pieces on me, so I stuck around.'

'I thought he was out of danger?'

'He is. But she's worried about the damage to his fingers, and what it might mean for his career.'

'Understandably,' Lawrence responded. 'Do they have any more idea about the long-term prognosis?'

'No. Apparently it'll be at least another few weeks before they know what tissue is or isn't salvageable. But they change the dressings each day, and from what Mrs Campbell was saying it's clearly not a pretty sight.'

Lawrence nodded.

'I get the impression she's very reliant on him.'

'What, financially?'

'No – well, I don't know – I meant generally. I don't think she really knows what to do with herself without him.'

'Where's his father in all this?'

'Sitting at home drinking, I expect,' Rebecca replied, before adding, 'He's an alcoholic.'

And presumably, Lawrence surmised from the little she had said the previous week, nasty with it. He didn't voice the thought, saying instead, 'Did Leighton have much to say?'

Rebecca shook her head. 'I tried asking him about Tuesday afternoon, but his recall of events was all very hazy. And I didn't like to push too hard because he was clearly feeling pretty rough.'

'No, fair enough,' Lawrence replied. 'With luck, ANPR data and IT records will give us some pointers.' He turned towards his office. 'If not, we'll have to think again.'

Lawrence had requested the loan of some office space at Birmingham Central Police Station in order to set up a local incident room, and by late morning most of his team members were gathered in the limited space available, perching on desks and cabinets for want of enough chairs. With the help of an enlarged version of Rebecca's illustration, Lawrence quickly summarised her theory before moving on to the tasks that lay ahead.

'Our first priority is to identify any terraced properties on Oakworth's books that are on or have access to the top floor, and set up around-the-clock surveillance by close of play today,' he began, resting an elbow on a nearby filing cabinet. 'There are bound to be some properties that aren't yet on the website, so our best bet is probably to ring around as prospective customers to ask what else they've got on their books and have them send the details to a Hotmail or Gmail address. And if that doesn't provide us with enough information, we'll need to schedule viewings.'

'Do they do sales, or are they just a lettings agency?' Jamie asked.

'We'll need to approach them on both fronts,' Lawrence replied. 'Using different email addresses, obviously.'

'For sales, we might have to look at other agencies, as well,' his colleague pointed out. 'Some people use multiple agents.'

'Good point,' Lawrence acknowledged, wondering how they might get hold of that sort of information, and whether his sister – an estate agent – might be able to advise him. It was over a decade since he'd had any involvement with the housing market. 'Hopefully we can get an answer to that with an online search of some sort.'

'Shouldn't be a problem,' Jamie said. 'I'll check it out once we've made the initial enquiries.'

'Thank you,' Lawrence nodded. 'Once we have a list of candidate properties, I'd like us to work on building up a picture of the other residents in each terrace, see whether any of them fits Williams' type. To some degree, that's a task we can combine with the surveillance, but we should also look at council tax records, the electoral roll and anything else that might provide a more comprehensive profile.

'Alongside that, we need to gather what CCTV we can from businesses in the immediate vicinity of each of Oakworth's three branches, going back weeks, if they've got it. As we can't discount the possibility Williams has already left town, we're also going to need whatever footage the train station and bus companies can provide for the past twenty-four hours. And we'll need to contact the HMRC to request tax codes and NI numbers for Oakworth's male employees, then work back from there to verify their identities.'

'D'you think there's any crossover between the branches?' Eva queried.

'We'll have to work on the basis that there is,' Lawrence replied. 'Even if the offices are ostensibly independent, I wouldn't put it past Williams to have found a way around that.'

'It's a shame he's not doing something more useful with his time,' Jamie remarked. 'He's bloody clever.'

'Yes,' Lawrence agreed. 'He is. But he's also – by at least some definitions of the word – human, and humans make mistakes. Hopefully he's arrogant enough to think he'll get away with using the same MO one more time.'

Lawrence had been in Birmingham for most of the day, so it was after eight by the time he was able to meet Rebecca outside Miranda's home in Southgate. The flat was minimalist and immaculate, the kind of set-up a friend of Rebecca's had once described as 'not very homely'. At one time, Rebecca might have agreed, but these days she found being in a clean and uncluttered environment very calming. That said, it wasn't enough of a priority for her to devote a substantial amount of her limited free time to domestic chores. Besides, if you didn't live alone the effort would only be frustrated by others' living habits, and there was no way she was going to pick up after anyone else, be it a flatmate or a partner.

Miranda herself looked tired and wan, and Rebecca guessed she hadn't had much sleep since being suspended from duty the previous afternoon. She had little to say as she showed them into her living room, perching apprehensively in a plush cream armchair as Lawrence and Rebecca sat on the matching sofa.

'I'm hoping you might be able to clear a couple of things up for us,' Lawrence began, conversationally, sitting back and crossing his legs.

'If I can,' Miranda nodded.

'Connall O'Leary was clearly involved in some of the illicit activities we've uncovered at Holly Brook Farm,' he revealed. 'And we suspect he was there the night he died.'

'Do you think he died in the freezer?'

'It's possible,' Lawrence replied. 'But from Leighton's research, it seems more likely he was hit by a vehicle. And according to ANPR records, your car was in the area the night O'Leary was last seen.'

Miranda swallowed, but said nothing, and after a while Lawrence added, 'That's quite a coincidence, wouldn't you say?'

She shrugged weakly.

'I'm guessing it was an accident,' he continued. 'Unlike Leighton's trip out that way. He's obviously lucky to be alive, although I'm not sure how lucky he's going to feel if he ends up losing his fingers. And I can only guess at what an experience like that does to a person.'

Tears pooled in Miranda's eyes. 'I never meant for him to get hurt!' She protested, her voice wavering.

'Forgive me for finding that hard to believe.'

'I didn't!' She insisted. 'I just thought that if someone connected O'Leary to the farm, they'd assume his death had something to do with whatever was going on up there. I didn't expect him to go alone! And I never imagined anything so barbaric would happen!'

'Because organised crime gangs are known for their benign response to interference,' Lawrence observed, sarcastically. 'On which note, how did you even know about that?'

'I didn't,' Miranda replied, weakly. 'I only knew that's where O'Leary had come from, and that the farm was owned by a company in Nevis. That, combined with O'Leary's record, made it a fairly safe bet something dodgy was going on. But it never occurred to me Leighton might go up there on his own. And I never, ever meant for him to get hurt! He's my *friend*!'

Lawrence raised his eyebrows. 'Your friend?' He echoed, incredulously. 'Even leaving aside the events at Holly Brook Farm, I wouldn't call lining someone up for disciplinary action very friendly, would you? And there's no question about your intent in that instance.'

'I just wanted Max to shut down his pursuit of the investigation.'

'But he didn't. So you had to take more drastic action.'

Miranda shook her head. 'When I was there – at the pathology unit – on Tuesday, he'd worked out an RTC was the likely cause of death, and he was hoping Clint would be able to help him narrow down where it might have happened –' she swallowed. 'I only ever meant to nudge him off course.'

'Really,' Lawrence responded, disbelievingly. 'How long do you think he would have remained off course? Clint was bound to have sent the genuine results though a day or two later.'

'I didn't have a lot of options. And if he hadn't got hurt, it probably would just have been put down to crossed wires. I doubt anyone would have looked very far into it. It's not as if you can check back on Lync messages as easily as emails.'

'That's true, but if he hadn't survived, it's unlikely we would even have known about the message,' Lawrence observed. 'Those seem rather better odds to me.'

'I honestly didn't mean him any harm,' Miranda insisted. 'I never meant to hurt anyone.'

'Well I'm sure that'll be a great comfort to Aileen Quinn.'

Miranda didn't respond.

'Perhaps you could tell us what happened to O'Leary? Or, rather, *how* it happened, given that we already have a fair idea of *what* happened.'

'He just suddenly appeared, out of the trees,' Miranda replied, with a slight shake of her head. 'It was really late – the road was empty – and then all at once he was just there, right in front of me.'

'If it was an accident, why didn't you report it?'

Miranda shook her head again. 'I don't know. I wasn't thinking straight. I panicked. And then – afterwards – it was too late.'

'Had you been drinking?'

'I wasn't drunk.'

'But you had been drinking.'

'Not much.'

'Enough to make disposing of a body preferable to contacting the authorities, it would seem.'

Miranda didn't reply.

'Where can we find the remains?'

'Epping Forest.'

'Clearly. But *whereabouts* in Epping Forest?'

'I don't think I can be more specific,' Miranda admitted. 'I wasn't thinking about where I was going, I was just driving around looking for somewhere –' she trailed off.

'Out of the way?' Lawrence finished, when she didn't continue.

She nodded.

'And then when his arm turned up, you pinned his death on Sean Quinn.'

'I didn't. Quinn got himself into that mess.'

'You allowed him to.'

'Him getting banged up was no bad thing,' Miranda returned, bluntly. 'You've seen his record.'

'Yes, and it makes for less than pleasant reading, but it doesn't include murder.'

Miranda didn't reply, and several seconds passed in silence before Lawrence said, 'I don't condone your actions, but as far as the accident goes – and allowing Quinn to take the blame – I can understand them. Where the events of the past week are concerned, though, I'm afraid you're on your own.'

'I didn't plan any of that,' Miranda protested. 'I swear. And I'd give anything to be able to undo what happened last Tuesday night. It's been destroying me.' She swallowed. 'I feel sick just thinking about it, and I can't think about anything else.'

'Oh poor you,' Rebecca snapped, coldly. 'Like you're the victim in all this.'

'That's not what I meant,' Miranda replied. 'I know I'm responsible for my situation. And not only mine.' She paused before meeting Rebecca's eyes and adding, hesitantly, 'Can you tell him I'm sorry? Please?'

'I don't think *sorry*'s quite going to cover it, do you?' Rebecca returned. 'But it might at least count for something if you had the guts to tell him yourself.'

'I know,' Miranda acknowledged. 'I know. And if I have the opportunity, I will do it myself.' She swallowed. 'But I'm guessing I won't get the chance.'

Thursday 29 April

Jamie was struggling to give the afternoon briefing his undivided attention, his mind repeatedly rewinding to the mischievous smile he'd awoken to that morning, and the ethical quandary it represented.

After their first meeting, Xanthe had instigated a flirtatious dialogue with him via text message, and a few days in suggested they meet up for a drink. Jamie hadn't expected things to go any further than that one night, but had found himself thinking about her for much of the following day, and when he had sent a message to tell her so, she had reciprocated. Several dates later, he was still thinking about her – and about the sticky career implications of carrying on a relationship with someone who was involved, however peripherally, in an investigation.

He had known he was overstepping the boundaries in responding to her very first message, but a brief flirtation – and then a one-night stand – with someone who was neither a victim of crime nor a material witness had seemed relatively low risk. For starters, nobody else needed to know. But if he continued seeing Xanthe, sooner or later he would be faced with the inevitable questions about how they had met, and lying about it could, in the long term, have more serious consequences than admitting the truth. Besides, it wouldn't be fair to drag her into a lie. The only alternative was to call things off, and he was loath to do that. Hanging out with Xanthe was like spending time with a friend as well as a lover, and it was a long time since he'd had that kind of connection with a woman.

'Jamie?'

He blinked. 'Sir?'

'CCTV?' Lawrence prompted, impatiently.

'Oh – um – we've managed to get plenty of footage in the relevant areas, but at least three of Oakworth's employees are the right kind of height and build, and it's perfectly possible none of them is Williams.'

Lawrence nodded, and Jamie guessed what he was thinking. The final point was what made simply pulling all three in for questioning – normally an obvious first step – problematic.

'And without a reasonably confident ID, knowing who to look for in CCTV from further afield is nigh on impossible,' Jamie added.

'Can the tech team not work some magic with facial-recognition software?'

'Nope. The footage from the original investigation doesn't give them enough to work with. Too much of his face is obscured by a baseball cap. We really need someone who's met him face to face.'

'His former landlady was very helpful during the original investigation, so we could see whether –'

'She's dead,' Jamie interrupted. 'And I've tried the locksmith who employed him, as well, but apparently he's overseas until next Tuesday.'

Lawrence sighed. 'Ok, leave that with me. Any word from the HMRC?'

'No useful words,' Jamie returned. 'I've heard the automated message they play while they keep you on hold about a thousand times.'

'But presumably you have spoken to someone in the past twenty-four hours?'

'Several someones,' he flicked to the relevant page in his notebook and proffered the list of names. 'But it's never the right *someone*, and thus far nobody's returned my calls.'

His superior looked exasperated. 'I'll see who I can stand on to get the message through.'

'Thanks.'

'Anyone have anything else?' Lawrence asked, casting his eyes around the room.

'Yes,' Daniel interjected. 'We've just had an email alert for another property that looks like it meets our criteria.'

'Taking the number needing surveillance to –'

'Seven.'

'Right,' Lawrence acknowledged, with an expressive lift of his eyebrows.

'Can we not move into a few of them temporarily?' Eva queried. 'It'd save on commuting time and reduce the number needing around-the-clock surveillance. Win-win.'

Lawrence shook his head. 'Not at this stage. It might cut costs, but we don't know which of the properties Williams might have a use for, either in terms of their architecture or residents, and we can't risk occupying the wrong ones.'

Eva nodded resignedly.

Lawrence turned towards the wall of information relating to the investigation, then stopped and looked back around. 'Have we managed to establish whether any of the properties is being marketed by multiple agencies?'

'Yep,' Jamie confirmed. 'The house in Myrtle Road is also on the books of Perfect Pad and Sandwells, but as far as I can work out, it's the only one. That's the good news.'

'And the bad?'

'Sandwells are also advertising a place in Richmond Terrace,' he revealed. 'Which means Oakworth's employees weren't the only ones who potentially had access to Laura's flat.'

Lawrence returned to London after the briefing, hoping to catch Rebecca before she left for the day: he really didn't want to have to broach the question he needed to ask over the phone. As it turned out, she was keen to have a word with him, too, although her news didn't come as much of a surprise.

'I've reached a bit of a dead end with the farm,' she admitted, as she sat beside his desk. 'The plant experts have ID'd most of the specimens, and I've managed to match a number of them with reported thefts, but I'm no further on with establishing who's behind the operation. I've been through the phone records for Healy and Falkner – he's the other guy whose prints we lifted from the house – but that yielded nothing of note, and it doesn't look like either of them is going to tell us anything.'

'They may not have much *to* tell,' Lawrence conceded. 'I suspect they're only foot soldiers, and they've been given the minimum of information by whoever is running the show. Do we have an ID for the body from the freezer?'

'No. SOCO have matched his fingerprints to one of the sets found in the house, but they're not on record, and I've not been able to identify him as a missing person.'

'And I don't imagine there's even any point my asking whether you've managed to dig up anything on the farm's owners?'

'No,' Rebecca confirmed. 'But I have learned how to go about hiding assets should I ever have any worth the trouble.'

'Well I'm glad you got something out of it,' Lawrence remarked, with a smile. 'MacClennan's keen to hand the investigation over to organised crime, and I'm inclined to agree. What do you think?'

'Seems sensible,' Rebecca agreed. 'They'll probably have more idea than I do what to try next. And perhaps some contacts that might take things forwards.'

Lawrence nodded. 'Ok. I'll speak to MacLennan and get back to you.'

'Ok,' Rebecca echoed, standing to leave. 'I'll see you tomorrow, then.'

'Before you go, do you happen to know whether Elliot is in London this week?'

'Yes, I think so,' Rebecca replied, clearly bemused by the question. 'He said something about working on a new album.'

'Do you have his address?'

Rebecca's puzzled look segued into a frown. 'Why?'

'I'd like to show him some CCTV clips to see whether he recognises any of Oakworth's staff.'

Rebecca's expression changed again. 'You can't ask him to do that.'

'I haven't any choice,' Lawrence replied. 'Williams' old landlady died last year, and the locksmith who employed him is out of the country. We don't have a long list of witnesses, and we need more than we can get from the CCTV.'

'What about the guy who sublet his flat to Williams?'

'He wasn't much help two years ago, and I think Elliot would be a good deal more reliable.'

'He barely spent five minutes with the guy.'

'I know, but despite the seemingly inconsequential nature of that encounter, he managed to give us a surprising amount of information. He may not be able to help us on this occasion, but I can't assume as much.'

Rebecca didn't respond.

'If lives weren't on the line, I wouldn't ask.'

'What, but it's all right for Elliot's life to be on the line?' Rebecca returned. 'You know what he's been through!'

'I know, and I'm sorry. But it won't be used as evidence, so if you think it might make it easier for him to have you there, I can allow that.'

'Easier for him, or for you?'

Lawrence sighed. 'I understand why you're upset, Becky, and I wish there was a viable alternative. I'm only telling you because I didn't want you feel I'd gone behind your back. If you'd rather not be involved, then that's fine.'

Several seconds passed while Rebecca clearly struggled with how to respond. Eventually, she settled on, 'If he wants me there, then I'll do that for him. But I don't think it's fair to make him relive everything.' She reached for the door handle. 'And I'm not going to pile on the emotional pressure by coming with you to ask for his help.'

'Wake up!'

Daniel jumped as Eva's elbow jolted his arm. 'I wasn't asleep,' he protested, automatically, shifting his position in the car seat.

'You were snoring.'

'I was not.'

'Get over it and check out the guy at two o'clock,' Eva returned, impatiently.

Daniel obligingly turned his eyes to the right, where a man stood almost in the bushes that separated a tiny front garden from the pavement, fiddling with his mobile phone. A moment later, he pushed the device into his back pocket, glanced quickly around himself and made for the front door of the house that had been the focus of their attention since dusk.

'Looks like we're in business,' Eva remarked, as the man drew a set of keys from his pocket.

Daniel held up a hand. 'Wait for him to go in,' he cautioned, before updating the rest of the team on the situation by radio.

It was only a matter of seconds before the front door opened and closed, and light filtered through the downstairs bay window. By the time Daniel and Eva were out of the car, the first floor was also illuminated, and they jogged across the street towards the building.

A unmissable knock drew no response. Daniel didn't waste time repeating the exercise, instead forcing the door and taking the stairs two at a time whilst Eva headed in the likely direction of a back door. He was more than halfway up when his quarry appeared on the landing, brandishing what looked like a metal pipe.

'Police!' Daniel informed him, sharply. 'Drop the weapon!'

The other man didn't move.

'Put it *down*!'

This time, the order generated a response and the man obligingly lowered the pipe before releasing his grip and letting it fall to the floor. He proved surprisingly compliant as Daniel pinned him against the wall and cuffed him, and it wasn't until Daniel informed him why he was being arrested that he reacted.

'Murder?' He exclaimed, incredulously. 'Are you fucking serious? Who am I supposed to have murdered?'

Daniel ignored him and finished reading him his rights.

'I don't want to remain fucking silent!' Came the furious reply. 'I want to know what the fuck is going on! And you'd better be fucking planning to fix my front door! Do you know how much white oak costs?'

'Your front door?' Daniel echoed in surprise.

'Whose door did you think it was?'

'Are you the owner of this property?'

'Yes!'

'Well if it is your house, then I apologise, but we're investigating some very serious crimes, and we're going to need more than your word for it that you're the owner. What's your name?'

'Robert Coulson.'

'How can I verify that?'

'If you take these cuffs off I'll show you my driving licence!'

'I'm afraid I can't do that. Where is your licence?'

'In my wallet.'

'Is that in your pocket?'

'Yes.'

'Would you mind if I took it out?'

'I would, as it goes, but I don't suppose I've any real choice, so why don't you just go ahead?'

Daniel carefully retrieved the man's wallet and flipped it open. The licence confirmed his name, and listed a different local address. By now, Eva had joined them on the landing, and Daniel passed the licence to her, saying, 'Can you have someone check the Title Register?'

'Sure.'

Daniel returned his attention to the man in front of him. 'How long have you lived in Elm Grove?'

'Seven years.'

'So what's this place, a rental property?'

'Not that it's any of your business, but yes.'

'Right. Presumably you've no personal belongings here, then, and you've clearly no tenants at present, so what brings you here at gone eleven? It's hardly the time for doing odd jobs about the place, is it?'

'Is there a law against it?'

'Are you saying that is what you're doing here?'

'There's a window catch needs replacing and tap that's dripping.'

'Does the estate agent not manage that sort of thing for you?'

'What makes you think I employ an agent?'

'There's a board up outside.'

The man grunted in response before admitting, 'I just use them to find tenants. Anything more's a rip off.'

If Oakworth was anything like as inefficient as the agent Daniel rented his flat from, he couldn't disagree. It had taken five weeks and multiple phone calls just to get a broken light fitting replaced, after which he had taken to sorting out similarly small jobs himself. He valued his time more than the cost of the materials. Which brought him on to his next question – the fact the man appeared to have no tools with him. But before he had a chance to ask, a fearful voice interrupted from downstairs.

'Is everything ok?'

The man swore under his breath.

'Should I call the police?'

Friday 30 April

Elliot hadn't been at the studio or his home in Camden on Thursday evening, and calls to his mobile had gone unanswered, so it had taken a good two hours and some assistance from the record company to track him down. Lawrence hadn't been sure what to expect of the meeting – or, more specifically, of Elliot himself. Given the enduring effect Rhys Williams' actions had had on the young man's mental health, any request to revisit the subject was clearly going to be wholly unwelcome, but quite how Elliot might react, Lawrence had no idea. On top of that, this time around Lawrence was dealing not with Rebecca's partner, but with a successful musician whose picture had been repeatedly splashed across magazine covers of late. Elliot was now, to use a description Lawrence knew he detested, a celebrity, and it was quite possible the acclaim had gone to his head.

In the event, although perceptibly on edge, he had been polite and personable, much as Lawrence remembered him from their very first meeting at a social event several years earlier. His response to the news of why Lawrence had sought him out had been surprisingly muted, perhaps because his first concern had been that something might have happened to Rebecca. He had raised no objection to the idea of viewing a selection of video clips that combined persons of interest with random members of the public, and having done so asked to watch the footage for a second time. During this process, he tentatively identified one of Oakworth's employees, saying that something about him 'seemed familiar' and apologising for the fact he couldn't be more definitive.

Lawrence had passed the information on to Jamie, who had spent much of the night wading through reams of CCTV, and turned up to Friday morning's briefing with reddened eyes and wearing glasses in place of his usual contact lenses. Lawrence arrived just as someone who apparently hadn't been on duty the previous evening asked, 'So what happened last night, then?'

'False alarm,' Daniel replied. 'The property owner was using the place as a shag pad while his missus was at home with the kids.'

'Twat.'

'Well at least that should put him off suing for wrongful arrest,' Jamie remarked, raising a laugh.

'Might put off his paramour, too,' Daniel returned. 'She looked guiltier than a nun in a cucumber field when she found out who we were.'

'In the interests of saving time in future, perhaps someone could get onto the Land Registry this morning to request the other property owners' details,' Lawrence suggested, by way of opening the meeting.

'I can do that,' Eva offered.

Lawrence nodded his thanks before looking to Roddy. 'Do we know what the chemical stain on Laura's sheets is yet?'

'No.'

'Can you chase that up, please? See whether the lab can get back to us today?'

Roddy looked perplexed. 'The turnaround time for that kind of thing is at least a week.'

'I know, but we usually get a preliminary analysis within a couple of days.'

There was a momentary pause before Roddy apparently registered what Lawrence was referring to. 'That's not from the lab. That's Leighton running tests himself because he's impatient for the results.'

'Oh, right,' Lawrence responded, realising that he'd given no real thought to what Leighton might have been using his cloned key card to do, and wondering just how much extra work the pathologist had taken it upon himself to do on a day-to-day basis. 'Ok, well if I clear it with Max, could you do it just this once?'

Roddy shook his head. 'It's beyond the purview of a pathologist.'

Lawrence sighed. 'I realise it's not your job, but we need all the help we can get tracking Williams down, and any clue could be –'

'I'm not saying I won't, I'm saying I can't,' Roddy put in. 'A medical degree doesn't cover advanced analytical chemistry. That's one of Leighton's pet things. The best I can do is ask Max if he can pull any strings with the lab, but I don't think they've a lot of room for manoeuvre, what they do is more sensitive and precise, and it takes longer. And some of it is sent elsewhere.'

'Ok, understood,' Lawrence acknowledged. 'But let's see what they can do.' He transferred his attention to Jamie. 'What's the latest on the CCTV?'

'The guy Elliot picked out was working at Oakworth's Caroline Street branch,' Jamie replied, presenting a printout of a CCTV still. 'But there's been no sign of him there for over two weeks. We checked out the home address in the tax records, but it's a B and B, and he only stayed there for a matter of weeks last autumn. We've been trying to work back from the CCTV to figure out where he might have moved to, but the area's pretty light on surveillance, so I think it's going to be a bit of a non-starter.'

'Any sign of him on public transport since Tuesday?'

'Not yet, but we've barely scratched the surface with all the bus footage.'

'Ok,' Lawrence replied. 'I think at this stage we're going to have to take the risk of involving Oakworth. I doubt they'll have an up-to-date address, but presumably they will have issued Williams with a mobile, and hopefully phone records might give us something on his movements.'

'If he had a personal one, we might even be able to match the two,' Jamie observed.

Lawrence nodded. It was possible, but privately he wasn't optimistic. He doubted Williams would ever have taken the risk of leaving a data trail between his workplace and home, and suspected the best they could hope for was that his efforts to maintain that separation might have fallen down somewhere along the line. Further than that, all they could do was circulate the man's picture among law-enforcement agencies, continue the surveillance, and hope both that Williams hadn't already moved on and that they got a result before the astronomical cost of the operation saw it downsized and then mothballed. Meanwhile, Lawrence would be left second-guessing himself, wondering what he might have missed and what he might have done differently. He had a sickening sense of déjà vu.

Wednesday 19 May

Rebecca arrived at the hospital to find Leighton up and dressed, sitting in an easy chair watching the small television at the foot of the bed. His hands were still swathed in bandages, but he had been disconnected from the IV line that had still been affixed to his arm a few days earlier, and his long hair had been neatly braided into cornrows. He glanced up with a smile as Rebecca approached, looking considerably brighter than he had on any of her previous visits, and greeted her with the words, 'Good job you're here, I can't operate the remote and there's some God-awful reality show coming up in ten minutes.'

'Nice to see you, too,' Rebecca joked, setting her bag down and sitting in a nearby chair. 'Although I nearly didn't recognise you, I've never seen your hair so tidy.'

'Jon's sister did it for me. Saves me trying to clear it out my eyes every five minutes. Now all I need to do is work out a hands-free way to operate a tablet and eat a bacon butty, and I'm sorted.'

'Well you've clearly got your priorities straight.'

'Yeah, you see, I *do* know how to prioritise. You pass that on to Forrester.'

Rebecca smiled. 'It's good to see you feeling better. You've had a rough few weeks.'

Leighton tipped his head to one side. 'I dunno, I think it's probably been harder on everyone else,' he observed. 'My experience has been more like edited highlights.' He paused momentarily before adding, 'Or edited highs. Mum said I was off my face.'

'Where is she?'

'Sheffield.'

'Oh,' Rebecca nodded. 'How long for?'

'For good, I think. She can't really justify being away any longer – she has work – and Dad –' he shrugged.

'So what's going to happen when you get out of here? You're not going to be able to look after yourself, are you?' She indicated his hands.

'I'm sure I'll figure something out. And hopefully I won't need the bandages much longer.'

Rebecca wasn't sure that was realistic, but she could hardly ask how he was going to manage if he didn't still have all his fingers by the time he was discharged. She suspected he had yet to fully take on board the gravity of the situation, and wondered whether anyone had filled him in on Miranda's part in his predicament, or the fact she would face no charges in relation to it. Rebecca herself had been incensed when Lawrence had admitted their former colleague's actions would go unpunished, but couldn't argue with his conclusion that there was nothing material for him to take to the Crown Prosecution Service. When it came down to it, they had no evidence Miranda had intended Leighton to go to the farm alone, or that she had known what would happen when he got there. The only charge that had any chance of sticking was the attempt to pervert the course of justice – a charge that had already been levelled, along with several others, on the basis of Miranda's actions the previous year.

'Thank you for being there for her,' Leighton added. 'Mum, I mean. She really appreciated it.'

'I didn't do much.'

'She says otherwise.'

Rebecca shrugged, feeling her cheeks flush.

'And all the staff keep telling me what a lovely girlfriend I have,' he added. 'So that's scuppered my chances of pulling any of the nurses.'

Rebecca smiled, grateful for the joke. 'Sorry about that.'

'It's ok, I told them you only date rock stars.'

'Because that worked out so well last time,' Rebecca returned, failing to achieve the jovial tone she had intended.

'Sorry,' Leighton offered, awkwardly, after a moment's silence. 'I didn't mean to –' he broke off. 'And I'm so sorry I hurt you. That really was the last thing I wanted to do.'

'I know,' Rebecca conceded. She hesitated before adding, 'But when you said you were afraid of hurting me, you didn't mean my feelings, did you?'

There was a pause before he shook his head.

'Have you ever hurt anyone? Outside the playground?'

'You don't need to get hooked on crack to know it's not a good idea to take it.'

'Sweetheart, you don't even kill spiders.'

'I'm not sure how that's relevant. At one stage, Charles Manson was vegan.'

'Charles Manson was a sociopath.'

Leighton apparently didn't have a smart answer for that.

'I do understand where you're coming from,' Rebecca continued. 'But you're punishing yourself for things that haven't even happened. Please don't write yourself off on account of other people's crimes.'

He shook his head slightly. 'I wouldn't be able to forgive myself if I hurt you, Bec.'

'Well, regardless of the low likelihood of that even happening, it's not as if I'm defenceless, is it? I could put you on the floor in three seconds.'

'I'll take your word for that. I think I've sustained quite enough injuries for one year.'

Rebecca smiled, wishing she could take his hand. She settled for resting hers on his forearm. 'And you always say a scientist should never assume,' she pointed out.

Leighton lifted his eyebrows. 'Me and my big mouth.'

'At least think about giving yourself a chance.'

'All right,' he conceded. 'I'll think about it.'

Rebecca leaned to give him a hug, wondering whether he really would. Once, when faced with a particularly disturbing crime scene, she had asked what his worst nightmare was. He had made a flippant remark about turning out like his dad. She hadn't realised until recently that that fear was controlling his life.

Just as she was about to release him, he stiffened and spoke her name, his tone urgent.

Concerned, Rebecca immediately pulled back. 'What's wrong?'

Leighton's eyes were fixed on something behind her, and he indicated the direction with a nod of his head. Turning, she realised he was looking at the television; more specifically, the text scurrying across the *breaking news* ribbon at the bottom of the screen. 'Latch-key killer detained, Scotland Yard confirms.'

'Did you know about that?' Leighton asked, as he looked back to Rebecca.

She nodded.

'Where'd they find him?'

'Estate agent.'

Leighton frowned. 'That should have been checked weeks ago, surely?'

'He wasn't accessing the flats directly,' Rebecca replied, before summarising Williams' modus operandi, and the surveillance operation that had finally succeeded in apprehending him in the early hours that morning.

'Impressive,' Leighton remarked. 'Who added that up?'

'That would be me,' Rebecca admitted, feeling herself blush.

'Wow, well done.'

'Thanks.'

'And what about Evan?'

'We've not been able to definitively connect Williams to Adriana's flat, but it does share a loft space with several other properties, and we've established that a house was for sale within the terrace at the time she died, so West Mids are having her body exhumed for a second postmortem.'

Leighton nodded wordlessly.

'Which wouldn't be happening if it weren't for you,' Rebecca added.

'It shouldn't have needed to happen at all.'

'Well, whatever the outcome, I doubt the case will ever come to court now.'

'As if that's going to convince people he's innocent,' Leighton returned. 'Maybe if the original investigation hadn't been treated as open and shut, his life wouldn't be in ruins. And I bet nobody will have to answer for that.'

'I know,' Rebecca acknowledged. 'I'm sorry.'

Leighton shook his head. 'It wasn't your doing,' he replied, trying to smile. 'You're the star of the show. You just caught a serial killer. I hope you'll be out for beers tonight?'

Rebecca returned the smile. 'A few drinks may be on the agenda.'

'Make sure you have one for me. In fact, get everyone to have one for me. I'll come and stand my round as soon as I can hold a pint glass.'

'Righty ho,' Rebecca promised. 'Anything else?'

Leighton gave the question a moment's thought before saying, 'Yeah, one other thing. Can you give Forrester a message for me?'

'Sure.'

'Tell him he owes me a macchiato and a jam doughnut.'

A note from Sadie

Thank you for choosing to read this book. If you have enjoyed *One in a Million*, I would be very grateful if you would consider rating it, or even writing a review – just a few words can make a difference in helping to persuade others to give my books a try!

On another note, given the nature of the Birmingham storyline, some of the street names used in this book are fabricated.

Made in the USA
Monee, IL
12 May 2023

33599851R00173